LIES IN CHANCE

By

Sarah J. Bradley

For Tom…who has waited very patiently for a Jeep of his own!

To Peter and Hannah: No matter how long it takes, no matter what anyone says, never, ever give up your dreams!

.

1: SHARA

Shara Brandt opened her eyes and stared at the gray clouds drifting overhead. More curious than concerned, she tried to blink away the gloom and change it to the ruffled pink canopy bed she'd awakened in every morning since she was ten. Not only did the clouds not disappear when she blinked, but Shara was suddenly very aware of the fact that her eyelids were covered with something sticky and, as she touched them gingerly and looked her fingers, red.

Am I bleeding?

The cobwebs brushed away from her mind and three facts became abundantly obvious. First, she had a cut, no, several, criss-crossing her face. Second, there was a spot at the back of her head and one just above her right eye that were very, very tender. Finally, she was sitting in cold, wet mud at the edge of a creek and ice water rushed over her feet, her bare feet.

Why am I outside? Where is Grandmother? Where is Richard? Where am I?

She tried to move, tried to get to her feet, but a sudden wave of dizziness washed over her. Closing her eyes to stave off the whirling white that threatened to spin her into unconsciousness, Shara took a deep breath and tried to remember the last several hours.

I was in a car.

I was in the trunk of a car.

No, that's ridiculous.

The scent of a new car fluttered in her memory, comforting only in that it was something familiar. She'd grown up around new cars. She always equated the smell with her grandmother. It was not a pleasant smell.

Okay, I was in a car.

She opened her eyes, but the unfamiliar creek and trees yielded no answers. Closing her eyes again she tried to picture her grandmother's office at the car dealership, the last place she remembered clearly.

I was at her desk, looking at magazines. At bridal magazines.

5

She eased one eye open and glanced at her left hand. *No ring.* There were plenty of red welts and a bright red spot on her knuckle just above where the ring should have been. *That ring was too small. Richard was supposed to get it sized over the weekend, but he forgot. I must have taken it off.*

She stared at her knuckles, as if expecting the bruised, torn skin to tell her where her engagement ring was. *I didn't take it off very gently, did I?*

Come on Shara, think! You were in Grandmother's office. You were waiting for Richard. You were working on plans for the wedding. And then someone came in.

An involuntary shudder of dread shook her. She hugged her knees and tried to focus.

Then Richard came in with Grandmother.

Richard…Grandmother…

There was a horrible flash of memory, and Shara opened her eyes, looking for the source of the screams that shattered the quiet morning air. She bit her lip, realizing she was the one screaming.

It's all a dream. It's got to be. It's all a dream. None of this is real.

She curled herself more tightly against the cold mud, waiting to wake from the nightmare.

2: BRYAN

Bryan Jacobs looked forward to mornings with a relish that made his students nervous. The thirty-two-year-old fifth grade teacher loved the early morning quiet in the halls of Rock Harbor Community School, the stillness of the teachers' lounge. He could not bring himself to tell anyone, not even his best friends, not Drew, not Joanna, and certainly not Molly, why. Not even they could understand how mornings reminded him of Jenny more than any other time of the day.

Bryan settled into his favorite leather armchair, and reached for the remote control. A news junkie who watched CNN religiously, Bryan once a week ignored the national news and focused on the local news for his Current Events class. Local news for Rock Harbor students meant Green Bay news, focusing on the Packers, or the grittier big city reports from Milwaukee. While Milwaukee was four hours and a cultural lifetime away from the rural confines of Rock Harbor, Bryan found that the students in his class felt in touch with any news that originated within the boundaries of their home state.

"Mornin'."

Bryan did not need to look up. The only other person awake and not milking cows at this hour was the principal of RHCS, Drew Shepaski, a quiet man who spent most of his life in the shadow of his perpetually verbal, and currently pregnant wife, Joanna. "How's Jo?" Bryan turned down the volume on the TV.

Drew switched on the coffee maker. "She sees a doctor today. A Green Bay channel? Did the cable go out again?" Drew tapped his coffee mug on the counter; a nervous habit picked up from every other teacher in the building who survived long night meetings by drinking a gallon of the bitter brew spewed out in the teacher's lounge.

"Current events class."

"Oh. So what's the big story?"

Bryan shrugged. "Nothing earth shattering. We have Packer news, of course. Sunday's win makes the whole season seem rosy again, what's new? I was actually about to change it to a Milwaukee station. You want four or twelve?"

"Doesn't four have that blonde traffic woman?"

Bryan grinned. "Yes."

Drew filled his coffee mug and stared at the dark brew. "Better go with twelve, then. Jo's got enough paranoia about how she looks right now. Word gets out I'm watching the blonde traffic woman on four, I won't be allowed in the house."

"Twelve it is." Bryan grinned as he changed the channel. "Here we go."

7

"Breaking news from the northern suburbs this morning. Prominent local businesswoman, Lydia Brandt, was found shot to death in the Shorewood Lexus dealership she owned early this morning. The cleaning crew found her body at about two…"

"It's always those poor cleaning people who walk in on stuff like that, isn't it?" Drew commented over the female newscaster's voice as he sat at the table.

"Seems that way, doesn't it."

"Police confirm that Mrs. Brandt was killed by a gunshot wound to the face."

"Oh that's messy." Bryan jotted a note on his note pad and looked back up at the screen.

"Also seriously wounded was Mrs. Brandt's sales manager, forty year old Richard Bennett. Mr. Bennett spoke to our reporter, Blair Dailey, from his hospital bed at Froedert Medical Center this morning."

"Ya know, I'll probably get in a ton of trouble for saying this, but there are days I almost wish Rock Harbor had some kind of interesting news going on, just so Blair Dailey could come up here and interview the locals." Drew stirred three sugar cubes into his coffee, his gaze never leaving the TV screen.

"You're worried Jo will find out you're watching the traffic girl on four and you're sitting here wishing from some kind of drama in this town just so you can meet—ho-ly hell!" Bryan leaped from his seat and turned up the volume to maximum.

"What?" Drew stared at the man's face on the screen. "You know that guy?"

"That's the guy…the guy from the loft." Bryan nearly gagged on the words.

"That's Jenny's guy?" Drew threw a glance at Bryan. "Sorry. I mean, that's the guy…from the loft? Someone shot him?"

"I'll bet it was some poor slob who just happened to have an attractive wife." Bryan backed up from the television and stared at the face. He tried to ignore the twisted sense of satisfaction that washed over him as he studied the man who stole Jenny from him three years ago. *Sucks to be you…*

"Yes, Blair, I am blessed to be alive. Losing Lydia like that…" Richard Bennett stared right into the camera lens, a tear glistening in the corners of his blue eyes.

"Were you able to get a look at the assailant?" Blair Dailey, roving reporter, stuck the microphone back to him.

"No. It all happened so fast. And now…Shara is missing. And if anyone has Shara, please bring her back…to the people that love her."

"Oh shut up you…you lying…sack of…bastard." Bryan's voice was a deep, heavy growl as he glared at the face on the screen. *So smooth, even from a hospital bed. Ass.*

Blair Dailey, obviously now outside the hospital, continued her report. "Mr. Bennett refers to Miss Shara Brandt, Lydia Brandt's twenty-three- year old grand-daughter, who is also Mr. Bennett's fiancé. Miss Brandt is wanted for questioning in the murder of Lydia Brandt, but she is currently missing. Police are asking for your help in locating this woman." Here a picture of what looked to be a high school senior portrait, of a thin, pale girl flashed on the screen. The face didn't register with Bryan, who was still stuck on the fact that Richard was engaged…and not to Jenny. "Son of a bitch."

"Hey, Bryan? Take a deep breath and remember we're at school." Drew said in a low voice as he looked over his shoulder at the door. "We don't need the rest of the staff thinking you've had a relapse, right?"

"Yeah, okay." Bryan turned off the television. "Pity they didn't get him in the face…One less wife stealing bastard on the planet wouldn't be a bad thing." His steps to the coffee maker were measured, almost painful. He noted the worried expression on Drew's face. "Sorry. I wasn't planning on airing out old wounds this morning." He gave Drew what he hoped was a reassuring grin.

"I'm thinking maybe you should stick with the Packer news."

"You're no fun." *But you're probably right.*

"I know. The fine families of Rock Harbor Community School appreciate that fact," Drew replied with a grin. "Not to mention the even finer folks of Rock Harbor Community Church, you know the group that pretty much signs your checks?"

"Daddy! Come quick!" Six-year-old Nathan Shepaski burst into the lounge. The dark haired boy was a younger, louder version of his father.

Drew, unflappable, reminded his son of the rules. "Nate, you're not supposed to come in here. And what do you call me when we are at school?"

Nate swallowed hard, trying to catch his breath. "When we're at school, I'm supposed to call you Mr. Shepaski. But Daddy-"

"Nate."

"Mr. Shepaski, Mrs. Hunter says to come quick. There's a girl, just walked out of the creek like a ghost or somthin'."

Both men followed him out the door without another word.

3: MOLLY

Molly Hunter, school nurse, health teacher, and girls' soccer coach, had early morning playground duty for the week, and now she wondered just whom she'd offended to deserve a morning like this. Trying to keep the older boys away from the creek bank was a difficult job on good days, but now that they'd found a young woman huddled on the muddy bank, Molly knew no one would ever heed her warning again.

Molly shooed away the boys who crowded the slippery grass above where the girl sat hugging her legs. This was a young woman, in her late teens probably. Kneeling next to her, Molly did a quick check for obvious injuries. *Chilled to the bone, and bruised, probably has a concussion from the looks of things. Someone worked her over.* "Sweetie, are you okay?" Molly glanced up at the young woman's face. A shiver of recognition flashed through her, like an icy bolt of lightning. *It's not possible.*

"What's going on, Molly?" Bryan asked.

Don't say anything until you know for sure. "I think she's a runaway. I don't know her." Molly did not miss the quick shadow

10

that crossed the girl's pale face. *Was that relief?* Molly looked up at Drew. "She's cut up some, but I don't think she's badly hurt. She's got some pretty serious bruises on her face, though, that I don't like." Molly looked back at her patient. "Do you think you can walk, sweetie?"

"I'll call the ambulance." Drew started back to the school.

Molly sighed. "I suppose we'll have to, won't we?" Her years as a trauma nurse in Milwaukee had taken their toll. Molly didn't like going to any hospital, though Rock Harbor Memorial, by big city standards, was little more than a clinic. "First we need to get the poor child out of the cold. Bryan, help me get her to the first aid room." She looked over her shoulder. "Oh, Drew, she'll need some dry clothes." She looked at the girl again. *It's got to be a monstrous coincidence. A look alike. After all these years, it cannot possibly be...* "Here Bryan, help her up."

4: BRYAN

Molly moved aside and Bryan knelt beside the girl. The heavy, wet smell of dead leaves and creek water fell from her like the water that dripped from her sweater. She shivered as Bryan helped her stand. She swayed a little and stumbled back

"Whoa, there," Bryan steadied her as they walked up the bank. The girl took four more steps and then stumbled back against him again. Placing steadying hands on her shivering shoulders, Bryan paused, waiting for her to take another step.

"Bryan, just carry her." Molly was several strides ahead and Bryan knew her tone well. Molly never liked keeping any patient, human or animal, waiting one second longer than they had to.

The girl whimpered softly as Bryan lifted her into his arms. He looked down at her and something drew his gaze away from the cuts and bruises that punctuated her childlike face. *Look at those eyes.* Something in her deep, black brown eyes spoke to Bryan words he would never be able to define, but knew all too well. For a heartbeat he understood this wounded stranger as well as he

11

understood his own endless heart's anguish. *Someone broke her heart.*

"I'm not going to hurt you. You can trust me." Bryan murmured against her matted, wet hair as he cradled the girl gently and followed Molly. He walked through the doorway to the first aid room, nodding thanks to the curious student who opened the door for him. Moving as gently as he could, he settled her on the ancient army cot that served as a bed in the nurses' room. Kneeling beside the cot, he studied her face. She was older than he'd first thought. And, in spite of her current circumstances, Bryan saw strength in the battered contours of her face. *She's hardly a child. She knows how to take care of herself.*

"It's going to be okay," he murmured, still spellbound by her eyes. "You're safe."

The girl blinked, breaking the spell, but Bryan did not miss the jumble of relief and doubt that played across her face.

"Okay, Bryan, we'll need a bit of privacy, if you don't mind?" Molly was full on in her nurse mode. She nodded dismissal to Bryan, who reluctantly stood, crossed the room, and closed the door behind him.

5: MOLLY

"All right my dear, let's see just how banged up you are." Molly took inventory of the girl in front of her while removing her sodden clothing. Molly was relieved to note that she was at least trying to move her arms to be helpful. A good sign.

Her clothes were of a high quality, from stores Molly vaguely recalled from the years she worked her way through nursing school as a clerk in a Milwaukee mall. She wore no jewelry. Molly looked carefully at the girl's neatly manicured hands. There was clear nail polish on each finger. And there, on the third finger of her left hand, was a slim ridge around the base of the finger, and torn bloodied skin up and down the finger, the knuckle was dislocated. *Was there a ring, maybe she was mugged for her engagement*

12

ring? She can't be old enough. Then again...if she is...who I think...then she'd be what, twenty-two? Twenty-three?

The girl pulled her hand away from Molly, wincing in pain. Molly stroked the girl's hair, still matted with mud from the creek bank. She spoke in a low tone, something she often did with a stray. "Don't worry; you don't need to be afraid. We'll get you fixed up at the hospital."

"Here are some clothes." Drew opened the door a slim crack and handed a sweat suit four sizes too big for the girl. "RHCS EAGLES" howled out in block letters from the red sweatshirt. Modestly, he closed the door again as Molly helped the girl out of her sodden clothes and into the sweats.

Once the task of dressing the girl was done, Molly opened the door and let Drew in. "Drew, did you find any socks in the lost and found?"

"Oh yeah. Here you go." Drew handed her a pair of grayish tube socks. "They're clean, Jo just washed everything in that box last week."

"Thanks." With great care, Molly slid the thick, floppy socks onto the girl's feet.

"How is she?"

Molly frowned. "The cuts on her feet are superficial, and I don't think hypothermia's set in. Nothing they can't handle at Memorial." Molly put a protective arm around her. "Is the ambulance here?"

"In a minute," Drew looked over his shoulder and down the hall. "I'll make sure they call us with an update later."

I really don't want to leave her, though. Molly bit her lip. *I need to know who she is.* "Tell you what, Drew. I'd like to ride along with her, if you don't mind?"

"Okay, I guess. Any special reason why?"

"Well," Molly looked at the girl who seemed to like the prospect of having her along. "It's not really nice to just dump her in the ambulance, is it? We don't know who she is, and she doesn't seem to be able to talk..." here Molly pointed to the girl's bruised jaw. "So let me just go along, sort of a friend. And then I'll just take her

13

home and make her some soup and we'll figure things out, won't we?" Molly smiled down at the girl and the girl nodded slowly. Molly did not need to see Drew's face. She knew he would wear no look of surprise.

"Are you sure?" His voice, graveled with the cigarettes he'd smoked in his younger years, was full of doubt. "Are you sure that's a wise decision?"

Still holding the younger woman's hand, Molly looked over her shoulder at him. "Well, where's she going to go? They might not keep her overnight. Look at her, Drew." Molly nodded to the girl. "She needs a safe place more than anything."

"Molly, this isn't one of your strays. This is a person." Drew put a fatherly hand on her shoulder; a gesture Molly watched him do a hundred times with troubled students. Not appreciating his approach, Molly pushed his hand away.

"Isn't it a good thing I'm actually trained to take care of people?"

"It's a talent we always appreciate." Drew took a step back into the room. He looked again at the thin young woman, who stared at him with round dark eyes. "Let me give the police a call. She might be lost and someone's looking for her."

At the word 'police' the girl shuddered and leaned against Molly.

"Drew, maybe we should talk about this outside." Molly patted her patient's hand. "I'll be right outside that door, sweetie. You just sit here and relax. No one is going to hurt you." Giving her one last reassuring glance, Molly stepped into the hallway. "Drew, I don't think we should call the police yet."

"Why not?"

"Look at her. She's not a danger to anyone, poor thing's scared. I'd like to know what her story is before I go turning her over to Kelly Fuller."

"There, everyone's back in their classrooms. I told them to be quiet, so of course, they're all talking…" Bryan walked up the hallway to them. "So what's going on?"

"I suggested to Molly that we give Kelly Fuller a call."

14

"Well, he is Rock Harbor's finest sheriff's deputy…and the only one. But Mol, you don't look sold on the idea."

Molly frowned. "No Bryan, I don't want to call Kelly. Not just yet."

"Well, Molly, don't we have to call him sometime? I mean, some girl shows up in the creek, beaten up, isn't that something we have to report?"

"You'd think that, but no. No, Molly's going to take our mystery girl home after they check her out at Memorial." Drew's voice now held a note of merriment that promised Molly support.

"Mol, this isn't one of your strays. This is a person." Bryan looked over Molly's shoulder through the first aid room window at the girl.

"You two are a pair." Molly had little patience with Bryan at the moment, though she knew he meant well. "I'm going with her to the hospital and then I'm taking her to my place. I'll try to find her family, and if there is anything to report to the police, I will do it. Is the ambulance here yet?"

"Uh, yeah." Bryan threw a look to Drew who grinned.

"So go make sure the medics find their way here. If anyone wants me in the next few days, I'll be at home. Drew, fire me if you want, replace me if you can, but this girl is going home with me."

Molly swept past them back into the first aid room. She knew they wouldn't argue with her about this. She always got her way with Bryan and Drew.

6: SHARA

"Well, hello there."

The gentle voice drew Shara out of the darkness. The soft, yellow light hurt her eyes, and she shut them quickly. *It was all a dream. I'm waking up now.*

"Now, now. You've got to wake up, young lady." The unfamiliar voice beckoned more forcefully this time. "It's time for some food."

Shara opened her eyes to unfamiliar surroundings. *Well, the dream continues.*

The woman in front of her was older than she sounded, maybe forty. Shara blinked and tried to focus in the dimly lit room. Warm smells hung in the air like a still summer day. The cozy comfort of the soft bed made her feel safe. Vaguely she remembered walking into this room, and lying on this bed.

"Well, your eyes are open, that's a good first step." The woman got up from the bed and left the room for a moment. When she returned, she carried a tray with a bowl on it.

"What I have here is my grandmother's chicken veggie soup, and it's never been known to fail. Not one time."

Grandmother. Where is my grandmother? Where is this place and why isn't she here bossing everyone around?

"You're going to be fine. You eat some of this, and you'll feel better, I promise."

Shara accepted a spoonful of the steaming soup. The liquid did little to make her feel better. Instead, she was suddenly aware of pain in her mouth and all around her face. Tentatively, she reached up to touch her cheek.

"Oh, no, you're not a pretty sight." The woman watched as Shara touched the tender spots all over her face.

I was at a hospital. This isn't a hospital. "Where-" Speaking was painful. She touched her jaw. *I was hurt. I remember…I was in a car…*

"No, it's not broken, dear. Close, heaven knows." The woman's voice lilted as she set the tray aside. "You were at the hospital, remember? You spent the night there. You have a concussion and they needed to keep you overnight, for observation. We got home early this morning." Here the woman looked at a small clock on the wall. "You've been asleep for almost four hours. I'm Molly, remember?"

16

Shara had little recollection of what the woman told her, but there was something in the woman's voice that was familiar. "Molly."

"I'm a teacher at the school where we found you."

Shara closed her eyes and struggled to call up shadowy images of a school yard. "Molly. Yesh."

Molly patted her hand. "Is there someone I can call for you? Is there someone I can contact, just to let them know you're going to be okay?"

Shara closed her eyes and tried to formulate and answer. Shadowy images punctuated with bright flashes of light made her head ache. *Grandmother and Richard...why don't they know where I am?* More light, this time with sound. *Gunshots. Grandmother.*

"Dead." A shiver of fear ran through Shara.

Grandmother is dead. Someone shot her.

"Your parents have passed?" Molly gave her a deeply sympathetic look.

"Yesh. Dead." Shara closed her eyes and tried to remember more. *Gunshots. Bodies on a floor. Noise. Screaming. I was screaming. I was kneeling next to Richard. Blood...*

Don't you dare tell. She shuddered again at the icy tone that uttered the command. *Don't you dare say a word.*

Who said that?

"How about if we just start with your name?" Molly put a hand on her arm.

Shara opened her eyes and realized that she didn't want to answer the woman's question. *Bodies on the floor. Gunshots. Grandmother is dead. Where is Richard? Is Richard dead?*

Don't tell. Don't you dare say a word.

"I-I don't know." She glanced quickly to see if the lie was detected.

Molly Hunter, the teacher, patted her arm and smiled a little smile. "That's fine, dear. The doctor expected that you might not recall everything just yet. You rest now. I'm going to clean up these dishes." She picked up the bowl and stood. "I'll be back."

Shara watched the older woman leave the room and shut the door. She touched her cheek once more and tried to think of something to tell the teacher, and anyone else who wanted to know about her.

Don't you dare tell. Don't you dare say a word, Shara Brandt, I'll kill you, too.

7: MOLLY

In spite of what the emergency room doctor said, Molly Hunter was not sold on the idea that the girl in her spare room had forgotten her own name. "But why? What's the point of hiding who she is?"

Time enough to ask her questions after she feels better. Molly put the dish and spoon in the sink and rinsed them out. Satisfied that the kitchen was tidy enough, she walked into the front room and sat down in her favorite lumpy recliner. She snapped on the noon news and absently toyed with the gold locket that rested, where it had for nearly fifteen years, at the base of her throat.

"Police in Milwaukee are looking for this woman." The television blared from the front room. Without really focusing, Molly looked up at the screen.

"Shara Elisabeth Brandt, heir to the Brandt Motors fortune, is missing and Milwaukee police are asking for your help. Miss Brandt is wanted for questioning in connection with the murder of Lydia Brandt and the shooting of Richard Bennett."

Molly sat forward in her chair suddenly as if struck from behind. The thin, pale teenager's face on the screen was not familiar, but the names she knew as well as her own. *Well, ding dong the old hag is dead!* She shook her head, trying to clear the decidedly uncharitable thought from her head, but the image of the tall, icy woman dragging that tiny little girl away from the hospital was one that Molly recalled with nothing less that pure, undiluted loathing.

"It is believed that while Shara Brandt is not armed, she has a history of mental illness and may be a danger to herself or to those around her. Anyone who finds Miss Brandt is strongly cautioned not to confront her. If you have any information on the location of Shara Brandt, please call Milwaukee Crime Stoppers at-"

As if there was really any doubt. Molly switched off the set and stared at the blank screen. *Of course it's her, lying in my guest room. I knew who she was the minute I saw those eyes of hers.*

She unfastened the chain from around her neck. The beveled edges of the heart shaped locket sparkled in her hand. Molly closed her eyes, seeing the child again, and the cold hearted woman who whisked her away. It was a memory that was never far from Molly's mind.

That night the streets in Milwaukee were terrible. Nineteen inches of snow had fallen over most of the city, the heavy, wet kind of snow that made shoveling and plowing a daunting, and sometimes, dangerous task.

Molly had worked in the emergency center of St. Luke's medical center for enough years. She'd built a shell around her heart. But that night, that snowy night, they brought in a couple, a man and a very pregnant woman, and their young daughter.

Why, why would they have tried to drive in such weather? They could have called an ambulance; they could have delivered that baby at home.

Molly snapped open the locket in her hand and stared at the picture of the happy couple one side and the grade school photo of a very young, very happy little girl with enormous dark eyes.

The father was dead on arrival. The mother died in delivery and the baby, a tiny baby boy, didn't live an hour. All of this happened while Molly Hunter, then Molly Collins, was patching up some superficial cuts on Shara Brandt and getting the child some cranberry juice. Molly remembered the cranberry juice clearly because the little girl had asked for it specifically. It was her favorite.

She couldn't picture the grandmother's face anymore, not after so many years, but Molly shivered at the memory of the woman's voice. A voice so cold the words were ice daggers, cutting wherever they landed. Even now, standing in her sunny front

19

room, Molly shivered, remembering that cold, hard woman who demanded the little girl.

"You may release the child to me." That's what she said. "Release the child." Like she was some kind of prisoner I was turning over.

Molly knew the woman's name. Everyone in the Milwaukee area knew the name Lydia Brandt of Brandt motors. Brandt Motors, a powerful string of car dealerships all through Southeastern Wisconsin, had weathered a Depression, two world wars, and countless recessions, very much due to the tireless work of founder George Brandt and the tireless iron fist of his successor, his daughter, Lydia Brandt. So determined was Lydia to rule her business, it was rumored that when she married, she demanded her husband take her name, a thing unheard of at the time. It was the only way she would marry at all, so the legend went.

And there she was, tall, slim, unbending like an iron rod, demanding that darling little girl be turned over to her like some piece of furniture

Molly smiled as she now studied the thin, cheerful face of the child in the locket. She had wide, dark eyes, eyes that bespoke a depth of understanding rare in child so young. They talked at length that night, after Molly hugged her and told her about her parents and her unborn brother.

And what did that child say to me? "They have a boy, but they'll miss me in heaven, won't they? A little bit?"

Raised Catholic, but lapsed for more years than she'd ever admit, Molly nearly staggered to her knees in the face of such simple, unquestioning faith.

Molly touched the picture in the locket again and wiped a tear from her eye. *I shouldn't have let her go with Lydia Brandt. I could have kept her at the hospital until another relative was tracked down. I could have called Social Services and gotten her into the system. At least someone would have watched over her.*

"You may release the child to me."

"I think there's some paperwork that needs to be filled out. And a doctor has to check Shara over one more time."

Lydia Brandt froze Molly with one look. "Do you have idea who I am?"

"I suppose you're a family member or a friend of Shara's family." Molly tried to stand her ground, but the contempt in Lydia's steel gray eyes weakened some of her resolve.

"I am hardly a friend. Shara is my grand-daughter. Now that her father is dead, I intend to remedy the damage that woman did to this girl."

"Woman?"

"The child's mother." Lydia cast a withering glass to Shara and sniffed. "If the child is even my responsibility, that is. There's no proof that my son wasn't trapped into marriage by that useless piece of white trash."

"Mrs. Brandt," Molly put her arm around Shara, who seemed to be watching her grandmother with a mixture of fear and curiosity. "Please, this isn't the time for…"

"Oh don't tell me what it's time for. My time is far more valuable than yours, Nurse, and I'm telling you right now to stop wasting my time and give me the child!"

I had no reason to keep her. She wasn't injured. I was just supposed to keep an eye on her until a family member came to get her. There wasn't much else I could have done.

Which is exactly what I've told myself all these years.

Shara wanted her mother's locket, and the grandmother refused to wait.

"I don't have the time to wait in this hospital for some useless trinket."

"Please, Mrs. Brandt, I'm sure I can have it sent to you."

Again Lydia Brandt fired off a freezing glare. "I'll thank you to have no further contact with me or with my grand-daughter. Unless you'd like to take on my stable of lawyers in the process." Lydia looked Molly up and down, and for a moment Molly felt like a horse being sized up by a buyer. "No, it's doubtful that's a fight you're up for."

Without another word, Lydia Brandt swept out of the room, with a submissive Shara trotting to keep up behind her.

Little Shara Brandt. A name Molly Hunter had not forgotten in the lifetime that lay between then and now. *I always promised myself I'd give you back this locket if I ever saw you again.*

And now, she's in there, scared to death and wanted for the murder of her grandmother. Molly closed her eyes and recalled the reporter's words. "A danger to herself and those around her?" Molly glanced again at the smiling child in the locket. "Not likely. Looks like someone was more of a danger to her."

I failed her that night. God only knows what sort of hell her life was with that woman. And now here she is. I have this chance to help her, or to at least make sure she's safe.

Molly Hunter snapped the locket closed and looked at her guest room door. *I'm not going to fail her a second time.*

8: BRYAN

Bryan pulled his well-used-much-loved Jeep into the yard. Briefly glancing at the barn as he got out, he realized that it had been several days since he'd ridden his horse, Pepper. A sharp twinge of guilt pricked his conscience. Brushing the feeling aside, he turned to look at the house. Jenny always used to say it faced backwards. She never understood the magic in watching the sun set behind the barn. *Which is why,* Bryan thought as he eased himself into his grandmother's rocking chair, *there's only one chair on the porch.*

Jenny.

He made a conscious effort every day not to think of her. Now the memories were not to be refused. Seeing Richard Bennett on TV brought back the old pain. Sitting with his head resting against the back of the rocker, Bryan stared at the loft window and saw it all again.

Jenny begged for that loft to be renovated. After three months of marriage, she needed space, or so she said. She wanted more privacy than the two-bedroom cabin they called home provided her. Bryan, blinded by love, acquiesced and renovated the loft in

22

his small barn. It took him a month of late nights and weekends and all of his savings, but he made a little nest for her.

Bryan never knew it was to be a love nest. *I never suspected that.*

Over and over, every night after he threw her out, or she left, the details did not matter; Bryan replayed that scene in his head. It was late that night. He'd had some meeting at school, he couldn't remember what. Jenny was supposed to be back from a little shopping trip to Milwaukee, a trip he encouraged because she told him she was meeting some girlfriends of hers from college. The house was dark, but her light was on in the loft. Even though he'd never been there since she moved in the furniture, he did not feel like a trespasser as he climbed the dusty stairs. He remembered the sound of Pepper and Rika, Jenny's mare, shuffling beneath his feet.

He opened the door slowly but confidently, a new husband about to visit his bride. Then Bryan saw *him.* Then Bryan saw Jenny. And he saw her eyes.

Jenny was laughing at me with her eyes.

Laughing at him over the shoulder of her lover. The man was laughing at him, too. Bryan heard him.

The whole scene was over in a flash. He shut the door and ran out of the barn. She never even bothered to follow him or try to explain. It was what it was, and she, apparently, felt no need to gloss over her betrayal.

The next day she was home, waiting for him.

"I love him." She stood in front of the big picture window, where the afternoon sun danced on her auburn hair, giving it the life a flame has. Over her left shoulder he stared into that very loft window, seeing the naked man laughing at him again..

"Whom do you love?"

"I love Richard."

"Just like you loved me?" His voice dripped with sarcasm, covering the sound of lifeblood draining from his heart. "Then it will pass, my dear, as your feelings for me obviously have."

"I don't expect you to understand. He and I are alike, soul mates." She pouted with those full end-of-summer raspberry lips. "You don't need to get mean."

Bryan fought a perverse urge to laugh. "I didn't think I was, but then, you would be the one to know. Hell, all I did was build you your love nest right here on my property. I encouraged you to go shopping in Milwaukee for a weekend." He paced in front of her, watching her face for some trace of remorse and, seeing none, longed to say something that would make her sorry. "Tell me, where did you pick him up? Clearance racks at Boston Store?" Still no response from her. "Did you plan to screw other men in that loft before I built it, or was Mr. Soul Mate the only one?"

Again, the pout. "You're gone a lot at night."

"So that answers that question. But be fair, Jenny. I'm not gone a lot. I have meetings periodically."

"You're a teacher." Now the whining tone in her voice, the innocent pout and the whining. Usually the winning combination for Jenny. "I didn't think teachers had meetings at night."

Bryan stopped his pacing and stared at her, momentarily surprised by her words. "You've never heard of a PTA or faculty meetings?"

The pout was gone, replaced by anger. "Bryan, I had every right to do what I did. You left me alone too many nights. That's not right for newlyweds."

"So now it's an attention thing? I didn't pay enough attention to you? You can't be serious, Jenny. You know full well I gave up my whole Masters' program for you this winter, and I won't be able to get back into it for who knows how long. That put my career on hold so I could spend more time with you. I did it because I love you and I wanted to give you everything you wanted. You're going to tell me that wasn't enough?"

"Oh, like your career is any big deal. You'll probably stay here your entire life, teaching at the dumpy school in this dumpy town."

"Rock Harbor might be rural, but I wouldn't call it dumpy."

Jennifer heaved a large sigh. "Call it what you want to. I'm not going to turn into some kind of drudge country housewife, all fat and nasty with a string of kids like that Joanna plans to have."

Bryan nearly hit her then. No one ever insulted Joanna Shepaski within his hearing and got away with it. "Joanna is one of the finest women I know, and you'd be better off keeping your filthy mouth shut." He was snarling then, a wounded animal cornered.

"Anyway, that's not what I want for my life."

Bryan took an adversarial stance in front of her, his hands gripped at his waist, his legs wide apart. "And what does your new man do?" *Besides you?*

"His name is Richard Bennett, and he's a sales manager at a car dealership. But he has ambition. And he's amazing in bed." She added the last fact with a-none-too- subtle lick of her lips.

The porcelain water pitcher on the mantel had been in Bryan's family for generations. At that moment, with that comment, Bryan's rage was such that family heirlooms meant nothing. Without even realizing he threw it, Bryan watched as the pitcher shattered against the opposite wall, inches from Jenny's head. He remembered feeling a great wash of relief.

"You're insane!" She ran at him, all fists and fangs.

Suddenly calm and purposeful, Bryan stopped her charge only his tone of voice. "Get out."

"What?" His two words held her frozen in place a foot from him.

"Get out now. Get into that new car I see in the drive and get away from me."

Jenny glared at him then, as if trying to find a reason to argue further. But, finding none, apparently, she turned on her heel and left, the screen door snapping closed behind her.

After that I've lived in three years of agony and darkness. Now he's in critical condition. And apparently, Mr. Soul Mate is engaged to someone who is not my ex wife.

All in all, not a bad day in a sort of weird, twisted way.

Bryan blinked into the last rays of the setting sun and got out of the rocking chair. He felt lighter than he had since the day Jenny left. *Maybe this is my chance to finally be free of those memories.*

9: MOLLY

"Drew, I'd love to tell you when I'm coming back to work, but I just don't know," Molly said into the phone. "And calling me nine times in seven days isn't going to get you an answer any faster."

"Mol, I wouldn't push, you know that, but I'm having a terrible time with those girls in gym class." Drew's voice was a little less than its usual calm.

"Poor baby. You should have Bryan take that class."

"Why Bryan?"

Molly grinned. "Drew, my dear, you are just a married teacher with kids."

"Molly, don't you dare say what I think you're going to say."

"Bryan is the school sex symbol."

"Oh brother!" Drew started to laugh.

"You know every girl in school has a major crush on him. On top of which he's got that whole wounded hero thing going for him. Those girls would not give him a minute's trouble. Whereas with you...well, you're the beloved principal, but when it comes down to it, you're just a married teacher."

"I'm going to ignore this topic of conversation. How is the creek girl doing?"

Molly stared out the window of her kitchen and spoke in a lower voice. "She's doing well, physically. Most of the swelling's gone down, and she can talk properly. She still doesn't remember much, though." *At least not much that she's telling me.*

Drew's voice held a note of parental warning. "Maybe she should see another doctor. Choose one that specializes in things less...physical. You know I respect your abilities, but this one may be beyond what you can handle. Besides, she's got to have a family looking for her."

"I'll take that into consideration. Now she's coming, so I have to go. I'll call you later, okay?" Molly hung up the phone and watched as the girl strode into the kitchen.

"Good morning, Molly." The girl opened the refrigerator and scanned the shelves before closing the door and then pouring herself a cup of coffee.

"Good morning." Molly picked up her own cup of coffee and sat down at the table across from the girl. "Are you looking for anything in particular?"

"Oh, I don't know. I think I was in the mood for juice."

"I have orange."

The girl looked at her and gave her an uncertain smile. "Oh, I know. Guess orange just wasn't trippin' my trigger."

Molly swirled her coffee in her mug. *Go ahead...ask her.* "Maybe you'd prefer...cranberry?"

"Yeah, cranberry sounds good. I mean, if it's not too much trouble." The girl smiled sweetly as she sat across the table from Molly.

It's time to ask her. "There's a bottle of it in the back of the fridge, behind the milk. You know, I met a girl once, long time ago, rather like you."

"What, she wasn't interested in orange juice?" The girl set aside the coffee and opened the refrigerator door.

"Well, cranberry juice was her favorite, she told me. She was in the hospital where I worked. She'd been in a car crash." Molly stirred her coffee with a spoon, a casual motion that covered the point of her statement.

"Was she hurt?" The girl poured herself a glass of the juice and sat down across the table from Molly.

"No. But her parents were killed." Molly watched her face closely for a sign of something, and she wasn't disappointed. The girl kept her gaze fixed on the tablecloth pattern, but her hand trembled slightly as she set down her glass. "Her parents and her unborn brother."

The girl picked at the tablecloth and kept her eyes averted. "That's a really sad story. But why tell me?"

27

Molly pulled the locket out of her collar. "She told me to collect this locket from her mother. I never had a chance to give it to her, but I swore that if I ever saw the girl again, I would be sure to hand it over."

The girl glanced up at the locket and her eyes shot back down to the table. Molly smiled and let the locket dangle free over the table as she leaned closer. "Would you like to look at the pictures? They really were lovely people." Molly held the locket up again.

The girl shook her head and stood up quickly. "I'm feeling a little too tired right now." She pushed herself away from the table and started down the hall.

"Shara." Molly's voice was firm and commanding.

The girl stopped in her tracks, but did not look at Molly.

"You're Shara Brandt, aren't you? You're the girl in the hospital." Molly watched Shara's back for a sign of anything. The girl was a statue. "You're the one they're looking for."

As an answer, Shara Brandt ran down the hall to her room and slammed the door.

10: SHARA

Pressing her back against the closed door, Shara's heart raced and she couldn't breathe. *She knows. She knows, and soon everyone will know and then-*

And then whoever killed Grandmother will kill me because they'll think I said something.

Don't tell. Don't you dare say a word.

If only I could remember who it was.

There was a light knock on the door. Shara turned and backed away from the door. She wasn't ready to face her accuser but she had little choice.

Only her accuser came into the room and gave her a big hug.

Wrapped in Molly Hunter's arms like a small child, Shara Brandt gave way to the sorrow she'd hidden for so many years. It was not for her grandmother that she wept. For the first time since

28

the car accident so many years before, Shara allowed herself to mourn her parents.

11: MOLLY

Half an hour later, they sat together at the kitchen table, poking at pancakes they weren't eating and trying to conjure up small talk in the wake of the revelation.

"This is ridiculous, Shara." Molly set down her fork. "We should really discuss what you should do next."

"I'm not sure I have a lot of options. I should go to the police. Turn myself in. Isn't that what everyone wants?"

Not what you want…not what I want. "Look Shara, when you left the hospital that day, I felt like I'd failed, you know? I never forgave myself for letting your grandmother just take you like that. " Molly took a deep breath. "I always promised myself that if we ever crossed paths again, I'd make it up to you."

Shara leaned forward, looking uncertain. "What are you saying?"

"What I'm saying is this: I'm not going to turn you in. Unless that's what you really want. Tell me what you really want, and I will do my very best to help you in any way I can."

Shara's eye widened with surprise. "Are you serious? Why on earth you would do that for me?"

Molly did not miss the shadow of distrust that darkened Shara's face. *Why should she trust anyone at this point?* "Shara, after you left with your grandmother, I sort of had an epiphany. I couldn't take living in a big city, working in a big city hospital where people were just faces, just numbers. I realized, after you left, that I'd lost any sense of true compassion. I was heartsick, so I left. I found a job far away from anything I'd ever been. I moved here. I married a darling man."

"You're married?"

Molly smiled, tears welling in her eyes. "I was. He was...taken from me several years ago. It was an accident, he was electrocuted."

"Oh, I'm sorry."

Molly waved her hand at Shara. "Not the point. The night Robert died, when he was brought into the hospital, I was working as an ER Nurse. We were so happy then. But then he died and I realized that I was done with emergency medicine. I took the position as school nurse at RHCS. I've been there almost ten years now. But the one thing I've never forgotten, the one thing I've carried with me for so long, is the knowledge that I didn't do enough to protect you all those years ago. So now," Molly reached across the table and took Shara's hand in her own, "Now is my chance to do just that."

"So you'll help me?

Molly nodded. "Whatever you need, however you want to approach this, I will help you."

Shara nodded, as if satisfied. "I need some time. Time to remember what happened that night. I need time to remember how on earth I wound up here, and who murdered my grandmother."

"You didn't do it then." Molly watched her face and saw no trace of guilt.

"Would it change how you feel if I did?"

"Not in the least." *I should really feel sorrier the old hag was murdered, I suppose.*

Shara heaved a sigh of relief. "No. At least, I can't imagine I did. I-I" Shara stopped and stared at the wall.

Molly leaned closer to her. "You may as well tell me everything at this point."

"I was getting ready for a wedding. For my wedding." Shara got up and started a slow pace around the table. "My grandmother...she didn't like the way I was handling things. She wanted a big social blowout. Not my style. And Richard didn't care."

"Richard?"

30

"Richard Bennett, my grandmother's dealership manager. Her right hand man. He was…is…my fiancé."

Richard Bennett…the man in Bryan's loft. "Isn't Richard a bit old for you?" Molly's words came out before she realized she'd spoken them.

Shara gave her a surprised look. "You know him?"

Molly weighed whether or not she should tell Shara about Jenny and Bryan. *No, focus on her story first. Don't add to her worries.* "We never met. But the news reports say he was shot, as well."

This seemed to surprise Shara. She stopped circling the table. "Is he dead?"

"I'm not sure. Could he have seen the shooter?"

Shara sat down and twirled her spaghetti on the end of her fork. "Not likely. He adored Grandmother. All I remember was being in the office reading wedding magazines. Grandmother and Richard weren't there; I was alone in the office. It was late. And then—"

"And then?"

"And then someone came in." Shara frowned and closed her eyes as if to see more. "Someone came in to talk to me." She opened her eyes. "That's all I remember. Everything else is just like grainy snapshots, and little pieces of noise. Nothing clear."

The telephone jangled, startling them both.

12: SHARA

As Molly held an animated discussion with someone on the phone, Shara closed her eyes again. *Bodies on the floor. One is Richard.*

Don't tell. Don't even think about telling.

You'll never get away with this, Shara Brandt!

Shara's eyes snapped open at the sound of the shrill female voice. *Get away with what? Did I shoot my grandmother? Did I shoot Richard?*

I couldn't have. Not Richard. Who else was in the room?

"Well my dear, that was Drew Shepaski on the phone. He's my boss, after a fashion. Seems his wife isn't doing too well again, and

31

I have to go back to work tomorrow because he can't cover for me. So we'd best figure out our plan today."

Shara shook herself out of her reverie. "Does anyone else know who I am?"

"Doubtful. The only picture anyone's seen has been the one on the news, and that one doesn't seem terribly recent."

Shara smiled. "I don't like getting my picture taken. They're probably showing my high school yearbook photo." She nibbled on the croissant on her plate. "That's what Grandmother and I were fighting about that day. The photographer. I didn't want one. She wanted a big spread in half a dozen papers."

Molly scooped some salad out of the big bowl onto her plate. "We could give you a new identity, a story to tell people." She looked at Shara. "We could give you a new look, too."

"Will that work? I mean, do people actually do that kind of thing and get away with it?"

"Maybe." Molly grinned. "I've never tried hiding anyone's identity before. But I know this much: This isn't Milwaukee. Rock Harbor is light years away from any big city. There aren't many who care about news much beyond what's happening in Green Bay. In a few days, I'm sure news coverage will die down and this town will pretty much forget about Shara Brandt."

Mr. Mittens, Molly's big tortoise shell cat, strolled into the kitchen and rubbed against Shara's leg. "What is it about animals? They pick the person who can't tolerate them, and they love them."

"You don't like cats?" Molly picked up her big tom and hugged him.

"It's not that." Shara sniffled. "I'm allergic to them." She sneezed, and wiped her eyes. "Big time. I didn't want to say anything because you've been so nice to me, but I don't know how much longer Mr. Mittens and I can cohabitate."

Molly hugged her cat again and gave Shara a sympathetic look. She looked over her shoulder at the phone. "You know what? I think I have an idea."

13: SHARA

After several hours of discussion, two boxes of hair color, and a fairly successful attempt at a haircut and home perm, Molly was confident they'd created a new look, and alias, for Shara.

But it this is going to work, it's got to be flawless. "Let's go over it one more time. Name?" She busied herself applying some soft pink blush to Shara's cheeks.

"Bethany Elias. I'm twenty-six. I've been living with my grandfather in Escanaba, Michigan since I was little. I wanted for the longest time to go to college, but haven't been able to because of money, and taking care of Gramps. Now Gramps is dead and I need a job." Shara looked uncertain. "I did actually just graduate from college."

Molly nodded. "Not everything has to be a lie. What was your major?"

"Business, with some pre-law thrown in…and education. Did it all at Marquette."

Molly arched an eyebrow in her direction. "That's quite the combo."

"Grandmother wanted someone to take over the business when she died…she insisted I get a business degree, and start working on a law degree, so I could save money on legal fees when I took over the business."

"And the education?"

Shara shrugged and gave Molly a smile. "Let's say I took some night courses. My father was a teacher. My mother was a teacher. I wanted to teach little children. Grandmother wouldn't hear of it, so I snuck around."

Of course Grandmother wouldn't hear of it. "So you have a degree in teaching? And business?"

Shara nodded. "I have all kinds of talents up my sleeve."

"Such as?"

"Such as I can play anything that has a keyboard. Piano, organ, harpsichord. When it comes to music, I have a memory thing, I learn pretty quickly, and once I've learned it, I never have to look at it again. Like some kind of computer program or something. Weird, right?"

Molly laughed out loud and the younger woman's self deprecating humor. "You are a mystery, Miss Shara, I will give you that. The piano thing may come in handy later. Now, one last question." She gave Shara a very serious look. "How did you wind up in the creek?"

Shara closed her eyes. "My boyfriend was terribly charming when gramps was around, but not so much when he wasn't. Once Grandpa died, boyfriend became even less charming. I tried to break up with him, I did, but he wouldn't let me." She paused, and Molly was about to prompt Shara when she noted a tear rolling down Shara's cheek. "We were in the car, headed south. Had a big fight. The rain was so bad, we had to stop. I saw my chance and ran." She opened her eyes, and blinked away more tears.

"Good, good." Molly tapped a pen against her lips for a moment. "One question?"

Shara wiped her eyes on her sleeve. "What's that?"

"How did you really wind up in the creek?"

Shara shrugged lightly. "I've gone over and over that. I remember being in a car, but I wasn't driving. That's all I remember. Why?"

"Because I think our story may be closer to your reality than we think, just from how you react when you tell it. This Richard you were engaged to, did he abuse you?"

Shara closed her eyes and smiled. "Richard? No. Richard loved me. He promised me everything I wanted. He was going to be my escape from my grandmother and the car business."

Yeah, Richard Bennett probably made you all kinds of promises he planned on keeping. I'll just bet. Molly held up a mirror to Shara. "Take a look and tell me what you think of the new you."

There wasn't much left that would remind anyone of the pitiful girl from the creek. Shara's hair was now a dark golden blonde, a halo of soft waves that barely skimmed her collar. With the added color of some light make up, she looked like a different person.

"Wow, Molly, I don't even recognize me. This is amazing. I don't look like I'm in junior high anymore!"

"That's good since we are trying to pass you off as a bit older than you really are." Molly nodded with satisfaction. "With your new look, I'm sure we won't have to tell your story more than once."

Shara frowned at her new reflection in the mirror. "You really think your friends will hire me as a nanny?"

Molly nodded. "I'll pitch it to Drew in the morning. Knowing how he feels about this baby, I'm confident you'll be Jo and Drew's nanny this time next week." Molly tapped her pen against her lips again. "Normally with Jo, I'd come right out and tell her what's what. She's as direct as I am when it comes to most things. But this nanny thing..." Molly shook her head. "She needs the help, but she refuses to admit that. So we'll have to be a bit more..."

"Sneaky?" Shara grinned at her.

Molly chuckled. "I don't love that word, but okay. Sneaky." She tapped her comb against her chin. "I've got it. The faculty fall picnic! She reached for a notepad and scribbled some reminders. "Madeline, she's the second grade teacher, she was supposed to host it, but the addition on her house is taking way longer than anyone expected... Bryan's place. We'll have it at Bryan's."

"Okay..." Shara didn't sound convinced. "Why not here or at the school? Why can't I just meet Joanna at her house? If she's supposed to be off her feet, wouldn't that be smarter?"

"No, because the fall picnic can't be held at school. No one wants to spend MORE time at school." Molly shot Shara a grin. "As for doing it at her house, that's no good, she'll feel the need to clean and cook, which is counter-productive. Can't have it here, no place to go with the group if the weather craps out. Bryan's got way more room at his place."

"Bryan... won't he mind us sort of dumping this picnic on him?"

He'll mind very, very much, but who cares? Molly waved the idea off. "He'll be thrilled. You just wait."

14: BRYAN

"Drew, what's up with you?" Bryan strolled into the lounge.

Drew was sitting at the table, staring at his half-empty coffee cup, a pile of worksheets in front of him. "Stuff."

Bryan understood. Joanna was ordered to slow down and rest every day, but with two young kids, and her job as church organist there was no way. "Have you thought about taking a leave of absence, maybe going part time, to help her out?"

"Impossible. The board would let me, but not with pay. And I'd have to pay a sub. We've pretty much accepted that she's going to have to quit her job and that makes things tight."

"And the idea of getting a nanny?" Bryan knew the answer to this before he asked.

"Joanna is not exactly excited about having a stranger come in and take care of her kids and house. You know how she gets."

"I suppose." Bryan looked behind him and saw Molly walk in. "Well, Molly, you old woman, how are you?" Bryan was genuinely glad to see Molly back at school. A week without the banter they had back and forth was too long. The best of friends in spite of the ten years between them, Bryan never liked to dwell on how many times, after Jenny's departure, he cried on Molly's shoulder.

"Who are you calling old?" She gave him a stern look reserved for only the worst behaved student. "Maybe I need more time off?"

"No way. This place is dull without you. Ooh, donuts!" Bryan grabbed the cardboard box she carried and ripped it open. "Molly, you are the best!"

"Why, Bryan Jacobs, is that some kind of declaration of love?" Molly batted her eyelashes at him. "Or just your lust for donuts?"

" More like I have no one to argue with." He spoke through a mouthful of cruller. "Everyone just agrees with me."

"We humor him." Drew took the box and picked out a jelly filled. The first bite dripped red ooze onto the stack of book reports in front of him.

Molly poured herself a cup of coffee. "It's that magic you have over other people, you know. You big heart breaker."

The three friends laughed at Molly's comment. Bryan was not comfortable with his position as school heartthrob, and Molly and Drew knew it. He felt easier in their company than anywhere else.

"So, how's the little girl from the creek?" Drew finally pulled his attention away from the papers. "Find out anything about her?"

"First off, she's not a little girl. She's twenty-six, or will be in a couple of months. Nice girl, pretty, too." Molly nudged Bryan with her elbow. "You come over and have dinner sometime."

"Don't start." He stared at his toes. *Seriously, is every single female a possible match for me? How desperate do I really look?*

"Anyway, she's fine now. Nothing a little good food and love won't cure."

"Molly and her lost causes." Bryan tipped his coffee cup back and swallowed the last of the dregs. "This is the worst coffee yet. Did Madeline make this? That's the last time we let her make the coffee after she's taught art to the second graders. This stuff tastes like paste."

"Focus here, Bryan. This is important. Our girl's got no family, but wants to go to college. She wants to be a teacher, of all things."

"How'd she get to the creek?" Drew wanted to know.

"When did she get to be our girl?" Bryan poured himself another cup of coffee. Bad or not, he'd had another dream about Jenny last night, a nightmare, and it kept him restless most of the night.

Molly shook her head. "I'm not sure. She's uncomfortable talking about it."

"Duh!" Bryan swirled powdered creamer into his mug. "And do you think you'd be real forthcoming if you wound up half drowned, half dead, in a strange town?"

"All I know is she needs a job and a place to stay."

"Why not at your place? You're the refuge for the lost and lonely." The creamer didn't help. Bryan made a face at his first swallow.

Molly drank from her cup, making the same sour face. "She's allergic to the cats."

"Is this a surprise to anyone? I've told you, your house is an allergy trap. People who aren't allergic to cats get close to your house, and poof! They have allergies."

"Bryan, you are just on a tear today, aren't you?"

"Just making up for lost time, my dear." He grinned at Molly.

Molly ignored his attempt at charm. "Not to change the subject, but how's Joanna doing, Drew?"

Drew sighed and looked up from his papers. "Joanna just keeps swelling and puking. The doctors keep telling her to slow down, to rest every day. She won't listen. She's in the church right now, practicing organ for Sunday services. I suggested a nanny again last night."

"Joanna hates that."

"Wouldn't you?" Bryan asked. Joanna was the mother lion type of parent. Maybe she kept Nate and Emma on a longer leash than most moms, but her territorial protectiveness was legendary.

"What can we do to help?"

"I'm not sure," Drew said, shaking his head. "I've been over a list of people we could have come to the house, but no one seems right. Jo, of course, won't listen. She's determined not even to quit her job. Says we can't afford to lose it in the long run. She says that if it's meant to be, the baby will be here. If not-" Drew broke off.

Bryan looked away from his friend. The loss of the baby the previous year devastated Drew. Drew loved children, and wanted a houseful. The doctors never explained the loss of the baby, as they could not completely explain the swelling and constant vomiting Joanna experienced now. Bryan hated the thought of his friend going through the same anguish again.

"So, let's find you a nanny," Molly said in a calm voice.

"How about Mrs. Galoff?" Bryan suggested. Mrs. Galoff was everyone's favorite adopted grandma. She had a smile and a very dry molasses cookie for anyone.

"Too old. Isn't she ninety or something?"

"How about Mrs. King?"

"Bryan, she'd be too expensive."

"Drew, she's the pastor's wife. She wouldn't take a dime."

Drew looked at the closed door and grinned. "I know that, Molly. But she's the local gossip mill. I'd pay every day in many different ways. Think about it. This nanny is going to have to look after the kids, do housework. Do the laundry."

"Do your laundry, you mean?" Bryan started laughing. "Yeah, I'm sure I wouldn't like the pastor's wife getting her hands on my delicates either." His laughter was infectious and soon both men were chuckling.

Molly gave them both a stern motherly look. "I have a serious suggestion to make, if anyone is interested."

The men, like two boys, looked at her quickly and stopped laughing. But their faces contorted wildly to control their mirth.

"How about Bethany Elias?"

"Can she start tomorrow?" Obviously not serious, Drew started laughing again.

Bryan's own giddiness cooled as he searched his memory for anyone he knew by that name.

"Of course. I'll tell her." Molly picked up her brief case and was about to leave.

Bryan noticed that she was serious, and Drew was not. He wondered if either of them knew what the other was talking about. "Who is this Bethany Elias? Is she new in town?" Bryan asked. "I don't know that name."

"At this point I don't know if it matters." Drew rubbed his eyes and took another bite of his donut, dripping more raspberry filling onto the doomed book report. "Molly's suggesting her, and if she's willing to work for free, she's perfect."

"Don't you think maybe you'd better at least know who she is?"

"Fine." Drew set down the donut and assuming his most serious face. "Mol, who is Bethany Elias?"

"The creek girl."

Bryan wasn't sure what was funnier: The ridiculous suggestion, or the fact that she seemed so serious. "Geez, Mol, are you kidding? Some transient you found in the creek? To watch Drew's kids?"

"Well, you could be a little more charitable. She's looking for work, like I said before. She could help Joanna at the house, and…" She paused and looked at both men, "I believe she plays piano. She's quite good, in fact. She needs a break. And if you make one comment about strays, Bryan Jacobs, I will club you over the head with my lesson plan book." She turned furious eyes directly at him.

"So let me get this straight." Bryan spoke all the calm he could muster. "You've apparently gone insane. How are you going to pitch this to Joanna? 'Jo you know how you need a nanny, but don't want one? Well, have I got a deal for you! She's young enough, and she'll work real cheap. Bonus, she's a local girl. Her last address was the creek behind school.' Yeah, I see Joanna buying this real fast." He could not believe that Molly suggested such a thing. He further could not believe that, looking at Drew's face, his friend liked the idea.

"I was thinking they could meet at the faculty fall picnic next weekend. Bryan, you'll be hosting it, since Madeline's house is still in construction limbo." Molly set down her briefcase on the table, opened it, and pulled out two pieces of paper. "I've made some calls and everyone's good to go. Kelly Fuller and his boys can still provide the music that day. Bryan, you won't have to do a thing. Sound good, Drew?"

Drew took the paper from her and studied it carefully. "Well it looks good to me, Molly. I'm not so sure about Jo, but it looks good to me."

"Can we back up a moment here?" Bryan's voice sounded strangled. "I'm hosting the fall picnic? How did that happen?" *How is any of this happening?*

"Don't get into a tizzy. You won't have to do much. We've got Dirty Dog Dave grilling burgers, which should make you happy."

"Take a look at this, Bryan." Drew handed the paper to him. "Molly's got a great thing planned here."

"I'm sure she's planned this down to the last minute." Bryan rolled his eyes and gave them both a look of disbelief before

40

glancing at the sheet in his hand. "the bigger question is, how and why did I get involved in this?"

"You have the most room. I don't have the space-"

"Drew's got a whole parking lot! With a playground!" Bryan pointed at the window that overlooked much of RHCS property. "And a gym!"

Drew nodded in agreement to Bryan. "That's true. This late in the year...maybe the weather won't be good and we'd need the gym. It's not like Bryan has a lot of indoor room."

"That's right! That's right! I have no indoor room at all! None!"

Molly turned a cold gaze on Bryan. "You have enough room for this and you'll have good enough weather. We always have good weather for the picnic. No one wants to have it here, that's the whole point of hosting it on a rotating basis. Besides, a cookout loses some of its charm when it's held on blacktop." She put her hands on her hips and glared at him harder. "This gets you out of your turn next year. And all you have to do is provide the place. I will take care of the food and the band and everything. Do you have any objections with that?"

"Uh...no." Bryan backed away from Molly. She always scared him just a little when she got like this.

"Good. I should hope not. Now, Drew," Molly turned her attention back to the table, "do you see anything I may have missed?"

Drew shook his head. "It sounds good. But the doctors really want Jo to take it easy. She was thinking she'd just send me this year."

"If the doc has any questions, tell him I'll be there, shadowing her every move, and there won't be many of those." Molly snapped her briefcase shut again. "I'll get these sent out. I'm thinking about forty people or so. You know, the teachers, their spouses, and we'll have to invite Pastor and Mrs. King."

"Hey, what if it's not great for me? What if I had plans for that weekend? Don't I get a say about the entertaining that goes on at my place?" *I wasn't even going to go to this, now I'm hosting it?*

Bryan tried one more time to stand up for himself, but even as the words left his lips, he knew it was a waste of air.

"You suddenly have a life that I'm not aware of, CNN-boy?"

"This from the crazy cat lady." Bryan tried to look pitiful.

Molly ignored him. "I'll get everything arranged. Drew, you tell Jo."

Bryan and Drew shared a pained look. "Want to trade with me, Molly? I can arrange everything. You tell Jo." Drew stuffed the last of the donut into his mouth.

Molly waved a dismissive hand. "Take Bryan with you. She likes him."

Bryan held up a hand in protest. "You just got done telling me I didn't have to do anything for this. Now you're sending me to announce this insanity to Jo and let her think I've lost my mind along with the both of you? "

"Yes!" Drew and Molly said together, staring at him.

"You can do it tonight," Molly picked up her brief case.

"Not tonight," Bryan attempted a defiant stance. "I'm watching 'Larry King'."

"Joanna's making her pork chops." Drew gave Molly a conspiratorial grin.

Bryan sighed. *They win every time with the pork chops.* "Fine. But I'm not cleaning my house for this."

15: BRYAN

The thing about the Shepaski house that always struck Bryan was the shoes. On a good day, everyone in the family lined their shoes up by the back door, the door that lead into the garage. There, in the little hallway leading to the family room, the shoes were lined according to size from Drew's size eleven wingtips to Emma's tiny saddle shoes. A second line of shoes, this for the everyday kind, ran along the opposite wall of the hallway, again arranged according to size. On a really good day, everyone in the house wore the slippers Joanna bought them last Christmas in an effort to

42

keep the carpet clean and ease wear and tear on the dozens of pairs of socks she washed every week.

Judging from the looks of the hallway, Bryan noted, this was not a good day.

"Uncle Bryan!" Nathan hollered from the dining room, which overlooked the family room in the split-level house.

Bryan was about to respond to the boy when a curly haired tornado jumped him from the side. "Uncle Bryan!" Emma squealed as she shimmied up his leg.

Bryan loved the Shepaski kids. He often thought they were the closest he would get to actually having children of his own. He truly liked Nathan, who, at six, had his father's sense of diplomacy and his mother's dark hair. Emma, at three, looked for all the world like Drew with her blond hair and cornflower blue eyes, but her mouth moved almost as quickly as Joanna's.

"Bryan, I didn't know you were coming."

Bryan looked up to the dining room and studied Joanna Shepaski carefully. He hated what pregnancy did to her. He felt traitorous to this lovely woman who was such a good friend, but he couldn't help it. Everyone said a pregnant woman glowed. Not Joanna. Her hair, normally a glorious, thick cascade of shiny chestnut locks, hung down her shoulders in dull, greasy clumps. Her peaches and cream skin was blotchy and the water she retained seemed to bloat her to twice her size.

Drew never seemed to notice, or be bothered by the fact that his wife was a sweaty, funky smelling, blotchy pile of bloat. He always looked at Joanna like she was the most beautiful creature in the room. Bryan longed to love someone like that. But, looking at Joanna, he doubted he'd ever be able to love anyone that blindly.

In spite of her outward features, Joanna's spirit was indomitable. Bryan often sensed that there were times when Drew was a little afraid of her. Like right now.

"Hi, honey. I thought you were going to lie down after work. The doctor said-"

"The doctor doesn't live with these wild animals." Joanna picked up a toy truck from the top of the steps, her face reddening to purple from the exertion. "Nate! Set another place at the table. Uncle Bryan is staying for supper."

Drew gave Bryan a look that mirrored Bryan's own thoughts. This was not going to be an easy conversation. Joanna was in the mother of all bad hormonal moods.

"Hey, Jo, you're looking…" Bryan couldn't finish the sentence. There was not one single thing he could comment on that wasn't negative.

"I know. I look like a heaving cow and I probably smell like Dead Sea scum or something. How are you? I heard Molly was back today. How's that creek girl?"

"Funny you should mention that, Jo-"

"She's fine." Drew threw a warning glance to Bryan. "Molly said she's coming to see you this week sometime. Why don't you sit down at least?"

Joanna sighed. "For you, my love, anything." She heaved herself onto the nearest unsuspecting dining room chair.

As she sat, Bryan caught a glimpse of her ankles under her floor length robe. They were swollen and red.

Drew tucked a footstool under her mottled feet. "Molly and Bryan and I came up with an idea for a nanny."

"We talked about this already. We can't afford a nanny. Besides, I can manage. Doctors like to be glum, it's their job." She flashed a smile at Bryan that looked more like a carnivore baring her teeth at him. Bryan shrunk from eye contact with her.

Drew hesitated. "Well, Molly-that is, we all thought of someone who would work out just fine. She's in her twenties and saving for college. She could fill in for you as church organist and secretary, and take care of things here so you could take it easy."

Joanna looked suspicious. "I don't know anyone like that around here."

"She's new in town." Bryan toyed with a bread crust on the table left over from breakfast. *Please let her love this insane idea. Please God, don't let her get more upset.*

"What's her name?"

"Her name? Her name is-is, ah…" Drew threw Bryan a panicked look.

What the hell did Molly say her name was? Bryan locked his attention on the bread crust.

"Her name is Bethany Elias, Mommy. Auntie Molly told me after school to tell you because she figgered Uncle Bryan and Daddy would forget. Bethany Elias. I think it's pretty," Nathan piped up from the family room below.

"Bethany Elias? Who is Bethany Elias?" Joanna arched an eyebrow at them.

Bryan tried to swallow, but any trace of moisture was gone from his throat. A quick glance at Drew confirmed that he, too, was suffering from a lack of spit.

Joanna sighed and shook her head. "Nathan? Your father and Uncle Bryan seem to have lost the power to speak. Tell me, sweetie, who is Bethany Elias?"

"She's the creek girl, momma. Auntie Molly says Bethany Elias needs a job, and that she can play organ at church and take care of us." The boy never even looked up from his toy truck as he spoke words that the men at the table knew would create all sorts of trouble.

Bryan hoped his smile didn't look quite as terrified as Drew's.

"What are you, insane?" Joanna's voice reached a squeaky level. "You expect me to have some stranger you fished out of the creek a week ago come and live here and help raise our children? Not to mention taking my job at the church? And you-" She pointed a puffy finger at Bryan.

"Me?"

"You! I can't believe you would support this!"

"Well, actually I-"

"I can't believe you two. I'm not going to allow some, some person to come in here and take care of the house and the kids."

"Jo." Drew took her hands and spoke with more force than Bryan had ever heard from him. "Jo, you are going to stop working, and we're getting a nanny. We have few choices, none of them ideal. But we are not going to lose this baby. Not this time."

45

Joanna looked as if she had been struck. "I won't talk about that."

Drew wrapped his arms around his wife. "I know. But it's time we faced this. Now, Bryan agreed to have the fall faculty picnic at his place. It's the perfect chance to talk to her. If she's not to your liking, Mrs. King offered to help us."

"Not Mrs. King!" Nathan wailed, running up the stairs to his room and hiding under the bed. "She's got gray skin, like a witch!"

Joanna looked defeated as Nate's door slammed. "You win, boys. I'll give her a chance."

16: BRYAN

Bryan hated picnics. He had a perfectly good kitchen table inside, why did he have to eat outside with the wind and the dust and the bugs? When he rode Pepper all day, then he packed a lunch of some sort, but that was different. This was eating outside and being polite. He hated having to be polite when he ate. It wasn't that he had bad table manners. He just hated having people watch him chew.

Now he had to host the picnic and be part of this ridiculous plan of Molly's. Unfortunately, no rain clouds seemed to be interested in showing their collective face. Odd, thought Bryan, a late October picnic was a sure target for rain and snow. But no, it was cool, but sunny. There was just enough of a bite in the air to remind everyone that winter was not far off. A sweater would take care of that. *Too bad.*

"Bryan, are you home?"

Bryan grimaced. *Where else would I be?*

"Whew! It's a good thing we planned this for today," Molly carried in several Tupperware bowls of salads involving marshmallows and fruit and set them on the table. "Winter's coming."

Molly always felt the seasons and Bryan often thought she should be a weather forecaster. She was never wrong. If Molly said

46

it was going to be wet, pack a raincoat. *Animals and weather. This is what Molly knows. Well, that and the foibles of men who love her.*

As far as Bryan knew, while every single man in the county over the age of twenty and under the age of ninety had in some way tried to woo her, himself included on one misguided evening blurred by red wine and a terribly boring Packer game, she showed not a whit of interest. If it was true that there was one great love for every person, then Molly Krueger and Robert Hunter had actually found each other. Molly, in spite of Robert's sudden death six months into their marriage, was satisfied with the romance he'd given her.

"It's also a good thing we're doing this fast. I don't think poor Bethany can take another day with the cats."

"You just keep convincing me that this is a good idea she's going to Drew's."

"Where else could she go? I think Drew said he cleared out that downstairs room he's been using as an office. He's so certain this will be a good thing, he's even moved a bed and dresser in for her."

"Where's his office going? That isn't that big of a house."

"Well, from what I understand, they put his desk in the baby's room, for the moment. Bethany will move out after the baby's born anyway, right?"

Unless you figure out a way to keep your stray with us longer. "I still want to go on record saying that this is the dumbest idea I have ever heard in a very long time, and I hope that Jo and Creek Girl show a little good sense and say no to the whole thing."

"So noted, you sourpuss," Molly said, smiling and tugging Bryan's hair.

"Where's this person?"

Molly frowned. "You really don't grasp the concept that she has a name, do you?"

"It's Bethany something, right?" Bryan's good humor returned. He loved teasing Molly. "It's Bethany Elias, quit getting bunched up."

47

"Are you going to behave yourself?" She tossed a bag of paper plates to him.

He flashed his most charming smile. "Of course. Now let me go get gussied up."

17: MOLLY

Shara walked in as Bryan shut his bedroom door. "Nice place. Kind of cozy."

"Bryan likes it."

"Do you need any help with that?"

"No, not at all. Oh, but sweetie your eye make up is drooping a bit."

Shara touched her eyelashes, where a drip of mascara was rolling down her cheek. "I can't get my eyes to stop watering. Can I go someplace and do a touchup?

Molly nodded down the hall. "The bathroom is there, first door on the left."

Shara closed the door behind her. A moment later, Bryan emerged, wearing a clean shirt but the same attitude. "Is the creek girl here?"

"Bryan! She has a name. Will you please use it?"

"It's a good thing I like you, Molly Hunter." He held the screen door for her as she carried a tray of picnic food out to the porch.

"It's a good thing I like you, Bryan Jacobs." She set the tray on the table and gave him a kiss on the cheek. "Now promise me you'll be charming and sweet."

"Cross my heart."

Molly went back into the cabin, but looked at him for a good minute. He was in a mood which could make things difficult. *Well, too bad for you, Bryan. This plan has to work. I have to keep my promise to that girl.*

18: JOANNA

Drew pulled the station wagon up to the top of Bryan's drive. "We're here."

Joanna looked out the window at Bryan's yard. "I don't see her."

"Since you've never met her, Jo, I think you wouldn't know what she looks like," Drew's voice held a touch of humor.

Joanna was not amused. "I don't see anyone I don't know. I think she'd be the person I didn't know."

"You wait, Mommy. I saw her when Uncle Bryan was carrying her out of the creek," Nathan said excitedly, bouncing on his seat. "She wasn't pretty then, but I'll bet she's prettier now. She's probably had a bath 'n stuff."

"Pretty girl!" Emma shouted from her car seat.

The Shepaskis got out of the car and walked up Bryan's drive to the yard between the house and the barn. Molly saw them and waved to Joanna to come into the house.

Joanna's heart pounded as she lumbered up the two steps to Bryan's porch. *Don't even think about running away. You'd look ridiculous. Besides, if Molly thinks this Bethany will be able to help us, maybe it's a good thing.* She ignored the stares from the two men and she stepped onto the porch.

"I thought you two should meet first," Molly murmured.

"Molly, I appreciate everything, but I don't know…" Joanna let her voice trail off.

"Jo, I'd like you to meet my friend, Bethany Elias," Molly ignored Joanna's comment and pulled her into the house.

Joanna studied the girl in front of her. Molly said she was twenty-six, but to Joanna she looked more like a young girl who'd played with her mother's make up. Joanna looked Bethany in the face, and the deep, serious light in the girl's eye pleased her. "Hello, Bethany."

"Hello, Joanna."

Joanna noted the Bethany called her by her first name right away. She had a confidence Joanna did not expect. The young woman was comfortable meeting strangers.

"Molly's told me a little about you, Bethany. Not very much, though."

"There's not much to tell," Bethany said, pointing to the couch. "I do know that you are supposed to be off of your feet. How about if we sit here?"

There was no sympathy in the girl's voice. She was stating a fact and providing a solution, and that simple gesture Joanna knew. *Like I would approach a problem.* "Bethany, I'll be direct. We need a nanny. Molly thinks you're a good choice."

"Well, I'll be direct. I need a job." Bethany focused her dark eyes on Joanna.

"Molly tells me you want to go to college and be a teacher?"

"I do." Bethany kept her gaze steady. "I should have done it out of high school, but there was my grandfather to take care of, and time sort of slipped by. I hope to one day get my degree. I think teaching would be wonderful. I adore children."

"Uh huh." Joanna braced herself for the most important question. "How did you wind up in the creek?"

The faintest of shadows fluttered over her face. "Molly didn't tell you?"

"Not really." Joanna looked toward Molly, whose face was still and blank.

The girl shifted in her seat, looking a tiny bit uncomfortable. "It's not a story I like to tell."

Oh, but you're going to tell it, sweetie, and I'm going to have to buy it. "I understand that. But if I'm going to trust you with my children, I think I have a right to know. Besides, I'd like to know if I should prepare for...any sort of drama."

"I understand, of course." Bethany Elias nodded in agreement. "Don't worry about family, I have none left. My grandfather...I was living with him until he died recently. He was ill for a long time, but he took care of me, too. I had this boyfriend." She paused and looked up at the ceiling. "My grandfather wanted us to get

50

married, so I would have someone to take care of me when he was gone. Only thing, I knew things about this man that weren't good. Money problems, legal things, that sort of stuff. I didn't want to make my grandfather worry, so I went along with his wishes for a while."

It was Joanna's turn to nod. The girl's story, if it was a story as Bryan suggested, was delivered with a sincerity few could fake. Joanna almost believed her.

"So when Grandfather died, I tried to leave Escanaba. But the guy," here Bethany sighed, "he didn't want me to leave him. I stayed. I didn't have any other place to go. I was working a crummy job as a waitress and had no money. I wanted to go to college, have some kind of chance." Here Bethany brushed a tear from her eyes and bit her lip. "Then one night, I just had to leave. We'd gotten into a huge fight and he threw a bottle at me. I was done with him, and I wanted to walk out and catch a bus. He apologized and said he'd give me a ride down to Green Bay, where I could find work. I believed him. On the road, it started raining like crazy and we couldn't drive. We pulled to the side of the road." Bethany traced the fading bruises on her face with the tip of her finger. "That's when he started in on me, really hitting me. I got out of the car and ran as hard as I could. He was laughing when I ran, said that it was okay for me to leave now because no one would want me, after what he'd done to my face. That he never wanted me again." She blinked back another tear. "I must've tripped in the woods or something and fallen down the creek bank."

How can anyone not be moved by this tragic story? Joanna looked at her face and saw no trace of deceit in the fading bruises. "Are you afraid he'll come after you if he knows where you are?"

Bethany glanced quickly to Molly, then focused those eyes back on her. "I doubt he'll put any more energy into me anymore. All I need is a fresh start. I've got plans, but the first step, that's the hardest, right?"

And I'm not going to deny her that. Joanna put a hand on Bethany's arm. "Bethany, I'll be honest with you. We can't pay you anything to watch the kids. We'll give you a room at the house, and any of the basics you'll need. Being the church organist and secretary, though, they'll pay you for that. It's a good first step to that fresh start. What do you think?"

"You trust me to watch your children?" Bethany looked genuinely surprised. "Just like that?"

"Joanna's a very good judge of character, Bethany. She's never wrong." Molly leaned over the couch. "Like me with the weather."

"Molly's no slouch in the character department, and I've known her a long time. If Molly vouches for you, that's good enough for me." Joanna grinned at Bethany.

Bethany looked back at Molly. "Does it matter that I've never really gone to church? I mean, Grandfather was a good man, but church, that sort of slipped through the cracks."

Joanna liked the girl's candid question. "Not a requirement, I guess, but something to work on. You do play organ, right?"

"Organ, piano, whatever has keys on it, I'll play."

"Then I wouldn't worry about it. You'll be going to church plenty while you stay with us." Joanna gave Bethany's hand a motherly squeeze.

"So I'm a mission project on top of it all. You get a bonus in heaven or something?" Bethany relaxed a little.

Joanna laughed out loud. "You'll do just fine. Can you start Monday?"

"Only if those guys with the grim faces lighten up a bit." Bethany nodded to the gathering in the yard, where Bryan, Drew, and everyone seemed to be very interested in something on the porch.

Molly left her post at the door. "Didn't I tell, you, Jo? She's perfect."

"You were right as usual. I have learned over the years to trust Miss Molly here." Joanna looked at Bethany. "It's something that gives me comfort."

"I know exactly what you mean." Bethany shared a smile with Molly that seemed a little too familiar to Joanna, but she didn't care to ponder it just now.

"Let's go tell the boys the news." Joanna took Bethany's hand and led her to the porch. All eyes turned to the porch as they emerged into the sunlight. *Maybe we should send up some white smoke instead.* "Hey everyone! Guess what? Bethany here is going to be our nanny!"

19: SHARA

All during lunch, Molly and Joanna clucked around her like mother hens while the children stared at her with big eyes. Shara didn't care for the attention, having every eye focused on her made her uncomfortable, especially given how frightening her bruises, even covered with makeup, must be to them all. There was something especially unnerving about the dark haired, dark eyed man who hosted the picnic. He was quite conspicuous about not coming into contact with her, and yet, every time Shara looked in his direction, he averted his eyes quickly.

Needing a break from the attention, Shara sought sanctuary in the cabin, under the pretense of finding a diet cola to drink. She located a can in the farthest recesses of the fridge and, snapping it open, took a minute to breathe and look out the small kitchen window at the country highway that ran in front of the cabin. The long shadow of a burned out farmhouse, seated a quarter acre beyond the cabin, stretched out over the pavement.

"They say it was burned down by the owner because his wife took a lover and lied to him about it, even though he had proof."

Shara whirled around to stand face to face with the host. "I-I'm sorry?"

"The old house. When I bought the place, that's what they told me. It casts a pretty cool shadow on the highway, doesn't it?"

"Oh, yes, it does. But that's an interesting story."

He set a bowl of unfinished potato salad on the counter. "I bought the place because I liked the land and the buildings. The story of the house...." his voice drifted off and he looked at the floor. "Well, isn't it Biblical for a man to be driven insane by a lying woman?"

Shara took a long drink from her cola, trying to pull her eyes from this dark, brooding man. "I-I wouldn't know much about that." He raised his eyes to her, a cold, glittering look that almost dared her to look elsewhere. "You must be Bryan. Molly tells me that you...that you were the one who carried me from the creek. I'm afraid, I don't remember much of that day."

"Yeah." Bryan scuffed his foot on the floor. "Oh. They need another garbage bag. Under the sink."

"I wanted to thank you, you know, for that." She bent down to find the bag and handed it to him, their fingers brushing slightly in the exchange. Their eyes met for a heartbeat, and a warm flow of electricity passed between them. Shara jerked her hand back and stared at the floor. "So, thanks."

"Yeah. Well, you're welcome." Whether he looked at her or not, she didn't care, keeping her eyes glued to the shadow of the old house until the screen door snapped shut.

20: BRYAN

In the solitary comfort of his overstuffed armchair, hours after the picnic, Bryan allowed himself to look at his hand, the hand where she touched him. Not a man given to imaginary sensations, he tried to ignore the fact that the tips of his fingers still tingled where her fingers brushed them. Her eyes, deep and wounded, haunted him.

Doesn't mean a thing. Everyone else has simply lost their minds. He looked at his fingers again. *She's hiding something.* He snapped on the television set.

"From his hospital bed today, Richard Bennett, wounded in the shooting spree that took the life of seventy-five-year-old businesswoman Lydia Brandt ten days ago, made a plea for his fiancé, Shara Brandt, to come forward. Miss Brandt, twenty-three, is a recent business graduate of Marquette University, and Lydia Brandt's granddaughter."

The next face on the screen was Richard's. Bryan wanted to look away, but could not, and everything was forgotten as he watched the man he hated make a speech.

"Shara, honey, come home from wherever you are. We all know it was an accident, you didn't mean to do it. Please come home so the people who love you can get you help."

The picture melted back to the news anchor. "In an off screen interview this afternoon, Mr. Bennett did say that Miss Brandt has been under a psychiatrist's care for several years. Authorities say that Miss Brandt is most likely not a danger to others, but if you should see this person you are to call Crime Stoppers at-" Bryan snapped off the set and stared out the window.

Well of course she's nuts. She was engaged to him.

He looked down at his hand again, a dark thought dawning on him. *Could the most innocent Bethany Elias be Shara Brandt? Is that what she's hiding?*

He reached for the phone, but thought the better of it. *I won't call the police just yet. But I'll be watching very closely. That's a promise, Miss Bethany Elias*

21: SHARA

From the moment Shara stepped foot inside the Shepaski home she knew the hardest part of her job was going to be dealing with the very independent Joanna.

"Your duties are simple." Joanna handed her some very well used Care Bears sheets to put on her bed in the room that used to be Drew's study. "You walk Nate home from school and help him with any homework. Watch Emma during the day, maybe do a little laundry. Amuse them while I cook dinner."

"You can cook sitting down?" Shara tucked the last corner of the sheet under the twin mattress and looked at her puffy employer.

"Listen, Missy, you're not the boss." Joanna's tone was kinder than her words.

Shara put her hands on her hips and tried to look as commanding as she could in front of the formidable Joanna. "No, I'm not, you're right. But I am supposed to do all household duties that involve standing or lifting." Shara grinned, remembered the long hours watching her grandmother's chefs prepare meals. "Don't worry. I do know how to cook." She matched Joanna's expression and stood her ground.

Joanna conceded the point, if only for the moment.

It was during her tour of the school and then the church later that day with Drew when Shara got more details about her new job.

"I know Jo gave you a short list of duties." He spoke softly, as if afraid of being overheard, even in a darkened school building. "That's not how things are."

"I know." With Drew, conversation was short and comfortable. She sat down at the piano in his classroom and started playing, quite unconsciously, while they talked. It was a habit she'd picked up as a child after hours of practice, which was far more enjoyable than other hobbies Grandmother chose for her.

If Drew was impressed with her command of the instrument, however, he wasn't letting on. "You'll need to run errands. You know how to drive, right?"

"Yeah. Of course." She stared out the window, and silently pleaded that Drew never asked her to produce a license. Even if she'd wanted to, which was unthinkable, Shara could not prove her identity. "I mean, I don't have a license right now. It was lost or, or something." It was one truth in a sea of lies and half-truths.

Drew gave her a quick smile. "Don't worry. Kelly Fuller's the only cop in town who might actually pull you over for anything, and he's a former student of mine."

"You're not saying you'd pull strings for me?"

"Maybe. But that depends."

"On what?" Shara liked the warm twinkle in Drew's eye.

"On your cooking." He grew serious. "Bethany, I'll help as much as I can, but my hours here are pretty long." He stopped for a beat. "I know this is a lot to ask of you." He shook his head. "It's not an easy thing to admit, not being able to care for your family."

"Drew," she stopped playing and turned toward him. "I understand the chance you're taking with me, and I appreciate it. I'll take good care of your family."

Drew gave her a quick pat on the shoulder and sighed. "Thank you."

The simple, fatherly gesture steeled Shara's resolve. *Whatever I did or didn't do before doesn't matter here. Bethany Elias is going to be good and honorable.*

* * *

The Shepaski family had an old piano in the family room, but no one had played it for years. "It came from my grandmother's house when she died," Joanna told Shara one night. "I haven't played it in ages because I'm usually over at church on that piano."

"Is it in tune?"

"We had it tuned when the school pianos were tuned. Maybe a year ago. Feel welcome to tinkle on it anytime you please. And if you need help with any of the choir pieces..." Joanna hoisted herself out of her chair and took a step toward the piano bench where Shara sat.

"No, I think I've got that all under control actually." Shara enjoyed her temporary position as choir accompanist. The music wasn't too difficult, and, though she'd rarely been in a church since her parents died, the creaky confines of Rock Harbor Community Church gave Shara a sense of security. She put her hands on the battered keys. *Maybe this loving God everyone around here believes in will take care of stuff for me.*

"Momma said tinkle!" Emma giggled from the dining room railing. Joanna patted the child's soft blond hair as she passed by on her way to her room.

"You hush, little girl, or I'll come up there and tickle you!" Shara called, making the child giggle more. Nate joined her and the sounds of children's laughter grew.

"You're funny Bethany!" Nate cried.

"I can be funnier." Shara started playing softly. *Kids are so easy.*

"Yeah?" Nate leaned over the railing and watched her.

"Underwear!"

Both children fell on the dining room floor in a heaving, giggling heap. Shara smiled and kept playing softly. This was their favorite game. As the laughter subsided, Shara didn't even look up from the cracked, yellowing keys. "Butt!"

The laughter echoed through the house. "What on earth are you doing out here?" Joanna demanded as she huffed out of her room.

"Bef'ny is saying funny words!" Emma chuckled.

"Really? Like what?"

"Nothing really, Joanna." Shara stopped playing and looked up at her. "All I said was something like, 'NAKED!'"

Both children roared anew and Joanna rolled her eyes. "You're all goofy. I'm going to lie down."

"I'll send Drew up when he gets in," Shara said over the din. "Now, you two, hush up and come down here. Instead of a story tonight I want to play a piece of music for you and see if you can make up your own story in your dreams." Shara waited as the two arranged themselves on the floor near the piano. She smiled, remembering herself, a child no older than Nate, watching worshipfully as her mother played some magical piece of music that gave her dreams of castles and princesses and stars.

"What's the name of the song?" Nate asked.

"This is called 'Moonlight Sonata' and it was written by a man named Ludwig von Beethoven."

"Beethoven? Like the dog from the movie?" Nate wanted to know.

"Nothing like the dog. This man was a brilliant composer and he was deaf."

"What's deaf?" Emma asked.

"It means you're not breathing no more," Nate informed her.

"No, that's death, Nate. Deaf means you can't hear."

"Oh."

At that moment, Drew opened the door and Shara stopped talking.

"Daddy! Bethany is telling us about a man named Beethoven, only not the dog," Nate ran up to his father and hugged him.

"Yeah, and he was death," Emma spoke solemnly from where she sat. "That means you can't hear."

"So, it's music appreciation night?" Drew leaned his briefcase on the banister.

"A little. I thought I'd play for the kids before they went to bed."

"Great. Bryan, you can put your stuff on the table."

Shara nearly choked on the lump in her throat as Bryan walked into the house. She turned to face the keyboard. There was something about him that unsettled her every time they met. Shara knew without a doubt he did not trust her. In her few weeks with the Shepaskis, Bryan had come over to the house at least a dozen times, always cold to her and always, always studying her with his piercing dark blue eyes.

"Play, Bethany!" The children resumed their seats.

Shara put one tremulous hand on the keys and played the first chord too lightly. She continued, calling the music from her memory, her confidence increasing with every note. Minutes later she finished and the final notes faded in the air to silence. She looked at the children who stared at her with enormous eyes.

"Wow." Nate could have been sitting in Sunday School; he was so still with his hands folded in his lap.

"Wow." Emma was his mirror image and his echo.

Upstairs there was a smattering of applause from Drew and Joanna, who leaned over the railing above to listen. She turned to thank them and her eyes met Bryan's.

"That wasn't bad." His words came in a flat tone. He gave her another dark look and climbed the stairs.

"Thanks." She was, as always, uncertain of what he was really thinking.

"I'm gonna dream about fireflies at night," Nate hopped up the steps to his room.

"Fi'fies!" Emma cheered, following him.

"Good night, kids." Shara closed the piano lid and followed them upstairs. Drew and Joanna led the children to their rooms for nighttime prayers. Bryan sat at the table and worked on the papers in front of him. Shara crossed the dining room to the kitchen to get a diet cola.

"Why do you drink that crap?" He arranged papers and books in front of him.

"I like it."

"No one likes it. You women just drink it so we all think you're on a diet."

Shara looked at him. Head bent over his books, Bryan wasn't even looking at her. "I don't know about other women. I know I drink it because I like it. It's not as sweet as regular soda."

"Whatever."

"I have to walk over to church and run through the hymns for Sunday." She passed by the table and went back downstairs.

"Don't get lost."

"I doubt I'll have trouble crossing the parking lot." She looked up at him as she put on her coat.

He gave her a quick glance. "You never know."

She shook her head and closed the door behind her. "How someone so rude ever got to be friends with Drew and Joanna, I'll never know," Shara muttered on her way across the parking lot to the church.

* * *

Working with the children, working at the church, Shara lost herself in the simple rhythms of the Shespaskis, and reveled in the acceptance and love that her new family showered on her. She dwelt as little as possible on the lie she and Molly shared, it was a distant memory that she shut out as best she could.

The week before Thanksgiving, six weeks after arriving in Rock Harbor, Shara took a rare afternoon off to go to Molly's house. It was time for her to get a touch up on her hair color.

"So how are things with Jo?" Molly donned latex gloves as Shara hung her head over Molly's kitchen sink.

"Jo's okay, I guess. She had another appointment yesterday. Everything seems fine. I mean, she's stressed about Thanksgiving, you know, relatives and all that."

"Bryan's coming?"

Shara sighed. "She says so."

"Okay, sit up. You don't sound thrilled at the idea of Bryan coming to dinner."

Shara sat up and wrapped a large bath towel around her head. "Well, it's just that…I mean…okay, what's the deal with him anyway?"

Molly laughed out loud as she gently dried Shara's hair. "I wondered when you'd get around to asking that."

"He's so…grumpy. And he doesn't like me one bit."

"He wasn't always like that. He hasn't been the same since the divorce."

"Divorce. Well, that means he was polite enough to a woman to get married at least once." Shara closed her eyes, enjoying the warmth of the blow drier on her scalp. "It's like every time he sees me, he's looking for something, waiting for something."

Molly turned off the blow drier and gave her a concerned look. "You haven't said anything…you know."

"Oh god no!"

"Well, then it's just Bryan being wary. Or he's jealous."

"Jealous? Jealous of what?"

Molly grinned. "Jealous of you. Since Creek Girl joined us, Bryan, the wounded hero, isn't quite as interesting."

"Molly! You can't be serious!" Shara laughed at the thought.

"Well, no matter what Bryan thinks, there's one thing no one can deny."

"What's that?"

Molly turned her so Share could see her reflection in the mirror. "I am getting to be a pretty good hand at home hair coloring. Looks quite natural if I do say so." Molly patted Shara on the shoulder. "And, you have to admit, there isn't a soul around here that would recognize you as the girl from that news story."

Shara smiled at her reflection, but with a slight pang, realized what Molly said was true. *Richard wouldn't even recognize me.*

If he's truly searching for me.

* * *

Mrs. King, the pastor's wife, had not missed playing the organ for a Thanksgiving Day festival service in twenty years, and just because Bethany Elias was, by all accounts, much better at it than anyone in church history, the woman was not about to give up her moment. That was fine with Shara, who was more interested in getting the dinner put together properly and letting the Shepaskis worship together. As a result, the house dripped with good smells by the time the church bells rang, announcing the end of the service.

Bryan arrived before the rest of the family. "Happy Thanksgiving."

Shara, surprised at the nearly polite tone from him smiled. "Thanks. You, too."

"Did you cook the whole dinner?"

Shara nodded. "I did. I mean, Joanna gave me her recipes, and she sort of supervised things. But I did the cooking."

Bryan leaned against the railing and watched her put the last place setting at the table. "Yeah, well, it won't be Joanna's cooking, but I'm sure it won't kill us, will it?"

Well, that took care of that, didn't it? She blinked a stinging tear. *Why does he always seem to want to find the harshest thing to say to me?*

And why on earth does it matter to me what he says?

Shara tried to look beyond the exterior, and into him. She heard he was the most desired male in the county, a profile he certainly didn't fit in her mind. But Molly loved him and she knew very well how much the children, as well as Drew and Joanna, adored him. He was family to them.

So maybe Molly was right. Just by being here I'm the problem he has. Well, whatever. I have work to do.

Drew's mother, a jolly old woman with powdery cheeks and pale blue eyes, greeted Shara like a long lost child. "I hear you are the angel from heaven." She kissed Shara's cheek.

"Mrs. Shepaski, you're giving me too much credit."

"Nonsense, and call me Mother S. Everyone does."

"Everyone who's family, that is." Bryan seated himself at the table. Shara did not miss the angry look Joanna threw at him.

With a twinge of sadness, as Shara surveyed the table heaping with wonderful food and circled with loving family, she remembered her own Thanksgivings with Grandmother. Quiet affairs, usually experienced at one of the finer restaurants in Milwaukee. Resentful wait staff bringing impersonal plates to their table. Grandmother grumbling because every year people wanted not only Thanksgiving Day off, but also the next day. That Friday was the biggest day of the year for sales. Didn't anyone understand business?

"What are you thinkin' about?" Joanna sidled up to her, carrying a bowl of yams to the table.

Shara sighed and brushed at the corners of her eyes. "It's just all so beautiful."

"Yeah, it is," Joanna agreed. She nodded to Bryan. "It would be perfect if Bryan wasn't in a mood."

"That's a mood? I thought that's how he always is."

"No. It's always worse on Thanksgiving." Joanna shook her head.

"Why today?"

Joanna studied Bryan across the room carefully before answering. "Bryan and Jenny got engaged on Thanksgiving. They'd only known each other a few weeks. I think they met at a Halloween party. Since she left, he's been a beast on Thanksgiving. Or, more so than any other day. Except Christmas."

"I see." She turned her gaze to the man in question. "What happened on Christmas?"

Joanna's smile held little mirth. "They got married on Christmas Eve."

"Wow." She ignored the brief thought of her own impending wedding, scheduled for Christmas Eve.

"Yes. She ruined him completely. Bryan used to be the sweetest guy I know. And I've known him for a very long time. Then she came along."

"He's not too crazy about me, is he?"

"Don't worry about that, Bethany. He'll come around." Joanna gave her a quick one-armed hug. "He has little choice in the matter, given just how great you are, and how much it will hurt if I smack him with my frying pan."

Shara returned Joanna's hug and tried to shut out the nagging feeling that her friend was wrong. *Bryan may never come around.* She glanced at him, standing at the other end of the table, just as he looked in her direction. Holding no warmth for her, his gaze felt like an icy slap. She turned away quickly. *I am not going to let him bother me.* She turned back and gave him a cold glare of her own. *You're attitude is not going to bother me, Bryan Jacobs.*

* * *

Shara ate until her stomach was more than full, reveling in the bond she felt with her adopted family. *Don't focus on what you didn't have living with Grandmother.*

"Drew, did you hear your cousin Randy is getting married in February? On Valentine's Day." Mother S. dug into her third helping of stuffing with gusto.

"No, Ma, I didn't hear that. Who to?"

"Well." Mother S. lowered her voice as if relating a scandal. "He's marrying a girl he met last month at work. Someone he was training at work. You can imagine his parents are up in arms. He hardly knows the girl."

"Well, Mother S., that doesn't seem to stop any of the Shepaski men from attaching themselves to people." Bryan spooned out more potatoes for himself. "The men in your family have a strange need to turn their lives over to complete strangers."

Shara's stomach twisted. His words reminded her too well that she did not belong with these good people. "Will you excuse me, please?" She scurried from the table , down the stairs, and out of the house.

22: BRYAN

"Bryan Jacobs, that was horrible." Joanna's hiss cut through the stillness.

"What did I do? Did I lie?" *And don't look at me like I don't know what I'm doing. This has nothing to do with Jenny and everything to do with that girl.*

Joanna rounded the table toward him. "Has it ever occurred to you that maybe she's here because she doesn't have a family?"

Drew stopped chewing and glanced up. The children stared in wonder. Mother S. helped herself to more stuffing. Bryan sensed a war with Joanna coming on and he knew no one ever won a war with her. *So what?* "Did it ever occur to you that she doesn't have a family because she killed them?" He crossed his arms and waited for her to volley back.

"Bryan Jacobs!" Joanna stood up, her rage purpling her face. "Nate, take your sister to your room. NOW!"

The children, wide eyed like rabbits, scooted away without protest. Bryan braced himself for the battle.

"Now, Bryan, you explain yourself." Joanna leaned over him, her puffy face a picture of barely controlled fury.

"Do any of you even care that she might be Shara Brandt?"

"Shara who?" Drew, for the first time, stopped eating long enough to speak.

"That girl from Milwaukee. The one that was engaged to Richard. The one that killed her grandmother in the car dealership."

Joanna slammed down into a nearby chair as if struck. "Do you taste the words that come out of your mouth, or do you just spread this poison on everyone without any feeling?"

"I'm serious. You all just took her in, and we know nothing about her. She shows up the day after this woman is murdered, and this Shara is missing. Not only that, but her fiancé says Shara Brandt is mentally unstable."

"Her fiancé, you mean Richard Bennett? Weren't you disappointed he didn't die in that attack?" Drew dabbed a roll into some gravy on his plate.

"You know, Bryan, you know that this is all about Jenny."

Bryan did not want to back down from Joanna's tiger-like frown. "It is not, Jo. This is about the kids."

"Well that young lady out there is pretty much a kid herself. She ran away from an abusive boyfriend, and all but died in our back yard. She's not from Milwaukee, she's from Escanaba. Molly vouches for her. Why would Molly lie?" Joanna sighed and dabbed some sweat from her face. "Bethany doesn't have a devious bone in her body. And since when do you believe a word Richard Bennett says? He's your advisor now? Then you have lost your mind, Bryan Jacobs and I don't want you here."

Looking in Joanna's eyes, seeing her conviction, Bryan mentally noted that it was unlikely that everyone he knew could be fooled. There was a chance that Bethany was genuine. *It probably is all about Jenny...and Richard Bennett.* "Maybe you're right, Jo. Maybe." He sighed and rubbed his head with his hands. "I guess I could be less of a jerk, couldn't I?" *And restore some peace in the process.*

Joanna softened visibly. The war was over. "I know you have a lot of hurt inside." She waddled over and hugged him. "But you've got to remember the great guy you really are, and be him once in awhile."

Yeah, but I don't have to be the nanny's cheerleader, either. "I'll go find her and apologize." *And that will keep the peace for now.* Bryan got up from the table and left the house. Dirty snow melted under the tires of Drew's station wagon. She wasn't in the garage. He opened the garage door and stepped out into the afternoon sunshine. Puddles formed on the sidewalks and driveways as snow melted in the forty-degree warmth.

She was sitting on the front stoop. "Hey." He sat next to her. "You didn't go far."

"Where exactly would I go?" She turned a tear stained face to him. Dark smudges under her eyes told him she had been crying hard.

Her eyes tore away another shred of his doubt. *Could she possibly be less sinister?* "Look, what I said was... uncalled for"

"It's not like you haven't been building up to it." She sniffled and buried her face in the crook of her arm. "I'd like to know what I ever did to you."

Nothing. Call it preemptive jerkiness. "It's not really you. I love those kids like they were my own. You just show up one day and no one ever questioned whether or not you were right for them." He shrugged and leaned his elbows on his knees. "I'm very protective."

"So you're saying you don't trust me." Her sniffle punctuated her pitiful aura.

"I'd like to know you better."

"Really?" Her tone showed no interest. "Aren't I the lucky one?"

Bryan frowned. He'd always had the opposite effect on women. Mostly, women wanted him to know them better. *Not this one.* "I don't mean in the way it sounds."

"Like what then?" The anger and hurt in her eyes tore away the last shred of pride he had.

If I shove my foot all the way in my mouth maybe I'll shut up and stop botching this apology. "I'd like to know more about you before I'm comfortable with you, you know, watching the kids."

"Fair enough." She sniffled again and wiped her eyes.

"So." He handed her a tissue. "What about it?"

"What about what?"

"What about your story?"

She shook her head. "You know my story. What's your story?"

And she's not going to let me off the hook easily. "Fair enough. Let's see: I was born, I grew up, went to school, got the job teaching here, got into trouble at dinner just now."

Her lips twisted into a half smile. "I like that version. Simple and short. I can do that. I was born, I grew up. I left home, wound up here, and just stormed out of the best Thanksgiving dinner I ever had."

"You missed the part about being in the creek."

"You missed the part about being married."

"Touché." He stared out over to the school and nodded. "I keep forgetting you don't keep too much hidden in a small town." He looked sideways at her. "How about a truce? A truce with ground rules. Anytime I want to know something about you, I have to tell you something about myself."

She nodded. "We don't ask questions if we aren't ready to answer any, right?"

"Deal." He stuck out his hand. She took it in hers, and they shook. "Now, how about some pumpkin pie?"

She gave him a worried look. "You want to know a secret?"

"Is this a freebie question for me? Because I don't think I'm ready to reveal much more this afternoon."

"Don't sweat it." She gave him a wan, yet utterly enchanting smile. "I'm actually a little afraid about how it turned out. I've never had pumpkin pie before. I don't know if it's right."

Her words startled him. "You've never had pumpkin pie?"

She shrugged. "My Thanksgiving Day dinners were always rather untraditional. Grand..pa wasn't big on pies."

"Well look, the rest of the meal didn't kill us," Bryan grinned at her.

"Oh thanks for the vote of confidence."

"Seriously. Dinner was great. I'm sure the pie will be great." He opened the front door for her. *I'll still keep an eye on you, though, Bethany Elias.*

Watching her walk up the stairs, Bryan realized that wasn't going to be such a terrible thing to do.

23: JOANNA

The restored good mood was not lost on Joanna. "They got on better, don't you think?" She adjusted the blankets around her mounding form in bed later that night.

"Yeah." Drew, almost asleep, dug deeper into his side of the bed.

Joanna sat up and frowned. "I was thinking about Christmas."

"We just got through Thanksgiving. Can't we rest for a day?"

"It's not that simple. We've got a houseful of relatives coming, like we always do, only this year we can't have people camping in your office, because your office is currently Bethany's bedroom. We really can't ask her to give up her room and bunk on the couch, you know. That wouldn't be right."

"No, that wouldn't be fair." Drew stared at the ceiling. "Maybe Molly's?"

"The cats, remember? Besides, Molly always goes to Chicago with her sister. I can't bear the thought of poor Bethany staying alone with the cats, suffering from allergies." Joanna put on a pouty face.

Drew didn't look fooled by her act. "All of a sudden I don't think we're really talking about Christmas."

No use sugar coating it and slowing the process. "I'm thinking that our nanny might just be the one to get Bryan over Jenny."

Drew sat up sharply and stared at her. "Has it occurred to you that it's only been about nine hours since he stopped treating her like a disease? That as recently as dinner today he accused her of being a murderer on the lam?" He shook his head. "Of all the women in this town who would give their eyesight to be with him, you choose the one he absolutely, positively does not like or trust? And is there any inkling at all that she even wants to be around him?" Drew stopped and took a deep breath.

Joanna waited, surprised he had so much to say. It wasn't often that her husband strung together so many sentences without a class of eighth graders in front of him. "From what I've seen, Jo, Bethany would rather be anywhere else than around him."

"Which is exactly why she's perfect." She picked up the telephone receiver and started dialing. "I'll talk to Molly. She'll love the idea."

Drew put his hand on her arm, and she stopped the call. "Jo, it's almost midnight! Molly probably isn't even back from her cousin's."

Joanna gave him a weary look and started dialing again. "Molly was probably home hours ago. There's little love lost between her and that cousin, and you know it!"

Drew propped himself up on one elbow. "How about this, then: If this thing, if there is a thing, is going to happen, shouldn't it happen slowly, maybe, you know, without a big push from you?"

Joanna sighed and looked down at her belly. "Drew, you and I both know that Bryan is never going to move quickly into the arena of romance without a push. Jenny cured him of that. So we can't wait for him to move at his own pace." She patted her stomach. "Once this baby is born, we won't need a nanny, and Bethany will probably leave Rock Harbor. And that would be a shame because I really do see in her a spark that might bring the old Bryan back to us. I don't know about you, but I'd never forgive myself if this is his chance to be free of the whole Jenny mess, and we let it slip away." She knew from Drew's expression that he agreed with her, however reluctantly. She finished dialing Molly's number and listened as the phone rang twice. "Hey Molly? I'm sorry to be calling so late, but I just had an idea."

* * *

That Monday afternoon, Joanna pondered how she would break the news to Bethany. She was bolstered by Molly's confidence that Bryan, would, indeed agree to whatever Molly suggested. He usually did.

An email from Molly at the end of the school day confirmed that Bryan, though plenty reluctant, agreed to having Bethany as a houseguest for Christmas Eve.

Now, as Joanna watched Bethany bring the children home from errands, she hoped she would be as successful with the nanny. She waited until they were in the house, the children squealing with delight as Bethany pealed layers of slushy wet clothing off of them. "Bethany, could you come up for a moment?" She called from the top of the stairs.

"Sure, let me bring these groceries up. We walked to the store." Bethany hoisted up two sacks from the Bag-n-Save grocery while Emma held on to her feet.

70

Bethany never seems to mind things like that. She giggles just as much as the kids. Like a kid herself.

Bethany dragged the groceries, and Emma, up the steps. "There." She set the bags on the counter. "Now, you wanted to talk about something?"

"Yes. Why don't we sit at the table?"

"Ooh, sounds serious. What's up?"

Joanna took in a breath and started the presentation she and Molly had prepared. "It's about Christmas Eve."

"I know, it'll be here before we know it. I have a couple of ideas for dinner, if you're having family over again."

"Bethany, stop a second." Joanna bit her lip, sorry she used such a sharp tone. "We always have relatives staying with us that night. They come down for the children's service and stay over until late Christmas Day. I mean, even with the baby," she patted her belly, "Christmas is such a big deal, we can't just cancel it, you know?"

Bethany nodded. "I know. The kids are all hyped about it, and we just got past Thanksgiving."

"Yes, well, normally we put at least some of the cousins in Drew's study..." Joanna let her voice trail off.

"Let me guess," Bethany nodded. "You're outta room for them with me here."

Although Bethany spoke without accusation, Joanna suddenly felt the need to explain herself. "It's just that I didn't like the idea of inconveniencing you by throwing you on the couch."

"So I'll go over to Molly's." Bethany toyed with a frayed end of the tablecloth.

This is the tricky part. Joanna took a deep breath and tried again. "You could, I suppose. It's just that Molly always meets her sister in Chicago for the break. Besides, your allergies." She smiled brightly. *Now, make it seem like it's really about her helping us.* "Look, to put it bluntly, we need you healthy and well rested if we're going to get through Christmas, so you can't stay at Molly's with those cats."

If Bethany caught all the emotion Joanna suddenly felt welling up in her, she gave little note. She instead smiled mischievously.

"How about the mothers' room at church. There's a nice couch in there. Besides, I'd get as much exposure to church as humanly possible, which is a bonus for you."

"Well that is an idea." *I didn't think about the mother's room. Damn!*

Bethany's dark eyes twinkled. "Joanna, it sounds like you already have a plan for me. Shall we just cut to the chase and hear it?"

"Molly and I thought it would be best if you stayed out at Bryan's."

"Interesting." Bethany raised one eyebrow. "Considering he's not my biggest fan."

Be casual. Joanna hesitated. "Molly asked him this morning."

"And?"

Joanna grinned and shrugged her shoulders. "If Bryan has ever said no to anything Molly's asked of him, I haven't heard of it. I got an email from her this afternoon. He said it was okay with him."

"I don't like the idea just marching into his house for an extended visit. Didn't you tell me that Christmas was a touchy thing for him since the wife left?"

Joanna bit her lip. *Is it even fair to drop Bethany into his mess?* "He's not the most social thing, that's true. He hasn't spent Christmas Eve with us the past two years, now this will be three, I'm sure. She shook her head. "I won't lie to you. He might be grumpy."

"Oh yeah, then sign me up!" Bethany's smile softened her sarcasm. "Thanks, but I think I'll camp in the mother's room."

Take one more shot. "Look, church is going to be non-stop from noon Christmas Eve until noon Christmas morning. You don't have a clue how busy that place is going to be, it'll be worse than here, especially since we're sending half the relatives to use the bathrooms over there. Bryan's got a nice spare room, it'll be quiet, and he's told Molly he has no argument for you staying over-night. Molly said he actually liked the idea." *Which, strangely enough, wasn't a lie. According to Molly, Bryan was actually pleasant*

72

about the idea. It was a complete about face on his part, but who's going to argue with it?

Doubt crossed the nanny's face. "I suppose...if Bryan really doesn't care."

Joanna patted the girl's hand. "Thank you, Bethany." She realized she spoke too eagerly, and looked away so Bethany couldn't see the color that rose in her face.

Bethany gave her a quizzical look, but did not comment. Joanna smiled at her again and watched as the younger woman returned to the kitchen to make dinner. *If you bring him back, we'll all be grateful to you, Bethany Elias.*

24: SHARA

Shara pulled up to Bryan's house with mixed feelings. On the one hand, she was happy to get out of the Shepaski house for the night. The kids worked themselves into a collective frenzy over the whole Christmas thing and the arrival of the multiple relatives only increased the mayhem.

On the other hand... Uneasiness she was used to, it was a way of life for her. This went deeper than simple uneasiness. She had not seen much of Bryan since Thanksgiving, and she was sure Molly and Joanna had a reason for wanting her to stay at Bryan's, but she could not figure out what. *I could tolerate the cats. This isn't just about the cats. It's not too late. I could be sipping a diet cola in front of Molly's television without being studied from every angle.* At the thought of Mr. Mittens and his friends, her eyes started to itch.

She stopped the Shepaski station wagon at the top of the yard, near the garage. *Christmas.* A single tear welled up in her left eye and she brushed it away absently. *Today was supposed to be my wedding day. Richard, do you think about me at all? How many nights do you lie awake, wondering if I'm dead or alive? Have you tried to find me? Doesn't matter what Molly says, Rock Harbor isn't so far from Milwaukee. Not really.*

But Shara Brandt is a lifetime away from Bethany Elias.

Glancing at her watch, Shara realized it was late. She pictured Nate and Emma, asleep and peaceful with dreams of magic and presents. *Yep, a whole lifetime away.* She reached into the back seat and dragged up the bag of presents for Bryan.

What did Joanna say? Bryan hadn't celebrated Christmas with them for the last three years. Shara surveyed the stack of presents, most wrapped and decorated by the children, and wondered what kind of horrible memories could keep someone away from such beautiful little souls on such a joyful holiday.

There was no answer to her knock. Shara tried the door and found it unlocked. Bryan had a fire going and the tree lights were on, but the rest of the house was dark. Timidly she pushed the door open and stepped inside.

"Who's there?"

Shara startled at his voice. *That doesn't sound like Bryan.* In the half-light of the fire his face looked puffy. Tearstains glistened under his red-rimmed eyes. "It's me, Bryan. It's Bethany."

"Bethany. Oh. I thought you might be…never mind." He stood uncertainly.

"Are you okay?" She reached out a hand to steady him, a reflex more than anything considering she was ten feet away from him.

He motioned for her to come in. "You have to excuse me. I'm afraid I've had too much Christmas cheer." He navigated himself to the kitchen counter, where a bottle of amber fluid twinkled half empty in the firelight. He filled his glass, not spilling anything, and made his way back to the big armchair with careful, measured steps. "And at this point you can join me or…not."

So this is how he spends Christmas Eve? Shara frowned. *Do Molly and Jo know this? Is this why I'm here?* She watched him drain a glass, get up, cross the room, and refill it without a word to her. *Doubtful. If Molly knew this is what he's doing, she'd never have gone to Chicago. She'd be sitting right here giving him hell.*

"Your tree is pretty." She took off her coat and draped it over the sofa, struggling not to stare at him.

He returned to his chair and stared at the tree as if for the first time. "Yeah, that. Molly comes over and does that. Insists I have a

74

tree." He took a drink. "And she'll be here sometime after New Year's to take it down."

Shara sat down on the sofa, and watched him drink. *This isn't the same loud, brash guy who plays with the kids and makes me feel uncomfortable with his direct stares and questions. This is a guy who's battling something. Like I am.* She tried to pull her eyes away from him. She felt like an intruder, seeing something she should not. The idea, though, that Bryan had hidden demons, had a strange, calming effect on her. She felt less alone.

"Little girl, you shouldn't look so shocked."

Little girl. The hairs on Shara's neck bristled and she instantly tensed. *I've been called that before...who called me that?* She frowned, trying, again, to put a face to the echo of voices that haunted her. Not eager to share her private thoughts with Bryan, she shook her head to clear her mind.

Bryan stared at the fire, seemingly unaware of her internal battle. "I suppose you want to know what I'm doing." He took another drink from his glass.

"Bryan, you don't- I mean, you know, we have that deal, right? I won't ask any questions. I'm just going to go-" She stood.

"Don't!" He jumped up and grabbed her arm. His force startled her and she sat back down. A shadow passed over his face and he released her arm. "I'm sorry." His voice was a contrite mumble as he slouched into the armchair again.

She slid over on the couch, closer to him. Something deep inside told her to stay close to him.

"No one has ever been around me when I'm like, well, like this."

She glanced at the bottle on the counter again. "Do you want to tell me what 'this' is?" She rubbed her arm, suddenly aware that his touch hadn't hurt her so much as given her a quick, strangely pleasurable shiver. *What is my basic defect?*

"This," he held his glass up to the fire, "this is what I am left with after my wife left me for another man. This is what is it to be the most desired man in the county and not to give even the tiniest damn about any of it. Do you have any idea how much pressure I have on me, to be this, this wounded sex symbol?"

Shara could not suppress her smile. "I can't say that I do."

"Don't you laugh, it's true. Ever since the divorce, everyone expects me to be this quiet, moody, but desperately handsome fellow, someone just looking for the right woman to come along and heal all my wounds."

"That's quite the opinion you have of yourself there."

He leaned forward and set his glass on the coffee table. "It's not my idea, I'm telling you. I may be quiet, I may be desperately handsome, but I am not moody." He gave her a sidelong glance as if daring her to disagree with him.

"No?" She tried to ignore the sympathy that welled in her as she toyed with a frayed thread on the arm of the sofa. "Because since I've known you, you have had your share of moods."

"No, I'm not moody, not by nature. I used to be a lot of fun. That's why I married her." Leaning forward, his elbows on his knees, Bryan's voice grew soft, almost dream-like and he stared out the picture window. "You should have seen her, she was one of these women who sparkled at a party, you know? Like a well stacked pile of diamonds in the middle of the room." He reached for his glass, studied its contents, and cleared his throat. "Of course, I thought she was fun because she loved me, and she was fun just with me."

"Not the case?"

He drained his glass before answering. "She partied with everyone all the time. Every night a party. Every morning a hangover. Didn't blend too well with work."

Shara nodded. "I can see that. It's like they always say, 'Friends don't let friends teach hung over.'"

He gave her a weak grin and sighed. "After a couple months, I got tired. I'd just turned thirty. I wanted to settle down, be a grown up. She got tired, too, of me. That's when she started going away for weekends, then days at a time during the week. Shopping trips, she called them. Didn't take her too long before she brought someone home, took him to her nest up there," he nodded to the dark outline of the barn, " and that's when it ended." He sat back in his chair. "I caught them, you know, together. Drew doesn't even know that. I just couldn't admit…that."

"Bryan-you don't-"

"I know, you don't want to hear any of this." He waved off her protest. "But you're here, lucky you." His crooked smile held little humor. "I told everyone that she told me about her affair, about what she did in the loft."

Shara looked at him with an understanding now the connection she felt with him. *We both know about having to hide things from others, don't we?*

"We had a good run, short, but fun. Met at Halloween. Engaged at Thanksgiving. Married at Christmas. Saw her true colors New Year's Eve, but ignored the truth until Valentine's Day. I don't even remember St. Patrick's Day that year. Divorce filed right after Easter." He shook his head and gave her another mirthless smile. " Our relationship covered, and ruined, most of the festivals in Western culture." He got up and poured himself another drink. "Want some?"

"No, thanks."

"Your choice." He filled his glass, drained it without a thought, and refilled it before walking back. Shara noted he walked with more concentration, each step a conscious thought, as keeping balance had become more difficult.

"So you hide yourself away on Christmas?"

"This is the one night a year I allow myself to wallow in it. Everyone else is so happy, it sort of amplifies how miserable I am." He sat down in his chair and faced the fire, away from her. "You ever love someone, Miss Bethany Elias?"

The question took the breath out of her. *He has no idea what he's asking. It's a question that can't hurt me if I answer.* "Sure." She nodded, more at the fire than at him.

"Ah, a great love in the life of our nanny." He lifted his glass in her direction. "So I told you my story, it's your turn."

"I'd rather not talk about it." She fought back the sting of tears.

"Fine, I'll fill in the blanks. I have a theory, you see, about you. You're not pining over the guy that dumped you and ran. There was someone else." He looked at her.

Her face must have registered surprise, because he laughed. It was a dry, sad sound in the still room. "Don't look so shocked. I may be on the verge of incoherence now, but I know what keeping something locked inside does to a person. You've got that look, like there's something way deep down that you're hiding." He swirled the melting ice in his glass. "You're a smart girl, I don't see you getting weak in the knees over a thug. No, I'll bet there was some slick guy, college type maybe? You loved him, but he decided he was out of your league." He turned bleary eyes to her and gave her a knowing grin. "I'll bet you haven't said anything about this, not to Jo, not even to Molly. But there was someone who promised you the moon and the stars and you bought the whole line. And now you're miserable, just like me."

Don't listen to him. He has no idea what he's rambling on about. Shara couldn't stop her hands from shaking. He went to fill his glass again. "Does that stuff really help?" She kept her face toward the fire, hoping he wouldn't see, that he wouldn't know how close he was coming to her truth.

"I don't know about helping, but it blanks things out a little. Softens the edges." He sat down again. "Erases some things you'd rather not remember. So if there's anything you'd like to erase, feel free to join me." He took a sip and set the glass back on the coffee table. "Or if you'd rather tell me about the someone you're remembering…"

I'm not remembering the one thing I need to remember. Shara closed her eyes and leaned against the cushions. "I'm not really in the mood."

"You're not playing fair, Miss Elias." He slumped in the chair. "I told you everything. It's your turn."

Shara closed her eyes and in her mind she saw Richard, her beloved Richard, gold hair gleaming in the sun, giving her his most charming smile. *Damn you, Bryan Jacobs, I don't want to remember this. I don't want to remember what was good about my past, and what I'll never have, unless I can remember everything and clear my name.*

Bryan let out a gasping sob that broke her thoughts. Head in his hands, his body shuddered with the power of his sorrow. Her heart welled up with forgiveness. She perched on the armrest of the chair, and put her arm around him in a gesture of shared heartache.

"I would have forgiven her anything if she'd just stayed." He wiped his face in his shirtsleeve. "People who love each other, really, really love each other, they can forgive each other anything, right?"

"I think anything is possible." She pulled him closer to her and buried her face in his hair. Her senses filled with his musky, clean scent. "You'll get past her, Bryan." She let go of her embrace and knelt in front of him. "You just need time."

"Has there been enough time for you to get over him?" Bryan raised his eyes, swollen and watery, to hers.

Something inside her urged her to tell the truth, to answer this one question honestly. "No. Not yet."

"It's not so easy, is it?"

She looked away. She could not face his sick, sad heart reflected so deeply in his eyes. *Those are my eyes, too.* Without another thought, she gathered him closer to her and rocked back and forth, knees to toes, soothing him with her motion.

"Could you ever love me?"

His words were soft, and slurred, and Shara gave them little credence. *He's gonna pass out in that chair right now.* "I think it's time to get you to your bed." She helped Bryan to his feet and led him to his room where he crumpled onto the broad bed. Shara eased his hiking boots off and covered him with a hand-made quilt she found on a chair. Making certain he was comfortable, she brushed a strand of hair out of his closed eyes.

"You didn't answer my question." His words were clearer, but his eyes remained closed.

Shara touched his face, traced his jaw line, with a gentle hand. *He has a good face, when he's not scowling. He could be loveable.*

She again stroked his cheek with her hand, a comforting, almost motherly, gesture. "Good night, Bryan."

"Because I think, maybe..." his voice drifted off before he finished his last words.

Maybe what? Maybe I should love you? Maybe I should worship you like everyone else? With a wry smile, Shara closed the door and returned to the living room. The spare bedroom held no interest for her. The fire was still going and the lights on the Christmas tree gave her a sense of security.

That sense of security did not translate into sleep, however. She tossed and turned on Bryan's couch, visions and shadows haunting her every time she closed her eyes.

Someone tapped the window. She got up and looked out. There was no one there, but squinting in the distance, Shara made out three people. She stepped out of the cabin onto the porch. There, in the yard, next to Bryan's Jeep, were the bloody corpses of Richard and Lydia. Standing over them, waving a gun in the air, was a woman.

"Don't you tell, Shara Brandt. Don't you dare tell or I'll find you and kill you." The woman waved the pistol in the air like some ancient gunslinger.

Shara sat up with a start, her body clammy with sweat. She paced the length of the room twice, then put another log in the fireplace and tried to lose her shadowy memory in the bright, dancing flames.

* * *

Morning dawned crisp and bright. Eager to shut out the events, both conscious and otherwise, of the night before, Shara got up to make breakfast. Bryan's kitchen was neat and obviously unused. A light film of dust covered everything. Rummaging around, she found a frying pan, pancake mix, and some bacon. The orange juice in the refrigerator smelled funny, but Bryan had several fresh oranges in the crisper, so she squeezed fresh juice. He had no Christmas CD's in his collection, a fact that Shara could not believe, so she tuned in radio station playing Christmas carols.

"Good morning." Bryans' voice, graveled, but closer to normal than last night, diverted her attention from the sizzling bacon.

"Merry Christmas." She turned her attention back to the skillet, unwilling to study him too closely.

He sat down heavily and surveyed the kitchen. "You've been busy."

She nodded. "Sorry. I made way too much. I'm used to cooking for the family."

"Don't apologize. I'll bet it would smell good if...I weren't under the weather." He rubbed his temples. "You got any coffee over there? And maybe grab the aspirin from the shelf over the sink?"

"Coming up." *He's back to his old self.* Nothing of the sad, heartbroken man remained. *How much does he remember?* She poured a cup of coffee and handed it to him. *How much do I want him to remember?* She stepped away from the table, hiding her face and the blush she knew warmed her cheeks.

"This and about fifty aspirin will fix me right up." He took a sip of the coffee and winced. "Thanks for putting up with my drama last night."

"It was nothing." *I hope that doesn't sound as weak to him as it does to me.*

"I doubt that." He poked at the pancake in front of him. "It's been a long time-I mean, I'm sorry if I said anything that was...untoward."

"You don't remember?" Shara busied herself wiping down the counter.

"I wasn't even sure how I got into bed until I remembered you were supposed to be staying here." He shook his head. "Don't know what I was thinking, letting you stay out here. Couldn't have been an easy night for you." He focused on cutting himself the smallest bite of pancake Shara had ever seen.

"No. No, you were fine. You went to bed right after I got here."

He tasted the pancake gingerly. "Liar."

She stopped wiping the counter and stared at him. "I beg your pardon?"

"I can tell you're lying to me." He opened the aspirin bottle and shook out three, which he swallowed with a quick swig of coffee. "So how about just giving me the ugly truth?"

You better not be able to tell when I'm lying. "You did mention...your ex."

"Uh huh, thought so. Told you the whole sad story, I'm sure. Sorry about that."

Shara hung up the dishrag and sat down at the table across from him. "It was nothing. You were...working through some stuff. I just listened. Then you went to bed and I slept on the couch because I liked the fire. Very peaceful night."

He took a sip of coffee and studied her more carefully. "See, now I know you're lying. That couch is really comfortable. I've never met anyone yet who didn't sleep like the dead on that thing. You look like you've been up all night."

Shara waved away his comment with a weak laugh. "Are you trying to tell me I look bad?" To cover her discomfort, she put two pancakes on her plate and spread a thick layer of butter over them. His expression of distaste as she poured syrup over the plate made her smile.

"No, I'm saying you look like you spent some quality time stressing over something. I'm saying I hope I didn't...share anything that...troubled you."

He sees far too much in me. She turned her attention back to her pancakes. "Don't sweat it. It had nothing to do with you." *At least this is partly true.*

"You know, some around here would say lying is a sin."

She couldn't resist smiling and turning to look at him. "Okay, there was a little bit more. I did help you down the hall, and I did take off your shoes off when I tucked you in. There. Happy?"

Bryan picked up a piece of bacon and studied it closely. "Well, I gotta say, you are an original, Bethany Elias." Taking a cautious bite out of the bacon, he kept his blue- black eyes trained on her.

"Why do you say that?"

"Because, under similar circumstances, I am confident many other women in this town would not have stopped at the shoes." His weary tone held no boastfulness.

In his eyes Shara saw the sorrow she'd often mistaken for cold heartedness. *I know better now, though, don't I?* "Well, I'm not every woman in town"

"I'm starting to realize that," Bryan shook his head. "I suppose I shared my most scandalous secrets?"

"Bryan." She reached across and put her hand on his arm. "You have nothing to worry about," she paused, watching a shadow pass over his face and gratitude light his face. "I won't tell a soul, promise. You're safe with me."

"Hope so." He picked up his fork. "These are really good. I may be able to eat something after all."

"Great." She flipped another pancake onto his plate. *You are safe with me, Bryan. I'm certainly not going to share last night with anyone.* She watched him take another tentative bite. *I wonder, though, can I be safe with you?*

He pushed away from the table. "I'm going to hit the shower. When do you have to be at Drew and Jo's?"

She checked the clock on the wall. "Around ten. After church."

He gave her a wry grin. "You're not going to services this morning?"

"I'm the agnostic, remember? I don't see you moving quickly to worship, either."

"Yes, but I have the flu." He rubbed his head and looked pitiful.

"Yeah, the self inflicted kind." She turned off the coffee maker and laughed as he gave her another sad look before leaving the room.

25: BRYAN

As the sizzling hot shower water hit his skin, Bryan's brain finally woke from the fog of his hangover. *Last night did not go at all the way I wanted it to. Instead of finding out about Bethany Elias, what, exactly did I do?*

Got myself blasted and probably told the one person I don't trust the one thing I don't trust anyone to know.

I'm such an idiot. He closed his eyes and let the scalding water wash over him. *There's gotta be a way to find out how far I can trust her. A way that doesn't involve me passing out before I find out anything about her.*

Turning off the water and stepping out of the water, Bryan studied himself in the mirror. *I look like hell. It's amazing she didn't run screaming from the house last night.*

Bryan toweled off, fighting away a nagging feeling that the opportunity he'd missed the night before was here again for the taking. *All I need is a little time alone with her, some time to find out, for my own peace of mind, just who this girl is. But if she wants to spend ten minutes alone with me ever again, that will be a miracle.*

Leaving the steamy heat of his bathroom for the cool air of his bedroom, Bryan shivered a little and reached for a clean pair of jeans. There, on the floor just beneath his bed, were his hiking boots, the ones he'd been wearing the night before. *She did just stop at the shoes, didn't she?*

Pulling on his jeans, the tickets tucked in his bureau mirror caught his eye. *There's the concert in Green Bay this afternoon. I could invite her to that. That would certainly give me some time to answer some of the questions I have about her.* He plucked the tickets from the mirror and headed down the hall.

"Yeah, Jo, everything is fine. No, no, he's fine. He's in the shower now. No, I doubt he's coming to church." Bethany put her hand over the phone receiver. "It's Jo. You're not going to church, right?"

Bryan shook his head and sat on the couch, busying himself with the task of putting on his boots, and trying not to look interested in her phone conversation.

"Nope, not coming. No, I don't know if he wants to stay for dinner. Yes, I'll tell him." She lowered her voice. "No, I don't think anything like that. I got here so late last night, he was already in bed. Okay. I'll see you in a bit."

84

Bryan couldn't suppress a grin. "You're lying for me now?"

She sat in the armchair and looked at him. "You want me to tell her the truth?"

"Um, no. Maybe not. So…thanks, I guess."

"You're welcome."

He shifted and put the tickets on the coffee table. "I got these, from a student, as a gift. I wasn't going to go, really, but maybe, if you'd like to come with me…" *Lame, Jacobs, very lame.* He cleared his throat. "What I mean is, if you want, if you'd rather not have the whole tribe of kids climbing all over you today, you could come along with me to this concert at the university. Sort of my way of saying, 'Sorry' for last night."

She looked at the tickets and smiled. "That sounds really, really nice Bryan, but I-" she looked at the phone, still in her hands. "The kids today. Jo needs me."

"True. Still, give me that." He reached for the phone. Dialing, he checked the clock. "No, they're still at home. Oh, hey Jo. Yeah, Merry Christmas to you. No, I'm fine. Really." He shook hid head and gave Bethany a look of mock anguish. "Listen, Jo, do you really need Bethany today? Well, I've got these tickets to the University concert this afternoon…you don't? Great. What? Oh, sure." He handed the phone to Bethany. "She wants to talk to you."

"Hey, Jo? Are you sure? Uh, okay. Yeah, I'll be home tonight. Okay, Merry Christmas." She hung up. "Wow. Weird."

"How so?"

She put the phone down on the coffee table and stared at it. "When Jo asked me to stay here, she said it was because she'd need me well rested for Christmas Day. Now she seemed really, really eager to get rid of me."

Well, that uncovers Joanna's motives, doesn't it? Molly's, too no doubt. Do those women never stop? Bryan shook his head. "I think maybe our friend is hoping to create something…you know?"

"What, something between you and me?" She laughed, tossing her head back in the full throes of mirth.

And so much for my ego. "So, let me finish getting dressed and we can leave."

* * *

Bryan took Bethany to the concert at the University of Wisconsin in Green Bay and then took in the Christmas decorations and lights of the ghostly quiet town. Through the course of the day, he'd asked her some questions, trying to uncover some deeper truth to her, and she answered everything he asked honestly, sincerely. Still convinced she was holding something back, he couldn't help studying Bethany's face when she wasn't looking, and wondering more than once if the thing he was looking for had more to do with the night before than with his overall impression of her. *It would be nice if I could remember just what I said last night.*

"You look serious." She fell into step beside him as they walked out of a diner. "Anything you can share?"

"Oh, nothing. Just wondering…you don't mind that I took you away from the family, did you?"

"No way. This has been so fun, and bonus, no one's begged me for a piggyback ride all day. Always a bonus."

"I would have asked for one, but I didn't realize that was part of the nanny package." *Keep it light, Jacobs, don't scare her off.*

Bethany laughed. "Oh, I'm a full service nanny, no doubt. But I doubt you were worrying about whether or not I was missing Nate and Emma." She cocked her head to one side, a mannerism he found attractive on her. "So what's the real reason for the serious face?"

Just spit it out. "I was wondering, uh, why you didn't walk out on me last night."

Her smile was gentle. "You're still worried about that? Fine, I'll 'fess up. You really seemed to need a shoulder, you know?" Her eyes reflected the twinkling Christmas lights lining the street. "Besides, you're a lot easier to be around when you're not so in control of things. You don't seem so, I don't know, up here?" She held her hand up above her head.

Oh, that makes me feel better. "You're not helping."

"Sorry. That's the best I've got." She bumped into his side as another couple passed them on the sidewalk.

Instinctively, Bryan put an arm around her and pulled her closer as the other pair walked by. The move seemed to be as much of a surprise to her as it was to him, and he jerked his arm away. He cleared his throat. "I would hate for…what happened…to get out, you know? Hard to perpetuate the image of a wounded sex symbol when everyone knows I'm a sad binge drinker."

He expected her to laugh. She did not. "Your secret's safe with me." She kept her eyes on the sidewalk. "But you know, there are a lot of people who really care about what you're going through. You don't have to be alone."

He stopped walking and laughed out loud. "Gee, I didn't realize Joanna was such a good ventriloquist."

"Yeah, okay, maybe she did mention it once or twice."

"So you think I should air my dirty laundry out and let my friends solve my problems?"

"It might be more constructive than sucking down your body weight in whisky and missing every Christmas Eve." A shadow passed over her face, and she suddenly looked serious, older. "They wouldn't hurt you. You could tell them the truth and they would still love you."

So I did give her all the gory details. Damn. "Maybe." They reached a small city park, where Bryan led her to a bench and they sat down. He draped his arm across the back of the bench and she leaned against his arm, a move that seemed completely natural, and forward all at once. "But some things, you know…" he sighed. "It's a very conservative little place you've fallen into, a very religious place. I'm not so sure the fine folks of Rock Harbor Community Church would like the fact that the town fifth grade teacher had some fairly unsavory things happening in his own house."

She looked up at the sky. "You don't have anything to be ashamed of. Lots of people get cheated on and get divorced. But they don't bottle it up. They find their friends, they open up."

"Okay, okay, I get it. I'll try and play nicer with others from now on. And to think that I was suspicious that Jo and Molly had ulterior motives in having you stay at my place. Boy was I wrong!"

"I think they wanted you to 'come around' to not hating me." Her tone was free of malice, still, her words held a surprising sting for him.

She hasn't given you one reason to mistrust her. Admit it already. "I'm sorry. I haven't exactly been kind to you, have I?"

"You have challenged my comfort level, that's for sure. I think though," She leaned forward and looked into his face, "I'm starting to see the guy I've heard so much about. He's not bad. I kinda like him." She leaned back against his arm, resting her head on his shoulder.

The move, so vulnerable and trusting, broke through Bryan's barrier of doubt. *So she's probably not some criminal on the loose. She's probably exactly what she seems; someone just looking for a chance at a fresh start.* With this realization, Bryan relaxed, letting his hand drape onto her shoulder. The strawberries scent of her hair gave him a peaceful feeling.

"So we're okay, then? You don't have anymore inquisition questions for me?"

"I was that obvious?"

She looked up at the sky and exhaled. Her breath was a frosty cloud in the night air. "Two days ago I would have hated it, I'll admit it. But last night I got a little more of a clue about you."

"I'll take that as a good thing."

She leaned forward and tucked her hair behind her ears. "We aren't so very different, you know."

"No?"

"We both have things we'd rather not have out in the public. You, well, you know what your secrets are, and I, of course, have the very pleasant secret of what you look like when you're peacefully sleeping off a bottle of Kentucky's finest." Her impish grin softened any reprimand he detected in her speech. "Watch yourself, Mr. Jacobs. Next time I might just have to remove more than your shoes." She bent down, grabbed a handful of snow, and threw it up in his face.

"Why you!" He scooped up a handful of snow and threw it at her. Her peals of laughter were musical, and, for the first time since Jenny, Bryan felt his heart beating.

26: RICHARD

Richard Bennett leaned over against the glass of the window and closed his eyes. "Are you sure it's her?"

"No, Mr. Bennett. That's why we called you." A short, barrel-chested detective offered him a Styrofoam cup filled with bitter smelling coffee.

Richard waved off the coffee and looked over his shoulder at Jennifer. She sat quietly in the corner, trying her best not to attract attention a feat, he knew, that was almost impossible for the six foot tall red head with a spectacular body.

Focus, Bennett. Focus on what you have to do here.

"Okay, Detective. I'm ready."

The detective tapped on the glass and the coroner pulled back the glass. On the table, a foot away from the glass, was a body covered with a white sheet. Swallowing hard, Richard nodded. This time the coroner pulled back the sheet.

The body wasn't human, couldn't be human. Every inch was bloated, gray and filthy. Bile bubbled up in Richard's throat.

"Mr. Bennett? Is that her? Is that your fiancé?"

Richard took a deep breath and looked at the mass on the table again. *This just needs to be over. It needs to be over now.* He looked closely, studying the repulsive figure. "Yes, yes it is. It's Shara."

The detective nodded to the coroner, who covered the body with the sheet again. "Thank you, Mr. Bennett. I'm very sorry for your loss."

"Yes, thank you, Detective." Richard looked past the man's shoulder to Jennifer, who remained still in the corner, but the energy around her was charged, energetic. She seemed coiled, ready to spring. Her ice green eyes fairly glowed in the dim light of the room.

At last. It's over. Time for me to move on.

27: SHARA

"What's New Ear's Eve?" Emma barely got the words out before a yawn split her tiny face wide open.

It was nearly eleven, but Shara was having so much fun with the kids, she lost track of time until Nate fell asleep in the middle of a rousing round of the Memory game. Drew, Joanna, indeed the better part of Rock Harbor's entire population was over at the RHCS gym for its big New Year's Eve party. The lights from the parking lot twinkled through the Shepaski's front window.

"New Year's Eve is the last night of the year." She tugged Emma's pajama top over the little girl's head. "It's the night that we all look back, think about the last year, and promise ourselves to make the next year a better one. A fresh start."

"Like a do over?"

"Yes, like a do over," Shara said with a smile. "Now, get into that bed. If your mommy finds out I let you guys stay up this late, I'll be looking for a do over!"

"G'night-Bethany-I-love-you," the girl mumbled sleepily.

Walking down the stairs to the family room, Shara paused at the wall of family pictures. *Maybe that's why I'm here. Maybe Rock Harbor is my do over.*

28: BRYAN

Bryan pulled into the Shepaski driveway, too engrossed in the radio news report to turn off the Jeep.

"Wisconsin's number one mystery of the year has been solved. The body of Shara Brandt, the young woman wanted in connection with the murder of businesswoman Lydia Brandt, was found today in the Rock River just outside of Watertown in Jefferson County.

Authorities received an emergency call just after noon today from a local man who discovered the body frozen in the ice near a city park. Brandt's fiancé, Richard Bennett, who identified the body at the Jefferson county medical examiner's office had this to say:"

"Shara was loved by so many people. While we may never know what struggles she faced that horrible night, we do pray that Shara has found the peace that avoided her in life. Those of us that knew her and loved her, we now must go on without her."

"Asshole." Bryan leaned back in his seat and stared at the ceiling of the Jeep, remembering Richard's sardonic expression peering over Jenny's shoulder. *Maybe he's feeling misery and loss tonight. Good.* He got out of the Jeep and the pale, sad face of young Shara Brandt crossed his mind. *Everything money could buy wasn't enough to save her.*

As he stepped into the house, Bethany looked up from the book she was reading. "Oh, hi. I didn't expect you here tonight. I thought you'd be over at the school, kickin' it up with everyone else."

He took in the image of her sitting, legs draped over the arm of Drew's favorite chair, completely at ease and happy. In the week since their trip to Green Bay, Bryan found himself mentally returning to the park bench and the feel of her leaning against him, smiling and laughing in the cold night. *How big of an idiot was I to ever think she was Shara Brandt?* "Dances bore me. Besides, I wanted to give you this." He handed her a package. Bryan liked the way her eyes sparkled as she took the box from him.

"Bryan, you didn't have to-" She got out of the chair, staring at the package as if it were gold.

"I didn't really. Just open it."

Bethany opened the present with controlled excitement. "It's a coat!" She held it up for his inspection.

"I figured you were tired of running around in Molly's old puffy monster coat."

Bethany held the dark denim coat and touched the pink corduroy collar and cuffs. "Bryan, it's so pretty." Her eyes glowed as she looked at him. "You shouldn't have-"

91

"Well, I didn't, exactly. I was cleaning out a closet yesterday, and I found this. I think I got it for my sister ages ago, but she moved to Hawaii. I never got around to doing anything with it. I saw it and thought you'd like it."

"I love it!" She held the coat in one arm and pulled him close in a forceful one armed hug.

Her sudden burst of affection surprised and pleased him. "Well, okay, good." He settled into the armchair and changed the subject. "So, what's for snacks? Need any help getting the kids in bed?"

"Thanks, but I got them in hours ago." She hung the coat on a peg near the door and grinned at him.

"Hours?" He arched an eyebrow at her.

"Fine. Minutes. And snacks are pretty thin, but I think there's a little confetti pizza left. The kids ate most of everything."

"Confetti pizza! I love that stuff! Let's have at it." She led him up to the dining area, but the last remnants of the dessert were hardly enough for him, and he pouted for a moment, just for her benefit. "It's a good thing I brought provisions, then." He ran back down the stairs and returned with a grocery bag. He pulled out several different bags of chips and crackers followed by a number of small containers of different dips.

"Let me guess. You mixed up Joanna's dream shopping list with your own?" She giggled, hiding her mouth behind her hand.

"Oh, fine. Ignore the fact that I went out into the wild and hunted and gathered all these provisions. You should have seen the grocery store. It was madness, madness I tell you!" He struck what he thought was a dramatic pose. "I had to bargain with some high school girl for this last bag of cheese puffs."

She attempted a straight face. "So, you're looking for an Academy Award for this performance, or are you going to open up that dip?"

"A true hero is never appreciated in his home town." Bryan gave her an exaggerated sigh as he opened a container of dip and grinned at her. "You have no idea the idle chit chat and the starry eyes I had to endure to get these cheese puffs."

"I thought you hated that whole 'wounded hero' thing. Or do you find it's to your benefit sometimes?" Bethany's laughter softened the teasing tone in her voice.

"Something like that." He got up from the table and looked in the fridge for something to drink. "Somewhere out there, is a high school sophomore who is telling all of her giggling friends about her almost romantic encounter with Mr. Bryan Jacobs."

"Lucky girl." Bethany busied herself with the dips, but her tone held a note of something…else.

Was that sarcasm or jealousy? Bryan watched her tear into the bag of cheese puffs with the all the self-consciousness of a starving convict. *I'm going with sarcasm* "Hey, there's a news story I'm following. Mind if I turn on the T. V.?"

"Go ahead." Bethany followed him down to the family room, and settled on the couch, tucking her feet under her.

Bryan sat in the armchair, pointed the remote at the television and pushed the power button. In a blink Shara Brandt's face stared at them. "Yeah, this is the story."

She jumped up so quickly, she nearly knocked over the stack of magazines on the coffee table. "Oh, um, who is that?" She picked up the magazines and held them, hovering over the table.

Bryan looked at her, unsure of why she sounded like she was being strangled. "It's that girl that shot her grandmother and fiancé and then disappeared."

"Oh, yeah, the killer you thought I was, right?" She'd regained her composure and gave him a humorous look, although there was still a glimmer of anxiety in her eyes.

"Very nice. Remind me of my most idiotic moment." He pointed to the television. "They found her body in the Rock River down in Jefferson County."

"They did?" Still holding the magazines, she stared at the screen, her expression now unreadable.

"Yeah. Her fiancé identified the body. So I guess the case is closed. Poor kid. Would have been twenty-four next month." He noticed that she kept slapping the pile of magazines against the coffee table. "I think those magazines are straightened up enough. Are you okay?"

Bethany gave him a blank look and set the magazines down. "Yeah, I'm fine. I'm…I'm going to check on the kids, okay? I'll be right back."

Bryan watched her go and wanted to kick himself. *Way to go, Jacobs. You don't know what happened to her parents, why she was living with her grandfather. Knowing your luck, they probably all drowned in some freak family vacation thing. Idiot.*

29: SHARA

Shara nearly fell over her feet getting up the stairs. It took every ounce of her self-control to keep from slamming Drew and Joanna's bedroom door behind her. In the dark she hugged a pillow and rocked back and forth on the bed. *Ohmygod, ohmygod, ohmygod.*

Richard just identified someone's body as mine. As far as he knows…as far as anyone thinks, I'm dead. Tears stung her eyes as she imagined Richards' devastation at her death. *My poor Richard.*

But how can Richard think I'm dead? How could he mistake someone else for me? She stared at her dark reflection in the mirror. *He's beside himself with grief. My poor, poor Richard.*

She rocked a few minutes more as all the ramifications of this information dawned on her. *If Richard thinks I'm dead…if the police think I'm dead…*

Maybe…maybe…

She stopped rocking. A sense of calm washed over her. *Maybe Shara is dead, and maybe* **she**, *whoever* **she** *is, will stop haunting my dreams. Maybe, just maybe, I can live in peace here and stop looking over my shoulder. If Shara Brandt is dead, that is.*

Shara switched on a bedside lamp and looked at her shadowy reflection in the mirror. She squared her shoulders and smiled. *Well, Shara Brandt, rest in peace. It's time for Bethany Elias to go back to work.*

94

30: BRYAN

Bethany returned a few minutes later, and seemed completely normal. "Did they say anything else about the cause of death? Of that girl?"

"Sounds like they ruled it a suicide. Apparently she was mentally unstable." Bryan watched a shadow pass over Bethany's face, and wanted to smack himself again. *Idiot. Just stop talking about it.* He turned off the television. "You know what? We don't have to talk about that."

She let out a heavy sigh and smiled at him. "You're right. I'd rather talk about the story the sophomore in high school is going to be spreading."

"And I'd love to share it with you, so how about if you sit down on the floor here, load up on carbs, and I'll spill my guts." He gestured grandly at the tray of snacks.

She rewarded his dramatic flourish with a dazzling smile. "Oh, that's a lovely visual." She sat down on the floor and started munching on cheese curls.

"Isn't it?" Bryan was in a marvelous mood. He hunkered down on the floor across from her. *She's got a great smile, even with the cheese powder on her lips.* He was about to launch into his story when a flash of light caught his eye.

"Is that a cop car?" Bethany looked out the window as she brushed cheese powder from her hands.

"Yeah, and an ambulance." He stood and moved closer to the window. "I wonder what happened."

The telephone jangled and Bethany jumped up to get it. "Hello…Molly…Oh my god! Is she okay? No…. No, I'll be fine with the kids. Yeah, Bryan's here."

Bryan glanced at her. *I'll be fine. Bryan's here.* He didn't analyze why he liked the sound of that. He didn't, however, like the look on her face. "What's up?"

Bethany was pale beneath her cap of curls and her eyes were more enormous than usual. "It's Joanna, she fainted. They're taking her to the hospital." She stood next to him, watching the ambulance roll out of the parking lot.

95

Not again. Not when everything was going so well for them. "That's the best place for her." He put a hand on Bethany's shoulder. She was trembling.

He watched the crowd in the parking lot while she rocked on her heels next to him. He wished he could say something that would make her worry, and his, go away. The commotion in the lot eased as people returned to the school. "You want me to go up to the hospital and see what's up?" *Or should I stay here, with you?*

"Do you think they'll tell you anything?" She raised frightened eyes to him.

If Bryan had any last doubts about Bethany's allegiance, they were erased with that one look. *She loves this family as much as I do.* "I'll go, and I'll make sure they tell me something." He reached for his coat. "I won't be long."

"Bethany…those lights outside woke me up." Nate staggered out of his room; his favorite stuffed teddy bear in tow, rubbing his eyes.

Bethany climbed the stairs but looked over her shoulder at Bryan. "You'll come back…and let me know, right?"

"As soon as I know anything."

She nodded and gave him a pleading look he could not interpret but could not deny. As he started up the Jeep, Bryan Jacobs tried to ignore the fact that, at this moment, he felt a very strong urge to stay and comfort the nanny.

31: JENNIFER

Of all the nights it had to happen, did it have to be tonight? Jennifer Tiel frowned out the car window. *It's New Year's Eve for god's sakes. I shouldn't be sitting in this car pretending to mope about Shara Brandt. I should be at some fantastic party, celebrating my ass off.*

Unbidden, a smile rose to her lips. *Still, you have to like my luck. Now even Richard truly believes she's dead, and we can start the life we were meant to have.*

Armed with this pleasant thought, she turned her attention to Richard, who had not said a word since leaving the police station. "Are you okay, baby?"

"I'm…I'm fine. I expected it, you know. I didn't expect…that."

Jennifer put on her sympathetic face. "I know baby, I know. It was horrible. But it's over now."

In the pale glimmer of the dashboard light, Richard Bennett smiled. He reached over and ran his hand up the length of her leg from her knee past the hem of her scandalously short skirt. Jennifer quivered at his touch. *The only man I've never had to pretend for.*

"Yes. It's over. And you, you should be at some party someplace, making all the men want you, shouldn't you?"

Jennifer shifted her legs slightly, warming to Richard's ever upward reach. "Well, I'm very sure you'll find a way to make it up to me, won't you?"

He eased the Lexus off the dark highway and pulled it to a stop. "I'm fairly certain I can start right now."

32: BRYAN

"Looks like Bethany waited up." Bryan nodded to the light in the window as he pulled up to the house. It was almost three in the morning; the parking lot was empty, the revelers long gone. The lone light in the house window cast an eerie glow on the snow in the front yard.

"You expected her anything else?" Molly gave him a sidelong glance of reproach. "You really don't give her enough credit, you know?"

Bryan recalled Bethany's frightened expression when he'd left. "I think I'm getting over that."

"Good. Because that girl is the best thing that could have happened for Drew and Joanna." Molly snapped open the Jeep door and hopped out. "I'm going to pack a bag for both of them. I'll drive Drew's car down to Green Bay, and catch a bus later today. We can work out a substitute schedule for Drew when I get back."

"Are you sure you don't want me to come along and drive you back?" Bryan kept his voice low and followed her into the house.

"No, you'll have to take care of the phone calls that will come in. Look at that." Molly pointed to Bethany and Nathan, curled together in the recliner, covered with the coat he'd given her. "And you doubted her."

Bryan smiled. *She really did like that coat.* "I'll carry him upstairs if you want to get packing." He set the coat on the floor and scooped Nate out of Bethany's arms. Bethany barely stirred as he and Molly walked up the stairs.

Ten minutes later, they came back down, Molly carrying two duffle bags slung over her shoulders. "I'll call you once I get to Green Bay."

Bryan hugged her. "It's going to be okay. Jo'll get the best care possible, so will the baby." He tried to shut out the vision of the miniature, wrinkled, bluish form they wheeled from the delivery room in an incubator. *Six weeks early...tough start for the kid.*

Molly leaned into his embrace, a rare show of weakness for her. "I've found that things always work out the way they should." She reshouldered the duffle bags. "Say a prayer, okay?"

"Yeah, sure."

He listened as Molly revved up the station wagon and pulled out of the garage. The garage door purred shut and the house fell silent. He walked around, double-checking the children, and draping a blanket over Bethany.

Confident that everyone in the house was settled for what was left of the night, he stretched out on the couch and clicked on the television, keeping the sound very low. *So this is that sense of peace Drew gets from having a family. Yeah, this doesn't completely suck.*

Bethany stirred and whimpered in her sleep. Absently, Bryan looked up from the television screen. Her face was pale, her brow knit as if in an angry frown. She muttered in a low, guttural tone

Bryan didn't recognize as human. She kicked the blanket off with a swift running motion.

What's going on in her brain? Bryan got off the couch and picked up the blanket. Gently, he tucked it around her small frame. She stilled at his touch, but her face remained frozen in a dark grimace and she continued to mutter words he could not understand.

Settling back on the couch, Bryan had no more interest in the television. Instead, he studied the restless woman in the recliner and wondered what ghosts haunted her dreams.

* * *

The sun rose, brilliant and full of promise. Bryan got up and brewed some coffee in the still silent house. Bethany was awake but silent when he returned, coffee cup in hand. "Good morning. You want coffee?"

"Oh, thanks. I can't believe I fell asleep. I really wanted to wait until I heard something about Jo."

"It was really late." He took a deep drag from the mug. "Molly and I got back sometime around three."

"Molly? Is Molly here?" Bethany brightened.

"No. She drove down to Green Bay."

"Green Bay? Why?" She seemed to lose steam and sank back in the chair. Their eyes met. Her face paled. "Something's really wrong."

Bryan tried to be nonchalant. "Nah. Mostly they needed to ship the baby to the Intensive Care Unit at Bellin. The hospital here doesn't have neonatal facilities."

"The baby? The baby was born? Boy or girl?" She sat cross-legged.

"They had a little girl." The telephone jangled and Bryan picked up the cordless receiver. "Hello?"

"Bryan? You're there already?" Drew sounded like he was in a tunnel.

"Still. I didn't go home last night. Is everything okay?"

"Joanna will be released sometime tomorrow, they think. Her blood pressure went back to normal and she looks good."

Bryan gave Bethany the thumbs up sign. "What about the newest Shepaski?"

"She's still in intensive care. The doctors say there's nothing to worry about, that all preemies have the same problems she does, and she'll be fine, in time. She's going to be here awhile. They say she needs to just get stronger."

"So take their word for it, and relax."

"We think we have a name for her, though."

"What, already? It took you three weeks to name Nate. And no one around here thought Em would ever get named." Bryan gave Bethany another reassuring smile.

Drew cleared his throat. "Well, when it didn't look good, last night, you know, we—we had her baptized by the hospital chaplain. We named her Bethany Grace."

"Bethany Grace Shepaski. I like it." Bryan nodded at Bethany, who blushed a little.

"I'm glad you approve." Drew cleared his throat again and this time sounded a bit more chipper. "Did I hear you right? You spent the night there?"

Bryan laughed out loud. "I slept on the couch. Honest, Pop. No funny stuff."

"You better hide your car. I can hear the gossip mill running already."

Bryan shook his head. "Okay, I think we've discussed this enough. Kiss Joanna for me, okay? And don't sweat school. We'll work out a schedule to cover your classes for a while." He hung up the phone and looked at Bethany. "It sounds like everything is going to be okay. And you have a namesake."

Bethany Elias gave him a shy look that was utterly charming and sincere. "They shouldn't have done that. They really didn't have to."

" I suppose they wanted to give her a name that meant someone…" he paused, hoping the right words would come out of his mouth this one time, "kind and loyal."

Bethany chewed on her lower lip and thought about this. "I suppose it's a pretty good name, isn't it?" She smiled at him as

100

Nate and Emma clambered noisily down the hall. "I better go tell the children about their new sister."

33: MOLLY

Almost a week passed before Shara mentioned her declared death to Molly. Molly hoped, in her deepest heart of hearts, that Shara would simply look on this as a blessing and move on with a life that so completely suited her...and didn't involve Richard Bennett. As she touched up Shara's roots, Molly listened to the younger woman ramble on about Richard and what this all really meant.

"So," Shara concluded, checking out her hair color in the mirror, "what do you think?"

I think that there's no need to return to your past, especially since the one person who is supposed to love you seemed pretty ready to declare you dead. Molly set down the blow drier. "How do you feel about this being dead?"

"How am I supposed to feel? I can't imagine how Richard would have made such a mistake, but then I think he was probably distraught, or the body was a mess, or something. It happens all the time on TV, right? People mistake someone who's dead and they're not really dead? I mean, maybe the body was really, really wrecked and they couldn't find dental records or something. I have been gone for almost three months." She paused. "This could be a positive, right?"

Molly remained silent for a beat, as if waiting to be sure that Shara was really done talking. "I think," she spoke slowly, her gaze fixed on the blow drier, "sometimes things happen the way they are supposed to, even though it's painful at the time."

"What do you mean?" Shara's tone was light, but didn't fool Molly. *She's got to be thinking that Richard's stopped looking for her, that he's moved on.*

"Why Richard declared you dead isn't up for debate. He did it. And I think that this is the best thing that could have happened.

You're free now, at least a little more so." She turned gave Shara a faint smile.

Shara sighed and smiled wistfully. "I always thought, maybe, Richard and I…"

"Put Richard out of your head." Molly instantly regretted her sharp tone. *It doesn't matter what Joanna and I want for Bryan, if Shara loves Richard, she loves Richard. And I pity her.* "I'm sorry. That didn't come out right."

"Uh, okay."

"What I meant to say is, maybe you should put that part of your life behind you. You've been declared dead. No one is looking for you right now. Now you have the time you wanted to put the pieces of that horrible night together. Or…not."

"You think I should stop trying to remember what really happened?"

Molly took a deep breath. *I'm supposed to be protecting her, not manipulating her to fill a void here in our lives.* "Look, ignore me. I'm being selfish. If you remember everything and clear your name, you'll leave us and go back to your real life."

"Molly!" Shara's expression was complete surprise, as if this fact had never crossed her mind. "I-I can't even think…I mean…" she stopped, looking completely perplexed. "I guess I see your point. And you're not being selfish. I feel more at home here in Rock Harbor than I ever did in my grandmother's world."

Something we've never, ever discussed. "You didn't like it with your grandmother?"

A shadow crossed Shara's face and she frowned. "You know the strangest thing? I don't remember big chunks of my growing up years. It's like with that last night…I get snapshots. I mean, I'm healthy enough. She fed me, I had a bed…" Shara gave Molly a weak smile. "What I do remember isn't all that bad. Oh, Grandmother wasn't the cookie baking type, and she was really, really focused on keeping me in the family business."

"You didn't want that?"

Shara shook her head, water from her wet locks spraying left and right. "No. I wanted more than anything to do something

102

important, you know? Grandmother loved the car business. I loathed it. I wanted to be like what I remembered my parents being. Good hearted people who gave back. We weren't rich, not in money, but I remember a lot of laughter and a lot of joy." She blinked and looked down at her hands. "It was not…quite like that at Grandmother's."

Molly studied Shara closely. *There's a lot she's not telling me about those years.*

Shara suddenly looked up, her tone far happier, her expression one of child like optimism. "But, do you think it's really over? That I'm truly safe, now that everyone thinks I'm dead?"

Molly shrugged, unwilling to darken Shara's relief with her own dark doubts. "It's a possibility, I guess. But there is that possibility that someone out there knows exactly what happened, and possibly where you really are."

Shara's eyes darkened with doubt. "You think that voice, that woman, whatever, she's knows I'm alive, even though Richard identified that body?"

"Well, let's look at what we know. You got from Shorewood to Rock Harbor. That's what, almost a four hour drive. You didn't drive yourself."

"Well, maybe I did."

Molly shook her head. "You were dumped, or you ran away from the driver. There was no unclaimed car anywhere near Rock Harbor. Someone drove you here. That someone knows it's not likely that a person dropped in Rock Harbor would wind up drowned in Jefferson County three months later. We have to at least keep that in mind." Molly looked up from her monologue and smiled. "Sorry. I'm not cheering you, am I?"

"Not really."

"Then let's focus on the positive: You've been given time, which is the best thing you could have. This is a chance not many get, a real live second chance at a new life."

Shara nodded, seeming to accept Molly's words. Yet Molly did not miss the melancholy expression on her face the rest of the afternoon. *The one thing that she wants back…Richard Bennett.*

The one thing that will kill any chance she has with Bryan.

34: JOANNA

Bethany Grace, "Gracie" to her family, was a month old before she came home from the hospital. While everyone in the Shepaski house adored the tiny baby, a cloud of dread seemed to mute their joy. It was clear, though no one would say it out loud, that Bethany's days as a live in nanny with the Shepaski's were coming to an end. It was a fact that troubled Joanna.

"We have to find her a job," Joanna said to Drew in the darkness of their bedroom later that night. "We need to find her a job and a place to stay."

"Can we discuss this when I'm not trying to sleep?" Drew burrowed into his pillow.

"We can't put this off, Drew, and you know it. Bethany's our responsibility, she's family. What, we're going to just kick her out like that? Would you let Emma just traipse around the world with no direction, an innocent child out there in the world?"

"Well, no. Emma is three. I don't want her traipsing down the steps by herself. But Bethany-"

"Bethany is just an older version of one of our own kids, and we can't let her go. You know you agree with me."

Drew huffed and rolled over to face his wife. "What I know is that I can't give yet another quiz on Bull Run in the morning just because I can't stay awake to teach actual new material. What I know is that you and Molly don't need my help with this."

"You old pooh." Joanna pushed his now turned back.

"Too many cooks spoil the nanny," Drew mumbled. "Go to sleep."

Joanna was quiet for a moment, a thousand thoughts rolling around in her head. "Aha!" She hit Drew again in the back. "I know where she can live."

"You can't wait until morning to tell me?"

"Sit up and listen to me, Drew Shepaski, or I'll make you get up with the baby."

"That's an empty threat. I'm not good at breastfeeding."

"This is so perfect. I can't believe I didn't think of it immediately," Joanna giggled, delighted at her idea. "She'll live at Bryan's."

Drew rolled over and looked at her. "Sleep deprivation has made you insane. Putting aside Bryan's privacy issues, let's focus on the concept of a single man, a teacher at RHCS, living with a single woman. I doubt the good people of Rock Harbor are ready to be that…liberated."

"Not in his house, of course. In his barn."

"With the horses?"

"Don't be dense. In the loft."

Drew was quiet for a minute. "I don't think anyone's been up there since Jenny."

Of course no one's been up there since Jenny. That's sort of the point. "Yes, I know." Joanna snorted impatiently. "But don't you see? This would be the perfect place for her. It's small, but comfortable, and she's got her privacy."

"And best of all, she's in close proximity to Bryan, so those sparks of love don't have so far to travel." Drew spoke in a fake perky voice.

"I believe I've noticed some interest in that direction." Joanna crossed her arms arm and smiled. "He's different with her since Christmas. He's certainly been around for dinner more often. Have we gone two days without him showing up on our doorstep?"

"So he likes being here. You've spent the last three years begging him to come over."

"He likes being here because of Bethany."

"He likes being here because of Bethany's cooking." Drew sat up against his pillows and grinned. "I'll be happy to build an extra room off the back of the house if she can stay here. That's a win-win for me."

Joanna elbowed him in the ribs. "Drew, don't be dense. They're friends, good friends. It could be something more."

"Yeah, they're friends because she's not interested in him." Drew gave her triumphant smile. "I can't believe you haven't noticed that."

"Oh please. You think a smart girl like Bethany is going to throw herself at him? He's so grouchy most of the time, and so obvious about how he hates the whole heart throb reputation. So she's taking a less obvious approach."

"Oh, but once they're out there at his place together she'll pounce," Drew shook his head and slumped back into a prone position.

"Well, let's just see how Molly feels about this." Joanna reached for the phone.

"What are you doing?" He lifted his head out of the pile of pillows.

Joanna held the receiver of the cordless phone in her hand. "Calling Molly."

"Jo, what is it with you and calling people late at night? I have to work with these people in the morning!"

"Hush. Hey, Molly, it's Jo. No, we're just fine. Drew and I were just talking about Bethany and what she's going to do now that Gracie's here. I know it's time, with the baby getting bigger, but we were putting off the idea of moving her out. Flat out, she needs a job and a place to stay. I was thinking-" Joanna broke off for a moment. "You thought it, too! I can't believe it! That's what I thought! Drew, Molly said the same thing about Bryan's loft!"

"I'm not having this conversation!" Drew pulled the blankets over his head.

"Don't mind Grouchy. So you'll talk to Bryan in the morning? Okay, I'll call you later." Joanna clicked off the phone and lay back. *This has to work. We're so close to having Bryan back, we can't lose her.*

35: BRYAN

Finally home after a day of squirrelly fifth graders diseased with spring fever and Molly hounding him about this new living arrangement with Bethany, Bryan was in a foul mood. It was a mood not improved by the phone ringing shrilly the minute he stormed into the cabin and kicked off his muddy boots. His greeting sounded more like a snarl than an actual word. "What?"

"Bryan? It's Bethany. I wanted to talk to you about this...arrangement that Molly and Joanna came up with. I-I wanted to know what you thought about it."

"Oh, someone's actually asking me my opinion about what happens on my property? How refreshing."

"I was afraid they'd pushed this idea on you." Her apologetic tone did nothing to shake him out of his mood.

"So what else is new?" He threw his coat on the nearby chair. "Those two have bullied me for years. Now they have a new recruit, someone they can train to continue their ways of evil."

"Well, I appreciate you telling me how you feel. I'm sorry they...I'm sorry." Bethany's voice got smaller and smaller with each word. "See you later." She hung up and the dial tone hummed.

Regret shot through him. *Crap, I should've been nicer to her.* Bryan stared at the receiver. *It's not her fault. It's Molly and Jo. Why can't they leave well enough alone?* He flopped down on the couch and clicked on the news. *Why can't they just let her go wherever it is she needs to go and live there? Why is that such a problem for everyone around here?*

He changed the channel a couple of times, then tossed the remote, realizing it was futile. *It's not just a problem for everyone else, is it? I don't want her to leave yet.*

Well, of course not. She's a nice person. She's easy to be around.

So let her live in the loft.

Bryan watched the shadows of trees dance across the face of the barn. He couldn't bring himself to look up at the loft window. *Why can't she live anyplace else? There are a hundred places in town she could live.*

Obviously Molly and Jo want her to keep tabs on me.

Cripes, those women! Can't they leave well enough alone! Now I need a babysitter?

Well, you haven't exactly been Mr. Stability in a long time, have you?

So what, I let her live out here and report back to them? Better yet, we fall madly in love because we're these two lost souls just waiting for each other?

Bryan rolled his eyes. *This is the most ridiculous thought process I've ever had. Bethany's not the least bit interested in me.*

And that bothers me…why does that bother me?

Oh shut up! Bryan got out of his chair and picked up his cordless phone. He stared at it for a moment, as if seeing a foreign object. *It's not bad, having her around. Besides, she hasn't breathed a word about Christmas Eve to anyone… And she's a good cook. Maybe she'll make those pancakes again.*

Fine! Make the call!

"Oh why, because everything I associate with the loft goes away because she makes really good pancakes?"

There are worse reasons to let someone into your life.

Bryan got up and paced back and forth in front of the fireplace. "This is ridiculous!" He picked up the phone and started to dial. "What am I thinking?" He stopped dialing and tossed the cordless onto the recliner.

I'm thinking about those pancakes…and how she always smells likes strawberries.

There's no way in hell anyone is going to live up there! What, then she lives up there one day she brings home a date…how's that going to feel?

That's going to feel sort of…sucky.

Well, there's no need to ponder it, because it's not going to happen because she's not bringing a date up to the loft because no one is living in that damn loft!

The matter settled, he crossed to the kitchen and opened up the refrigerator. *Why is it I don't have a thing to eat?*

There, at the back on the bottom shelf. One diet cola.

Oh hell.

Knowing the battle was over, Bryan returned to the recliner, and picked up the telephone. He dialed quickly, and forced himself to keep from hanging up.

Drew answered. "You are either the bravest man in town, or the most stupid."

"Why?"

Drew chuckled. "The women folk are clucking like angry hens because you were rude to Bethany. Emma's even in on it. I'd be mad about all the noise here, but it's kind of funny, since they aren't mad at me. It's pretty entertaining, actually."

Bryan rubbed his temples. In the background he could here a commotion of voices, mostly female, mostly unhappy. "So what's my punishment?"

"The jury's still out." Drew put his hand over the receiver and Bryan heard muffled conversation. "I'm supposed to ask if you still have a pile of dirty laundry in your hallway and no food in your fridge."

This caught him by surprise. "Why is that anyone's business?"

Drew chuckled again. "Jo wants to chat with you."

"Drew! Don't put Jo-"

"Bryan Jacobs, you mean thing!"

"Hi, Jo." Bryan rolled his eyes in mock exasperation. "How're things?"

"You hush and listen to some sense. Bethany could be your housekeeper. Doing the cooking, cleaning, in return for the use of your loft. She'd get another job, you know, to make money, help with groceries, that sort of thing. The work she would do for you would be sort of like paying rent."

Remembering too well the vacant space in his fridge, Bryan sighed and glanced at the pile of dirty clothes in the hallway. *I could use a hand around here.* "Jo, I was calling to say-"

"You can't argue about this Bryan! You need a housekeeper, and she needs a place to stay."

"Jo, I-"

"And you're so mean to her on the phone when all she was doing was making sure you weren't being bullied into something you didn't want."

At this Bryan grinned. "Yeah, who would ever think I got bullied into anything?"

"Very funny."

"Look, Jo, calm down. I was calling to apologize for being rude to Bethany on the phone and to say that sure, she can stay here. But does it have to be in the loft?"

"Do you really want to bear the wrath of Rock Harbor Community Church, having a single woman living inside your bachelor pad," Joanna's tone softened. "Don't worry about a thing. You won't have to lift a finger. We'll take care of everything."

"Of course you will." Bryan rolled his eyes again. "You and Molly win. Wipe that smug look off of your face, woman, I can see it from here. Molly's too."

"You are not going to regret this, Bryan."

"You two would rule the world if you used your powers for good, you know." Bryan shook his head and stared out the window at the barn. His eyes watered as if pricked with a pin. "And I think I already do regret it."

* * *

As promised, Bryan was not required to do anything in the loft. Almost worse was the army of women from the church Joanna enlisted to help with the clean up and redecorating. Hiding in the house each evening, Bryan tried to ignore the curious faces that passed by his window. *You all just love this, don't you? Rummaging through the worst bits of my past.* He was immeasurably glad that only Bethany knew the truth about the loft and why he really hated it. He doubted, had anyone else known, that there would have been enough parking space in his yard for all the curious onlookers who wanted to get a glimpse of the scene of the crime.

The process took two weeks. Bryan stayed in the back field of his property, riding Pepper, his big quarter horse stallion, and working with Marva Blakely, his neighbor, to train Spice, Pepper and his cranky mare Rika's filly. He stayed outdoors as much as possible in the unpredictable early spring weather, especially the day Drew loaded the last of Jenny's furniture into the Shepaski station wagon. Even from a distance, Bryan's stomach churned at the memory of the last time he'd set eyes on that bed set.

March fifteenth was officially moving day. *Beware the ides of March.* Bryan watched the Shepaski station wagon pull into his yard, this time filled with Bethany's few belongings. Absently, his hand dropped to the soft handmade quilt draped over the couch. His grandmother made it years ago. It was a dozen different shades of pink, a color that reminded him of Bethany for reasons he could not explain. He knew she would need it, given winter's reluctance to leave Rock Harbor. *The heating in the loft was not always enough to keep one person warm.* He did not miss the irony in the thought.

"Hey, Bryan," Drew called from the drive as Joanna and Bethany climbed into the car. "We headed down to Dave's to meet Molly for dinner. Wanna come along?"

Bryan patted the quilt. *This will wait.* "Let me get my coat."

"Dirty Dog Dave's" was a dark, seedy bar and grill three miles south of Rock Harbor and right next to the state highway. Dave, the proprietor, was a large, hairy man with an improbable Southern accent. Dave made the best cheeseburgers and onion rings in the state and the teachers of RHCS couldn't stay away. More than a few faculty meetings were held at Dave's because Dave was partial to the teachers and, contrary to the reputation perpetuated by the owner, the place was completely harmless.

Even though Dave does put on a good show with his wait staff running around in those campy, trampy outfits. Bryan absently wondered if Bethany's opinion of them would dive when she saw Dave's "triple D" girls.

"Well, it's mah favorite teachers!" Dave greeted them with beefy arms wide open as they hustled into the dark, cavernous bar. "Y'all's brought a friend."

"Dave, this is Bethany Elias. I'm sure you've heard she's been helping us out."

Dave looked at Bethany up and down with a practiced eye. "Ah, yes, the mysterious Creek Gal." Dave bowed low over Bethany's hand with great flourish. "But you, dahlin', are much prettier than they tell me."

"Comes from clean living and regular church going. You should give it a try." Molly quipped.

Dave chortled deep in his throat. "Molly, mah love, Ah have missed you." Dave looked up from Bethany and flashed a brilliant smile at Molly.

"It's not like it's been that long. I was here last night."

"Yes, but not as a group. Les' jus' say it's been a long winter without mah favorite teachers all together."

"Well, we've missed the food." Drew grinned at Bethany. "Nothing against Bethany's cooking, but I could do with a big pile of fries and one very greasy, very cheesy burger."

"In a minute, mah friend. I mus' get a better look at this little gal here." Dave held on to Bethany's hand and looked her up and down again, this time with more of an interest.

Bryan noticed that, while Bethany seemed surprised and a little uncertain about the direct attention, she was not completely displeased. Her smile warmed and her eyes danced under Dave's studied look. *So why do I care?*

"Well, Mr. Dave, do I pass muster?" She gave him a twisted grin.

Dave chuckled. "You are easy to look at, young lady, Ah will say thet. You got a fella? Or is there hope for slobs lahk me?"

Bryan did not miss, but tried to ignore, the look Molly and Jo shared.

"Well, I am moving in with Bryan today." Bethany gave Dave a coy look that surprised everyone at the table, not the least of all Bryan. *Is she flirting? With Dave?*

Dave seemed to feed off her mood. "I thought y'all were against that premarital stuff." He winked at her. Bryan's stomach lurched.

"Only if there's actually stuff involved." Bethany giggled, still holding Dave's hand.

Why doesn't she let go of the big oaf?

"So, whut are y'all doing for Bryan thet he let you into his fortress of privacy?"

Bethany smiled that same warm smile. "I'm going to be his housekeeper."

Dave's roaring laugh was infectious and the whole group burst out in loud guffaws. Bryan tried to look insulted, but he knew it was hopeless. Relieved that Bethany now let go of Dave's hand and sat down, he joined in the laughter.

"Bryan with a housekeeper! Ah must say, that is rich!" Dave chortled through teary eyes. "So you're celebratin', is that it?"

"In a way." Drew toyed with a napkin. "We're also brainstorming."

"Bethany needs a job." Joanna closed the menu. "And I need a cheeseburger."

"I thought she wuz your nanny." Dave kept his paw on Bethany's shoulder. "And your housekeeper. So she needs a third job?"

Bryan ran his hands through his hair. *Do you really have to touch her every time you speak?*

"Dave, I'm capable of taking care of things at home, now that Gracie is here, and Bethany is ready to move onto something more challenging than just taking care of Bryan."

"Bryan's not enough of a challenge?" Dave's face settled into a more serious expression and he leaned on the table, bracing his bulk on his meaty fists. "Ah tell you whut. Ah'm short a gal. Y'all recall Starlett?"

"What happened to Starlett?" Dave's hands were off of Bethany and Bryan's good nature returned. *Weird.* "I liked her. She actually brought food to the customers."

"Keep yer pants on. Chanel's put yer order in. As fer Starlett, Ah caught her tryin' to borrow some money from the register. The one rule Ah hev 'round here. So Ah need a new girl. Let's have a look at you again, gal." He pulled Bethany out of her chair and spun her around with his big, furry hand. "A little on the small side."

"Thank you very much!" Her tone was indignant, but her dark eyes sparkled.

"That's not always a bad thing, gal." Dave patted his chin. "Ah'll just have to think of an angle with you. Y'all look too young an' innocent t' be a Triple D gal."

"A Triple D gal?" Bethany looked at each of her friends.

"A Triple D gal is what Dave calls his waitresses." Molly explained.

"Ah also hold that it's the ideal cup size," Dave said. "It's a goal Ah try t'have all mah gals obtain. Y'all are just a little short there."

"I think I'm supposed to be insulted." Bethany backed away, her eyes wide and her face flushed. "I'm not so sure I want to be a Triple D gal."

I'm not sure I want her traipsing around as a Triple D gal.

Okay, since when is she my concern? She needs a job, he needs a waitress. Stop with the weirdness, Jacobs.

"Honey, every gal under the age of eighty and over the age of eight wants to be a Triple D," Dave said warmly. "Ask anyone."

"Fine, I will. Molly?" Bethany tapped the older woman on the shoulder.

"Don't ask her. She worked here," Bryan let out a short laugh. "Hey, Mol, what was your nickname?"

Molly held her face firm. "I'm sure I don't recall. It was right after I moved here, before I married Robert. I needed to make a little extra money. And it wasn't too humiliating." Molly kept her attention on the dried out spot of ketchup on the plastic table cover.

"Not too humiliating?" Dave roared. "Let me just tell y'all about mah dear lady here. You went by Nightingale, didn't you? You gave comfort to the customers!"

"Molly, you didn't-" Bethany broke off, unable to ask the question.

"Do you really think we'd come to a place that allowed anything illegal or immoral?" Joanna leaned against Drew and laughed. "Dave's is completely harmless. You'll be in good hands. Trust me, I even worked here a brief bit."

"You?"

"Of course. Of course, it's how I put myself through college." Joanna laughed. "Of course, once I got married and pregnant, my career was over!"

Dave let out a warm, deep-throated guffaw. "You, gal, you did a thing with your hips that made the men howl. Drew is one lucky man."

"I do not want to hear this!" Bethany covered her ears and shook her head.

Dave chuckled. "She's hired. Those land developers who come up here to look at mah gals will jus' eat this cute little thing up!"

"You know, Bethany has a skill beyond being cute."

Everyone looked up at Bryan, who couldn't believe he'd actually spoken out loud. "She plays piano. You've got that big old thing on the stage there. You could class the joint up with some music, you know?" *And maybe, if she must work here, it can be away from the customers, and wearing actual clothes.*

It's gotta be the starvation talking. Where is Chanel with the food?

Dave rubbed his stubbled chin with his paw-like hand and studied Bethany more closely. "Hmm, now that is somethin'. Hop up there, gal. Give us a listen."

Bethany followed Dave and Bryan, who now felt responsible for the pained expression on her face, to a vacant stage where a battle scarred baby grand sat, dusty and alone. She seated herself on the bench and opened the keyboard. Bryan watched as she closed her eyes and the notes melted from her fingertips onto the keys. He didn't recognize the music she played, but it conjured up thoughts of a soft smelling spring day in his mind. As she finished, her face now peaceful, the room was silent.

Nonplussed, Dave looked over the crowd. "Y'all play anythin' other than that?"

"Of course. Bach or Beethoven?" She positioned her hands over the keys again.

"No, no, child. Ah mean, anythin' besides that classical crap. Look around. These ain' whatcha wanna call a high brow crowd."

Bethany looked uncertain. "Sure, she can." Bryan jumped in. "She's a whiz at learning stuff. Jo, didn't she learn all that stuff at church right away?"

"No time flat." Jo barely looked up from her onion rings. Now that the food was at the table, Bryan knew any support he'd get for this suggestion would have to wait.

"Ah don't know. Church stuff an' classical crap? Ah'm thinkin' more along th'lines of Jerry Lee Lewis and whatnot."

"Oh, I can learn anything." Bethany stood up. "I'd just need a little time."

"Fahn, then first you wait tables. And don't fret. Dave's is all about good food for good old boys, thet's all." Dave gave her a warm, almost fatherly look. "When you get some good music in those fingers, then y'all can play. Do we have a deal?"

"Don't I need to fill out an application or something?"

Dave grabbed her up in a big bear hug. "Isn't she the funniest lil ol' gal? No, dahlin', you'll be workin' for tips. An' neither Ah nor Uncle Sam want t' know nuthin' 'bout what you make every night."

As Dave set her on her feet, Bryan did not miss the look of sheer relief on Bethany's face. *Is she that happy to be working for the old bum? Or just happy he's stopped manhandling her?*

Because I sure am.

36: RICHARD

Richard stared at the man across the desk from him in disbelief. "You cannot be serious, Archie."

Archibald James, Lydia Brandt's long time lawyer and confidant, folded blue file folder and stuffed it back into his brief case. "Certainly not, Mr. Bennett. Mrs. Brandt's instructions were

116

quite clear on this point. I found it odd at the time, but Mrs. Brandt did always have an uncanny way of knowing things that were going to happen. I imagine it's what kept her business so profitable for so many years."

"Yeah, yeah, whatever." Richard stood up from his chair and paced back and forth between his massive dark cherry wood desk and the matching credenza. "So what you're telling me is that it doesn't matter that Shara's obviously, completely and, most disgustingly dead? I still have to wait?"

"Well, the police ruled the matter a suicide."

"Precisely. And they closed the case. Shara is dead. Has been for some time, by the looks of her." Richard ran his hand through his thick blonde hair. "Lydia told me that if Shara wasn't…around…I would be the one to inherit."

Mr. James nodded, seemingly undisturbed by Richard's agitation. "And so you shall, Mr. Bennett. Once it's been proved that, first of all Miss Shara is, indeed, dead and second, that she was not murdered. And, of course, there's the little matter of the wait period. "

Richard glared at the lawyer, wishing he could smack the older man's completely peaceful expression right off his face. *A waiting period before I can inherit? What the hell, Lydia?*

"So, once the police have ruled that Miss Shara is truly dead, and once we've ruled out foul play, then it will be nine months' time before you completely inherit Mrs. Brandt's entire estate."

"Well, Archie, you can start counting as of New Year's Eve because that was Shara on that table, and she was definitely not alive, and the detectives I spoke to said it was either an accident or a suicide."

Mr. James remained unruffled. "And if that is so, Mr. Bennett you will indeed have everything sometime shortly after Labor Day. Until that time, you can continue to live in Mrs. Brandt's house, and act as caretaker there, and you may continue to run her businesses. I will, of course, act as counsel and you will need a vote of the board of directors to enact any business changes you wish to make prior to taking over the business. But the nine

117

months starts the moment I have a phone call from the police ruling out anything other than suicide or accident, and not one moment sooner."

Nine more months! Well played, Lydia. Well played. Keep your friends close and your enemies closer, and your protégé closest of all.

Richard took a deep breath and sat back down. "Fine, Archie, fine. I know you don't like me. I know you never liked me with Shara."

"I have no opinion to offer on either matter, Mr. Bennett."

Insufferable old fart. "Whatever. I also know you are going to call those detectives in Milwaukee and make them keep the case open because you can't believe your precious Shara would ever kill herself."

Mr. James blinked, and Richard noted with some satisfaction that there was a tear in the old man's eye. "If you wish nothing further of me, Mr. Bennett, I have other business to attend to." Mr. James stood up and took a step toward the door.

"Just remember this one fact, Archie: Your precious Shara was on some heavy duty meds just to keep her from clawing the walls. Even you can't deny that it's more than likely she threw herself into that river after a couple of days without her happy pills."

Mr. James slammed the door closed behind him. It was a sound that filled Richard with immense satisfaction.

37: SHARA

Shara looked around her new home and smiled. She wanted her bed next to the window, but the sloping roof of the barn made a headboard for the bed impossible in that spot, so Shara placed a mattress and a box spring on the floor and covered them with blankets. Polished wood milk crates lined the seam of the wall where the floor and the ceiling met, and all sorts of books filled the crates. Next to her bed was an old steamer trunk where she kept her few clothes and a small locked box for her saved cash. Next to

118

the trunk was a short lamp table and on it stood a small Tiffany lamp.

Shara was especially proud for finding the smoothly polished bentwood rocker at a garage sale. She tossed colorful pillows and cushions on the floor along the wall leading to the bathroom. The bathroom was actually just a small washroom with a very small shower stall.

Best of all, there was the roof. She crawled out the window and sat on the awning that overlooked the yard and the cabin. The breeze was cool, but she liked the view of the front part of Bryan's property, including the old, burned out farmhouse close to the highway. She hugged her knees to her and inhaled the cold, clean air. Sitting on the roof like this, Shara felt finally, and completely, in a place of her own.

"You know, I have chairs on the porch here, you don't have to sit on the roof."

Shara looked down to see Bryan, standing in the middle of the yard, something draped over his arm. "I like the view from up here. Why are you up so late? Don't you have school in the morning?"

"I, uh, I thought I'd see if you were up, maybe we could go over a few things."

"Sure, come on up." She crawled back through her window and listened as he entered the barn. Crossing the loft to the door, she looked down the stairs and saw him, one foot on the bottom step, frozen. "Bryan?"

He shook himself out of some kind of fog and looked up at her. "Oh, sorry. It's been some time since I've been…up there."

I'll bet this is impossible for you. She held her hand out to him. "Come on up. I think you'll like it."

Bryan moved slowly, as if each step made his joints hurt, but finally reached the top and ducked away from the slope of the roof. Giving the place a quick glance, he nodded. "Yeah, it looks nice."

"Thanks. So what, you wanna go over some ground rules?" She pointed to the rocking chair. "Have a seat."

"Oh, okay." He sat, still holding what looked like a blanket.

119

She sat, cross-legged, on the bed. "What's that?"

"Oh, right." He held it out to her. "It's a house warming gift, I guess."

Their hands brushed as Shara took the quilt from him and opened it up. It was lovely, soft and pink. "Bryan, this is so pretty. Thank you."

"My grandmother made several of these before she died. She said it kept her fingers moving and her mind alive. I-I thought you might need something a little warmer yet until summer comes."

"Well, thanks."

He nodded to the bathroom. "That shower's not great. Water pressure's pretty bad, and I think the hot water's iffy. Feel free to use the guest bath in the cabin."

She set the quilt aside and smiled at him. "Thanks. I'll keep that in mind. And on that note, I guess, we should probably talk about…you know…what places might be out of bounds?"

He gave her a dark look. "You're pretty much in it right now."

"I guess I knew that." She uncrossed her legs and leaned forward. "I know this is a huge thing for you, letting me stay here. I really appreciate it, you have no idea."

"But…"

"But, if this is going to work, you and I need to dispense with manners and be honest with each other."

He nodded and looked around the loft again. "You're right. So I'll be honest. I don't plan on coming up here ever again."

"Fair enough."

"As for rules, you have any thoughts?"

"How about this: I won't be a spy for Molly and Jo…and you don't give me any reason to be." She arched an eyebrow at him. *That should put him more at ease.*

"Uh huh. I knew they'd put you up to that." He grinned at her and rocked in the chair, plainly relieved. "Fine. Rule one. Rule two: I do my own laundry."

"Not a good rule."

"Why not?"

"I saw the pile in the hallway. You'd rather run around in skanky clothes than let your housekeeper get her hands on your dainties? Isn't that counterproductive to having a housekeeper?"

"Yeah, you're right. But I don't want you to think you're suddenly this slave or something. You'll be working a lot of weird hours at Dave's…"

"Not so different from running the Shepaski house. Easier, actually. You're just one guy, and a couple of horses. Way easier."

"Yeah, okay, I've got rule two: Don't touch the horses until I say so."

Shara scrutinized his face. "Okay, no problem."

He stopped rocking, and the deep lines in his face eased. "Sorry. I'm a little defensive with them. They're kinda like my kids."

"Got it. You take care of the horses. I'll take care of you." She glanced at the quilt next to her and stroked it with her hand. "What about your…bedroom?"

"What about it?"

She kept her eyes averted from him, suddenly feeling shy. "I mean…" *Oh what is wrong with me?* "You want me to clean the master bedroom and the bath, right?"

Bryan paused in his rocking again. "It's not like you haven't been in there before."

"True. I'm just thinking about…the people here in town…you know, how it looks with me living out here?"

He laughed, a warm, cheerful sound that put her at ease. "You've officially figured out the biggest pitfall of this place. I know Jo brought all those women here to do the remodel and to diffuse the ideas that you and I are doing something…torrid…" He grinned and she laughed out loud. "How about this: Your room is off limits to me at all times. My room is off limits to you unless I'm not home. Let that drop in a couple of conversations with Mrs. King, and we'll clear up any remaining gossip."

"Okay. Good."

"One thing I thought of. You'll need a car. It's not like you can walk to work now, and my hours aren't exactly predictable." The merry twinkle faded from Bryan's eyes.

His change of mood was not lost on her. Shara glanced out the window at the garage. "There's a cute car in your garage, besides the Jeep. Does it run?"

"Probably."

Shara studied him, then glanced out the window again. "It was hers, wasn't it?"

Bryan nodded. "She had it when we first got married. She bought something...else. I assume it runs. I haven't touched it in three years."

"It's a bug, isn't it? A VW?"

"Yeah. But not the new type model. It's an original. Probably why I kept it. It's sort of a weird green color..." his voice faded and he stared at her, through her, as if seeing something beyond the walls.

"Tell you what, Bryan. I'll take it down to Smitty's Car Lot tomorrow and trade it in on something else, how about that?"

Bryan shook himself, as if from a dream. "You don't have to do that. It's a good car. I had it tuned up...before...and the mechanic told me it was sound and would run for twenty more years. I think the keys are in the house. I'll find them."

"Okay, great. Any other rules?"

"You'll make those pancakes for breakfast once in a while?"

"Liked those, huh? Sure. At least once a week."

"Then nothing else that I can think of." He stood and took a step toward the door. Stopping, he looked over his shoulder at her. "Our other deal, that's still good, right?"

"What, 'I don't ask unless I'm ready to answer' agreement? Sure."

"Okay. Good." He put his hand on the railing and paused again. "We should...I don't know...shake on it or something."

She got up and crossed to him, and put out her hand. "Here's to a successful avoidance of gossip."

"And to finding the one other person in Rock Harbor who respects privacy." He shook her hand and grinned before leaving.

Even now, hours later, Shara still felt his hand pressing her own. She lay down on the bed and noticed the quilt still held a faint trace of the warm, musky scent of Bryan's house.

This won't be too bad, living here. She smiled at the ceiling. *And Dave will give me some terrible tacky name, which puts me one step farther away from the past. I can live my own life. Well, not exactly my life, but a life that I'm borrowing.*

Shara stared out the window. Bryan was still up. She could see directly into the living room where he watched television. She turned and looked at her darkened room. *Well, I could have borrowed worse lives, I guess.*

38: JENNIFER

Jennifer Tiel walked the long halls of the first floor and smiled. *A cat always lands on her feet. And this kitty is living in the big house now.*

The wealth of Lydia Brandt's expansive home was not lost on her. The views of Lake Michigan out the floor to ceiling windows were magnificent, as were the furnishings. *Especially the ones in the master bedroom.*

And this is all going to be mine, mine, mine legally in less than nine months. Again a smile played on her full lips. *Can I pick the right ones or what?*

Oh sure, Richard's in a foul mood because he doesn't get everything officially for a while. Staring out over the rugged lakeshore, she absently toyed with a heavy gold curtain cord. *It could have been a lot worse.*

It still could be.

Jennifer blinked away the dark thought. *No. Shara Brandt is gone. She's gone. She's not coming back. Not now, not in nine months, not ever.*

Not if she knows what's good for her.

39: BRYAN

"I think it's time we go for a horseback ride."

Bethany looked up from the stir-fry she was making and grinned. "So, I passed your tests for the last two weeks and now I get the keys to the kingdom?"

Not a formal test, but you haven't poisoned me or turned all my socks pink, so let's go the next step. "Not, at all." Bryan really hoped his lie sounded more truthful to her than it did to him. "It's more like, I have the spring quarter parent teacher consultations next week, and there's no way I'm getting home before ten any night."

"Okay."

Bryan glanced up from the paper he was reading and studied Bethany's face as she continued making dinner. *Did she sound disappointed?* "So anyway, after dinner, we'll go out to the barn."

"Sounds like a plan. Hey, can you toss me the soy sauce from the fridge?"

Later that evening, before saddling up, Bryan gave Bethany careful instructions on the care of the three horses, Pepper his beloved quarter horse, the mare, Rika, and the filly, Spice.

Once out on the trail, Bryan continued his lecture. "That mare you're riding's got a skittish streak. She hates me. I've been meaning to sell her, but just when I had a buyer I found out she was carrying that filly, and I just didn't have the heart to sell her then." He glanced back at Bethany. "You sit well on her, though. You've been riding before?"

She eased Rika alongside Pepper. "Not really. I mean, I took riding lessons in 4-H, but I guess I'm good with animals."

"Animals and little kids. What else do you know?" Bryan kept his tone even, conversational. *May as well dig a little deeper.*

Bethany paused. "What do you mean?"

Don't scare her off. "I know about teaching and horses and network news." He slowed Pepper to a slow walk and looked at her. The evening air was warm and she'd unbuttoned her jacket. Beneath she wore a pale pink tank top that hugged her smooth, fit figure. With each step Rika took, Bethany's jacket flapped open, giving Bryan a glimpse of her gentle curves. *Stop it!*

"Um, kids and cooking, I guess. Cooking on a budget." She glanced at him and Bryan snapped his attention back to the path in front of them.

"Yeah, but I mean before. Like your family. What did your parents do? Or your grandfather, the one that raised you. What did he do?" *Keep your eyes on the path, and quit staring at her, you idiot.*

"My parents were teachers. Grade school teachers."

"That's why you fit in so well here." He nodded in her direction, keeping his eyes firmly averted.

"Do I?" The hopeful note in her voice was unmistakable.

Bryan nodded. "Like you don't know. Joanna and Molly love you, the kids worship you. Drew likes your cooking, which is pretty much the best compliment you'll get out of him. And hey, I'm letting you handle the horses. You're golden." He allowed himself one glance in her direction. *Cripes, pink is really a good color on her skin.*

Bethany smiled and brushed a strand of hair away from her face. "Nice to know."

"What about your grandfather? Was he a teacher, too?"

Bethany nudged Rika to a trot and grinned back at him. "My turn. Question for question, why do I have to keep reminding you?"

"Come on Pepper," Bryan urged his horse to a trot to catch up. Once back with her, he grumbled, "You don't need to get defensive. I figured I'd make some small talk. Now that we…you know, are living in such close quarters, we'll be spending more time together…you know, alone, without other people. I'm trying some conversation."

She grinned at him. "Yeah, well, you're pretty lousy at small talk."

"I know." He studied the deepening pink and blue hues of the sky. "So, what's your question?"

"Don't have one at the moment." She laughed out loud. It was a warm, musical sound that eased Bryan's tension. "My parents were killed in a car accident when I was a kid."

Bryan blanched. "Geez, woman! You can't give me a beef about small talk and then land something like that on me!" He shook his head. "Sorry. I think what I meant to say was, 'I'm sorry to hear that.' That's what a polite person would say, right?"

Bethany nodded in agreement. "Probably. And don't sweat it. I was little; it was a long time ago."

"Let's try something a little less dramatic. Who taught you to cook?"

"At some point I 'm going to ask you about fifty questions in a row, rapid fire." She slowed Rika to a walk again. "My grandpa was a good cook. And I had a really excellent home ec class. How about you? Who taught you everything you know about housekeeping?"

Bryan liked the sparkle of mischief in her eyes. *Give her a reason to keep answering your questions.* "My sister tried to teach me how to cook, but it didn't take."

"Obviously. You don't talk about your sister much. What's she like?"

He chuckled deep in his throat. "Get ready to start shooting those questions. My sister Mikayla lives in Hawaii."

Bethany brushed at Rika's mane. "If you have a sister, you must have parents."

"I do." It was his turn to attend to something other than the conversation. Her question hit a nerve.

"Lame response,"

"Sorry. I answered the question, right?"

"Yes, you did. Look, Bryan, if you're tired of talking, we can probably go back. It's getting late."

"No, no I owe you a better answer."

"That's more like it." She sat back in the saddle and waited.

Bryan relaxed in his saddle, trying to put together the simplest explanation for his lack of close family ties. "My parents are on eternal vacation. I'm never sure where they are. I talk to my mother twice a month, if she calls. My sister is very busy being a career girl in Hawaii running a couple of my father's hotels. She lives there with her husband. Her first and only husband."

"Ah," Bethany nodded. "Not a real liberal family about divorce?"

Bryan shook his head. "Getting divorced was just another failure on my part." He steered Pepper away from some loose gravel. "One in a long line."

"I can relate to that. The failure stuff, I mean."

"Not like mine, I'll bet. Get this: My father owns a string of hotels and resorts all over the country. I was expected to follow in dear old Dad's footsteps."

There was a long pause before Bethany spoke. "You didn't like the idea?"

"Can you see me running a hotel? Being polite to rich people who have nothing else better to do than spend money being waited on by people who all but whore themselves out for a tip?"

She laughed then, a shallow, nervous sound. "Not really. It would definitely cut into your heart throb time."

"Very funny." He tried to sound grumpy, but Bethany started laughing for real, a warm, joyful sound, and her expression encouraged him to keep talking. "Mikki's the golden child. Moving here and teaching at a small town school after college pretty much did it for dear old Dad and me. He couldn't get that I'm not about money, that this was something I wanted to do because I wanted to do it." Bryan paused, feeling his face flush as it always did when he thought of his father. He glanced at Bethany who was studying him with dark, unreadable eyes. "So Mom keeps me filled in. Mikki I hear from sometimes." Bryan shook his head. "As far as I'm concerned, my family's right here." Bryan brushed a fly from his face and leaned against the saddle horn. "This is a good place for orphans and outcasts, you know? Half the people in this town got here because they failed at something, or were running away from something, or someone." He stopped, realizing he was staring hard at her. "I'm sorry. I wasn't talking about you."

She put a hand to her cheek as if to hide the flush on her face. "Oh, no. I-I was just thinking you were right about Rock Harbor...you know, being a place for outcasts and orphans. I never really thought of it that way."

A rabbit darted out in front of Rika's hooves, sending the mare into a frightened frenzy. Rearing up, Rika didn't unseat Bethany, but the sudden motion loosed her grip on the mare just enough for the mare to get her head and race into the darkening field.

Fear flooded Bryan. "Go Pepper!" Bryan howled, jamming his heals into the stallion's sides. Pepper leapt into a full gallop, but in the darkness, Bryan couldn't see Bethany or the mare. Straining to hear them over the thunder of Pepper's hooves, Bryan detected the sound of splashing water far to his right. *They've gotten to the creek! It'll be over its banks with the thaw, and very fast. If Rika throws Bethany in that water...*

Even the unfinished thought sent a wave of horror through him. Turning Pepper toward the creek bank, Bryan was forced to slow the pace of the horse, but was unable to slow the pounding of his heart. "Bethany!"

The only response was another heavy splash in the snow swollen creek water. "Bethany!"

Let her be okay. I'll shoot that damn mare if she's not!

"Bryan?"

Bryan halted Pepper at the edge of the shimmering black water. "Bethany? Where are you?"

"Don't come any closer...the water is really deep about ten steps in front of you."

Bryan squinted into the darkness in the direction of her soft voice. "Are you okay?"

"I will be..." her voice quivered with cold. There was another splash and Rika whinnied sharply.

A sense of fearful familiarity washed over Bryan as he slid off Pepper and made his way down the muddy creek bank. "Bethany? Where are you?"

"Aren't you supposed to say 'Marco,' and then I say, 'Polo' until you find me?" Bethany's words were cheerful, but the shiver of chill in her voice was unmistakable. "Can you see anything at all?"

Bryan's eyes were used to the dark and the rising moon gave him a pale glimmer of light. "I can see you now. Are you...swimming?"

"Not really. I just slid off Rika. I thought I could walk her up the bank, but this water is really deep...and fast."

Bryan stepped ankle deep into the creek. Icy cold shot up his legs. *Damn.* "Okay, can you reach out and catch my hand?"

"Not-not without you losing your footing. Just r-reach out and grab the reigns." There was a soft slap of leather against the water, and Bryan saw the reigns floating like a snake toward him. He tugged the reigns and Rika took a grunting step forward.

"Don't lead her up too f-fast. I n-need to hold onto the stirrup until I can g-get my f-footing." Bethany was calm, but Bryan knew, in water as cold as the newly thawed snow, hypothermia wasn't far off.

With Bryan's lead, Rika took a few reluctant steps forward, then walked easily up the bank toward Pepper. Bryan dropped the reigns and slid a foot down the muddy bank to Bethany, who was staggering unsteadily out of the water.

"I-I j-just can't s-s-seem to st-stay out of that d-d-damn creek," she grinned at him, her teeth chattering wildly.

Bryan hoisted her into Pepper's saddle, and then swung up behind her, wrapping as much of himself around her to ease her shaking. "Home, Pepper."

"W-what about Rik-ka?"

Bryan glanced over his shoulder at the mare, who followed behind. "Don't worry. She'll be fine. You we need to get warmed up fast."

"I'll b-be..." her voice drifted off.

"Bethany? Bethany!" He gave her a shake.

"Okay. I'll b-be okay." She slumped back and shivered against him.

"Just stay with me, okay? I'll get you home and warm in just a minute." *Stay with me. Just stay with me.*

The ride back to the cabin, though it only took ten minutes, was a torturous eternity for Bryan. Once to the paddock, Bryan eased Bethany, who was silent, but shivering, off Pepper. Leaving both horses in the paddock, he carried her into the cabin and back to his bedroom.

"Bethany? Listen, I have to…" he set her on his bed and tugged off her jacket, then ran into his bathroom to start filling the Jacuzzi tub with warm water. He returned to the bedroom, and stared at her sodden form, wishing there were a more modest way to go about what he was going to do. "Look, I've got to get you warmed up, okay?"

Still conscious, she nodded. "J-just…"

"Just what?" He leaned closer to hear her faint voice.

"J-just st-stop with the sh-shoes." She smiled through chattering teeth at him, her dark eyes laughing in spite of the violent shaking of her body.

In spite of himself, Bryan laughed as he undid her boots. Then he eased her, fully clothed, into the warm water of the tub. He sat on the edge of the tub and watched her closely.

Within a few moments, color returned to her porcelain white skin. "Feeling better?"

Bethany nodded, her teeth still chattering. She slid under the water and her hair floated away from her head like a halo. Sitting back up, she wiped water from her eyes. "Do you people keep your creeks that cold all year round?"

"That's what happens when you go swimming in melted glacier water. You're from Upper Michigan, you should know that river water is always freezing in the spring. Let me take off your socks."

"Mr. Jacobs? Are you getting fresh with me?" She smiled, her lips still quivering with cold.

"No, I'm checking for frostbite." He pulled off her socks and dropped them on the floor. "Don't worry about the mess. My housekeeper will get that." He grinned at her.

"Very funny," she wiggled her toes at him. "So, am I going to live?"

Bryan looked her up and down, suddenly very aware that the pink tank top she wore was translucent and the lacey outline of her bra caught far too much of his attention. *What am I twelve?* "I think you're going to be just fine." He let her foot drop back into the warm water. *Stop thinking about her bra!* "Hey, I do have to ask you one question."

She gave him a look of mock wariness. "I'm in a weakened state, that's not fair."

"No, I gotta ask. Why did you ride Rika into the creek?"

"Hmm. Well, a horse can't very well throw you if she's too busy trying to swim, right?"

"You didn't learn that in 4-H or home ec."

"No, that trick I think I got from some movie. It worked, though, right?" She blinked her wide eyes at him.

"Well, except for the part where you nearly froze yourself to death."

"Oh yeah. That's definitely the last time I take a dip in that creek. Nothing good comes of it!" She giggled and slid under the water again. Surfacing, she gave him a nudge with her foot. "Hey, we broke a rule."

"Which one?"

"The one where I'm not supposed to go anywhere near your bedroom when you're home. What will the fine folks of RHCS say?"

Probably not as much as they'd say if they knew what I was thinking about that pink tank top.

"Tell you what. I'm going to run up to your room."

"Breaking another rule." Her grin widened.

"And get you some dry clothes. And here are some towels and a robe. I'll be right back." Bryan left the bathroom, closing the door behind him and attempting, with only moderate success, to shut out the image of Bethany and her soaking wet pink tank top.

* * *

Alone later that night, Bethany safely and warmly tucked into her bed, and the horses cared for, Bryan replayed their conversation over in his head. *Someone beyond small town high school home*

131

economics taught Bethany Elias how to cook. Where did she learn to handle horses so well? She acts like she's never been in a barn, yet Rika didn't throw her. There are just some things you can't learn from 4-h and the movies.

The more questions she answers, the more I come up with. What is my problem?

She's either telling the truth, or she's the most practiced liar in the world.

God, let her be telling the truth.

40: SHARA

Easing the VW up the muddy drive in the wee hours of a May morning, Shara cursed her throbbing feet, and Dave, for the millionth time since she started working as a Triple D Gal. *It's not the ridiculously stupid outfit, or even my nickname..Daisy Mae. It's the darn shoes.* She rubbed her heel and glared at the open toed spikes sitting on the passenger's seat. *He just likes the way my ass looks when I wear them. Beast.*

Cold rain soaked through her blouse as she hobbled, barefoot, up onto the porch. Pain seared up her legs. *How much more of this can I handle?*

She shook mud off her toes before going into the cabin. The door was, as always, unlocked, and she smiled, recalling how cold Bryan had been to her when she'd first come to Rock Harbor. Now, living side by side, they shared an easy, peaceful rhythm of normal, day-to-day life. *Well, as normal as it gets with me, I suppose.*

Since the night she rode Rika into the creek, Bryan seemed to watch out for her. It wasn't unusual for him to be awake when she got home from Dave's, surfing the television channels, even on a school night. He never locked the cabin door, and, as the weeks went by, Shara found it easier to cross the yard late at night for any small reason. Often they would sit, absorbed in an old movie, while Bryan rubbed her feet.

Bryan's hidden talent; a master foot massager. I could totally use one tonight.

She found herself looking forward to these quiet moments with him. Between his schedule at school and hers at Dave's, it was rare they saw each other during the daylight hours. Shara always made breakfast, and they always ate breakfast together, but Bryan preferred quiet in the mornings. It was at night, when the rest of the world was silent, that the two of them seemed most comfortable together.

On this night however, the house was dark. Shara did not turn on a light until she crossed the living room and was in the kitchen, then she clicked on the dim kitchen sink light. Aided only by the weak fluorescent glow, she glanced at the refrigerator. *A snack and a little television sounds about right.*

Pulling the peanut butter from its place in the pantry, Shara grabbed the bread and jelly from the fridge. Not wanting to rattle around in the silverware drawer for a knife, she used one of the steak knives in the carving block. As she spread the peanut butter on the bread, the floorboards creaked behind her. The hair on the back of her neck stiffened. Another creak. Shara froze, gripping the knife in both hands and stared at the glob of peanut butter on the end. *Someone's right behind me.*

Frozen in fear, Shara's thoughts ran wild. *It's not Bryan. Bryan would have said something by now.*

Don't you dare tell anyone, Shara Brandt.

Shara hadn't heard that voice since Christmas Eve. But now, hearing the woman's voice so close to her, Shara's beating heart crushed her ability to breath. *She's finally found me.* Panicked, Shara whirled around and pointed the knife at the shadowy figure. In the process, the glob of peanut butter flew off the end of the knife and landed squarely in Bryan's face.

"What the devil are you doing?" He was too shocked to wipe the peanut butter from his face. "Holy cow, woman!"

Shara's hands still trembled as she clutched the knife. "What are you doing here?"

"I live here." He raised an eyebrow at her. "You can put the knife down. What's the matter with you? You look like you've seen a ghost. And why are you all wet...again?"

If I could see the ghost that haunts me, I would be the happiest person in the world. "You shouldn't be sneaking up on a person."

"Who's sneaking? I heard you come in, so I came out to see if you needed anything. Next thing I know, you're screaming and flinging crap at me."

"Yeah, well, next time, be noisier." Looking at him, she burst out laughing as he reached for the peanut butter on his forehead. "Sorry."

"So you're home later than normal."

"Dave had me closing, and there were some guys down from Fish Creek...they were getting away from their weekend getaways with the wives." She leaned against the counter and watched him clean the peanut butter off his face. "I was just gonna have a snack and maybe watch some television."

"Sounds good. You, uh, you wanna change first?" Bryan nodded to the wet clothes that clung to her body. In the dim light of the kitchen sink, her blouse was all but transparent.

"Oh, yeah. I got soaked running to my car after work. I'll be back in a minute." She took a step to the door when a brilliant flash of lightning cut through the darkness.

Bryan raised an eyebrow at her wildly startled reaction to the lightning. "I don't recommend going out in that, not as jumpy as you are at the moment Go take a hot shower in there," he pointed to the guest bath, "I'll go find you some clothes. And, bonus, I'll rub your feet when you're done."

She attempted a shaky smile. "That's definitely a plan I can live with."

Once in the bathroom, Shara turned on the shower, letting the water run for a few minutes before stepping in. The forgotten pain in her feet was back, throbbing under the spray of the water.

The door opened and her heart fluttered for a beat. *Bryan's coming in here?*

"I found you some things to wear. Hope they're okay. I'll throw the rest of your clothes in the wash." Through the privacy glass of the shower door, she saw that he stayed in the hall and tossed some clothes on the counter.

"Thanks." She waited for him to shut the door, but something woke inside her and thrilled that he remained in the doorway.

"Don't mention it." He cleared his throat as if searching for something more to say. "I thought I'd put in a movie and pop some popcorn."

"Bryan, it must be three in the morning."

"Well, if you're tired…"

Excitement flushed her skin. "No, not tired. I'm definitely not tired."

"I'll see you in a bit, then." He closed the door behind him.

The living room was cool compared to the steam of the bathroom. Dressed in a long t-shirt and a pair of basketball shorts that looked more like a long skirt on her, Shara padded out on to the carpet, warm in the generous folds of Bryan's robe. She smelled on the clothes the warm, spicy scent she knew as Bryan's.

"Have a seat." He pointed to the couch. "I can give you a foot rub while we're waiting for the popcorn. You want some of that muscle stuff that stinks?"

"No. I think a rub will be enough, thank you." Obligingly, she sat on the couch and stuck out her legs. With gentle hands he rubbed her right foot with a soft, sensual motion. It was then that Shara remembered her feet were bare. Bryan always rubbed her feet through thick, protective socks.

He studied her foot as he rubbed it. "Those shoes are ruining your feet."

"I don't mind." His touch in her bare skin woke something inside her. *A foot rub never felt like this before.* She closed her eyes, unwilling admit the warm feelings of arousal. *Richard never made me feel this way.* Briefly Shara tried to conjure up some memory of Richard, but the sensual rhythm of Bryan's hands on her feet erased the image of her fiancé.

"You don't paint your nails."

She opened her eyes. Bryan's non sequitur did little to break the spell, and Shara struggled keep her tone conversational, in spite of the fact that something dormant within her had just been turned on. "My toenails? No, I don't. I rarely even do my fingernails."

"Joanna paints hers."

"Really?" *What has that got to do with what you're doing to my feet...to me?*

Bryan didn't look up from his task, his face stayed shadowed. "Yeah. Drew says she paints them bright red. Some kind of rebellion thing."

"What, like she can't be uncool, she's got red toenails?"

"Something like that. Does this foot feel any better?"

Shara realized, as he switched feet, that her right foot no longer throbbed with pain, although, elsewhere in her body, there was a throb of a different kind. She cleared her throat and nodded, unable to trust herself not to let out some sort of moan of pleasure as he went to work on her left foot. *Toenails. Keep talking about toenails.* "So, um, hmm, what color should I paint my nails?"

"Pink." He spoke without hesitation. He spoke so easily, without thought, without missing a beat with his hands, he might have been discussing the weather. "My grandmother always said everyone has a color that's all theirs. Pink is yours, as I see it."

"Hm. Really." She found it odd how quickly he gave his answer. *And yet...* the image of her pink quilt, the pink trim on her coat flashed before her. *He's been thinking about this for a while.* She shut out any further conscious thought as she let herself revel in the feel of his hands stimulating the joints of her foot.

The popcorn stopped popping in the microwave. Bryan rested her foot on the coffee table and got up to go to the kitchen. He returned, a bowl of popcorn and two cans of cola, one diet and one regular, in his hands. "Still up for a flick?"

Whatever you want to do with me is fine. The sudden thought, so clear and undeniable, shocked her. She sat up straighter. "Uh, yeah. Sure."

He sat next to her, very close, his leg brushing against hers. She shifted quickly and he looked at her, surprised. "Oh, sorry. I figured you wouldn't want to have to stretch over to the coffee table to get the popcorn. He set the bowl on her lap. "If you don't mind sharing the couch."

His easy manner relaxed her. *I'm reading way too much into any of this.* "Oh, no. Not at all. What are we watching?"

Bryan picked up the DVD case. "Oh a lovely story about a plucky lad stuck in terrible circumstances. He manages to win the heart of a fair lady and save the day, though, so you should like it."

"Fair lady?" Shara raised an eyebrow at him. "That doesn't sound like something you would pick. Let me see that case." She reached over him and grabbed it off the end table. "Oh good lord, we're watching 'Gladiator' again?"

"What, you have a problem with Russell Crowe? I thought women liked him."

"I have zero problems with Russell Crowe." She laughed and settled back against the cushions. "But what is this, like the hundredth time you've watched it? People may wonder a bit about why you like Russell Crowe so much."

"Oh please. I see myself in the film."

"As the hero or the creepy guy? Or the completely overlooked servant guy with the weird scars on his face?"

"The hero, of course."

She flicked a piece of popcorn at him. "You see yourself as a Roman general sold into slavery and made to fight in the Coliseum? Really? I gotta be honest with you, I don't see it. You have a better hair cut, for one."

"Yes, yes I do have a better hair cut. But come on, that whole doomed, brooding hero thing, you gotta give me that." He twisted open his cola and took a swallow before giving her a mischievous sidelong glance.

"Oh, and bonus, you'd probably look good in that short little tunic thing." She giggled, hiding her face behind her hand.

Their conversation quieted at the movie started. Once the popcorn bowl was empty, Bryan set the bowl on the coffee table and, sitting back, rested his arm on the back of the couch, across her shoulders. A comfortable sense of familiarity washed over her.

She allowed herself to relax into the niche of his body. The soft flannel of his shirt warmed her cheek. *Whatever else I may feel, I'm safe here.*

41: BRYAN

Bryan opened his eyes and blinked away the fog of sleep. The television screen glowed at him as the music from the movie played. *I must've fallen asleep.* He moved to stand up and realized that Bethany was curled up next to him, snuggled against him. He smiled and rested back on the sofa cushions. Without thinking, he nuzzled the top of her head, inhaling the smell of strawberries in her freshly washed hair.

What are you doing to me, Bethany Elias?

She stirred and her hair fell away from her face. With light fingers, he stroked the clean, soft skin on her cheek. With his other hand, Bryan clicked on the movie again, muting the sound. A sense of completion, of perfect ease, washed over him in this still, simple moment.

What am I letting you do to me?

He'd almost drifted back to sleep when she sat bolt upright. "What do you want?"

Her posture, more than her words, surprised him. She'd leaned forward, her hands balled up in fists on the coffee table, her arms rigid, as were her back and shoulder. *She's dreaming.*

He put a hand on her shoulder and she startled awake. "Bryan?" A cloud passed away from her eyes. "What time is it?"

"It's early. Are you okay?"

"Sure." She ruffled her hair with both hands and looked at him. "Why?"

"You were having some dream or something."

Her cheeks colored a little, something Bryan found charming. "I guess so. Probably something related to late night popcorn and gladiator movies." She looked at the screen. "Are you watching this again?"

"Why not? I know I missed at least half of it last night."

"Yeah, well, don't you have school or something?"

Bryan looked at his watch. "Nope. It's Saturday."

She stood up and grinned at him. "In that case, how about I make some breakfast and I'll veg out too? I'm off the whole weekend."

"Sounds like a good idea." He caught himself watching her move around in the kitchen. Watching, wondering what nightmare had burst her so harshly awake.

Just a bad dream. He turned back to the movie, and realized, that he didn't care what caused the nightmare. He was more interested in protecting her from whatever demons haunted her sleep.

42: SHARA

Typical of most days, Shara's ankles ached mercilessly by noon. She stepped behind the bar and slipped off her high heels. She twirled her foot around, feeling a lovely release with every snap and pop of protest from her ankles.

"I think it's a violation of some sort to be barefoot behind the bar."

Shara looked up and smiled at the speaker. Kelly Fuller, Rock Harbor's youngest cop, and graduate of RHCS, was a regular at Dave's. "You turnin' me in, Deputy?"

He blushed a little, and looked away. "Not today. I'm no health inspector."

"Good to hear." She slipped her shoes back on and pulled out her order pad. "What'll it be? The usual?"

"I guess. I'm meeting the guys here in a little bit. Can I get a table?"

Shara looked over the deserted room. Noon on a Tuesday was never close to busy. "Ummmm, I'll have to check. You mind waiting forty minutes?" She smiled and tore the order from her pad. "Sit wherever. I'll find you."

Ten minutes later she set a plate of steaming chili fries in front of him. "So what's up? Why chili fries on such a beautiful spring day?"

"It's the band."

Shara nodded. Kelly's group of friends played for every moderately social event in Rock Harbor, including the faculty picnic at Bryan's. *A lifetime ago.*

"We've been playing together since we were all at school, more than nine years." He dipped a fry into the greasy red-brown chili. "But our keyboard player got accepted to grad school in Madison. We'd just lined up a gig at his dad's supper club, you know, soft Sinatra for the folks in the bar over Memorial Day weekend. This was a big deal for us."

"Let me guess. Dad doesn't need you now?"

Kelly Fuller stirred pooled chili with a fry. "Exactly." He looked up. "It's not like I was hoping we'd get discovered and make it big. We've all got good, real life jobs. I just love playing with those guys." Kelly shook his head and stared back at his plate.

Shara tapped her pencil against her cheek. "Kelly..." she spoke slowly as an idea opened up in her mind. "You don't play Sinatra all the time, right?"

"We mostly do covers from the 70's and 80's. Jake's a real fan of those monster stadium bands, like Journey and Kansas. Since he's the lead singer, we sort of do what he wants. But we can play country, folk, polkas, jazz whatever, if given time to practice." Kelly gave her a shy smile. "But this might be the end of the road."

Shara smiled back, as she always did with Kelly. She knew he had a crush on her. It was flattering, especially since no one had ever had a crush on her. A tiny vain corner of her mind liked it. "You know, Kelly, I may just be able to help you guys out a little."

"Really? How?"

"I might be able to get you guys a regular place to play." Shara looked over her shoulder, making certain that Dave wasn't listening. "I've been telling Dave since I started here; he needs to do something here to bring in more people. Well, maybe not more, but better people, people not so bent on trying to pinch the waitresses' bottoms. Who better than a home-grown group who can pretty much play anything?"

"Really?" Kelly jumped up out of his chair. "You think Dave would let us play here?" He sat back down, but the adoration on his face was not to be ignored.

Shara nodded hard, hoping Dave wasn't overhearing the conversation before she had time to present the idea to him. "Well, he's got that stage area up there. And I know there's a big room in the back that's just sitting empty except for a piano. Perfect for practicing, you know, after hours or before they open." She shrugged apologetically. "The piano's beat up, but is sounds fine. I tried it."

"Bethany, that's great! Wait until I tell the guys!"

"Tell the guys what?"

Shara and Kelly both turned to look at Jake Winter. Jake was tall, probably six foot six, and took it upon himself, whenever he wasn't working at his father's dairy, to wear nothing but black leather and rock band t-shirts.

"Hey Fuller. Dan and Tony got held up at work, so whatever we decide here, I'll take back to them." Jake sat, straddling the chair, crossing his arms on the back of the chair. "Hey there Creek Girl." He nodded to Shara.

"Jake." Shara didn't care for Jake Winter. She really didn't love how he insisted on calling her 'Creek Girl.'

"Bethany here thinks she can get Dave to let us play right here!" Kelly nodded to Shara and grabbed another fry.

"That so." Jake was unimpressed.

"Bonus, she's a great keyboard player. She can replace Mitch!"

Shara looked over her shoulder again. "Oooh, Kelly, I don't know about-"

"Kelly, dude, you wanna add a girl to the band? Did Journey have a girl? No. Foreigner? I don't think so. Aerosmith? Not a chance. Bon Jovi, Van Halen, Nickelback, Metallica," he ticked off each band's name on his fingers. "The great bands don't have chicks." Jake looked up at her and smiled derisively. "Sorry Creek Girl."

"E Street had a girl," Kelly put in hopefully.

"First of all, she wasn't in the band, she played the tambourine. Second, Springsteen was doin' her, so it doesn't even count." Jake barely glanced at Shara. "Nope, rock and roll is a man's world. Chicks just make it more fun."

"Jake!" Kelly blushed three shades of red.

Shara wanted to slap Jake, more for the mortification she knew Kelly was suffering, but she held back. "Hold on, Jake." She kept her tone even, and friendly, in spite of her distaste for the man in black leather. "There are plenty of great women in rock and roll, and I'm perfectly capable of playing any music you put in front of me."

"Yeah. Church music."

Shara bit her lip, but the words kept pouring out of her mouth. "Yeah church music. And other stuff. I've played recitals for hundreds of people."

"Oh yeah? You play some dusty piece all perfect and then you get applause. Well rock and roll doesn't work that way. You gotta feel it in your soul. You've gotta suffer for the music you just don't get it, man." Jake leaned forward, his face twisted with intensity.

"Jake, you are such a moron." Kelly shoved a fry in his mouth. "It's not like you've suffered all that much, you run your dad's dairy. Bethany can play anything." Kelly nodded to Shara. "She can sing, too."

"Oh, wait a minute Kelly. I can't-"

"Sing, huh?" Jake Winter looked slightly less disgusted with her. "A back up singer, that could be cool."

"She's got a great voice." Kelly nodded vigorously.

Jake stood up and pushed the chair away with his booted foot. "Okay, Creek Girl, I'll give you a chance." He took two strides toward the door. "I'll bring Dan and Tony in next week and we'll listen to you and then we'll vote. Be sure we're solid with Dave."

As he left, Shara stared at Kelly. "Shame on you Kelly Fuller! You go to church every Sunday with your mother and you do this?"

"What? What did I do?"

"You tell me. I thought lying was a sin!"

"How did I lie?"

"First of all, I don't know a thing about rock and roll. Second, I don't sing."

Kelly wiped the last bit of chili from the corners of his mouth. "I'll get you some sheet music. I'll work with you. It'll be fine." He got up and dropped some dollar bills on the table. "I'll come back in tonight and we'll go over some stuff."

Well, it would beat waiting tables, every night. Shara watched him leave the bar and wondered, exactly, how she was going to break the news to Dave. Squaring her shoulders, she marched straight to his office. "Dave, we need to talk."

"So talk dahlin'." He didn't lower the paper he was reading.

"You know how you've been wanting more people in here? I've got an idea."

"Gonna cost me anythin'?"

"Of course not."

Dave set the newspaper down. "Ah'm listin'."

"You know Kelly Fuller and his buddies, and how they have a band? They want to play and they want me to play with them. You know, keyboards."

"No." Dave picked up his paper again.

Shara choked back her surprise at the quick dismissal. "I'm sorry. Did you just say no, without even thinking about it?"

"You said it wasn't gonna cost me nothin'. Lettin' mah best waitress, the Creek Gal, go, that's gonna cost me. You're good for business, you're a celebrity."

Shara put her hands on her hips and shook her head. "Okay, first of all, stop calling me Creek Girl. You and Jake Winter are absolutely the only two people who still call me that. Second, if I were a celebrity, capable of bringing people into this shady dump, don't you think it would be better for business if I were on a stage where everyone could see me?" She leaned against the doorframe and waited as the idea settled on Dave.

He set down the paper again. "Fine. Join the band. You play a coupla nights. Then we'll see. Maybe you make me more money on the stage than off."

"Give us a few weeks to get it all together. We'll rehearse in the back room."

"Not during business hours, yer not."

Shara crossed her arms and looked at her boss. "Wouldn't think of it, Dave. Before we open and after we close, of course."

"And you'll work for tips."

"Dave, be fair. The guys in the band need something. You gotta pay them something, if they're any good and bring in business."

Dave looked her up and down. "Fine. If they's any good, and if they bring in business. Then Ah'll toss 'em somethin'. But you..." He stuck a beefy finger at her, "are working for tips." He snapped his newspaper open again. "Ah don't want it getting' around to the other gals that Ah'm payin' anyone anything. Bad for business."

"Tips will be fine." Shara returned his grin and started out the door. "Is there any other way to work here?"

43: BRYAN

"Bethany has a boyfriend." Bryan slammed the door to the teachers' lounge.

"Well, good morning to you." Drew glanced up from the stack of sample textbooks he was reviewing. "You don't approve, I take it?"

"I guess that would depend on who it is." Bryan paced back and forth in front of the coffee maker. "Not a piece of information she's sharing at the moment."

"So what makes you think she's got a boyfriend?"

Only everything for the past week. "Did she ever stay out all night when she worked for you? She hasn't been home to make breakfast for the last three days."

Drew put his pen down and smiled at his friend. "So, is it the fact that Bethany has a life that doesn't involve you that bothers

144

you or is it the fact that you're not getting your eggs and bacon on a regular basis anymore?"

"You're hilarious." Bryan started pacing, dragging his fingers through his hair.

"Bryan, calm down. She's an adult. She's working for you, plus a full time job for Dave. If she finds time to date, wonderful. It's a good thing for her to find someone closer to her own age anyway. Hanging out with us, can get old."

"Please, I'm not that much older than she is."

"You have the social life of an old man. She's twenty-six. Give her a break."

Bryan shook his head. "I don't get it." He recalled the smell of her hair. "How could she? How could she after-" He broke off.

"After what?" Drew looked up, curiosity creasing his face.

Bryan paused in his pacing and rolled his eyes. "Nothing."

Drew sat back in his chair. "Okay then."

"Well, maybe. Maybe I thought…something. Last week I rubbed her feet and then she watched 'Gladiator' with me…" Bryan sat down in his customary armchair and then stood up right away. "I don't know."

"I see your point. In some cultures, that kind of courtship means automatic marriage."

"Shut up or be helpful!" Bryan paced back and forth in front of the coffee maker.

"This is when Jo or Molly should be here." Drew bit on his pen. "I'm not equipped to deal with your woman angst."

"If you breathe a word of this to either of them…" Bryan broke off.

"A word of what?" Molly walked in.

Drew kept his eyes on Bryan. "Bryan thinks Bethany's got a boyfriend."

"You don't say twelve words a day, but you feel the need to spread my personal life out for everyone?" Bryan glared daggers at Drew, who sipped coffee and chuckled.

"Your personal life?" Molly looked at Bryan calmly. "I thought it was Bethany who had the boyfriend."

"You're loving this, aren't you?" Bryan snapped at both of them. "Look, she's out too late, running around with some stranger, doing God knows what. But if you don't care about that, then I'm sorry I mentioned it." He thumped back down into his chair.

"What's with him?" Molly poured herself some coffee and looked at Drew.

"Cholesterol withdrawal. Apparently this new interest of Bethany's has her out late and she's not home to make his breakfast anymore."

"Poor baby." Molly gave Bryan a sympathetic look. "It could be something completely innocent, you know."

"What could be innocent that keeps her out all night?"

"Well, you have heard she's trying to put together a house band at Dave's right?" Molly grinned took a sip of her coffee. "But hey, your idea is far more interesting, let's explore that."

"Okay Miss Know-it-all. Tell me this: Why out until four in the morning and then out again before eight in the morning?" Bryan crossed his arm and stared at Molly.

"I think he's got you there, Mol." Drew bit into a cruller.

"How about she's probably practicing after Dave closes up, and before he opens. Now pass the donuts." Molly took the box from Drew and pulled out a cruller

Did she mention being in a band? Maybe. "Still, she shouldn't be hanging around Dave's all night. It's not safe."

Molly laughed out loud. "If I remember right, you lived at Dave's, literally, that first year you taught here. Dave hardly ever leaves. And I know for a fact that Kelly keeps his car parked out front when they're there. She couldn't be safer. "

"Yeah, but you go ahead and ground her." Drew reached over and patted Bryan on the shoulder. "That's what a responsible parent would do."

Bryan ignored Drew, but stared at Molly, processing her words. "Kelly Fuller?"

"Yes, Bryan, you know him. Graduated from here, what, eight, nine years ago? His band played for the picnic last fall? His mother works over at the-"

"I know who Kelly Fuller is!" Bryan's voiced was strained as he interrupted Molly. "Bethany is spending late nights and early mornings with Kelly Fuller?"

"You know, if you say his name three times right in a row, he'll appear and give you magical powers." Drew never looked up from his stack of book reports.

"Drew, my friend, you are on fire today." Molly laughed and shot a gleeful look to Bryan. "Yes, Kelly Fuller. He's in the band, and he's working on music arrangements with her. What's wrong with that?"

"Nothing. Of course, nothing. If she thinks it's proper to go traipsing about at all hours of the day with the likes of Kelly Fuller and heaven knows I don't have a problem."

Drew looked up from his book reports. "The likes of Kelly Fuller? He's a cop!"

"Yeah, okay, but you know who else is in that band? Jake Winter."

"Oh, Bryan, please. Little Jacob Winter is such a nice boy!" Molly used her most annoying old lady voice. "Those boys are all lovely young men." Molly shot Drew a conspiratorial grin. "They're really a bit younger than Bethany, and they share this interest in music-"

The school bell rang shutting off Molly's teasing tone. "Don't we all have classes to get to?" Bryan ignored his friends' barely suppressed smiles.

"We do." Molly closed her notebook with a snap. "And stop getting so worked up about Bethany. People might get the wrong impression."

"Whatever." Bryan stood and started for the door. "She's not the innocent nanny you guys had living in your house." He looked to Drew.

"No, she's an adult responsible for herself. She's not caring for small children anymore," Drew replied. "Then again…" Drew let his words hang in the air as he gave Bryan a pointed look.

"You're a riot." Bryan watched the door shut behind Drew. He noticed Molly was staring at him. "What are you looking at?"

"You like her. Admit it." Molly gave him a tiny smile.

"Of course I do. She's a good kid. Or she was until a few days ago."

"Don't be obtuse with me, Bryan Jacobs." Molly cocked her head to one side and studied his face. "I'm not talking about friendship. I mean you LIKE her."

Bryan rolled his eyes and picked up his briefcase. "You're starting to sound like my fifth graders. Pretty soon you'll be chanting that stupid kissing poem."

"Well…."

"Don't even." He started out the door and paused, giving Molly a quick look over his shoulder. "I'm just concerned for her safety."

Molly's smile was one degree short of triumphant. "Okay. Fine."

Bryan shook his head and shut the door. *Time to be the teacher and forget about…other things…for now.*

* * *

Midnight came and went and no sign of Bethany. Done waiting and wondering, Bryan walked into Dirty Dog Dave's and stormed right past the hostess stand and the bar without looking left or right at anyone. Only Chanel slowed his determined march to the back room.

"Bryan Jacobs, just what do you think you're doing?"

"I'm looking for Bethany, Chanel. She hasn't been home since she left for work yesterday morning, and I'd like to know that she hasn't been tied to a chair in the back."

"Oh please!" Chanel laid a red-clawed hand on his arm. "First of all, Bryan, you know full well that Dave is not about to let any customers back there. Second of all, Bethany is just fine. She was here for her shift, then she practiced piano until almost sun up. Dave told her she could sack out in the office until her next shift, which is what she did. She's been workin' real hard with Kelly Fuller to get ready for her audition."

"Audition?"

"For the band. You didn't think that Jake Winter was about to let some girl just be in his precious band, never mind she got them the job playing here." Chanel let out a deep, throaty laugh. "Please."

"So she's back there with Kelly Fuller?"

"Yeah. Has been for just about all week. And they are workin' on something big, I can tell you that!"

Bryan clenched his jaw. "I'll just bet."

Chanel directed him back to the bar. "Bryan Jacobs, if I didn't know better, I would swear on my mama's biscuits that you were jealous."

Bryan seated himself on a stool and rubbed his eyes. "I'm not jealous."

"Yeah, that would sound a little more real, honey, if you weren't stomping in here past midnight all wound up. It's a school night. You should be mindin' your homework." She pushed an icy glass of cola at him. "You want me to go get her?"

"No!" He realized, from the look on her face, that he'd spoken too quickly and too sharply. "I mean, no, that's okay. I just want to-" *What exactly do I want to do?*

"Tell you what. Dave's not here, he's at a lady friend's for the evening. That's why I'm closing up early. Place is deader'n a ghost town. Go ahead, go back there and listen. I'm telling you, that girl is pretty good."

"Thanks, Chanel." Bryan drained the cola and set the glass on the bar before going behind the curtain. As he got closer to the far back room, Bryan heard Bethany talking. He hid in the shadows and listened, hating himself the whole time.

"You know, Kelly, this song is really, really good. I can't believe you wrote it yourself. You should tell Jake you want to sing it."

"Not a chance. We do good, solid, party stuff, and the guys all love that. Jake especially, since he sings it. He's the star, not me."

"You don't give yourself enough credit. Let's run through this one more time."

Bethany's piano and Kelly's smooth tenor voice were the perfect duet together. Bryan closed his eyes and tried to ignore the nagging feeling that he was spying on something deeper than two people performing a song together.

They finished and Bethany applauded. "I'm telling you, Kelly, this is the song I should play for the audition tomorrow."

"Then you're doomed. And you'll take me down with you." Kelly looked at his watch. "Holy cow, is that the time? I've got the early shift in the morning." He laid his saxophone in its case. "You coming?"

"I think I'll practice just a little more," Bethany thumbed through the book on the music stand. "I can't think how to thank you for finding all this sheet music."

Bryan frowned, noting the encouraged glimmer in the younger man's eyes. *I'll just bet Kelly Fuller has a couple of ideas about that.*

"It was nothing, really." Kelly looked at his feet and blushed a little.

Good lord, he's blushing.

"No, really. I've never looked at pop music. Lots of classical, baroque stuff, you know? Jake was right about that."

"Not about you, though." Kelly leaned against the piano. "This music, it's not about reading notes. It's more about what's here." He put a hand over his heart. "And you've got that." He put a hand on her shoulder.

He's touching her. Bryan swallowed hard and screwed his eyes shut, wishing Kelly's hand away from her. Opening his eyes, he breathed out with relief as Kelly turned to buckle his instrument case.

Kelly looked at the music in front of her. "You're going to be fine. The guys are going to love you… like I do."

Bryan stared at the younger man for a full minute before he realized his own hands were balled into fists.

150

"Don't stay up too late, okay? Tomorrow is the big day." Kelly patted Bethany on the shoulder one more time before leaving the room.

Bryan tucked himself back from the doorway, allowing Kelly to brush by without seeing him. Alone, Bryan peeked into the room again to watch her. There, under the glow of a single light bulb, was Bethany, sitting at a battered old bar piano. She sang the song Kelly had just sung, but with a sweet, clear voice that gave the lyrics a spirit, a soul. *Does anyone know she can sing this well?*

He watched her, unable to move away from the door and unwilling to enter the room and disturb her. Her fingers glowed on the keyboard, glossy pale pink fingernails flashing over the keys. Her voice mesmerized him until she stopped and broke the spell. He ached to step out of the shadows, to let her know that he had heard her singing and that he thought she was amazing. Before he got up enough courage, she started playing again, this time something a bit more classical, dark and brooding. At first it seemed like she just toyed with the keys, touching them without a thought to the sound they made. But as she progressed into the piece, her shoulders stiffened. As Bryan watched from his hiding place, the notes seemed to fly from the piano more like shrapnel than music. She no longer played an instrument, but wielded a weapon, pounding key after key, firing bullets into the darkness. Stunned, Bryan watched with a growing sense of helplessness as she battled against demons unseen, but palpable even to him.

44: SHARA

Where the music came from, she didn't know. Some piece her grandmother threw in front of her, no doubt, proving to her friends that her granddaughter was a genius. Even as the notes flowed from her fingers, the resentment of those afternoon teas when she was trotted out like some trained monkey to perform for the dusty old elite friends in Lydia Brandt's circle, heated Shara's hands. She closed her eyes, unable to shut out the pictures, the snapshots her mind took of everything. *Grandmother holding up some impossible sheet music. Plunking it down in front of me for less than a minute, then ripping it away and demanding I play. And later, in my room, crying on my bed, exhausted from the experience.*

But singing, singing was something else. Grandmother hated her singing. Too well Shara remembered a day when she, at thirteen, arrived at the breakfast table, singing some song from the radio. Grandmother, Lydia, stared at her as if she'd taken leave of her mind and commanded her to never sing again. *I argued with you that day, didn't I, Grandmother? We argued and you made a phone call to-*

Unbidden, a flash of red flooded her mind. *Red. Blood. Gunshot. Richard lying on the floor. Grandmother, too.* Her hands raced from chord to chord, the piano shuddering in time with the pulse that throbbed mercilessly within her.

You made me hate you Grandmother. You ruined or took away anything I loved and made me hate you.

She pounded out chord after chord, her hands flying up and down the keyboard.

Did I hate you enough to kill you?

Don't you say a word, Shara Brandt.

The woman's voice, sharp and clear, shook Shara out of herself. She jerked her hands off of the keys and stared hard into the darkness of the room, looking for the one face she ached to see clearly.

45: BRYAN

The sudden stop to the music jarred Bryan out of the trance Bethany had woven around him. Something in her posture beckoned him to her, but held him back at the same time. Without seeing her face, Bryan sensed a change in the atmosphere around her. *Something is really, really troubling her.* He reached a hand out to her, but even from his hiding place, he realized there was little he could do.

His feet, however, did not agree with his mind, and without knowing how he got there, Bryan stood behind her, and tapped her shoulder. "That was, uh, really great."

She shuddered and turned to stare at him. "I-I didn't realize you were there."

The pale glow on her face startled him. "Guess I have to stop sneaking up on you…you've got that 'I've just seen a ghost' look on your face again. You okay?"

"What? Oh, yeah. I'm fine." She managed a weak smile and slid over slightly on the bench so he could sit next to her. "Just a little tired, I guess."

"Working hard like that, I can imagine."

She shrugged. "That was nothing. I've been playing that stuff since I was little."

"That didn't sound like nothing. Sounded like you were mad at somebody."

She let out a short, high-pitched laugh. "Please. That's how it was written. Blame the composer, not me." She gave him a sidelong glance, her color normal. "So what are you doing here so late?"

"Late supper. My housekeeper hasn't been around much the last few days to make dinner, you know."

"Oh sorry." She nudged him playfully. "Molly says you're jealous."

"Cripes, there really are no secrets in this town!" Bryan felt his face warming and was grateful for the dim light.

"You know that better than I do. Besides, you wouldn't be the only one to lose a," here she paused and studied the silent keys before looking up at him, her eyes aglow with mischief, "a housekeeper to the magnetism of a rock and roll star." She laughed out loud, tossing her head back with mirth.

"Yeah, I can see that song at the top of the charts. 'I Lost my Housekeeper to Kelly Fuller and His Band.'" He tried to laugh, but the sound stuck in his throat, so he looked at his hands, limp and purposeless in his lap, and sighed. "Hey, well, I'll let you get back to practicing, right?"

"I suppose." She nodded and watched him get up. "Hey, Bryan?"

"Yeah?" He nearly tripped, he whirled around so quickly.

"I- uh- Once we get this audition over with, things will probably be back to normal, okay? I mean, Jake hates me anyway, so I don't even know why I'm bothering, how Kelly convinced me to do this."

Her expression, more than her words, shot daggers of guilt into Bryan's heart. *I'm such an idiot.* He shook his head. "You have a gift, Bethany. When you have something like that, you have to take any chance that's given you. No matter how small it may seem at the time." He took a step right behind her and put a hand on her shoulders. She seemed to relax against his touch. "I don't mean just the piano."

Her shoulders tensed again. "How long were you back there?"

"Long enough to know that Jake Winter is a moron if he doesn't bring you on as a major part of the group. Long enough to know you've been holding one amazing talent pretty close to the vest." He absorbed the furious glare she shot him over her shoulder. "Sorry. I didn't want to disturb you. But that was the best singing I've heard in ages."

"Since you're saying such nice things, I suppose I'm going to have to forgive you. But don't you say anything, okay?" She smiled, but her eyes pleaded with him.

"Why not?"

Bethany sighed and leaned her back against him again. "I love playing. Playing comes so easy, and it gives everyone joy. Singing…that's another story."

"If it's a confidence thing-"

"Hardly!" She covered her mouth with her hands, her face registering shock at the force of her interruption. "I mean, I'm happy to let Jake have that joy, or Kelly, who is great."

"Yeah, Kelly's fantastic." Bryan couldn't stop a single drop of sarcasm from coloring his words. He tried ignoring the curious look she gave him. "You're the one who's got the voice." *Of an angel.*

"Well, thanks." She glanced up at him again; this time there was a warm light in her deep eyes that touched him. "I don't think anyone's heard me sing...except for you."

"Then I'm honored." He noted her grin. "Seriously, you have a gift and you should share it. But for now, it can be our secret." He rested a hand on her shoulder.

She straightened up again. "Like everything else?" Her voice was soft, and held no hint of teasing. "Your turn next time, Mr. Jacobs."

His hand moved of its own accord to stroke her upturned face. She did not pull away, and he held his breath, waiting to see what either one of them did next. She covered his hand with her own fingers, and the chill of her skin startled him. "Your hands are cold." His voice was husky, straining to hold back words he suddenly ached to say. Instead, he took both her hands in his and warmed them.

"Cold hands, warm heart, isn't that what they say?" She held his gaze, her dark eyes mirroring his own sudden tumult of feelings.

"They say that." Unwilling to let go of her hands, he sat next to her on the bench and leaned closer, his face inches from hers. In this moment, he felt safe, and dangerous. He ached to reach out and touch the part of her he could only see inside her eyes, the part that asked every question and offered every answer. "Bethany..." he leaned forward, a whisper away from tasting the sun warmed strawberries that seemed to be part of her.

"Bryan Jacobs, are you still back here?" Chanel's angry voice shook them apart. "Dave's back and he's in a foul mood and if he catches you back here he'll tar you until you're as dark as I am!"

Bryan dropped Bethany's hands as if they were on fire. "I'm going. I'm going." He stood and gave Bethany one last lingering look. "See you at home?"

"Yeah, okay." She brushed some hair out of her eyes and turned back to the keys.

He nodded to Chanel and slipped out into the bar and out the door.

46: SHARA

"So I suppose you're going to get mad at me for breaking up that little moment of romance." Chanel strolled over to the piano and leaned on the big instrument.

"Romance? Not hardly. Bryan was just-"

"Bryan was just about to lay some big long love line on you."

Shara tried to laugh, but the sound squeaked out too sharply. "Please. My hands were cold. From practicing."

Chanel nodded and gave Shara a wise look. "Oh yeah, the old cold hands routine. Girl, you are missing out if you're not seeing what I'm seeing."

"Chanel, there's nothing to see. Bryan and I are friends. I'm his housekeeper. That's all."

Chanel clucked her tongue against her teeth. "Every woman in the county would give her eye teeth to have the 'friendship' you've managed to stir up in that man. Oh don't look at me all innocent."

"You don't understand." Shara stared at her hands. *There's no chance for that, not with the lies I'm living.*

"I understand more than you think, sweetheart." Chanel put a hand on her shoulder. "I know what it's like to feel unworthy of something because of what's happened to you in the past. But it doesn't matter; don't you see that? Everyone's got something in the closet. That Bryan Jacobs could write a book, I just bet. This is your time, sweetie. Your time to come out of the shadows and shine."

Shara shook her head and started playing scales as Chanel walked away. *I'd love to come out of the shadows. I just don't know what I'll find. Or what will find me.*

47: MOLLY

"Has anyone seen Bethany yet tonight?" Joanna leaned as far across the table as she could to be heard over the rumble of the packed bar.

"Nope. She didn't even tell me she was leaving. I looked out and the VW was gone." Bryan leaned back in his chair, attempting a casual air, but Molly noted his hand trembled as he picked up his beer.

Molly fanned herself. "I swear it's a furnace in here."

"What's she wearing?" Drew wiped his forehead with a paper napkin.

"You remember that my old prom dress, the one with the rhinestone straps?"

"I remember that one. Oh, she'll be gorgeous!" Joanna clapped her hands.

"A prom dress? Do you people even know what kind of band this is?" Bryan set his beer down and stared at the stage. "It's not some genteel orchestra. If Dave gets wind of the fact that she's wearing some big formal pile of taffeta, he's going to howl."

Molly arched an eyebrow at his protective tone. "Would you settle down?" She swirled melting ice in a watery drink, staring at Bryan. "She knows what she's doing. She said it was going to be perfect, given what the guys were going to wear."

"I'm glad it's not me, that's all." Joanna looked up to the curtained stage again. "This huge crowd, and it's so hot in here. I hope she's not nervous."

"We're about to find out." Drew nodded to Dave, striding across the low stage.

"Ladies and gentlemen!" Dave took the microphone from its stand. "It is mah supreme pleasure t'introduce y'all to Dirty Dave's latest improvement. While yer enjoyin' the fine fare we have to offer, we are bringin'on a little group that calls Dave's home. Y'all may think you know these kids, but Ah'm here to tell ya, this is a new and improved band...thanks to yours truly!"

"Shut up and bring out the band!" Someone yelled from well in the back.

Dave waited until the laughter died down. "Fine. Without further ado, here they are...Teacher's Pets, featurin' our very own Creek Girl!"

The applause was thunderous. The curtain rose to reveal Bethany sitting at a piano. The noise died down and a hush covered the large room. The lights dimmed to a single spot over Bethany, a vision in the pink satin that hugged her form and floated like a cloud from her trim waist. The rhinestone straps twinkled like stars against her smooth skin, already lightly tanned in the spring sun. She adjusted her position on the bench, held her hands over the keys and waited.

The audience held its breath.

She's gorgeous. Molly scanned the faces of the crowd and knew they were in agreement. *She's not the waif we pulled from the creek. She's a beautiful woman.* Molly's gaze rested on Bryan. *And he knows it.*

With a deliberate slowness, Bethany turned her head to look at the crowd. She smiled, winked and slammed into the opening chords of Bob Seeger's "Old Time Rock and Roll." The lights shot up and the four guys, all dressed in tuxedo shirts and ratty jeans, jumped into the song with wild abandon.

Molly ignored the crowd and watched Bryan. He never looked away from the stage. His food sat, untouched. She couldn't miss the pride that glowed on his face. Molly caught Joanna's eye, and the women shared a knowing smile.

The multitude that crowded Dave's got their money's worth. Teachers' Pets knew their audience and let loose a barrage of songs that kept the mob dancing and cheering, and, most important to Dave, eating and drinking.

Finally, after nearly two hours of garage band heaven, the music stopped. Everyone in the band except for Kelly and Bethany took a step back. Bethany took a deep breath and spoke into her microphone.

"Ladies and gentlemen, we sure do appreciate you coming out tonight. Now we're going to give Jake's voice a little break and play something new." Someone in the back groaned loudly and Bethany grinned into the spotlight. "Someday you'll be able to say you were there the first time Teacher's Pets performed their hit song."

Silence hung heavy in the room. Molly glanced at Dave, who looked less than thrilled. No one danced, ate, or drank. Bethany squared her shoulders and looked to Kelly who'd set his saxophone aside. He stood behind a microphone stand, his face a strange shade of gray.

"That boy's going to faint, isn't he?" Joanna nodded to the stage.

"In my professional opinion, yes." Molly bit her lip. "Anyone know where Dave keeps his first aid kit?"

"It's going to be okay."

"Sorry, Bryan, I'm with Molly. This is going to be a whole different show." Drew took a sip of his cola and, like everyone else, waited.

"Just wait, and listen." Bryan didn't take his eyes off the stage, but his voice was firm. "It's going to be okay."

Bethany played a few opening chords, lovely, sweet notes that eased the tension in the room but only a little. She looked to Kelly, who didn't seem to be breathing. Behind them the other band members shuffled restlessly as they looked from Bethany to Kelly and back to Bethany for some direction. Bethany took a deep breath and started the chords again, with the same reaction from Kelly.

"Jake is going to kill that poor boy," Joanna shook her head.

"Go on." Bryan's whisper was so low, only Molly, sitting next to him, even knew he'd spoken.

Molly followed his site line right to Bethany, who looked more indecisive than nervous. *Is he talking to her?*

"Go on. It's okay."

As if she'd heard Bryan, Bethany smiled at the crowd, and took one more deep breath. This time the chords she played were over scored by her own lilting voice, soft at first, but stronger with each passing phrase. As if shocked out of a dream, Kelly joined in, harmonizing beneath her. It was far more original and sophisticated than anything they'd played all night. But Molly knew no one cared. Doing a quick study of the room, Molly knew the only thing anyone heard was Bethany Elias, the Creek Girl, opening her heart to them all with a voice that soared over and around them all, like a graceful bird, looking for a place to land. The final chord wasn't finished echoing before everyone rose to their feet and cheered wildly. Kelly, with a grateful nod of his head, held his hand out to Bethany, who stood, took his hand, and walked to the center of the stage.

She bowed to the thunderous throng, along with the rest of the band, but seemed to be searching for something in the throng of people crowding the stage. The vacantly pleased expression she wore broke into a soft, almost shy smile when she caught site of Bryan. She tipped her head to one side as if asking a question. Molly noted that Bryan gave her a subtle nod and a quick, nearly imperceptible smile. Bethany's whole face glowed in response, and in that silent exchange Molly heard everything she needed to know.

As the crowd settled back down, the rest of the band played another set. Molly excused herself from the table and went out to the parking lot.

The stars in the midnight blue sky were every bit as brilliant as the rhinestones on Shara's dress, but Molly noticed nothing, even as she stared upward.

"Well, I got what I wished for." Molly kicked some gravel up. "I wanted the girl to be safe. God almighty, if Bryan truly loves her, hellfire won't touch her."

She leaned against her car and kept her eyes locked on the clear heavens. "But he loves Bethany Elias. What if he finds out the truth?" She smiled wryly. "In this town, it's more of when he finds out, isn't it?"

You know full well what will happen, don't you?

Molly sighed and kicked another bit of gravel. *Then, when he knows, will he be able to survive the truth? Will she?*

"Have I failed her again?" Molly shook her head and jammed her hands in her jeans pockets. "Have I set her up for yet one more abandonment?"

160

48: SHARA

Shara crossed the yard to the cabin and wiped her forehead. *Another scorcher, and not a drop of rain in site.* The summer was hotter and drier than anyone could remember. June brought only sparse moments of rain, and July and August brought none. Grass everywhere was brittle and brown. Now, a week past Labor Day, Rock Harbor Community School delayed the start of school two weeks to conserve water.

"Mornin'." She let the screen door bat her backside as she stepped into the cabin.

"You're up early." He glanced up from his newspaper. "Considering how late you pulled in."

"Yaaah, dat big city crowd in Green Bay dere, hey." She grinned at him as she mimicked the accent common to long time residents of Northeastern Wisconsin. "We didn't get out of that place until almost three. Ladies night and they were all over the guys. Too bad you had homework, you would have loved it." She grinned. "I think Jake may have...met someone."

"Oh yeah?"

"Yeah, I couldn't see her from where I was on stage, but apparently she was in the back, making eyes at Jake. Dan said there was no question what she was after. Personally, I can't believe, with all the religious training you give these boys get in church, such a thing would happen!" She gave him a mock look of disapproval.

"Yeah, well, all those 'Thou shalt nots' are no match for some hot looking babe in a bar." Bryan grinned at her.

Shara wiped her hands on a towel and leaned against the counter. "Yes, but when word gets out about this, you may lose your title. That, my friend, would be a shame."

"I've already lost my title."

Shara did a quick study of his expression, but found no sign of mockery on his smooth features. "Really? When did this happen?"

He turned the page of the newspaper. "Well, I got older last week."

"I remember. I was there. What are you, seventy three, seventy four?"

"Very funny from someone on the sunny side of twenty-seven. Besides, since this town got the Disney channel, I'm yesterday's news. I can't keep up with those tweener kids. I've got facial hair older than they are."

"You are just determined to feel sorry for yourself, aren't you?"

He lowered the paper just enough for her to see the twinkle in his eye. "There is of course, the fact that you are living here. All of a sudden, I've achieved some weird sort of married status in the eyes of the fifth grade girls. That makes me boring."

"And their mothers?"

He took a long sip of coffee before answering. "And their mothers. You've been garlic to the vampires."

"Nice imagery. That reminds me; when you're in town, pick up some cloves of garlic. I'm making a cold pasta salad for dinner and I want to use fresh garlic." She looked at the clock. "What's on your docket for today?"

"I should've gone to Green Bay with you. I didn't come close to finishing that paper for the correspondence course. Figured I'd get in to school early before it got too hot." At Shara's insisting, Bryan had resumed his Master's program, taking some classes at the University of Wisconsin, Green Bay, and some through the mail. The delayed start to the new school year made things easier for him.

"Too late for that. It's already over 90." Shara looked at the thermometer outside the window as she washed her hands in the sink.

"You still okay sleeping up in the loft?"

"It's not so bad when you sleep naked." She glanced over her shoulder to catch his reaction.

"Ooh baby." He gave her a mischievous grin over the top edge of the paper.

She squirted him with the sink sprayer, laughing as he jumped out of his chair and swatted the water away with the newspaper.

"Hey!" He wiped water out of his eyes. "You're supposed to be rationing that!"

"Yeah, well I'll make up for it. I won't do laundry."

"Again?" He gave a meaningful look at the growing mound in the hallway. "Not to put too fine a point on it, but isn't that pile the whole reason you're here?"

"That was just an excuse Jo came up with to get me into your house. Besides, what's your grief about laundry? Out of underwear?"

"Hardly. I've stopped wearing it." He arched an eyebrow at her.

"Ewwww!" She covered her face with her hands in a dramatic display of disgust.

"Hey, all in the name of being a good citizen, right?" He folded his paper and took a last sip of coffee before getting up from the table and putting the cup in the sink. "Besides," he rinsed out the cup and washed his hands as he spoke, "as long as we shower once in a while we don't really need clean clothes, right?" He whipped the sprayer out and gave her a cold stream of water right in the face.

"Nice. Real nice." She grabbed a dishtowel from the stove and wiped her face. "Don't you have a paper to write somewhere?"

"Yeah." He slipped the sprayer back into its holder and headed for the door.

"Hey, wait, you're forgetting something."

He stopped and took a step back. "Sorry. Have a good day, honey." He kissed her forehead and locked his gaze with hers.

Shara's heart fluttered. *What are you doing?* Unwilling to let him look into her eyes for fear of what he'd see there, she stared at her shoes. "I-I was talking about your lunch. It's in the fridge."

Stepping back easily, as if unaware of the chaos he'd stirred in her, Bryan opened the refrigerator and pulled out a brown bag. "What is it?"

"Your favorite." She took a deep breath, willing her heart to stop racing.

"You mean?" He gave her a hopeful, child-like look that made her laugh.

"Yes, double-decker peanut butter and jelly on homemade bread. I used the last of the spring berries to make a freezer jam, so savor it." She wagged a finger at him, relieved to return to their easy banter.

"Whoo hoo!" He grinned at her before bounding out the door.

Shara watched him get into the Jeep and pull out of the drive before touching the spot on her forehead where he'd kissed her. *That was quite the domestic moment.* She looked at the kitchen and mentally ticked off her list of chores to do before the afternoon sun blazed too hot. *Of course, I am a domestic.*

For the hundredth time in a week, Shara marveled at her life. Teachers Pets was a roaring success, playing at Dave's on the weekends and at various bars and clubs in Green Bay and Door County as everyone's schedules allowed. The added travel was exhausting for the guys, but Shara loved the whirl of it all. Now fully accepted by the guys, she sang at least one solo per show. Best of all, she was down to one night a week waiting tables at Dave's. Even then, she rarely got through a shift without hopping up to play and sing on her own for the demanding crowd. The tip jar on the piano overflowed and Dave told everyone he'd created a star.

Sweeping dust from the front porch, Shara allowed herself a small thrill of triumph. *See Grandmother, I can sing, and people do find it worthwhile.*

She closed her mind to more memories of her grandmother before any darker memories clouded her cheerful thoughts. Instead, she pushed Bryan's rocking chair aside to sweep behind it and her thoughts turned, very easily, to him.

With school out for the summer, Bryan made a point of traveling with the band frequently. Kelly teased her about having her own groupie, but Shara liked the moment in a show when she would catch Bryan's eye. In the jumble of hot lights and raucous partiers, his smile took her back to the quiet, dark room at Dave's, and they were alone, and she sang for him. Only from her place onstage, separated by throngs of people and hiding behind a piano, would

Shara allow herself to embrace the feelings that swelled within her whenever she thought of Bryan. *Someday.*

Someday, maybe there won't be anything left to worry about, and I will be free to be Bethany Elias. And Bethany Elias loves Bryan Jacobs.

She paused in her sweeping and scanned the cloudless sky.

Maybe being Bethany Elias is who I really am supposed to be after all. I found myself and I'm someone else.

"Hello there, dreamer!"

Shara looked up. Molly stood right in front of her. "Oh hi. I was just thinking...about something."

"Let me see, I'll bet it was something tall, dark, and driving away in his Jeep." Molly walked into the cabin and set a stack of books down on the counter.

"I have no idea what you're referring to, Molly." Shara followed her and opened the refrigerator door. "Lemonade?"

"You know very well what I mean." Molly sat down and accepted a tall glass of lemonade from her. "How are things out here?"

"Bryan's been great, with me being gone so much. Even cooked his own breakfast without whining the other day."

"That's not what I mean, and you know it."

"Molly. I don't know what you think you've been seeing lately, but it's nothing. Bryan and I are friends. Good friends. Period. That's where it ends."

"Really?" Molly sipped from her glass and did not look convinced.

"Isn't that where it has to end?" Shara sat down and opened a diet cola. "Given the fact that he's really all about complete honesty and I'm...really not?"

Molly looked deep into her face. "You do know he's fallen for you, right? It's been pretty obvious since that first concert at Dave's."

"Even if I did believe you, there isn't a thing I want to do about it." Shara stared at the ceiling. "Molly, every day is like a gift, and I'm still afraid it'll be taken away from me. I've got the best life I

could possibly hope for, and I'm not going to chance losing it."
She blinked. "Okay, yeah, it would be great, it would be
spectacular if he were falling for me, because I…really like him."
Shara picked up her cola and took a long drink before setting the
can back down. "But so what? None of it matters because I
remember all too well how he used to look at me? That was when
he just thought I was hiding something. I'm not going back to that.
I'd lose everything because he would never, ever forgive me for
lying to him." She blinked away a tear.

Molly put a comforting hand on her arm. "So what now?"

Shara wiped her eyes and smiled. "Well, right now I'm going to
finish in here and then go clean out the stalls. I told Jo she could
bring the kids out later this morning so we could ride down to the
creek and let the kids wade in whatever water might be left."

"And Bryan? If I'm right about him and he makes some sort of
move?"

"I'll have to shut him down." Shara picked up her broom.
"Because living here, being Bethany Elias, at least I have some
part of his life. I guess that makes the lie worth living."

\49: BRYAN

School was almost as stifling as his house. Bryan looked up from
his textbook and watched Drew and Nate trot down the hallway.
"Welcome to H E double hockey sticks," Bryan said with a grin,
editing himself for the boy's sake. "What brings you here?"

"I'm planning out the bulletin boards for the first quarter. If we
ever have a first quarter." Drew flopped a plastic box brimming
with cut out construction paper shapes on the table. "Nate wanted
to play on the playground before Jo takes the kids out to your
place. The ladies are too dainty for the heat." Drew tousled Nate's
hair.

"Hi, Uncle Bryan."

"Hey, Nate."

"Now, stay away from the creek, you understand?" Drew wagged a finger at his son. Nate nodded. It was their ritual. Bryan knew Nate would head for the creek immediately after leaving the building.

Nate left the teachers' lounge and ran down the hall. "Walk!" Drew shouted after him with a grin. "So, how was summer school?" He looked at Bryan.

"Almost done. I've got one last correspondence course to finish. The best thing I can say is the classrooms were air-conditioned. We should look into that for this place."

"Please! You mean you don't love this heat?"

"But it's a dry heat!" Bryan mimicked the weatherman.

"It is not a dry heat. It's a dry everything. I think the creek dried up."

"Yeah, it's pretty bad out by my place." Bryan shook his head.

"How's Bethany?"

Bryan tapped the end of his pen against his cheek. "I will never admit it to Molly or Jo, and I'll kill you if you do, but I do like having her out there. She's been great…you know, with the horses."

"Ah, yes. With the horses, of course." Drew gave him a quirky little smile, his light blue eyes twinkling. "I swear I'll never breathe that secret. The women will be unbearable to live with if they knew they were right."

"Thanks." Bryan leaned back in his chair and stared at the textbook in his lap, but in his mind's eye he was back in the back room at Dave's, warming Bethany's hands in his own. *What could have happened that night?* He shook his head and tried to focus on the textbook in front of him. *Stop it!* He liked their comfortable existence. He rejoiced in finding someone who felt no need to analyze a past best forgotten. *Don't ruin a perfectly…perfect situation by…wondering.*

Still, the feel of her hands in his stayed with him like a whiff of long forgotten perfume. *Someday…maybe.* The simple thought made him smile.

"Daddy! Daddy!" Nate burst in, shattering Bryan's reverie. The boy waved something over his head.

"Nate, settle." Drew didn't look up from his construction paper.

"I found something!" His enthusiasm was undimmed.

"And what would that be?"

"This!" Nate handed Drew a slim brown leather wallet. "I bet there's a hundred billion dollars in it!"

"Nate this is really gross," Drew pried the scum covered wallet open and thumbed through it. He stared at it and frowned. "Bryan, catch." Drew tossed the wallet to Bryan. "Nate, where did you get this?"

The boy squirmed, obviously uncomfortable under his father's unexpected scrutiny. "Nowhere." He stared at his feet.

Bryan flipped open the wallet. He scratched the dried mud scum from the plastic cover. The face on the driver's license was as familiar as his own. The name he knew well enough. "The creek." His voice cracked under the weight of the discovery.

Drew put a hand on his son's shoulder. "Nate. Go on home."

"Am I in trouble?"

"Go home now." Drew's voice was tight. Nate ran out without a second look.

It's her. Of course it's her. I know it like I'd seen it from the very first minute. Bryan gulped in ragged breaths of air. His heart raced. "I knew it."

Drew stared out the window at Nate, who ran to the playground. "Bryan, there's an explanation for this. We can't just assume-"

"No we can't, can we? We should never, ever assume anything!" Bryan jumped up from his chair and threw the wallet against the door. "You tell me how this could be anything but what it is." He grit his teeth, unable to stop the outpouring of angry sarcasm. "Maybe Shara Brandt happened through the creek just like our Bethany? Maybe they have the same face? Maybe it's just a coincidence of gross magnitude?"

"Slow down." Drew raised a cautioning hand.

"Slow down? I knew it! I knew it and everyone said," he couldn't finish, pain spread through his body like a fiery toxin.

168

"Come on. We'll go and talk-"

"Oh, we will talk, that's for sure! Right now." Bryan crossed the room and picked up the wallet. "Yeah, we're gonna do a lot of talking." He opened the lounge door. "Someone is going to tell the truth. For once." Before Drew could move to join him, Bryan turned and slammed the door behind him.

50: JENNIFER

Jennifer Tiel checked her make-up and hair in the rear view mirror of Richard's Lexus before roaring out of the hotel parking lot. "Who needs beauty sleep?" She smiled at her reflection one more time before she pulled the silver vehicle onto the two-lane highway. "Sex is so much better for the skin."

She drove the scenic road to Rock Harbor with no radio. She needed the quiet to think. It wasn't a complete surprise to find that Shara Brandt was alive, but it was a major inconvenience. *At least I saw her before Richard did. That would be the worst.*

I just have to fix the situation, and before Richard finds out that his little fiancé has a pulse, and therefore a grip on the fortune I'm days away from enjoying.

She clicked the air conditioner up another notch and tapped her perfectly manicured nails on the steering wheel, hoping a plan would pop into her head.

She hardly paid attention as she drove the roads that were familiar to her. Once on the outskirts of town, Jennifer toyed with the idea of stopping at Dirty Dog Dave's for more information about Shara. She rejected the idea quickly, however. *Best to stay away from anyone who might recognize me.*

Jennifer wasn't one given to marveling at how things worked out. Things happened for two reasons: She made them happen, or someone got in her way, and she still made them happen. The fact that Shara Brandt was still alive was troubling. The fact that Shara Brandt was performing in a cover band at a club in Green Bay, while Jennifer herself was making some business connections for

169

Richard, well that was simply everything in the world righting itself.

Jennifer mulled over the conversation she'd had with the lead singer, the one dressed in black leather, the night before. Jennifer licked her lips at the very thought of him. *What was his name? Not that it matters.* In the scope of things, one tasty looking young thing from the back woods was hardly remembering. *Still, he did look really good in black leather. And out of it.*

Said her name was Bethany and she was living at Bryan's house. Jennifer shook her head. She wasn't sure if it was monumental bad luck or a gift that she would now have to revisit her ex husband's home to find Shara Brandt. *I could kill two pain in the ass birds with one stone…* The thought amused her.

She pulled her car off the road and into a tractor road in a cornfield a quarter mile from Bryan's house. Dust was thick on everything, and the farmland was a dry brown. The hot, fragrant air reminded her of a bakery as she stepped out of her air-conditioned car. Jennifer looked both ways on the deserted two-lane highway. *Good.*

The walk to Bryan's would be hot, but necessary. *Can't very well just drive up to his house and expect a warm welcome.*

The sound of a car behind her broke Jennifer's concentration. A sheriff's car pulled alongside her. "Are you okay, Ma'am?"

Jennifer peered into the rolled down window. She instantly recognized the sax player from the night before. "I'm just fine, Deputy… Fuller." She leaned against the car, her firm breasts eye level with the young deputy as she read his nametag. "I was just out for a little walk."

"Ma'am, it's a little hot to be just out walking on the highway. Can I give you a lift somewhere?"

Jennifer tossed her hair back and laughed. *No, but I'm sure I could give you the lift of your life, Deputy Fuller.* "That's quite all right. I'm actually staying at Marva Blakely's house." Jennifer pursed her lips slightly, praying old Marva Blakely, Bryan's neighbor, hadn't died in the last three years.

"Oh, that so? I didn't know she had company." The deputy looked her up and down, and Jennifer smiled sweetly, acknowledging the appreciation in his eyes. "Well, don't be out in the sun too long, okay?"

"I won't, I promise, Officer." She draped her fingers lightly on his arm, amused as his skin warmed in response.

"Okay then." He gave her one last look and eased the cruiser onto the road and was gone.

Jennifer strolled a few more steps until she was satisfied he was out of sight and then she ran the last several yards to Bryan's drive. She skirted the tree line along the drive and hid behind a hundred year old oak tree as Bryan's Jeep spat dust and gravel swinging around the corner and up the hill to the yard.

Jennifer peered around the tree and watched with interest as Bryan leaped from the Jeep and raced into the barn. *This could be good.* Slinking behind the tree line, she crept up behind the back corner of the barn, crouching just below the open window.

51: BRYAN

Bryan froze in his tracks at the sight of Bethany shoveling new sawdust into Rika's stall. "You and I need to have a conversation." He bit his lip and tried to hold himself in check. *Steady. Don't let her know how she's destroyed you.*

She stopped her work and set down the shovel. "You look terrible. Why don't you come on inside and I'll get you some lemonade."

Damn, she's good at this game. Bryan put his hands on either side of his head to shut out the fury throbbing inside. "I don't want lemonade!" He slammed his hand against the stall divider. Pepper shifted and snorted. Rika pawed the floor. Bethany loosed the mare from the crossties and put her back in her stall.

"What's up with you?" She stared at him, her dark eyes wide with something akin to fear, but not yet fearful enough for Bryan's satisfaction. *She has to know it's over.*

171

"The creek dried up." He stood in front of her, his arms crossed, his whole body trembling. *Keep it together. Don't let her know she tricked you into loving her. Make her pay for lying to you.*

Make her pay for loving Richard Bennett.

"And?" She drew the word out to three syllables, her eyes searching his face.

"And Nate was down there playing this morning." Bryan threw the wallet at her. It snapped against the wall and fell to the floor of the barn.

She did not bend down to pick it up. Her face paled. "Then you know."

Yes, I do. I know everything. I'm nobody's fool anymore. He ran his hands through his hair. "I said, 'We don't know anything about her.' Everyone else telling me I'm crazy, that I'm the jerk, and you're so innocent. Poor little Bethany Elias, running away from an abusive boyfriend. Orphaned. Wants to be a teacher but never had the money for college." He paced in front of her, not looking at her, not seeing her. "You certainly hit all the marks with that story."

"Bryan, wait."

He waved his hand to stop her. "I started to believe it myself. I wanted to believe it because" he stopped, and glared at her. "You're the one who's engaged to…you're wanted for murdering your own grandmother." He spat the words out like bile.

"Bryan, I can explain." Tears welled in her eyes and overflowed.

"I don't want explanations!" He flew at her, the weight of his body pinning her against the wall. "Your whole life here is a lie, an act. You used us!" *You used me. You led me on. You loved Richard Bennett the whole time.*

"Bryan- please!" She couldn't move. He had her pinned against the wall.

"We all trusted you! I trusted you and you lied to me. You're a liar just like-" He choked on his words. *Jenny.* "Damn it!"

His lips were on hers, devouring, angry. She tried to pull away, but he gripped her tighter, suffocating her, bruising her. *Destroy something Richard Bennett loved.* He dug his fingers into her

172

wrists. "It was very convenient that they had you declared dead. Was that a happy accident or part of your plans?" He hissed the words close to her face, close enough to feel the heat of fear radiating from her skin.

"Bryan-please." Her words were little more than a whimper.

Her voice touched the last reasonable corner of his fevered brain. With a deep-throated curse, he ripped himself from her and pushed her away. The force was sudden, violent, and she fell to the floor. Her expression, one of wounded fear, incensed him. *Lies! All lies! Don't look at me like that, with those eyes, and lie to me more!* Cat-like, he was on her, pushing her deeper into the straw

She struggled against him, weeping his name and begging him, over and over to stop, to let her go. He sealed his mouth over hers to quiet her cries and still the anguish in his own soul. He held her down with the full weight of his body, pinning her arms over her head with one hand. *Why? Why?*

Why did you have to be another liar? Why did you have to be another one of Richard Bennett's lovers?

There was no answer to his heart's cry. Done pleading, she lay silent under him, and Bryan paused in his onslaught. He gasped for air, staring into the face of the woman beneath him. *Jenny...*

"No!" She pushed him off of her with a burst of strength. "I will not take this from you! Not from you!" The force of her shove sent him slipping back to the wall.

Don't let Jenny do this to you again. He wiped the back of his hand across his mouth. "Listen here, you little-"

"No, you listen to me!" She stood and leaned her back against the wall, keeping him directly in front of her. "My whole life, people told me what to do, where to go, who to be." She glared at him, rage simmering in her eyes. "Under the same circumstance, you would lie, too. You'd do what you had to, if it meant saving yourself." Panting, she wiped a drop of sweat from her face.

He stood, also panting in the heat that hung like a cloud between them. "I have always been completely honest with you. I would never lie." *Not to you.*

She slid sideways and leaned against the back door of the barn. "You know what they say about me. You don't know the truth." She bit her lip. "I don't know the truth."

"I know what I need to know." He did not miss the flash of disappointment crossing her face when she pushed on the latch of door and found it to be locked. *There's no escaping what you did, this time.* "I know you slept with him. I know you loved him. I know that much."

She nudged the door again, this time with her foot. "What are you talking about?"

"Stop playing games." He took three steps toward her and raised himself to his full height, a clear seven inches over her head. "I'm talking about Richard Bennett." He took one more step; close enough to see her body tremble in spite of the defiant look in her eyes.

She put her arm straight out, her hand flat against his chest. "Stay away from me, Bryan."

"Or what?" He loomed over her. *You're not going to hurt me again.*

"Bryan, please." This final plea was weak, defeated.

"No!" He pinned her against the wall again and for a moment hovered next to her, panting. "No more!" Sweat rolled down his face to hers. The drops mingled with the tears that spilled onto her cheeks. *No more lies, no more pain...*

"Bryan, look at me, please. Look at **me**."

In those still, soft words, Bryan blinked away the fiery image of his ex wife and found a wide-eyed Bethany. *Bethany.*

He sealed his lips to hers again, no longer to punish, but to claim. He loosened his grip on her wrists, and she let her hands fall to rest on his waist. Her touch, her heady scent of sun warmed strawberries, softened the edges of his rage. He took hold of the nape of her neck, felt her heat and sweat. She melted to him as he buried his face in her hair. "Bethany..." He whispered her name as a prayer. *My Bethany...*

"Bryan..."

His name never sounded so sweet as she returned his kiss. Joy and desire flooded through him, warming his soul, frozen for so long. He kissed her again then looked into her eyes, his heart racing beyond the confines of his own body. *My beautiful, beautiful Bethany.*

Only-

Only she's not Bethany.

And she will never be mine.

She belongs to Richard Bennett.

Jarred by the thought, Bryan searched her face for something, anything, to wake him from this nightmare. Everything faded and fell away, leaving only the insistent throb of want pounding through him. *Again, I lose to him.*

But his mouth tasted bitter and his skin burned as if touching something hot. *How could you have done this to me...to us?*

Not willing to do battle against a passion that could only ruin him, Bryan pushed himself away from the wall, still grasping her wrists. "Get away from me!" With one final, furious gesture, he pushed her to the floor and left the barn. Once outside in the scorching sunlight, he slammed the rolling door shut and snapped the padlock closed. Spinning on his heals, he ran back to his Jeep. Once in the drivers' seat, he jerked the car into gear and tore backwards down the drive, leaving his property is a cloud of gray brown dust.

52: JENNIFER

From her position behind the barn, nothing was lost on Jennifer who lit a cigarette and smiled at her perfect timing. She stayed hidden as Bryan sped back down the drive and squealed a two tire turn onto the road.

So Bryan's in love with his housekeeper, but just can't deal with the fact that she's the evil Shara Brandt. And now he's probably off to cry on good old Molly Hunter's shoulder.

Realizing both entrances to the barn were locked, Jennifer felt the onset of a plan. She crept beneath the site line of the high, narrow windows. Now that Shara had no escape, even if she did see her, Jennifer strolled to the front of the barn. She flicked her cigarette butt onto the drive where it stuck on a crisp patch of grass and scorched it black instantly. Jennifer stared at the black earth and back at the barn. *This is too easy.*

Her stride still casual and unhurried, Jennifer walked around the barn, setting her lighter flame to the tall grass and shrubs surrounding the structure. Satisfied with the half dozen flickering fires working their way up the sides of the barn, she stood on tiptoe beneath one of the open windows, and watched Shara, who leaned against a stack of hay bales in the far corner, her face hidden in her arms. Smiling, Jennifer lit a cigarette, then a second, and flicked both through the open window.

She lit another cigarette, which she smoked as she waited a few moments to be sure that she'd done enough. *No use making a mistake of half measures this time.*

The horses stirred and snorted. Jennifer stood on tiptoe again to look through the window. She took a long drag on her cigarette and stared straight into the panicked face of Shara Brandt.

"You..."

"Good bye, Shara." One more drag and she threw the butt on the ground, stubbed it out, waved at the ghostly face in the window, and strolled back down the driveway.

Can't make it look more like an accident than that does, can we?

Better yet, Bryan might get blamed for this one. Dear, sweet, sanctimonious, boring as hell Bryan is going to pay for something I did.

How perfect is my life?

53: BRYAN

The drive to Molly's was a furious race against his heart-rending rage. The four miles of roads that separated his home from hers did little to calm him.

"Molly, you will not believe what I just found out!" Bryan stormed up the steps to Molly's porch and into her kitchen. He circled the table twice before sitting down.

"Bethany is Shara Brandt." Molly opened the refrigerator door. "Thirsty?"

"You know?" Bryan tapped out his pulse on the table. "Did Drew call?"

"I've known since the day she got here. Lemonade?" She held up the pitcher.

"Everyone offers me lemonade! I don't want any damn lemonade!" He swatted his hand backward in the direction of the pitcher. "What do you mean, since the day she got here?" Bryan's lungs tightened with his shock. *Has everyone lost their minds today?* "She told you?" Swallowing hard failed to ease the awful strangling sensation.

"She didn't have to. I knew the minute she opened her eyes." Molly poured a glass of lemonade and pushed it toward him calmly, as if they were discussing standardized testing.

The room spun around him. "You kept quiet while she lied to us?" He wiped sweat from his eyes, hoping to clear his vision and understand Molly.

Molly sighed and crossed her arms on the table. "It wasn't exactly her lie. The poor child didn't have the wits about her to come up with a story anyone would believe."

Bryan leaped out of his chair, knocking it over, and paced like a caged beast. "You made up the story?" White noise raged in his head, pounding his pulse beat against his temples. "Why?"

"I was protecting her."

"You never thought to protect Drew and Joanna? The kids, for God's sake, Molly. You let a killer take care of those kids. What the hell were you thinking?" It was a struggle to keep from shouting.

"I was thinking Shara needed to be protected from attitudes like yours right now." Molly's eyes blazed with indignation. "Now sit yourself down and listen to me."

Even in his agitated state Bryan couldn't disobey Molly Hunter.

"Take a look at this." She pulled the locket from out of her collar.

"Your locket? I've seen it a hundred times. What has that got to do with the fact that you've aided a wanted criminal for almost a year?"

"Shut up and look at the pictures." She opened the locket. Bryan leaned in and studied the pictures for a moment.

"Okay. It's a couple and a little girl. So?"

"So doesn't that girl look the least little bit familiar?"

What's the point of this? Bryan looked again. "Should she?"

Molly snapped the locket shut and gave him a tired look. "I should have told you this story long ago." She tucked the locket back in her collar. "Shara's parents were both killed in a car accident when she was a bit older than Nate. That night, the night of the accident, Shara came in to the ER where I worked. I sat with her until her grandmother came to get her."

Bryan ground his teeth at her calm demeanor. "Skip to the part where you helped that murdering liar hide herself in our lives!"

With a fluid, effortless motion, Molly slapped his face. Bryan leaped out of his chair, knocking it over on the floor. The room stood still as they both stared at each other in disbelief, rage simmering in their eyes.

"You will not speak of her that way again!" Molly pointed to the overturned chair. "Now you will sit there and you will listen." She inhaled and was silent until Bryan obeyed. "The grandmother was horrid. Cold and demanding, not a shred of love or warmth in her. I tried calling one time, to return this locket. That woman informed that if I ever called again she could report me to the authorities for harassment. All I wanted to do was return a piece of jewelry." Molly wiped a strand of hair from her face. "And this little girl, Shara, had to live with that. It was like abandoning her, letting that sweet soul walk away with that icy old woman, but there was nothing I could do. I couldn't save her, couldn't protect her from what I knew was going to be, at best, a loveless life. I made a vow. I vowed if we ever crossed paths, I would not fail her again. So be sure of this, Bryan Jacobs, I will protect her now, from you or anyone else." Her eyes glittered like two blocks of ice and for a moment Bryan wondered if she would hit him again. For a moment his anger gave way to a quiver of fear at the thought.

"Could be that you're right, of course. Maybe she murdered her grandmother." Molly took a sip of lemonade. "It's possible. She has little memory of that night."

"Well, that makes it all right, then! She can't remember shooting her grandmother to death, so let's keep her. Cripes, Molly! We're talking about murder!" Bryan jumped up and paced the width of the room once.

"Oh stop it, already!" Molly gave him a pointed look. "I think if you search your heart, you know she's very well not guilty of anything. Except maybe, wanting to live a safe, happy life." Molly took his hands in hers. "I don't believe that's a crime."

No, that's not a crime. Bryan's heart softened as images of Bethany…Shara crossed his mind.

The telephone jangled them out of the moment, and Molly reached over to answer it. "Hello? Yes, he's here…it what?" Molly's expression melted into a mask of worry, and her voice softened, alerting Bryan to trouble. "Yes, I'll tell him. Thanks Marva. Thanks for calling the fire department."

"Fire department?"

Molly set the telephone on the table. "That was your neighbor, Marva Blakely. Your barn is on fire."

One heartbeat, then two passed in deathly stillness.

Bethany. His knees threatened to crumble beneath him.

"Bryan?"

He couldn't move. The room started to spin around him.

"Bryan, what is it?" Molly stood and put a hand on his arm. "Where is she? What did you do to Shara?"

Bryan stared at Molly as if seeing her for the first time. His mouth went dry and words caught in his throat, choking him.

179

Unable to give voice to the fear that surged through him, Bryan raced out of the house, Molly close behind.

With Molly in the seat next to him, Bryan threw his Jeep into gear and tore down the drowsy hot street. *What have I done?*

54: SHARA

Shara squinted at the departing female figure. *Who is that woman? Why does she look so familiar?*

"Don't you tell, Shara Brandt. Don't you say a word."

Her chest tightened. *It's the woman. It's the woman…*

… in my nightmares..

Shara closed her eyes and saw it all again. *We're in the office. Grandmother is lying on the floor. Richard lying on the floor, and I'm kneeling next to him.*

And the red headed woman, dressed in black, wearing black leather gloves, holding the gun over us all.

A burning smell snapped her out of her reverie. Smoke floated around her. Looking over each shoulder, she noticed the flicker of flame here and there, and a small fire smoldering alive at her feet. Calmly, she walked the length of the barn, testing both doors. *Locked.* Reaching to the shelf above the door, she grabbed the fire extinguisher and smothered the weak flames inside the barn. Smoke started to clog the air.

She looked around again, to each corner of the barn and up the sides of the building and realized that fighting this fire would be useless in another five minutes. The horses pawed nervously at their stall doors. *I have to get them out. This whole place is going to go up.*

Barn windows are too narrow for me to get out.

I can jump out the loft window and unlock the door from outside.

Bryan keeps the spare keys in the cabin, just above the sink.

She raced up the stairs, two at a time. Her window was open, and she looked down to the ground, measuring the distance.

It's the only way. She slid out to the awning. Squeezing her eyes shut, she pushed away from the barn, floated for a moment, and hit the ground. She gasped for air after the impact, then stood and checked for injuries. *Nothing broken.*

The high-pitched whinnies of the horses jerked her into action. Racing across the drive to the cabin, she made short work of finding the never used barn keys on their hook. Back in the sunshine, she squinted at the barn and noted that, while the sidewalls were burning quickly, the front door itself was not on fire. She grabbed the lock, ignoring the heat that seared into her hands as she tugged at the stubborn padlock. *Here goes nothing.* She inhaled and opened the barn door; giving the fire inside more oxygen, more fuel. Shielding herself from the flames, Shara grabbed Bryan's old denim jacket from its hook and ran to Pepper's stall. The big stallion fought her until she tossed the jacket over his eyes. Calmed, he followed her out, past the smoke billow in the drive, to the sunny yard.

Slapping Pepper on the rear, Shara watched the horse run several paces then stop under a tree before she ran back into the barn. Spice was as easy to get out as Pepper once the comforting darkness of the jacket was over her eyes.

In the far stall, Rika was a different story. The mare reared and slashed out her hooves. Shara used the jacket, but Rika tossed her head back and the jacket fluttered, useless, to the ground. Choking in the smoke, Shara climbed up the stall wall and leapt onto Rika's bare back. With a vicious kick to the mare's sides, Shara grabbed the mane and held on. Rika burst out of the stall, but turned left instead of right, colliding into the door. A ceiling beam crashed down, pinning them between the back door and the flames. Rika reared from the flaming embers, throwing Shara to the floor. *This can't be it. I will not die in this barn not now. Not when I'm so close to remembering everything.*

Another beam fell, this one on top of Rika, who collapsed next to Shara. Shara shielded herself with the mare's body as best as she could. Rika's shrieks were the last thing Shara heard before smoke filled her lungs and she slipped into unconsciousness.

55: BRYAN

As Bryan wrenched his Jeep to a halt at the bottom of his driveway, the Shepaski station wagon pulled in behind him. Slapping open the Jeep door, he raced past Pepper and Spice, grazing next to the cabin. He stopped and stared at the barn, which belched smoke and heat into the already scorched horizon. Molly followed a few paces behind.

"Bryan, Molly! No!" Joanna screamed, leaping out of the station wagon. She grabbed hold of Molly's arm, but missed stopping Bryan. "What are you doing? You can't go in there!"

A violent crashing sound silenced them all. He looked back at the two women. "I have to! Bethany's in there!"

"Bethany!" Nate burst out of the car, closely followed by Emma, pigtails streaming like a banner behind her.

The momentum of the two small bodies spun Bryan in a circle as he trapped them in his arms.

"Bef-any!" Emma reached out to the barn. The heat rolled over them and flushed their skin.

Bryan set them down and knelt in front of them. "Listen, I have to go get Bethany now, okay? You need to go back to your momma and stay there. Nate, take Emma."

"But Bethany's in there!" Tears streamed down the boy's face.

"I know. I'll get Bethany. You have to watch over Emma." Bryan stood up and turned the children towards Joanna, who took them by the hands. "Bryan, you can't—" Joanna didn't finish the sentence. Another crash of ruined timber was all the punctuation she needed.

Flames shot out of the roof of the barn, out of the loft window. "Jo, I have to. Molly, go tie up the horses, okay?" Bryan looked over his shoulder at Molly, Joanna and the kids. "If I don't—" He nodded to flashing lights of the fire truck barreling down the road, still a mile away. Molly said nothing, but ran to the clump of trees in the front yard where Pepper and Spice kept skittish watch. Joanna nodded in answer and turned the children's faces away from the heat of the fire.

Bryan hesitated before taking a step into the black, smoky furnace that was the barn. A high-pitched scream emitting from deep inside the inferno jolted him forward as another beam crashed to the ground. Through the thick smoke, Bryan scarcely saw the struggling form of a horse, and nothing more. Two steps, three, the searing heat attacked his body as the roar of destruction deafened him. He knelt beside Rika, badly burned and crushed to her knees beneath a beam. Soot and heat blinded him. Bryan brushed his hands on the floor near Rika, and struck something. A shoe. A foot.

"Bethany!" He choked on the single word filling his lungs with smoke. Clawing at the ruined rafter, Bryan lifted a small corner of the flaming mass, fiery shards of woods embedding themselves into his hands. Hoisting the beam up a few inches and rolling it away from her, Bryan dragged her out of the hollow created by Rika's body. He lurched to his feet, as more flaming debris rained down, and, cradling her limp body close to his chest, he staggered out of the barn.

Bryan managed a dozen steps away from the blaze before the voices of firemen reached him. Someone took Bethany from him. Relieved of her weight, he crumpled to the ground.

* * *

"You're a complete fool, you know that?" Drew sat at the foot of Bryan's hospital bed.

"I'm aware…" Bryan's throat blazed raw as he tried to speak above a hoarse whisper. "Bethany-"

"You're not supposed to talk." Drew shook his head. "Molly's with her." He patted Bryan's foot. "I'm sure she'll be fine."

"She's alive?"

"She's very much alive, Mr. Jacobs." Kelly Fuller walked in, followed by a nurse who took Bryan's pulse, checked his IV, and smiled too warmly at him. "Thanks to you."

"Not that the sheriff recommends a civilian running into a burning building, though, right, Deputy?" Drew tried to smile.

"Certainly not. Although in this case, you did save her life. Which is pretty cool."

Her life wouldn't have been at risk if I hadn't lost my mind and put her there.

Kelly cleared his throat. "I have to ask you a couple questions, Mr. Jacobs."

"Here? Now?"

"Yeah, Mr. Shepaski. There are some things we need to know...about the fire."

"What ...questions?" A coughing fit seized Bryan.

"There now, Mr. Jacobs, you really need to rest yourself." The nurse, a perky little brunette Bryan recognized vaguely, entered the room and shooed the men away from the bed. "You men need to wait before you make him answer all your questions."

Bryan turned his head slightly to look at Kelly Fuller. *This is serious.* There was an expression on the young officer's face that was new to Bryan. "It's okay. Ask me anything." He spoke slowly, fighting off the pressure in his chest. The pollution in his lungs was not to be denied, and he shuddered with the coughing. Lifting his hand to his face to cover his mouth, Bryan saw the burns on his hands for the first time. "What happened?"

"Well, Superman, apparently you are not immune to fire." Drew shook his head as a wry smile played on his face.

"Mr. Jacobs-"

"Kelly, for Pete's sakes, give the man a break and ask him later." Bryan now realized the nurse was a former classmate of Kelly's from RHCS. She spun the young deputy around on his heal and pushed him toward the door. "And you, too, Mr. Shepaski. Our patient here needs some rest."

56: SHARA

Shara opened her eyes and closed them immediately to shut out the blinding white of the hospital room. *If I keep my eyes closed maybe it will all go away.*

"Doctor, she just opened her eyes."

Molly. Molly's here. Molly will stay with me.

"Miss Elias? Miss Elias, please open your eyes again." The warm voice of the old doctor drew her out and she opened her eyes again. "There you are."

"Welcome back." Molly stood at her side. "You gave us quite a scare."

"But you're going to be fine." The doctor flashed a light in her eyes. "Good news. No concussion. Your lungs are another story. You inhaled a lot of smoke." He scribbled a note on a chart and smiled at her. "We'll keep you over night just to make sure all's clear. Your left arm is broken in two places, and you have a second-degree burn on your left hand. But, since there's no head injury, you get to enjoy pain medication just as soon as I can get someone in here to give it to you." He patted her on the shoulder and left the room.

As the door swooshed shut behind him, Shara reached for Molly with the arm that wasn't in a sling. "Molly." Her voice was raspy and hoarse. She opened her mouth to speak more, but coughing racked her. Molly handed her a glass of water.

"Molly-" She held on to Molly's arm tight and coughed harder.

"Bethany, you did an amazing thing today. Pepper and Spice are just fine." Molly's voice was firm and her eyes never broke from Shara's. "Stay quiet now. There will be plenty of time to talk later."

No! Listen to me! This is important! She opened her mouth to talk again, but Shara coughed harder, her lungs expelling the poison. "I saw—her."

Molly looked over her shoulder, and then leaned closer. "The woman you can't remember?" Molly kept her voice calm, belying the intensity that glowed from her eyes. "Where?"

"I think...she set the fire." Shara inhaled clean air through her nose, trying to control the gagging cough that slowed her revelation. "She said, 'Goodbye, Shara,' and threw a cigarette through the window."

"Who is she? What did she look like?"

Shara closed her eyes and tried to call up the name that eluded her. "I-can't remember. But I saw-red hair." She coughed until she gagged. Lying back, exhausted, Shara adjusted the position of her slinged arm and winced.

Molly fidgeted with the sheet and blanket. "Does your arm hurt much?" Her voice was kind, too kind.

Why is she suddenly changing subjects? Shara shifted in her bed and tried to breathe slowly. "I'll live."

"Let me run out and see where the nurse is with your meds, okay?" Molly patted her shoulder. "I'll be back in a shake."

"No, Mol-"

"No I'll be back in just a moment."

Maybe some pain meds would be a good idea. Shara settled on the pillows and closed her eyes. *The red headed woman, what is her name? How did she find me, why does she want me dead?* Shara squeezed her eyes tighter and saw only the woman's cold, green eyes glittering at her through the window. *I'm so close to the one thing that could clear my name and bring Bryan back to me.*

57: MOLLY

Sitting at a cafeteria table an hour later, Molly stared at Drew and Kelly wondering how much she should tell them. Two cups of coffee later, she told them everything. "She doesn't know the name of the woman, you understand. All she remembers is that the woman had red hair." She glanced at both men, noting Kelly's expression. "Obviously you have some ideas, Kelly. Are we thinking the same thing?"

"Possibly, Miz Hunter, but it's a hunch. Something this serious, I can't just go around saying out loud."

"Spit it out, son." Drew drained his coffee and leaned back in his chair. "Now's not the time to hold back."

"Okay. I saw Mrs. Jacobs, I mean, Mr. Jacobs ex, twice in the last twenty-four hours. Once at the club we were playing last night. She was the one that..." he stopped and blushed.

"She was the one that what, Kelly?" Molly frowned at him.

"Well, you know women always go for Jake Winter and last night he stayed over night...you know...with a woman. Bethany...I mean...Shara...she never saw the woman, but I thought last night she looked just like Miz Jacobs."

"You thought that and you didn't say anything?" Molly glared at the younger man.

"I swear Miz Hunter, I didn't think for certain that it was Miz Jacobs! I thought she just looked like her. And Jake didn't say a word about it, I don't think he remembered her at all."

"Jake Winter should be flogged." Molly shook her head. "I'm calling his mother."

Drew swirled coffee in his cup. "Molly, these boys are grown men, you can't call his mother because of something he did in a bar."

"Can and will, just watch me." Molly turned her full attention back to Kelly. "So when was the second time you saw Jennifer?"

"The other time was this morning, maybe an hour before the fire. She didn't recognize me, but I knew who she was, no mistake. She wasn't breaking any laws, so it wasn't like I could arrest her." Kelly rubbed his eyes. "She said she was staying at Mis Blakely's place. I knew she was lying, but before I can say anything, I have to ask Mr. Jacobs if he was maybe expecting her for some reason."

"Very doubtful." Molly grumbled.

"I know. That's why I think maybe she set the fire."

"But you can't say anything until you're positive," Drew sat up straight.

A sharp pain pricked the back of Molly's eyes and she winced. *This makes no sense. And yet...* "You saw her this morning?"

"Walking on the road near Mr. Jacobs house. Not an hour before we got the call for the fire."

If Jennifer was so close, she must have been the woman Shara saw. And Shara believes she's the woman from her nightmares. Molly set her cup down too quickly, the strength gone out of her hands as a lightening bolt shot through her mind. Coffee splashed up over the lip of the cup and Kelly sopped up the mess with paper napkins. "You haven't mentioned this to Bryan?"

187

"No ma'am, I got kicked out of his room, just like Mr. Shepaski. I was thinking maybe she was here because of Mr. Jacobs and Beth-Shara, their relationship."

Molly glanced around the room, making sure no one could overhear them. "We may as well use her real name. Just don't use it too loud." She got up for more coffee. "You think they have a relationship?"

"Just assumptions." Kelly blushed to the tips of his ears. "Not like I'm happy about it." He gave Molly a wry smile.

Molly smiled and shook her head. "Like everything else we know, we can't prove it." She sat down. "Look, here's what we know: Jenny saw Shara last night at the club. She shows up near Bryan's house today. A short time later, Bryan's barn goes up in flames, with Shara in it. Shara sees a woman set the fire, the woman talks to her. Now, Shara's convinced that it's the woman from her nightmares, the woman she believes shot her grandmother." Molly clicked her tongue against her teeth. "I highly doubt Jenny gives two figs about Bryan's personal life." Molly rubbed her eyes again. "All the pieces are here, but I don't see why they fit together. If Jenny's not after Bryan, why would she care one bit about Shara? Why would she have shot Shara's grandmother? Where's the connection?"

"Richard Bennett."

Both Molly and Kelly stared at Drew, standing next to the coffee maker, pouring himself another cup. Without looking at them, he continued. "That was the guy Jenny ran off with, right? That newspaper story that first day, Bryan said Richard Bennett was-

Molly broke in, the thought dawning on her. "-Shara Brandt's fiancé. He was shot, too." She leaned back, rubbing her eyes with her hands. "That goes a long way to explaining a number of things. Jenny was always unstable; it's not a stretch to think she'd be jealous of someone taking Richard from her. That also explains why Bryan was so furious at my house. Richard Bennett."

"This is all about some guy named Richard?"

"Kelly, think about it: Shara shows up here in October, beaten up, no car, no anything. Just shows up here."

"Yeah, we all believed you when you said her boyfriend dumped her here." Kelly gave Molly a stern look. "We never looked for a car."

"Scold me later. Let me finish this thought: New Year's Eve, Richard Bennett identifies a body hundreds of miles away as Shara Brandt. Now, months later, Jenny sees Shara, alive, at a club. Suddenly Jenny's back, an hour before Bryan's barn burns down with Shara in it? Jenny's afraid she'll lose Richard if he finds out Shara's alive."

"But we're talking about murder, Molly. Do you think Jenny is capable of simply locking someone in a barn, and setting fire to it, out of jealousy?"

Molly grimaced. "I think she's capable of anything."

"But Miz Hunter, she slept with Jake. How can she be jealous enough to kill Shara if she's picking up guys in a bar?"

"If you had a rival for something, something you were willing to kill for, would you stop at anything to remove that rival?"

Kelly rubbed his hands over his face. "Jake had no idea what he was doing. I may flog him myself."

"I believe Jenny's capable of anything to hold on to Richard." Molly's tone turned urgent. "How long do you have before you have to report any of this?"

Kelly Fuller toyed with his paper cup. "From a cop's standpoint, we've got a pile of nothing. We can't prove Jennifer did anything wrong. It's not illegal to pick up a guy in a bar. It's not illegal to walk down a county highway on a hot day."

"But it is illegal to lock someone in a barn and set fire to it."

"That it is, Mr. Shepaski. But the only witness we have to that is Shara. And we can't question Shara without this whole…thing coming up. And that gets Shara into trouble. Someone else can turn her in." He sighed. "I can't."

"Molly, we have to contact the authorities in Milwaukee. If Jenny had something to do with that murder, and with burning down the barn…" Drew stopped himself. "You said it yourself…she's capable of anything."

"You think the Milwaukee police are going to protect her?" Molly bit her lip. "No one outside this town cares about her. The whole state wants Shara Brandt for murder. We need to make very sure we have all the facts that prove she's innocent before we open her up to the general public."

"But Molly, what if-"

"There is no what if!" Molly stood up quickly, her chair falling behind her. "There is that girl down the hall, hurt and scared and certain that whoever killed her grandmother is out to get her, but she doesn't know who and she doesn't know why. Now, maybe Jenny isn't the one. Maybe it's the world's biggest coincidence. But we are not going to alert any Milwaukee authorities. Not yet."

"Are you sure?" Drew put her chair right, then put a calming hand on her arm.

Molly glared at him and brushed his hand away. "I swore I would protect that girl from anything. I am not about to let her down now, not again." She looked over her shoulder where a woman sat in a chair, writing something on a legal sized pad of paper.

"It's already started." Drew nodded toward the woman. "You know who that is? That's Blair Dailey."

"Who?"

"Blair Dailey is a reporter for the channel twelve news in Milwaukee. I heard they were sending a reporter up here to do a story on the drought."

Molly smiled in spite of her mounting dread. "And I'll just bet she got wind of the barn fire and the horses and the rescue, so she's sticking around to get a jump on a great human interest piece." Molly clicked her tongue against her teeth again. "She doesn't know she's sitting forty feet from the biggest story in the state. The minute that gets out, this place is going to be crawling with all kinds of people who are not interested in the truth, only in the story." She stopped and took a breath. "Then, there'll be no saving Shara."

"Then what do we do Molly?"

Molly looked over her shoulder at Blair Dailey again. "We wait."

"For what?" Kelly watched the reporter as well.

"We wait for Shara's memory to come back completely. We're so close."

Drew cleared his throat and swirled the last dregs of coffee in his cup. "It's been almost a year...what if it doesn't?"

"Then we do what we must to protect Bethany Elias."

Kelly fidgeted with his keys. "What if she does remember... and it's...not good?"

"Then you do what you have to do." Molly rubbed her eyes and leaned her elbows on the table. "But you'll be doing battle with me. And I'm not going to fail her."

58: BRYAN

Bryan stared at the ceiling of his hospital room and sighed. *This is ridiculous.*

Slowly, painfully, he slipped out of the bed. *I can't sleep, doesn't matter what they give me. And I'm not lying in this room by myself.*

Ignoring the relentless throbbing pain in his scorched hands, Bryan focused his concentration on moving one tired, aching leg in front of the other. Crossing the room, the first hurdle. The second, opening the door. *This is going to be interesting.*

He held his hands up to the faint light that streamed in through the narrow window in the door. Yellow burn salve wept through the light wrapping of gauze, only partially covering the ruined skin. *That's what you get for being a hero.*

Wouldn't have to be a hero if I hadn't locked her in the barn.

I had no way of knowing.

You had no reason to endanger her like that.

Weakened by the accusations of his conscience, Bryan leaned against the door and screwed his eyes closed. There, in his mind's eye, the image of Bethany weeping on a hay bale pained him. *I didn't think there would be a fire. I would never-*

You would never what? Hurt her? Use your superior physical strength to threaten her? Betray her?

Stop! Bryan pounded a fist against the door, and cried out as shards of pain shot up his arm. Biting back any further sound, Bryan jerked the door open and stepped into the dimly lit hallway. The hallway spun around him as he struggled to absorb and eliminate the anguish in his hands.

I have to be sure she's okay. Steadier on his feet, Bryan looked around. *It's not that big a place, she has to be nearby.*

Progressing slowly, stiffly, Bryan glanced in sidelight windows, searching for Bethany. Keeping his hands still, and close to his chest, Bryan silently prayed that he wouldn't have to pass by the nurses' station to find her. Each sidelight window brought him closer and closer to the nurses' station, where he knew someone would stop him and send him back to his room.

At the corridor intersection, Bryan glanced left and right. *Where did they put her?*

What if she's not on this floor? What if she's in ICU?

No, no, she couldn't have been that badly hurt.

Was she breathing when you got to her? How much of her body was burned? How much was broken?

Bryan grit his teeth. Looking left and right again, he turned right, staying far away from the nurses' station. *She's on this floor, and I'm going to find her.*

Window after window, there was no sign of her. About to give up, Bryan paused at the last door. Holding his breath, he peered into the window.

The bed light was still on, glowing like a halo over her head. With her eyes closed, Bryan saw no life, no animation in her porcelain countenance. With great care, he eased the door open to get a better look at her. *She's so small.*

Two steps, three, and he stood beside her, aching to touch her colorless cheek. Only the faint rise and fall of the blanket covering her bespoke any sort of life within the shell of her body.

How much damage did we do to each other today?

His body suddenly exhausted, Bryan slumped into the chair next to her bed, never taking his eyes off of her. The anger that threatened to consume him such a short time ago, a lifetime ago, was gone. In its place was something cold, something forming a shell around his broken heart. He studied her with as cold, as objective an eye as he could muster. "You should have been honest with me," he whispered to her.

So you could turn me over to the police sooner?

Leaning forward, resting his head on the edge of the bed, Bryan closed his eyes and tried to shut out her voice that echoed in his head. "You should have told me. You could have given me the benefit of the doubt."

It wouldn't have changed a thing. You'd still hate who I am.

He kept his head down. "Probably, but I might not have fallen in love with you if you'd told me sooner."

She whimpered, a soft, anguished sound, but now he knew the ghosts she battled in her dreams, and he had no strength for them. Looking up at her, the smooth lines of her face twisted in pain, in fear, he longed to erase her nightmares, because they were also his. *But it's no use now, is it? It's too late. There's no taking back who you are, or what I did.* He stood to leave, took a step to the door.

Bryan, don't leave me, please.

He looked over his shoulder. Still asleep, wresting demons unseen, demons that now included him, her head twisted side to side as if turning away from oncoming horror. *How can I leave her alone? I put her here. She shouldn't be alone. I owe her that.*

Bryan turned and leaned close to her ear. "I'm here. It's going to be okay." So close to her, he caught a faint whiff of strawberries, under the layers of disinfectant and smoke. A sense of loss stirred in him as he sat down in the chair and watched the lines on her face relax and fade into peaceful sleep. *If only I could believe my own words.*

* * *

"Well look there wouldja? Here's our missing patient."

193

Through the fog of drugs, Bryan was vaguely aware of two voices behind him.

"We should've known he'd be here."

"We can't leave him here, can we?"

"No, of course not. I can't believe he managed to get here on his own. We gave him enough to drop an elephant."

"Well, that's love, isn't it?"

"Love, schmove, it's one more thing we gotta do before first shift shows up. Go get a wheelchair and we'll get him back to his room."

Too numb from the pain meds to put up an argument, Bryan kept his eyes closed and followed the orderlies' commands to get in the wheelchair, and then, to get into his bed.

* * *

The next morning, Bryan winced as the nurse wrapped layer after layer of gauze on his hands. "Do you really need to do all that?" He grimaced past her shoulder to Drew, who wore a look of quiet amusement as he stood in the corner of the room.

"Only if you want them to heal." The nurse batted her eyes at him. "You know, that was really brave, saving your housekeeper yesterday."

Your opinion of me would change if you knew why I had to save my housekeeper.

"There you go. You're all set." The nurse wheeled her stool back from the table. "You have someone to take you home? You can't drive, not with those hands and not with the meds they've got you taking."

You mean you're not volunteering?

"Yeah, I'll drive him home." Drew scuffed his shoes on the gleaming tile.

"Okay then. I want you back in here tomorrow and we'll look at those again. And be sure you see me." The nurse blinked one more time and left the exam room.

"Unbelievable. Did you see that?" Bryan nodded at the closing door.

Drew grinned at him. "Yeah, the mystique that is Bryan Jacobs just went up a notch. Now, you're a wounded, brooding, heartthrob...and you're a hero."

If they only knew. Bryan shook his head. "Can we get out of here now?"

"Don't you want to talk to...Shara... before we go?"

Bryan closed his eyes and saw her again, lying in the hospital bed, tortured and alone. *Of course I want to see her. I want to tell her how sorry I am for...everything. I want to see her beautiful face and beg for forgiveness. I want to forget who she really is and just live happily ever after. But that's just not going to happen, is it?* "It's probably best to let her rest. I'll see her soon enough." *If she ever allows me near her...*

Drew held the door open for him. "You're not still angry, are you?"

No. Yes. Bryan kept his eyes away from Drew. "No, of course not."

"Good, because Molly says-"

"Drew. I really don't want to go over what Molly says right now." Bryan held a hand up. "I don't want to discuss any of this right now."

"Fine. But I have to warn you: The press will be in the lobby."

"Are you kidding?" Bryan stared at Drew as they stepped into the elevator. "It's eight in the morning. They don't know-"

"No, nothing like that. Blair Dailey was up here yesterday doing a piece on the drought and fell on the whole rescuing the horses and the housekeeper thing."

"Well, isn't this a gold letter day for you, then."

"Don't blame me. The Packers are off to a slow start this season. The only thing going on is your heroics." Drew threw him a twisted grin. "It's dream come true!"

More like a living nightmare. Bryan cast a bewildered glance around the elevator, trying to prepare himself for the worst.

59: SHARA

Shara closed her eyes as Molly wheeled her into the elevator. Her arm throbbed and fear pulsed through her. As the elevator sank floor by floor, dread filled her at the prospect of coming face to face with reporters. "Tell me again, Mol. Who's out there?"

"Couple of paper people, Milwaukee, Green Bay. Bennie from the 'Rock Harbor News.' When this is all over, give him an exclusive. He's a big fan. Told me he knows Shara Brandt is innocent."

"Could he tell everyone else for me?"

The elevator doors opened. Molly peered out into the lobby. "I see a camera crew. We have to avoid them. There's that woman from last night, Blair Dailey."

Shara shook her head. "If Blair Dailey is here, it's big news already."

"Well, she might be the luckiest reporter in all the land. If you give yourself away, that is." Molly looked down at Shara and smiled. "You ready?"

"I guess." Shara nodded and managed to eek out a weak smile. Fear twisted her stomach in a knot.

"All you have to do is look down and say nothing. Don't look at anyone."

Again she nodded. Tucked in the wheelchair, half-covered with the sling, Shara steeled herself. Molly pushed forward several steps before anyone caught sight of them.

"Miss Elias! A minute, please?" Reporters blocked their way. "Can we just get a word with a local heroine?"

The other elevator opened, and Bryan and Drew stepped out. Molly glanced back at them, but kept moving without a pause. "Miss Elias is going home, folks."

"Come on, one shot with the two of them together!"

Drew dragged Bryan past Molly, making a path for the wheelchair. Reporters followed them, shouting question after question. Shara stared at her lap and counted the steps until the main doors slid open. Raising her eyes for a moment, she caught Bryan glancing over his shoulder at her, his eyes unreadable.

Bryan. Lifting her head she locked her gaze with his. For a heart beat everything was silent and in slow motion. *Forgive me. Please.* She could not silence the cries of her heart as she tried to find any warmth in the hopeless depth of his eyes. A tear ran down her cheek and, as she wiped it away, Drew gave Bryan a push out the door into the sunshine.

Don't leave me, Bryan.

She blinked once before she realized that there was a camera just outside the sliding doors, pointed right at her. "Molly!" she hissed in a panicked voice.

"Get away from this girl right now!" Molly yelled, shoving three photographers away. She ran the last few yards out the door, where her car was open and running, Joanna at the wheel. Molly helped Shara out of the wheelchair and slid her into back seat. Molly hopped into the front passenger seat. "Drive!"

Joanna jerked the car into gear and they rolled away from the hospital.

Molly looked over her shoulder. "Damn."

"That good, huh?" Jo glanced in the rearview mirror.

"Depends on who had the camera and how good an angle they got."

Shara, listening to her two friends, closed her eyes as tears wet her cheeks. *What does it matter who saw me? The worst of the damage is already done.*

60: RICHARD

Today's the day I get everything. Always an early riser, Richard Bennett loved mornings even more when he smelled a lucrative business deal. With Jennifer's return from Green Bay and the notes she showed him on the dealership she scouted for him, he reveled in the thrill of visceral excitement that always signaled money. Buttoning up his perfectly crisp white shirt, he shot a last careless glance at Jennifer's naked form in the bed. *Everything money can buy.*

Downstairs he fixed himself an egg white omelet and listened absently to the morning news. Some female newscaster chirped, "We have breaking news out of the Green Bay area this morning. While doing a piece on the effects of this summer's drought on Door Country's cherry crop, our own field reporter, Blair Dailey, stumbled on a truly touching love story. Blair?"

Blair Dailey, *screaming hot field reporter*, popped onto the screen. "Thanks Janie, I'm here in the tiny farming community of Rock Harbor, about thirty five miles northeast of Green Bay. The drought this summer has been pretty brutal on the normally moderate weather up here, and the proof is the barn, or what's left of it, that you see behind me." Blair pointed to a charred pile of wood. "This barn belongs to school teacher Bryan Jacobs, and housed his three horses, until yesterday afternoon when a blaze, thought to have been caused by a careless cigarette smoker, brought the whole thing down."

Richard stared at the screen; his body quivered like a wire. *Bryan Jacobs?* He fixed his eyes on hot Blair Dailey, field reporter, and waited to hear more.

"Mr. Jacobs' housekeeper, a young woman named Bethany Elias, lived in the apartment above the barn and was home alone when the blaze started. She jumped out of the upper window, but went back in three times to save the horses."

"Three times, that's amazing Blair!" Janie, the anchor, blathered.

"It gets more amazing, Janie! The third horse got trapped under falling debris, with Miss Elias on her back. Miss Elias would have been crushed by the falling beams of the burning building, had she not been rescued by Bryan Jacobs, who got to the scene of the fire before the local volunteer firefighters did."

"That's unbelievable, Blair!" Janie chirped, dabbing an eye with a perfectly manicured finger.

"Both Mr. Jacobs and Miss Elias were treated at Rock Harbor Memorial Hospital last night, and released this morning. I have footage you'll see only on channel twelve of Miss Elias, thronged by reporters as she's leaving the hospital, catching a glimpse of

Mr. Jacobs. They can't get close because of the crowd in the lobby, but the look on her face tells the whole story."

Here Blair Dailey, hot field reporter, ran a short clip of a young woman in a wheelchair staring directly into the camera. Her deep, dark eyes filled the screen. The picture stunned Richard. *What the hell...*

"Miss Elias suffered a broken arm saving those horses, Janie, and Mr. Jacobs has severe burns on both his hands from saving her. These are two very brave people very much in love. We wish them well. Back to you Janie."

A smaller version of the still frame of the woman they called Bethany Elias was still on the screen as Janie smiled into the camera. "Thank you, Blair. You let us know how those two wonderful people are doing. And now in more local news-"

Richard slammed his coffee mug down on the stainless steel counter top. *How the hell is she alive?*

He looked at the ceiling and, yet again, cursed himself for allowing Jennifer Tiel any part of his life. Furious, he left the kitchen and ran up the stairs two by two. "Get up!" Richard dashed into the bedroom. He shoved the door, and it slammed against the wall. Jennifer stirred and sat up. "Wake up!"

"What is it, baby?" Jennifer rubbed her eyes and tossed her head, giving him the most provocative look possible considering she'd just been asleep. "You up for a little breakfast before you leave for work?" She sat up straighter, letting the satin sheet fall away from her bare body.

The scene cooled the venom of Richard's invective for a step. *Damn.*

"Come in babe." She beckoned him with a shiny red nail.

His fury cooling, Richard could not deny the arousal she always stirred in him. Unbidden, Shara's face flashed through his mind. *Stay focused, or you're going to lose everything.* The mere idea of what having Shara alive meant rekindled his rage. "Shara's still alive. How do you explain that?"

"What?"

To her credit, Richard had to admit she looked truly surprised. "She's still alive. Alive and well and living in Rock Harbor, with your ex husband!" The bed creaked under the sudden thrust of his weight. Richard grasped Jennifer by the chin and drew her face close to his. "So I have to ask you, Jennifer my love, how did that happen? You swore to me she was dead. Drowned in a river months ago. I identified a body. A body in Watertown, which is, let's see…oh, about six hours in a completely opposite direction from Rock Harbor!" He grasped her by the shoulders and gave her a shake. "So how the hell did she wind up in Rock Harbor, living with Bryan Jacobs?"

"She is dead. Of course she is." She batted her long eyelashes at him, an act made less effective by the remnants of mascara crusted in the corners of her eyes. Still, Jennifer wore an air of calm and, more infuriating, innocence. "Is Mr. James hounding you again that she's alive? I swear, Richard, you need to let that old lawyer go."

"Mr. James didn't say anything, I saw it for myself. She's all over the news. Survived some fire and left the hospital before anyone figured out who she really is." He tightened his grip on her chin. "I'll ask again. How did that happen, Jennifer?"

Innocence slipped from her face like a putty mask. A venomous light glowed in her green eyes. "You can't blame me for this, Richard." She jerked her head back, loosing his grip on her. "I couldn't very well shoot the little bitch, could I?"

"You said she was dead. Said you saw the body yourself, floating in a river. Which is why I identified a body they found in a river. Only two problems with that…either she was dead when you dumped her, and she floated halfway across the state upriver, a series of rivers that don't actually connect with each other and wound up, magically, ALIVE with your ex husband. OR you, you stupid, stupid woman, actually drove her to your old home town, to a place that could very easily be connected to *me!*"

"Oh please. Don't call that collection of shacks and losers my hometown. I certainly never think of it anymore. Not since I have you, baby." She ran her bare foot up the inseam of his trousers.

200

Arousing men, was Jennifer's best talent and her most powerful weapon, and Richard felt his resolve crumble at her touch.

"Stop it Jennifer, this is no joke!" He stepped away from the bed and took a deep breath, clearing his head. "How in the hell were you so stupid as to go in the one direction that could get us into trouble?"

Her green eyes chilled to a hard, glittering light. "Well, Richard, I was working under the assumption that you didn't want me stopped by the police. And you know the cops line up between Milwaukee and Chicago. Same for the Milwaukee to Madison drive. I couldn't go east…that would put us both in the lake."

Richard strained to keep his temper in check. "Jennifer, let me explain something to you. My fiancée, a woman I identified as being dead, is living with your ex husband. Now, don't you think, somewhere along the line, they maybe had a conversation?"

"Oh I'm sure they've had many conversations." She tossed her hair and smiled at him with an air of confidence. "I wouldn't be worried about anyone believing what she has to say, once they find out who she is."

"You really are an idiot." Richard shook his head. "Tell me, Jennifer, tell me something: When you drove her up there that night, looking for a place to dump her, did you actually think to yourself, 'Hey, I know, let's drop the body of an heiress in the one little shit hole town in this state where they know just enough about Richard Bennett to hate him.' Was that a conscious thought or do you just continue to screw up my life by accident?"

"Make it look like an accident. That's what you told me. So I couldn't shoot her. I couldn't very well drive down to Chicago and just toss her in some ally, could I? The odds of getting stopped by the state patrol going that way are pretty good."

"Mostly because you're too damn dumb to drive without attracting attention."

Her green eyes blazed at him as she got up from the bed and stood eye to eye with him. "Listen to me Richard, everything I did, I did because it was your plan."

"No, Jennifer, everything you did you did in spite of the plans we had. Everything you did has turned this into the complete disaster it is."

"Don't blame me. I wanted to shoot her dead on the spot that night. Kill both those bitches right there. But no, you have to have an attack of a conscience or some other sissy assed thing, and you can't get your hands dirty. So I'm the one, Richard, I'm the one that drove her away. I'm the one who was going to take her all the way to Michigan, until your beautiful baby of a car blew a tire on the interstate in the middle of the biggest damn downpour in history. So don't sit there in your clean clothes with your clean hands and tell me I've screwed up, because, of the two of us, Richard, I've proven I'm not afraid to get a little dirty."

Richard swung his hand at her face and connected with a vicious backhand that slammed her to the floor. Blood trickled from the corner of her mouth as she stared at him. "I don't have to tell you what this means, do I?"

"No, of course not." Tears sparkled in her eyes, but her face hardened into a mask of haughtiness.

"So you need to get your ass to Rock Harbor and do what you should have done a year ago."

"Don't be a fool." Jennifer cringed, but her tone remained defiant as he rose from the bed and raised his hand again. "I can't just show up in Rock Harbor. People know me there, as you just pointed out."

"Then don't be seen. And this time, do it right." He stormed out of the room and slammed the door closed. *Meanwhile, I'm going to probably have to work up the loving fiancé act again. Damn it.*

61: BRYAN

The glow of the morning sun illuminated a scorched horizon as Drew drove Bryan to the cabin. Bryan tried very hard to focus on everything Drew told him, but felt mostly relief when he finished with, "So that's everything."

202

"So what do we do now?" Bryan really didn't care about the answer, but he didn't want to look at the charred remains of the barn.

"Molly and I are convinced that Jenny's behind everything, we just don't know how to prove it without putting Shara at risk. And-" Drew put a hand on Bryan's arm, "we have to remember that, no matter what, Shara is the same person she's always been to us. No matter what others think."

"I'd like to forget she's a part of any of this." Bryan didn't realize he'd spoken aloud until he looked at Drew. "What on earth are you grinning at?"

"You've come a long way since she first got here."

"Not really. I was right all along." He closed his eyes again.

"But now you don't want to be, do you?"

"No. Of course not." *I don't want her to be yet another of Richard Bennett's lovers.* "I don't want anyone to be in any danger." Speaking this much wore him out. He squinted into the sunlight as they drove into his driveway. "I also don't want that to be a reporter sitting on my porch."

Drew squinted into the sunlight. "That's not just a reporter...that's Blair Dailey."

"Well there you go, tiger. Your big moment to talk to Blair Dailey."

Drew eased the car up the drive. "You sure you don't want to?"

"Just go already." Bryan tried not to make eye contact with the woman as Drew spoke to her. Blair smiled, nodded, and gave Drew a hug. Then she walked past the car, down the drive, to her own car.

"What did you tell her?" Bryan stared at Drew, as Drew opened the car door for him.

"I told her that you weren't in any mood to talk to anyone right now and that if you did decide you wanted to discuss this very stressful event, I would give her a call."

Bryan coughed out a short, smoky laugh. "There you go. Ya got her number."

"Because she's interested in you. Or at least, in your story." Drew opened the door for Bryan and stood close by as Bryan slowly walked to the house. Bryan nudged the screen door open and hobbled into the house, immediately slumping onto the couch.

"You sure you want to stay here?"

"I'll be fine. I want to be alone."

"I could stay, fix you some breakfast or something." Drew grinned sheepishly. "Jo won't forgive me if I just leave you."

"Jo won't forgive you for that stupid grin you have on your face." Bryan held up his hands. "Besides, how much trouble could I possibly get into? Tell Jo she can come and twitter over me later. Much later."

Drew nodded at the window. "What about the horses?"

Instinctively, Bryan looked out to the charred ruins, then to the paddock, where Spice and Pepper stood, staring back at him. "Can you call Marva? She'll take them."

"Until you rebuild."

Can I rebuild what I've destroyed? Do I even want to? "Right."

Drew was about to open the door, but paused, his hand on the knob. "You should probably expect Jo over here later this afternoon, once they've got Shara settled at Molly's. Call us if you need anything. Dial with your toes or something."

"Yeah. Thanks."

"Oh, Bryan?"

Bryan barely acknowledged him. "Yeah?"

"You did an amazing thing." Drew opened the door, but still hesitated.

You have no idea what I've done.

"Every man hopes he has the courage to act if his loved ones are in danger."

Bryan snorted and slumped lower on the cushions. "Sometimes courage has nothing to do with anything."

Drew stepped out the door. "Get some rest."

Bryan waved a mittened hand at his friend, who closed the door and drove away.

* * *

Just before noon, Marva Blakely came to take the horses. From his rocking chair on the front porch, Bryan watched without emotion as she loaded Spice into her trailer. The filly, still skittish from the events of the previous day, didn't load easily, and Marva, a sturdy third generation horse breeder, worked up a good sweat in the process.

"Okay now, Pepper, you're turn."

The normally docile stallion jerked back on the lead and snorted in protest. Bryan closed his eyes and heard, again, the heart rending shrieks of Rika as the fire consumed her. "Wait, Marva." He stood up. "Let Pepper stay here."

"Heaven's sakes, Bryan, what do you think you're going to do with a big horse like this in your state?"

Bryan rested his arm around Pepper's neck while the caramel colored horse nuzzled his shirt pockets. "I don't know. It's just a thought."

"You know as well as I do, Bryan Jacobs, that you can't take care of yourself much less a big beast like this." She shook her head, and this time loaded Pepper very easily. "Now you go and rest yourself. Remember, I'm just babysitting." She waggled a calloused finger at him. "You're going to rebuild and go on with your life."

"Thanks, Marva." Bryan watched her truck roll down his drive. The pain in his hands roared. *Time for another pill. Maybe two. Why not? I'm not going anywhere.*

* * *

He dozed on the couch, lulled by the television and the painkillers flowing through his system, when the screen door squeaked open and snapped shut.

"Well, well, Bryan, you've really let yourself go."

Jenny. He knew her voice, and struggled to open his eyes. He regretted doing so; the revulsion at the site of her was instant and harsh. "You'll excuse me if I don't jump for joy." He looked her up and down, but saw no waning of her blinding beauty. *Damn.*

"You look like hell." Jennifer sat down in the recliner and leaned over the table, reminding Bryan of a predator on the scent of prey.

He reached out blearily and patted her face. *Not a hallucination.*

"What are you doing?" She backed up and gave him a look dripping with disdain.

"Just checking. I was hoping you were just a nightmare." He leaned against the cushions of the couch again, dizzy from the exertion. "Do you have a purpose for this visit, or are you just here to cap off a perfectly hellacious day?"

"Oh, I have a reason for being here." She arched a perfectly plucked brow at him.

"Well, I don't care. You know where the door is. Use it."

She ignored his direction and instead slid onto the couch next to him. She bent and spoke into his ear. "I have a question for you." Her voice was a purr, her fingers velvet against the back of his neck.

"Ask someone else." Her touch burned him, but he didn't have the strength to push her away.

"I don't know where anyone else is." She continued her rhythmic stroke up and down his neck and across his shoulders. "You have what I want."

His resolve waked and he shrugged her hand away. "Get off me, woman!"

"You don't need to be rude." She sat down in a chair across from him and stared at his hands. "What's with the mittens?"

"Long story and I'm not telling you. Whatever you want, the answer is no."

"Fine. Since you're in no condition to answer complicated questions, I'll keep it simple. Where is Bethany Elias?"

Bryan blinked again and sat up, struggling to focus on Jennifer and her question at the same time. *"Why do you care?"*

"She's an old friend, from before I met you. I saw her on the news this morning. As you can imagine, I'm so worried about her. I rushed right up here to make sure she's okay." Jennifer stuck out her perfect red lips in an attempt at a concerned pout.

Drew said something...in the car. What did he say?

He watched her pose in front of him, near the windowsill that had once held the antique water pitcher. A battle raged in his fogged mind.

Bethany saw a woman at the fire...Drew said Kelly saw Jenny...

Over Jenny's shoulder, beyond the window, the sunset illuminated the charred remains of the barn. Angry words, an echo of an argument, roared in Bryan's head. Bryan stared at her, truth striking him like lightening, sharp and undeniable. "It's you."

"Of course it is, dummy." Her tone was derisive. "Have you been drinking, or are you just more stupid than usual?"

"She can't remember." He rose to stand on wobbly legs, holding her gaze as she moved from the window toward the fireplace. "You know her...from before?"

"I told you, we were old friends, Bethany and I." She tucked her hands behind her. "What can't Bethany remember?"

"You set the fire." He took a step, but stopped, unable to move closer to her.

"Bryan, I really have no idea what you're babbling about." Jennifer assumed a bored expression.

Kelly saw her. Shara saw her at the fire. She set the fire, tried to kill Shara. The floor spun under him, but he steadied himself with a hand on the back of the recliner. "You can't see her, Jenny. I won't let you."

"You won't let me?" She tossed her glossy curls back and laughed. "That is funny. If I recall, yesterday you couldn't stop me. In fact, you were very helpful. The little snot should be dead right now. She's not, but it won't be long before she is, especially since you're barely a speed bump today." She slammed the fireplace shovel into the side of his head. Bryan stumbled back into the couch.

I've failed her again.

Jennifer hit him one more time before darkness washed over him.

207

62: JENNIFER

Jennifer stepped past Bryan's still form and searched each of the rooms. "Well, not that I expected her to be here. She's at Molly Hunter's then, for sure." She looked at Bryan's face, blood streaming down where the corner of the shovel caught his forehead. "Sorry, baby. I almost feel bad about doing this." Finding the whisky bottle in the cabinet, she opened it and poured the amber liquid over Bryan and the furniture. Reaching into her purse, she pulled out a pack of cigarettes and a lighter. She opened the cigarettes, lit and stubbed out two on the coffee table. A third she lit and set on the couch near Bryan's right hand.

She then snapped on the lighter and set fire to a quilt draped near Bryan's still form. Jennifer couldn't keep from smiling as she played out the scene in a singsong voice. "Poor Bryan Jacobs. Distraught over the loss of his barn, his horse, and his sweetheart, he decided to drown his sorrows with a drink and a smoke. But a lethal combination of alcohol and," she picked up the brown bottle of pills, "What seems to be some very, very nice pain meds made him an inattentive smoker and he set fire to his house. Poor, poor Bryan Jacobs."

Satisfied that the quilt was burning quickly enough to do damage before anyone knew to come and help, Jennifer returned to her car.

She checked her makeup in the rearview mirror. "And that is how we make it look like an accident, Richard." She reached into her handbag and pulled out a gun. "Unfortunately for you, Shara Brandt, I just don't have time for accidents."

63: SHARA

Shara was back where she started: injured and frightened and in Molly's guest bedroom. Molly puttered around, wiping everything clean of cat dander, and the former residents of the room howled in protest outside the back door.

"They'd better shut up, or the neighbors are going to start throwing shoes at them," Molly fluffed the pillows on Shara's bed. She stopped for a moment and studied Shara, then removed the locket from around her own neck and fastened it around Shara's, resting the locket itself right on her breastbone. "I think, maybe, you should have this now, don't you?"

My mother's locket. Shara drew some comfort from the reminder of her beloved parents, so long gone. *Even this can't help me now.* She inhaled deeply; drawing courage for a question she ached to ask. "Molly how's Bryan?"

Molly sat at the side of her bed. "He's going to be fine. Jo drove over there just now to check on him."

"That's good, but- but that's not really what I wanted to know." She inhaled again. "Why-why was he so…"

"I imagine he was hard on you when he found out?" Molly didn't wait for an answer. "I should have known Bryan would take it very hard once he learned you and Richard are engaged."

"Richard? Why would Bryan care?" Shara sat up a little higher on the pillows.

Molly sat next to her and patted her hand. "Did you love Richard?"

Shara picked at the soft, pilling blanket. "What has that got to do with anything?"

"Maybe nothing. Maybe something. Did you love him?"

Of course I loved him. Didn't I? "He was handsome and charming. He said he loved me. He was kind to me. He said he'd take care of me, far away from Grandmother. He promised I wouldn't have to work in the car business, that I could do what I wanted to do, be a teacher, whatever."

"Did you believe him?"

"I had no one else to believe, and no reason not to believe him." Shara sighed and closed her eyes. "I know he was a ladies man. No woman could help but love him, you know? He has eyes the color of a summer sky. He has a way about him that draws women to him, and I doubt he ever said no to any of them. But he always treated me well. And once we got engaged, he stopped

209

his…activities with other women." She opened her eyes and noticed Molly's worried expression. "When he was with me it was like I was the center of his universe. He never gave me a reason not to trust him." She smiled. "He was hope for me."

"I doubt Bryan would share your impression of him." Molly frowned. "In answer to your question, Bryan cares about Richard because of Jenny."

"Bryan talked about her, once."

"He did?" Molly raised both her eyebrows.

"Christmas Eve." Shara smiled at the surprised look on Molly's face. "He was…not exactly himself." She closed her eyes.

Could you ever love me, Bethany Elias?

I wonder, Bryan, will you ever ask me that question again?

Molly nodded and clicked her tongue against her teeth before speaking. "Jenny left Bryan for Richard three, almost four, years ago. She ruined him. That much you know, I'm sure, from Joanna. Bryan's whole world just stopped. He just stopped being." Molly gave her a sidelong glance. "Until he met you and fell in love again."

Maybe before the fire, but not now. "It was weird, Molly. Like I was some cheating wife." Shara shivered, recalling the dark expression on his face as he pinned her down. The memory of his kiss, angry as it had been, gave her a shiver of another kind. *Stop it. What might have been is over. He'll never forgive me.*

"Well, in a way, you did cheat on him."

Shara dragged herself from her thoughts. "How can you say that? I mean, don't you have to be a couple in order to cheat on someone?"

Molly chuckled and fussed with the blankets. "Shara, be honest about it: He is in love with you, just like you are with him." She patted Shara's face lightly. "It stands to reason that the minute he found out that you're engaged to Richard Bennett, well, it was like losing Jenny all over again. To the same man."

Shara shook her head. "That's where you're wrong, Molly. It couldn't have been the same woman. Richard always left married women alone. He had a lot of affairs, before we were engaged, but

210

never with married women. He always said…" Shara's hand froze over the blanket and her mouth went dry. "Wait…What was her name?"

"Jenny. Jenny Tiel, I think her maiden name was." Molly clipped her words, as if it hurt to speak them.

"Jennifer Tiel?" Shara leaned forward, straining for something that was just beyond her mind's eye.

Molly leaned in closer to her. "What is it, Shara? What are you remembering?"

"I can't believe I forgot this." Shara swallowed and closed her eyes, trying to picture every detail of the memory. "Ages ago Richard brought her to work at the dealership. Grandmother didn't like them dating if they were going to both work there, so she told Richard to break up with her. He did." She opened her eyes, and laughed out loud at the expression of surprise on Molly's face. "That's how Lydia was. She didn't like something, she fixed it to her liking. Richard never disobeyed her."

"He never disobeyed your grandmother, how was he going to keep you out of the car business?"

Shara shrugged. "No clue. But, Molly, if you heard him, you'd believe anything he said. When we got engaged, Grandmother liked the match, even though he's so much older than I. She probably figured he'd keep me in the business, and the Brandt name would be secure for another generation."

"How much do you remember of Jenny and Richard when they were together?"

"Not much." Shara closed her eyes and tried to recall what the woman looked like. "I do remember, when Richard broke it off with her, she ran a car through the show room window." Shara looked up and smiled at the distant memory. "I never saw her again…" a shiver of recollection ran through her. "Molly, she was the woman at the barn. I swear she was!"

"She was on Bryan's property right before the fire. Kelly thinks she may have set it." Molly frowned. "But why would she want you dead?"

Don't you tell…

"I-don't-know..." Shara tried to stay awake, but her eyelids were too heavy. The medication was taking over.

64: JOANNA

There was a strange, unsettling quiet about Bryan's place as Joanna pulled the station wagon into the drive. No cheerful call from Bethany in the barn. No songbirds twittering in the shrubs around the yard. *Death itself has settled here.*

She climbed the short steps to the door of the cabin. "Bryan?" She tapped at the screen and waited for a moment. "Oh heavens, he's probably sleeping."

She opened the door and the acrid smell of smoke struck her. "Bryan!" She did a snap study of the room before seeing Bryan splayed on the couch. Smoke and flames rose from the quilt draped over his legs. The stench of whisky and smoke welled tears in her eyes. "Bryan." She shook his shoulders harshly. "Wake up!"

"Hmmmm." He waved a mittened hand at her, like some fly. She grabbed the quilt and dragged it out of the house where she stomped out the flames. Racing back in, she filled a pitcher with water, and promptly doused him.

"What?" He struggled to sit up and stared at her, eyes glazed.

"Bryan Jacobs, just look at you."

Bryan shaded his eyes from the sunlight streaming into the room. "What? What did I do?"

"You set yourself on fire." Joanna filled another pitcher and doused him again.

"Hey! What's that for?" He sputtered and shook water out of his hair.

"That's for being a fool. Look at you. What, things don't go your way and you dive right back into the booze and the cigarettes? Thought you were past that crap once you and Bethany got together!"

"Whoa now, power down a little." He sat up fully and studied the coffee table. "First of all it's Shara, not Bethany. Second, we

212

never 'got together.' Third, I wasn't drinking. I haven't touched it since she moved in and you should know that since you know everything."

"Then what's this?" Joanna held up the empty bottle. "And that stink? Since when do you smoke?"

"Since never. Geez Jo, how about if you leave and send the real you in here? You know, the one that likes me?"

Joanna sat in the recliner and glowered at him. "There are a lot of people in this town who will forgive you anything and everything, Bryan Jacobs. I used to be one of them, but not anymore. You've got us, you've got Molly, you've got the kids and Beth-Shara…. yet here you are." The speech exhausted Joanna and she sat back.

"Did she say that?" Joanna didn't miss the hopeful tone in his voice. "Did Shara say I had her?"

"Heaven's no. She's about as open as you are. I'm piecing a puzzle together, that's all. Give me some credit for having eyes and ears."

"Fine. You're a genius, Jo. And I'm an ass. There, I said it. But," he surveyed the mess on the table, "you shouldn't point a finger. You're assuming the worst about me without letting me get a word in. How is that fair?"

Her heart melted at the agony she saw in his eyes. "You're right, of course. So what happened here then? Why try and kill yourself?"

"I'm telling you, I wasn't. I took one…okay, maybe two… of those pain pills they gave me and then I was lying here, watching TV." He brushed his hair back from his eyes. "What the-"

Joanna looked down at his bandaged hand, the white of the bandages now red. "Bryan, that's blood!" At his side instantly, Jo brushed more hair away from his face. "Bryan, you've got a really bad cut right here on your scalp. What did you-"

"Jo, I swear, I didn't-" he broke off, his face paled. "Oh, no."

"What? How did this happen?"

He stood up, wobbled, and fell back on the couch. "We have to get-" he ran out of breath, and, panting, gave her a look that cried for help.

"We have to get what?" She moved next to him and stroked his face, this time noticing the dried blood. "What happened here, Bryan?"

"Jenny. Jenny was here."

"Jenny was here?" Joanna glanced around the room wildly. *Of course. The cigarettes. The whisky, the fire.* Her gaze fell on the fireplace shovel, out of place on the floor near the sofa, and tinged red. *She's out for blood.* "Okay, let's go." She hoisted him off the couch and helped him take a few weak steps to the door.

"We have to get there. I have to tell her-" He broke off again, sinking into unconsciousness as Jo shoved him into the back of the station wagon.

Joanna picked up her cell phone and dialed Drew. "Honey, I'm at Bryan's, where are you?"

"Just dropped the kids at Chanel's for the afternoon, now I'm on my way to Molly's to stand guard duty." There was a note of humor in Drew's voice.

"Get to Molly's as fast as you can. Speed if you have to."

"I'm in the car now, but won't speeding attract the police?"

"You need the police at Molly's. Hurry up! Call Kelly Fuller."

The humor left Drew's voice. "What's going on?"

"Jenny's been here, Drew, and she beat the crap out of Bryan, tried to kill him. I'm on my way to the hospital with him right now. He's unconscious." Fear choked her as tears welled in her eyes. "Drew, I don't think Shara is safe at Molly's."

65: SHARA

She woke with a start. Turning her head slightly, Shara noted the sky had clouded over. A cool breeze caressed her face and a low rumble of thunder promised rain. *The weather's changing.*

What was I thinking about before? I had to tell Molly…something. She tried to shake the cobwebs from her mind.

It was raining that night. The trunk, I was in the trunk of a car. The car broke down, or something. She opened the trunk and I fought away from her.

Don't you dare tell Shara Brandt!

Shara squeezed her eyes tight shut and gripped the quilt to her chin. "I didn't tell. I didn't tell anyone."

"Who are you talking to, sweetie?"

Shara jerked her head toward the door, where Molly smiled at her with calm, gentle eyes. "I thought I heard someone."

"Well, you did. Drew just pulled up." Molly helped her sit up a bit more. "All you have to do is rest right now. Let us worry about everything else."

Shara leaned back on the pillows. "I had to tell you something."

"What's that?"

Shara frowned. "I-I can't see it all." She turned tortured eyes to Molly. "I see her, I see Jennifer Tiel. But I don't know for sure… Why can't I remember?"

Molly patted her hand. "Your brain is protecting you from your worst memories, which include that night. Yes, it would help if you knew if it truly was Jenny who was there that night, but the best thing is to not stress about it." Molly gave her a tight smile. "Rest while I go talk to Drew."

"Are you sure?"

Molly gave her one more smile before leaving the room and closing the door. Shara's eyelids drooped as she listened to murmured conversation at the end of the hall. She looked out the window and the gathering clouds lulled her further into a dream.

"Goodbye Shara."

Shara's eye flew open. There outside the window, some ten feet away, there was Jennifer Tiel, staring right at her window. Jennifer held something in her hand, something aimed at her. Shara closed her eyes and shook her head trying to wake from the dream. She opened her eyes again. Jennifer was still there, a little closer, still holding something in her hand. Shara leaped out of bed, and flung

215

herself against the farthest wall, screaming for help until everything spun into darkness one more time.

66: BRYAN

"I'm fine. I'm FINE! Jo, tell her I'm fine."

"Mr. Jacobs, please hold still." The doctor sat back from her squirming patient. "You are not fine. You have a concussion. You need seventeen stitches. And you aren't exactly treating your hands with tender loving care. You are the opposite of fine."

"Jo, tell her I'm fine." Bryan turned pleading eyes to Joanna.

Jo stood in the corner of the room and bit her lip. "Can't do it, Bryan."

"We're going to admit you overnight, Mr. Jacobs."

"Jo, tell this woman I'm perfectly capable of taking care of myself."

"Like you did this morning?" Jo nodded to the nurse who left the room. As the door closed, Jo leaned closer to Bryan. "Don't you think this is the best place for you, given the fact that Jenny is back?"

"She's not after me. She's after Shara. We have to get to Molly's because that's where she's going." Bryan tried to sit up, but the room started spinning and he fell back.

"And you'd be right. Drew called ten minutes ago. Apparently, Shara started screaming then fainted. And..." Joanna bit her lip, "A shot was fired. Kelly found tire tracks behind the house, and a bullet hole in the siding, near the spare bedroom window. Molly's going to tell the doctor Shara's got a bunch of symptoms that will keep her here for a bit." Joanna tucked a blanket around him, "She'll be safe here until we can figure out what to do next."

"Just what do you think that's going to be?" Suddenly exhausted, Bryan lay back on the exam table. "I mean, so far, this has been a lot of running around for no purpose."

Joanna patted his shoulder. "We're not good at this cloak and dagger stuff, are we? But we'll think of something. Molly is trying to get hold of a lawyer."

Bryan winced as the doctor knotted off the first stitch in his head. "A lawyer? On a Saturday? In this town?"

"Bryan Jacobs, don't tell me you're back to see me already?" The perky brunette nurse from earlier bounced into the room. "I just can't let you out of my sight, can I?"

Bryan didn't miss the amused look on Joanna's face. He sighed heavily and gave up fighting for the moment. "Apparently not."

67: SHARA

She opened her eyes to the now familiar sterile white of a hospital room. Molly was patting her arm and humming a low tune. "Mol, what happened?"

"You fainted sweetie. Jumped out of bed and fainted."

"Jennifer!" Shara sat up quickly. "She's got a gun! She's here! She's outside-"

Molly bit her lip. "There's no doubt. For whatever reason, Jennifer Tiel is trying to kill you.."

The room faded to white and Shara gasped for breath. *Don't pass out. Don't pass out again. Listen. Listen to what she's saying.* "So I didn't imagine it."

"She …paid a call to Bryan this morning." Molly looked away.

"And?" Shara poked Molly with her cast.

"And she asked for you. Then she beat the crap out of Bryan, tried to make that look liked a suicide. He's down the hall."

Not Bryan. Not again. "Is he okay?"

"He will be. He's got a concussion."

"Mol, it's been a year almost. How did she find me?"

Molly gave her a wry grin. "She was at that club the other night, in Green Bay. She got…friendly with Jake Winter."

"And Jake probably told her everything. That boy should be flogged."

"That is the general consensus. Once she realized you weren't dead, and Jake mentioned Bryan, it was nothing for her to find you."

"Molly." Shara didn't recognize the firm tone coming out of her mouth. "I can't let any more people get hurt because of this. It's time to contact someone and let them know I'm here. I can't let her hurt anyone else."

"You think Jennifer's the shooter?"

"I know she is." Shara nodded. "But I can't think why." Shara looked to Molly. "It's like she's hunting me."

"Of course, you're right. I hate to have to do this," Molly looked away, tears glistening in her eyes. "I haven't protected you very well, have I?"

"You've done more than anyone else in my life has. You've saved my life in more ways than I can count." Shara struggled to a sitting position. "My grandmother's lawyer...Mr. Archibald James. We should call him."

"Do you remember his number?"

Shara closed her eyes. "Of course." She repeated a number, long stored in the deep recesses of her memory. "If you tell him that I'm here, he'll come."

Molly gave her a quizzical look. "Are you sure you can trust the lawyer?"

"I can trust him." Shara stared at the wall. "And there's always Richard."

Molly paled. "You want me to contact Richard?"

Make it look like an accident.

The hair on the back of Shara's neck prickled as the words seemed so clear in her mind now. *Who said that? That wasn't the same voice. That wasn't a woman.*

Molly didn't miss her expression. "Are you remembering something?"

Shara shook herself out of her reverie. "Uh. No. I don't think so."

"You looked a little strange just then." Molly arched an eyebrow at her. "What about Richard?"

"I suppose Mr. James will call him, won't he? Just call Mr. James."

"I'll go give this number to Drew. He's down the hall with Joanna. "

"Jo's here, too?"

Molly smiled and patted her arm. "She brought Bryan in. Chanel's got the kids."

"Is he going to be okay?" Shara grabbed her wrist to stop her from walking away. "Molly, tell me the truth. How bad is he hurt?"

"He'll be fine, he's got a hard head. I'll be right back." Molly slipped out the door and the room settled to quiet.

Shara stared at the ceiling. *So Jennifer Tiel has some score to settle with me. Enough to burn down a barn and beat up Bryan. Soon everyone will know, and the police will pin the murder on me. Everything, everything hinges on Mr. James... and my malfunctioning memory.*

A single tear rolled down her cheek as she realized that everything would be much better if Bryan would walk through the door.

68: JOANNA

"Excuse me. I'm looking for a Drew Shepaski?"

"Mr. James?" Drew stood up from his seat in the lobby as the distinguished, older man spoke to a nurse. Joanna followed him. "Are you Mr. Archibald James?"

"I am, sir. You must be the gentleman who called me?"

"Drew Shepaski. This is my wife Joanna." Drew shook the small man's hand. "I'm glad you could make it so quickly."

"Mr. Shepaski, I've waited a long time for such a call. Where is the patient?"

"Upstairs. The elevators are that way." Joanna pointed away from the nurses' station. *At least he understands we can't say her real name here.*

Once in the elevator, Joanna studied the aging lawyer closely. "You think you can help our girl?"

Mr. James patted his briefcase. "Madam, if your girl is my Miss Shara, then yes. I believe I have here something that, coupled with her memories of that awful night, will clear her completely."

Joanna bit her lip. *No use telling him that she can't remember much of that night. Let's see what he can do for her first.*

The elevator doors slid open and Drew lead the way to Shara's room.

The expression on Shara's face was all Joanna needed to see to know they'd done the right thing.

"Mr. James!" Shara beamed from ear to ear.

"Miss Shara!" Mr. James stepped forward and patted Shara on the shoulder. "You are a sight for weary eyes." The affection in his voice was unmistakable.

"Let me introduce you. Mr. James, these are my friends, Molly Hunter, and you've met Drew and Joanna Shepaski."

"We have. Ms. Hunter, hello." Mr. James sat in the chair closest to Shara. "I want to thank you all for taking care of Miss Shara."

"Well, we haven't done such a great job recently." Molly spoke softly.

"Nonsense, Ms. Hunter. Three hours ago Miss Shara was dead, drowned in a river. I would say, without hesitation, she looks significantly better at this moment."

"Mr. James, you know I'm innocent."

Shara's words were a statement, not a question, meant, Joanna had no doubt, for them. The bond of trust between lawyer and client was undeniable.

"You needn't even ask, Miss Shara. How about if you tell me, quickly, everything you need to tell me. We may not have a lot of time to talk. I believe you will have another visitor quite soon."

"Richard?"

Joanna did not understand the expression on Shara's face as she spoke Richard's name, but she was certain of one thing: Shara was not a woman in love about to be reunited with her lover.

"Yes, Miss Shara."

And Mr. James seems to share her mixed feelings.

"He contacted me this morning. Apparently he saw someone who looks like you on the news this morning. He wanted to see what I thought. I, of course, was already in the car on the way here. I'm sure he'll arrive shortly."

Jo shot Molly a fearful look.

"The Milwaukee police also saw the news report. They have reopened your case. Mr. Bennett indicated two detectives were riding up with him."

Jo waited for Shara to show a hint of fear at the mention of police. There was none. Shara nodded and squared her shoulders. "Then I will talk quickly."

For the next half hour, Shara told him about her life in Rock Harbor, about the fire, and about Jennifer. Mr. James took notes, but said little. When she was done, he looked up. "Well, Miss Shara, you seem to have found your place here, haven't you?"

"Like nowhere else." She smiled at him, the first real smile Joanna remembered seeing on Shara's face since the fire. "But I can't have any more of my friends hurt, and it's a matter of time now before this story blows up."

"One thing troubles me: You mentioned Jennifer Tiel is this Bryan's ex wife?"

Drew nodded. "You'll meet Bryan later. He's being treated for the injuries Jenny inflicted on him today."

"She's here, then? In Rock Harbor?"

"We think she locked Shara in the barn and set the fire." Molly seemed to imitate Shara's sense of calm, in spite of the horrible events they discussed. "Do you believe that's possible?"

"I don't know for certain. What I am sure of is this: If Jennifer Tiel knew of your whereabouts two days ago, I have no doubts that Richard Bennett knew as well."

The air sucked itself out of the room. Joanna watched as a shadow crossed Shara's face.

"Then they're back together?" Shara's voice was wispy, laced with emotion.

"It pains me to tell you this, of course. Since you were declared deceased, Mr. Bennett resumed his relations with Miss Tiel."

Joanna watched Shara's reaction to her lawyer's words and wondered if this was Mr. James' version of an 'I told you so.'

Here Mr. James pulled a blue file folder from his case. "This is your grandmother's will. She made it out shortly after you and Mr. Bennett got engaged. I've spent the last year trying to persuade the detectives assigned to your case that there is evidence here proving you are not to blame for your grandmother's death."

Instead of looking relieved, Shara's frown lines deepened.

Joanna could no longer wait for an answer to her question. "Mr. James, who do you think is responsible for the shootings?"

At that moment the door snapped open. "Hello, Shara, my dear."

Joanna's stomach churned at the sight of the smooth features of Richard Bennett.

69: BRYAN

Bryan paced the length of his room again and again. *Where is Drew?*

What is going on with Bethany?

With Shara, idiot.

I'm not an idiot.

Yes I am.

Drew opened the door and Bryan all but pounced on him. "What is going on? I'm going crazy in here!"

"I can see that." Drew managed a grin and pointed to the bed. "All those with head injuries inflicted by their ex wives, get into bed."

Bryan obeyed, but grumbled. "I'm glad you can find humor in this."

"Lot funnier in here than it is out there." Drew nodded to the door. "We found Shara's lawyer. He believes he can help us."

"And...."

"And Richard's made an appearance."

"Great. Richard's here. Jenny's here. It's big old reunion." Bryan crossed his arms over his chest and stared at the wall. "And since I have a bump on my head, I don't get the fun pills to turn this into a real party."

"The good news is that the doctors figure you can go home in the morning. Seems your concussion isn't as bad as all that, and as long as you promise to come back on Monday, you and your mittens can be trusted outside the hospital."

"Great." Bryan didn't take his eyes off the wall.

"Okay. Well, I promised Molly I would go entertain the detectives Richard brought…" Drew opened the door part way and paused.

"You never heard how Richard talked about her on television. About Shara. Like she was lunatic, a raving danger to everyone." Bryan blinked back an angry tear and faced Drew. "So this is how it ends? He swoops in and takes her?"

Drew scuffed his foot on the floor and shook his head. "I honestly don't know right now." He looked at Bryan. "But remember this: just because the loudest people in the room are saying it, doesn't mean it's true." He cleared his throat. "A nurse will be in soon with your dinner. I'll check in before I leave tonight, okay?"

"Yeah. Fine."

The door closed behind Drew and Bryan lay in the bed, staring at the ceiling. *So Richard's here to take her away. It's over. Whatever it was, it's over.*

"Dinner time!" The chirpy brunette was back, wheeling in a cart of covered dinners. "I know, I know, some aid from Dietary was supposed to bring up dinner, but you know, I couldn't leave for the night without seeing my favorite patient one more time." She shot Bryan a high wattage smile that made his stomach churn. "Let's see what we have here tonight….mmm…ham steak and mashed potatoes with green beans and red jell-o for dessert. Now be sure you finish your veggies before you eat your dessert!" She straightened his pillows, her long hair brushing his cheek. He could tell she used the same shampoo Shara did, her hair smelled of strawberries.

But it's not the same.

He let the nurse fuss around him for a few minutes, grunting short answers to her multitude of questions. When she tired of his mood, she bid him good night and closed the door behind her. Not really caring about the dinner in front of him, Bryan uncovered the plate to reveal a mushy, room temperature mess that made him ill. *Bethany used to cook up a great ham steak and make the best mashed potatoes.*

Only her name's not Bethany, you idiot. And she won't be cooking for you again.

Anger added heat to the misery that simmered deep inside him. With one motion he kicked the dinner tray to the floor. Looking at the spilled mess on the floor, the ache of homesickness filled him. It didn't matter anymore that he was supposed to stay in the bed. He needed to go home. He needed to hide in his own private fortress again.

Steeled with this decision, he got out of the bed, and rummaged around for his clothes. With difficulty Bryan managed to put his shirt on, but donning the jeans was a more involved, more painful, experience.

The fire exit was just a few steps from his room. Bryan pushed the door open and, ignoring the blaring alarm, stepped out into the humid night. Somewhere in the distance, thunder rumbled.

70: SHARA

Shara insisted everyone but Richard leave the room. *Now, Richard, you're going to tell me the truth about that night...I may not remember everything, but I'll know if you're lying to me or not.* She set her face in what she hoped was a sunny, sincere smile. "I've missed you, Richard."

"Oh, Baby Doll, I've missed you, too." He sat on the edge of her bed and leaned close to her, locking his clear blue eyes with hers.

"How about if we dispense with this unpleasantness and go home?"

Weird. I always thought you had pretty eyes, Richard. Have they always been so empty, soulless? "This shouldn't take long, then. Mr. James says he has something that may prove someone else killed Grandmother. Isn't that great? I mean, with what he has and what you know about that night, all we have to do is tell the police the truth-"

"Truth? What do you mean?" His face frozen in a smile, Richard's words shot out too sharply and betrayed his cheerful demeanor.

Shara hesitated. *Careful. Don't let him know you're looking for something.* "The truth. You know, the other person who was in the office that night, the one with the gun. I can't remember everything clearly, but I'm certain it was a woman…might even be Jennifer Tiel." She watched his face but his expression remained smooth, unreadable. "Now, I know, you probably think I'm saying it's Jennifer because Mr. James told me you two were together again, but that has nothing to do with it. I mean, you thought I was dead, after all, how were you to know? I can't very well fault you for anything like that." Forcing herself to sound so cheerful wore her out.

"Shara, stop. Stop now."

I struck something there. "Richard, what do you mean?" Her voice, high pitched and sugary sweet, hurt her ears.

"I mean, stop the storytelling." He leaned closer, this time taking her hands in his and brushing some hair out of her eyes. "I'll take care of you, baby. You don't need to worry anymore." His voice was sing-songy.

Have you always been so creepy? "Those detectives with you, they are going to arrest me."

"It's all part of the process, but I promise you, Baby Doll, I won't let anything hurt you anymore." He stroked her cheek with the back of his hand.

Stop calling me Baby Doll. "But that's what I'm talking about. Mr. James has evidence that'll clear me. We just have to look at

225

this, he said." She held up the blue folder in her lap. "Mr. James says this will is all we need to clear me."

Richard cleared his throat and looked away from her to the folder. "Baby, you have to stop talking like this." His eyes never left the folder.

"But why, Richard?" *Why is there fear in those eyes of yours?*

He resumed his gentle tone, but was obviously distracted by what she held in her hand. "Baby, I don't like to bring up bad memories for you. You haven't had…your medicine for a very, very long time." He covered her hand with his and yanked the will out of her hands.

"Richard! What are you doing?" Shara could not bite back the anger in her voice. She grabbed for the will with her good hand, but Richard held it out of her reach.

"See, Baby Doll, you're agitated now. You need rest. I'll go right now and find a doctor who can prescribe the proper medication for your…condition." He stood and patted her shoulder, but did not hand the papers back to her.

A chill went through Shara. *Medicine? What medicine? What are you talking about?* "Richard, give me those papers. They're mine."

"Oh no, Baby Doll. You don't need this now." He tore the folder in half and in half again and tossed it into the hazardous material bin. "You don't need to worry about anything now that I'm here." He leaned over and kissed her on her forehead, his lips cold on her skin.

Without another word, he was gone, leaving Shara with more questions than answers. *Why is he treating me like an invalid? What does he mean about medicine?*

Something inside her stirred uneasily. Shara closed her eyes and tried to shut out the nagging tug of memories long buried. In her mind's eye she was back in her grandmother's mansion, her own room. The room was large, cold, furnished with pieces far too austere for a child's bedroom. But beyond the bed there was a light, a private bathroom. Deep inside a voice warned her not to go beyond the door.

There's something in there. Something I've forgotten...

The bathroom light glowed around a mirror. The mirror, a door to a medicine cabinet. In the dark of her hospital room, Shara reached out with her good hand as if to open the little door. And there, behind the mirror, there they were. Two small, brown bottles. Bottles with her name on them. Bottles she'd hidden, destroyed, forgotten.

Her name was on those bottles.

I don't want to remember this.

I must remember this.

"Take these, Shara. It's for your own good because you're such a bad child. Take them and you won't be bad anymore and I will love you."

The doctor, one who sat in a brown leather chair and wrote notes as Shara sat in a chair and tried to recount her many sins against her grandmother. "We'll make you well, Shara. We'll make sure you grow up a good girl."

She wanted to be a good girl. She wanted her grandmother to love her. She took the pills, the white ones with the funny name. Lith-lith-ium. That was the name. They made her groggy during the day, made the edges of everything soft, fuzzy.

Four years. For nearly four years she wandered around in a haze.

Her senior year in high school she guzzled coffee to hide the exhaustion from all the sleepless nights when she tried to break free from the pills that stole her soul. Pretending to swallow them, knowing the maid reported back to Grandmother every night. How many nights? How much pain, feeling reality for the first time after four years of drug induced peace?

Mr. James was my friend. Grandmother didn't know he was helping me get off the pills. Mr. James gave me cranberry juice, my favorite. He said it was good for my kidneys. He knew I wasn't sick.

Shara shook herself out of the memory. *I wasn't sick then, I'm not sick now.*

227

Still alone, she crawled out of the bed and hobbled across the room to the garbage can. The exertion drained her, and she had to lean against the wall and give her protesting muscles a rest. *Wonder what I'll infect myself with if I stick my hand in here.* She lifted the lid of the hazardous waste can and noticed there was nothing else in the can. *There's your mistake, Richard.* Looking over her shoulder at every sound, she reached in again and again and retrieved the shreds of the one piece of evidence that perhaps held the key to freeing her.

You identified that body as mine on New Year's, Richard. Why are you so eager to have me dead or mentally unstable? Why don't you want me to see what's in my grandmother's will?

71: JENNIFER

Jennifer waited outside the hospital. What she waited for, she couldn't tell, but she knew she couldn't go inside. She'd watched, fuming, as Joanna Shepaski dragged Bryan through the emergency doors some time earlier. *Another idea screwed.*

Bad, but not the worst.

The worst was later, when Richard showed up. *Of course he has to. With Shara alive, he has to play the part of the loving fiancé. Otherwise everything will be ruined.*

Jennifer bit her lip, anger bubbling in her. *Of course, with Shara alive and perfectly capable of telling her story, everything's probably ruined anyway.*

"No, nothing is going to be ruined. My life with Richard is not going to be ruined. Not by the likes of Shara Brandt." Jennifer cackled at the thought of Shara actually beating her. *Especially where Richard is concerned.*

She couldn't have Richard seeing her hanging around. She had to finish the job he'd given her. She didn't dare disappoint him again. What she needed was one thing, one little sign, and she'd fix everything. Richard, and the fortune, would be hers for good.

All she had to do was wait. *I will get one more chance to make everything right.*

72: BRYAN

Bryan almost made it to the highway before the rain started. The pelting drops chilled him and he wished, not for the first time since he'd left the hospital that he had better sense and stayed in the hospital.

He sensed the car driving up behind him but tried to ignore it, hoping whoever was driving would go around him.

"Mr. Jacobs?"

Kelly Fuller. Crap.

"Mr. Jacobs, it's raining really hard." Kelly pulled the patrol car up next to him and opened the passenger window. "You shouldn't be out here. I'm sure they're all real worried about you back at the hospital."

"Kelly, I want to sleep in my own bed. I don't want to be part of that…circus anymore. Okay?"

"Fine with me, but Miz. Hunter and your doctors are pissed, pardon my French."

There's a newsflash. Molly is pissed at me. "Go away Kelly."

"I can't do that, Mr. Jacobs. Please get in. You're not supposed to be out of the hospital until the doc says so. Don't make me have to arrest you, okay?"

Bryan stopped. The rain ran rivulets down his face. *Don't look back. You can't look back.* He started walking again. "I'm not breaking any laws, Kelly."

"I know that, but you're not doing yourself any favors at the moment, either. I can put you in protective custody. "

Bryan ignored Kelly Fuller and the patrol car and the lights, *but not the image of Richard Bennett taking Shara in his arms, and…* So deep was his reverie, and his focus on his pain, Bryan put up little fight when Kelly pulled up and dragged him into the car.

"I'm really, really sorry about this, Mr. Jacobs." Kelly looked in the rearview mirror at Bryan. "I didn't want to have to do it."

"I'm aware of that, Kelly. Nice of you not to use the cuffs." He sat quietly, defeated. "So this is protective custody then?"

"Yeah, I guess."

Bryan grinned at the absurdity of the whole situation. "Kelly, it wasn't that long ago that you were failing Drew's grammar class and I had to tutor your butt after school. You were my first tutoring gig at RHCS."

"I know that, Mr. Jacobs. And I appreciate that." Kelly pulled the car up to the main entrance of the hospital.

"I promise." With assistance, Bryan got out of the car and let Kelly help him into the hospital. A sudden wave of pain in his hands made him dizzy.

"Easy there, Mr. Jacobs." Kelly supported him as they walked into the lobby.

"Bryan! Bryan you're back!" Jo rushed to his side.

Oh lordy, here we go. "Hey, Jo. How are things?"

"Are you okay? Is he okay, Kelly?"

"He's fine, Ms. Shepaski. Found him walking in the rain."

Jo threw her arms around Bryan's neck, nearly toppling him. "Bryan I could just kill you! We were so worried!"

"So I feel." Bryan struggled to steady himself. They turned the corner to his room, and there, right in front of him, there he was.

Richard Bennett.

"Excuse me; I'm on my way to find a doctor." Richard didn't even look at the small group crowding the hall. "You people do have a psychiatrist in this hospital?"

"Oh sure." Bryan tossed his wet hair out of his eyes and glowered at Richard. "We've got electricity, too. We do have to wait until next year for indoor plumbing, other than that we're just like big city folk."

Richard stopped and gave him an amused look. "I'm sorry." He studied Bryan's face a little more closely. "Do I know you?"

"Bryan…" Joanna's tone was cautionary.

"It's okay, Jo. I can answer the question." Bryan put on a pleasant expression. "I don't think you and I have been properly introduced, but you are familiar with my wife."

"Why? Did I sell her -oh hell," Richard's oily smile faded. "You're Bryan."

"See, Jo, it's just not true what they say about blondes being stupid, is it?"

"Look, buddy that was a long time ago. I've got nothing against you."

Rage pricked behind Bryan's eyes, and he let out a short, angry laugh. "Nothing against me? NOTHING AGAINST ME!" He broke away from Kelly's grasp. "You have nothing against me? That's really, really funny."

"Marriages break up. It happens. Sad that you've kept such a grudge all this time, though, isn't it? Although," Richard looked him up and down with a judgmental attitude, "Perhaps you're not playing with a full deck. Is that it, buddy? Are you a little cuckoo?"

"I am not your buddy." Bryan stepped in front of Richard and glared down at him.

Richard's grin returned to its normal position on his face. "Of course, from what I hear, you were fond of my Shara, too, weren't you?" He reached up and brushed something from Bryan's shoulder. "Sad, isn't it? Losing two women. To the same man." He leaned closer to whisper. "I'm the one who gives them what they need. Jennifer, Shara, they all want me."

Richard's breath still warm in his ear, Bryan let one bandaged fist fly. The connecting punch sent blinding waves of agony up Bryan's arm, but he didn't flinch until Richard slid to the floor.

"Bryan! What on earth?" Molly burst out of a nearby room to stare at the scene in front of her. "Joanna, what happened? Kelly Fuller, what did you let them do?"

Bryan didn't hear the conversation that buzzed around him. Kelly pushed him toward Molly, who shoved him into a room. The door hissed shut behind him.

There in the bed was …Shara.

They stared at each other for what seemed like a lifetime to Bryan. *Say something. Say something!*

"That was Richard?"

Her eyes stayed locked with his, but told him nothing. "Yeah. Sorry. I didn't mean to hit your fiancé."

"Yes. You did."

"You're right. I did." He looked over his shoulder, but no one was pushing through the door. He took a step closer to the bed. "Listen, Bethany-"

"Shara."

The one word was a slap to him. "Fine. Shara. I-"

"Come on Mr. Jacobs, you're going to your room." Kelly slammed the door open.

"And put him in restraints!" Richard shouted from somewhere down the hall.

Bryan turned and backed away from Kelly, bumping against the bed. "Kelly, I'm not-" he paused. Shara was shoving her hand in his back pocket. He glanced at Kelly, who didn't seem to notice. *What on earth is she doing?*

Stall Kelly. "Can't I stay here? We have a lot of catching up."

Kelly shook his head and looked very serious. "Mr. Jacobs, seriously, if you haven't lost me my job I'll be very surprised. And I'm really sorry about this, but we're going to have to put you in restraints."

"Restraints? Kelly, really?" Bryan held up his hands. "How much trouble could I possibly get into with these?"

"Exhibit A." Kelly opened the door, where Richard was still sitting on the floor, and orderly attending to his bloody nose. "Not to mention that you managed to leave the hospital all by yourself and got halfway home."

Shara stopped pushing her hand in and out of his pocket. *Whatever she's doing, she's done with it.* "I see your point, I guess." He peered over his shoulder at Shara, who lay in the bed as if nothing had happened. Kelly grabbed his arm and all but dragged him out of the room. Bryan glanced back one more time to see Shara's empty expression.

Once back in his room, Bryan hopped onto the bed, feeling a little exuberant, in spite of everything. "Can I at least stay in human clothing? If you make me were those pajamas again I'll feel enough like a mental patient to be one for real."

Kelly pondered this a moment. "Fine. Lie down." He and an orderly buckled the wrist restraints. "Just for a bit, Mr. Jacobs. Just until that Bennett guy stops howling." Kelly grinned. "You did clock him a good one, didn't you?"

"I did." Bryan winced as the last buckle was fastened a bit too snugly. "It felt really, really good."

"I'll bet it did." Kelly nodded to the orderly, who took a post near the door. "I'll be back to check on you, Mr. Jacobs. You may as well get some sleep."

Like sleep is going to happen for me at all. "I'll give it my best shot."

73: MOLLY

"**I**'ll say this again. We need to take her into custody."

"No, she's insane and she needs a proper doctor."

"Gentlemen, she's neither insane nor guilty."

Molly shot a tired look at the clock and then at Drew. They'd been sitting there for almost two hours, listening to the debate about what to do with Shara. Joanna, exhausted and lactating, went home to nurse Gracie and feed Nate and Emma dinner. But Drew sat next to Molly, and together they absorbed what they could of the argument.

Richard Bennett, above the others, fascinated Molly. *I can see the attraction. He does have a way about him...if you don't get too close.* The most interesting point Richard repeated was his concern for Shara's mental health. It was a new wrinkle that surprised and confused Molly, but didn't seem to faze either the detectives or Mr. James at all. By the time they broke for the night, Molly was sick of the debate and sick at heart. She bid Mr. James and Kelly a good night and walked slowly to Shara's room.

The guilt she carried for so long weighed heavy on her, and Molly paused at Shara's door. *Could I have saved her from this mess if I'd protected her that night?* Molly heaved a heavy sigh and walked in. "How are you doing?"

"That depends. What's going on out there?" Dark circles under Shara's eyes echoed the defeated expression on her face.

Molly sat on the edge of the bed and patted Shara's leg. "Everyone's gone someplace for the night. I had Kelly take Mr. James and his driver to my house. I think the others are going out to Judy Weller's bed and breakfast." She settled herself better on the bed. "You, my dear, have a true friend in that Mr. James. He's taking on the detectives and beating them every which way from Sunday."

"And Richard?"

Molly searched Shara's face for a clue about the girl's feelings for Richard Bennett, but there was none. Whether on purpose or because she was exhausted, Shara wore nothing but a mask of weary defeat. Molly put her hand on Shara's good arm. "Honey, everyone just wants to do what's best."

Shara gave her a wry smile. "You're a bad liar, Molly. I know he's trying to convince them I'm a lunatic." Shara wilted against the pillows. "But he knows, he knows I'm not crazy."

"What did your grandmother's will say?"

"I didn't read it. I don't have it."

"Where is it?"

Shara sat forward and rested her chin on her knees. "I gave it to Bryan."

"What? When did you do this?"

"Right after he hit Richard." Shara's voice was still devoid of emotion, but she toyed with the edge of a blanket, hiding her face from Molly. "He was in here, and then Kelly wanted to take him back to his room. I stuffed it in his pocket. I couldn't read it."

Molly sat on the edge of the bed and smoothed Shara's hair. "Why not, honey? Too many painful memories?"

"Too many pieces."

"I'm not following you."

Shara sat up straighter and nodded at the garbage can. "When I was in here alone with Richard, I showed Richard the will and said that Mr. James thought it might point a finger to someone else. Richard sort of freaked out, and he took the will and tore it up." She hung her head back down on her knees. "I dug the pieces out of the garbage. I didn't have any place to hide them that Richard wouldn't see. When Bryan got pushed in here, I stuffed them in his pocket."

Molly tapped her on the arm. "Do you want to tell me what Richard's talking about? What meds were you on?"

Shara wiped a tear from her eye. "That was something…I didn't remember until today…" Her facade broke and she started crying.

Molly gathered Shara into her arms. *What kind of hell did you have to live all those years?* "Shh. We don't have to talk about it right now." She wiped tears from Shara's eyes. "How about good news? Any from the doctors?"

"I can get out of here tomorrow morning. They say there's nothing wrong bed rest and your soup won't cure, except for this," she held up her cast.

"Good." Molly sighed. "Now if managing that group out there were so easy."

A nurse entered the room, rolling in the medicine cart. "Hey there Miz Hunter. Time for a pain pill. Our patient needs some real rest."

"I agree." Molly stood up.

"Molly!" Shara put a hand on her arm to stop her. "You're not leaving me."

"No, no. I won't leave. I thought I'd get a cup of coffee and maybe an extra blanket. I'll be back in a moment."

As the door closed behind her, Molly looked through the window and watched Shara take her medicine obediently. *There's so much we don't know. If only you could remember everything…and quickly.*

74: BRYAN

Bryan lay in his bed, timing his pulse beats with the throbbing in his hands. The door creaked open, and he turned his head, hoping against hope someone would bring him something for his pain. *At least the pain in my hands. That would be a start.*

Drew stepped into the room. "If your students could see you now."

"Nice empathy there, pal. You could unbuckle me."

"I don't know. You're not going to pop anyone in the nose again, are you?"

"No, of course not."

"Okay then." Drew unbuckled the restraints.

"Thanks." Bryan rolled his wrists around, wishing he could rub the aches away.

"Don't mention it." Drew pulled the institutional arm chair close to the bed and sat in it, resting his feet on the bottom rung of the hospital bed. "May as well settle down for the night. Everyone's gone home, or something like it."

"Not you?"

"Just talked to Jo. She'd rather I kept an eye on you."

"She, ah, she doesn't still believe that I did any of this to myself, does she?"

"Of course not." Drew opened a magazine in his lap and started paging through it. "But finding you like that..."

"Freaked her out?"

Drew didn't respond. Bryan turned his head and studied his friend in the dimly lit room. "Drew?"

"I have to be honest, Bryan."

"I should hope so."

"The way she found you..."

"Spit it out."

Drew closed the magazine and set it on the floor. "You, dead to the world, looking suicidal. That's been her...our... worst fear in the last couple years."

Drew's words, no matter how calmly spoken, were an icy shock to Bryan. He pushed the automatic button on the hospital bed and sat up to better look at his best friend. "You're not serious."

Drew nodded. "Jo's worried about you since Jenny left. You have no idea how hard that woman has prayed for you. Molly, too."

"Drew, those women-"

"Those women love you!" Drew stood up suddenly and turned his back to Bryan. "Those women love you, Bryan, and they watch over you. They've watched over you since the day you showed up in Rock Harbor. At first it was easy." He turned to look at Bryan. "Remember? Everyone thought you and Molly-"

"The rumor that would not die," Bryan laughed at the memory. "But we never-"

"I know that. I know that." Drew leaned at the foot of the bed. "I'm just saying, at first it was easy for those two to twitter over you because you were good looking and uncomplicated. That's what they said anyway."

Bryan was grateful for the dim lights in the room as he felt color creep from his chin to his hairline. "Uh, thanks."

"And then you changed."

"What, I got ugly?"

"Very funny. No, you got complicated."

"I got a divorce. It sucked. I wasn't happy about it. What's wrong with that?"

"Nothing. Not a thing. But it was more than that. You sank. You spiraled. Bryan, you've been divorced for three years and it's only been in the last six months that anyone's been able to let you go home without worrying about what you might do to yourself." Drew seemed to sag, spent from putting so much into what he said. "Jo begged me to bring you home for dinner, and when you wouldn't come to our house, Molly dragged you to Dave's."

"All those nights…all those meetings that you had to have with me about sports teams or whatever?"

"All to keep you from being alone." Drew leaned back in the chair and stared at the ceiling for a beat, then looked back to

237

Bryan. "After those meetings, I'd watch you leave and wonder if I'd see you the next day."

"Drew, I-"

"You kept moving, somehow. Only it wasn't you. It was some shell of you, until last fall."

"And then?" *Like I really need to ask this question.*

Drew straightened up and stretched his arms over his head. "And then Bethany…Shara is in the creek. One day that battered, frightened, slip of a girl shows up and our worst nightmares are suddenly a thing of the past. Jo is able to take care of herself. We have Gracie. You became a human person."

"So when Jo saw me today she thought I'd spiraled back because of who Shara…of what she is." *Richard Bennett's fiancé…lover.* Bryan felt ill at the very image the words conjured in his mind.

Drew shook his head. "She's guilty until proven innocent, Bryan. Everything I've heard today, I would have pulled the trigger."

"You're buying her claim that she can't, or didn't, recall everything until now?"

Drew looked very disappointed. "I'd think you would get that a lousy past shouldn't ruin your future."

"I do." *It's just easier to believe she's a killer. Then I don't have to face the fact that I endangered an innocent woman.*

"The mind is a delicate thing, and hers has been messed with for years. I think the grandmother was everything Molly says. I believe Jenny is involved. And I know Richard does not have Shara's best interests in mind."

"Well, I've never been a fan of his work."

"Molly says you have the will."

"Will? What will?"

Drew sat back down. "Lydia Brandt's will. Mr. James believes it'll clear Shara and point the finger elsewhere."

"Why hasn't he shown it to the cops?"

"He has. They aren't listening. "

Bryan shifted on the bed and rolled on to one hip as best he could. "You may want to pull the paper out of my pocket there."

Drew gave him a quizzical look and reached into his pocket, drawing out the shreds of paper. "Shara gave this to you?"

"Right after I punched Richard Bennett, I sort of got pushed into her room. She didn't say anything, just shoved it in my pocket."

"Molly said Richard ripped it up and threw it away."

"You know, there's something not right about him, and it's not just my bias."

"I agree." Drew laid the pieces out on the bed, like a big puzzle. For several minutes the two men worked intently on reconstructing the legal document. Drew crossed back over the room and turned on the light. "What does it say?"

"This is some serious legal crap." Bryan frowned. "Like they get paid by the word or something." He shifted so Drew could read over his shoulder.

They read silently together for a moment. Bryan looked over his shoulder at Drew, who wore the same puzzled expression Bryan did. "You done?"

"Yeah."

"Do you see anything here that makes any sense?"

"Seems like the old woman was really thorough, particularly about who inherits."

"Richard inherits if Shara is dead...or mentally incompetent. The news reports last winter made her out to be some crazed danger." *So why didn't she act crazy here all these months?* "What's the lawyer like?"

"He's been with the family for years. Good man. No question he's in Shara's corner."

"When did he draft this?"

"Right after Shara and Richard got engaged."

Bryan rubbed his eyes. "That makes sense. I mean, make room for a new family member, right? Make allowances for any mental or physical illness." He poked at the paper. "I feel really stupid, like we're missing something." He stared at the paper a moment longer. "Wait a minute."

"What, you found something?"

"Maybe. Can you get some tape? There's something right here on the tear line." Bryan picked up two pieces of paper and waited as Drew searched the cabinets.

"You'd think in a place like this...oh, here." Drew brought a roll of white tape to the bed. He taped the two pieces together and stared at them. "What does it say?"

"Well, it says here that Richard inherits if Shara is declared mentally unstable, or is dead, but not if she is murdered."

"I'm not following."

"Dead, but not murdered. Why doesn't he inherit if Shara is murdered?" Bryan studied the paper again, drawn in by the mystery of it all. "What, like she expected Shara to be murdered?" Bryan pointed to the sentence. "Here, it says if Shara is murdered, then the money and the business go to some cousin or something. Richard gets a monthly allowance to run the business, but not the big jackpot."

"Maybe-"

Bryan looked up at Drew, who wore a serious expression. "Maybe what?"

"Maybe Lydia wanted to protect Shara from...from Richard."

Bryan wanted to laugh out loud. "He strikes me as someone more likely to be a victim rather than one who would commit a murder. Too messy for his perfection."

Drew sat on the edge of the bed. "Let's look at this another way: Maybe, instead of thinking Shara shot her grandmother and Richard, maybe Shara was the target."

"Drew, this whole cops and robbers thing is going to your head." Bryan grinned. "We have to face the reality that she might be guilty." Bryan spoke slowly, struggling to believe the words he said.

"You also need to leave room for the possibility that she's innocent."

"But all the evidence points to her, not to mention she's basically been in hiding for almost a year. That's not the action of an innocent person."

"No, but think about it: She shows up, in rough shape, and no one finds a car sitting at the side of the road. She had to get here somehow. She didn't fly."

Bryan nodded, pushing his mind to bring up arguments faster than his heart could agree with Drew. "Yes, but Molly's cover story for her was so good, no one thought to go look for a car. Maybe Lydia put up a fight. Shara shoots her, shoots Richard, and runs. She could've gotten hurt running through the woods. She leaves the car, runs around in a rainstorm, falls into the creek. Someone comes along and steals the car."

Drew started laughing. "This is almost funny, if it weren't so horrible."

"What's that?"

"You, putting out a theory that casts Richard Bennett in a positive light."

"Okay, that is a bit out there." Bryan laid back and sighed, drained of energy. "I guess I'd like to talk to her."

Drew chuckled. "That's not going to happen. Last report was she's sound asleep, Molly's in there with her, and you're not even supposed to be out of restraints." Drew opened the door. "I'll be back in a minute, I gotta call Jo. You may as well get some sleep. Tomorrow's going to be a long day for everyone."

75: RICHARD

Richard cruised through the rain, scanning the streets and parking lots. The thrill of his hunt was tempered by disgust at his own weakness. *I should have taken care of everything myself. Then I wouldn't have to tie off loose ends.*

There, at an outdated motel on the other side of town, he found what he was looking for. His own car's twin, the Lexus he sold to Jennifer Tiel Jacobs four years earlier. *So predictable.*

It was no trouble to ease the Lexus around to the swampy back lot behind the motel. Taking quick steps, careful to avoid the largest puddles, he walked around the end of the motel to the only room with a light on in the window.

Richard had only to tap the door once and she opened it, just as he knew she would. *So predictable. Makes it that much easier for me.*

"Richard. Darling!" Jennifer, dressed in nothing but a short satin robe that left little to the imagination, greeted him with a smile that bespoke a powerful energy simmering just below the surface.

Richard knew, too well, the nature of that energy. He stepped out of the rain and closed the door behind him.

"How did you find me?" She settled on the ancient bedspread and crossed her long legs, revealing a flash of something…else.

Richard cleared his throat. *Focus. That's what got you into this mess in the first place.* "Wasn't too hard. It's not as if your car is hard to find in a town like this."

"And your cop buddies?" She tossed her head back, laying bare the length of her creamy white throat. Richard's eyes followed the line of bared skin downward, mentally cursing himself and the thin folds of the robe.

He again cleared his throat and fixed his eyes on her face. "I left them at the bed and breakfast on the other side of town. They'll be expecting me later, I'm sure. I won't be staying here." He watched as she processed this information. Mixed emotions flashed across her face. He was thwarting some idea of hers and that pleased Richard.

"Then we should make the most of the time we have, don't you think?" Her emotions reigned in, Jennifer's face settled into an expression Richard knew too well: predatory feline on the trail of prey. "I ordered pizza, should be here soon. I know it's not prime rib from Mo's," here she licked her lips at the mention of Richard's favorite high end steak house in Milwaukee's theater district, "but it'll fill…whatever spot I can't." She leaned back further on the bed, this time letting her robe fall loose, revealing yards of glorious, perfect, female form.

Richard stared at her, and did nothing to stave off the desire that welled in him. Gifted at multitasking, he was able to let his body

242

enjoy the site of her, while his mind worked furiously on a new sprouted plan. *This could be the opportunity I need.* "Pizza sounds just fine. When did you say it was coming?"

"I expect it any minute."

"Let me go get my suitcase from the car." Richard glanced out the window. *This could not be more perfect.* "I'll be back in just a moment."

"Don't take too long, lover." She licked her lips, reminding Richard again of a cat on the prowl.

Richard closed the door behind him and ran the short distance back to his car. Once inside, he eased the Lexus, lights off, into a position where he could watch her door, but not be seen. A flash of headlights through the rain announced the arrival of the pizza. Richard pictured the scene he knew would play out.

She'll meet the pizza guy at the door in that robe of hers. She might look out the door, wondering where I went, but she won't see me. If the poor hick looks even moderately human, she'll flirt with him. He'll like the attention, and it won't matter that she doesn't tip him. Richard swallowed an impulse to laugh out loud.

Most importantly, he'll assume she's alone, because who flirts with the pizza guy if they've got someone else waiting. So, when he's questioned later, he'll swear she was alone. He'll also swear that there was one Lexus in the lot, not two. Richard smiled. The pizza delivery car pulled out of the lot, and Richard counted to ten, slowly, before returning to her room.

"You were gone long enough." She met him at the door, and wasted no time unbuttoning his damp shirt.

Richard let go of his suitcase and closed his eyes as she slid his shirt off and dropped it to the floor. Her touch always inflamed him. *Don't lose focus.*

With smooth precision, she slid his belt free of his pants. *Oh, what the hell. Once last time.*

He sealed his mouth to hers as he loosed her robe and slipped it off of her shoulders. Richard opened his eyes and surveyed her naked body with a burning hunger. Whirling her around in a circle, he pushed her to the bed, where she lay in all her glory, watching him with those cold, green eyes. *How many men have you damned with those eyes?*

One last time, and then, Jennifer, my love, I will show you how to make something truly look like an accident.

76: SHARA

"**D**rew says we're meeting at school." Molly walked in with her breakfast. Shara took little notice. "Come on, eat. You're going to need your strength. We've got just enough time to get you into something…less institutional before we have to be there."

"Why are we going there?" Shara never took her eyes off of the single raindrop rolling down the windowpane. A single raindrop in the midst of hundreds that batted at her window, this once held her gaze as it rolled down the length of the glass.

"Drew said that's where the cops are going to question you."

Shara blinked. "So this is the end, then." Her voice registered no emotion. She felt deflated. Lifeless. Dead.

Molly helped her to her feet. "Not if you believe."

"What exactly am I supposed to believe in?" Shara turned tortured eyes to her friend. "Outside those doors are police who are going to be thrilled to arrest me and put me in prison for a crime I didn't commit. Beyond them is a whole crowd of reporters who are salivating, or will be very soon, at the thought of getting a piece of the notorious Shara Brandt. Beyond that is Jennifer Tiel, who is probably guilty of murder, but I can't prove it. Oh, and she wants me dead, for reasons I can't understand. And beyond that-" she stopped, her words catching and sticking in her throat. "Beyond that is nothing."

"We're here for you. Jo, Drew…" Molly guided her slowly down the hall to the elevator. "I mean, we can't be in the room with you, but we'll be nearby. Bryan, too."

"Did he say that?" *Don't sound so hopeful. You know what the answer is.*

Molly bit her lip. "Well, no, not to me. I haven't talked to him since the fire."

Then you don't know just how much he hates me right now. "Mol, you and Drew and Jo have been great. But you can't put yourself in danger anymore."

"The danger for everyone will be over once you tell your story." Molly stopped and took a deep breath. "What about Richard? What are you going to do about him when this is all over?"

What about Richard? Who cares? "That's over. I don't think I can trust him. I certainly don't want him."

"What is it you do want, Shara?"

Shara blinked. *No one has ever asked me that.* She smiled wistfully. "Molly, there's only one thing I want: All I've ever wanted was a chance to be my own person. I found that here. Unfortunately, I had to be someone else to get that chance." She sighed and squared her shoulders. "Oh well." She looked glanced at the clock. "Let's go, Molly. It's time."

77: BRYAN

Bryan sat on the edge of his hospital bed and toyed with a frayed end of one of the bandages on his hand. He knew Drew would be in soon to drive him home. Then Drew was headed to RHCS, which, Bryan knew was where Bethany Elias' life would officially end. He watched the weather outside his window grow more and more stormy, the clouds heavy with rain that fell as if it were trying to wash away the anguish of the last few days. The heat of the previous months was gone, washed away in the sudden weather change. But the anguish, Bryan noted, stayed behind.

"Are you ready?" Drew pushed the door halfway open, and did not walk in. "I've got to be at school by one."

"I know." Bryan slid off the bed and followed Drew out of the room.

Once in the car, Drew turned on the engine and the windshield wipers. "Good to see the rain, isn't it?"

"Probably too late for the farmers, though."

"Probably. Still, it means life can get back to normal, at least a little." Drew's tone was hopeful, and irritating.

Bryan closed his eyes. "Drew we can chit chat all day, but frankly, we suck at it. How about if we don't discuss the weather?"

"Fine. You want to come to school with me?"

What would my purpose be? "No."

Drew kept his eyes on the road. "I think you should be there."

Oh great. Joanna and Molly picked this moment to rub off on him. "There's no reason for me to be there. Why should any of us be there?"

"The truth is going to come out."

"You think that's what this is about today? Truth? No, this is about justice."

Drew stomped on the brakes, bringing the station wagon to a sliding stop. "You can't accept that Shara might be innocent? After everything?" Drew's normally even tone quavered. His blue eyes flashed with an anger Bryan didn't recognize.

"Drew, it doesn't matter what I think. What matters is she's someone else. She belongs to someone else." *She is Shara Brandt, and she belongs to Richard Bennett.*

Drew put the car in gear and continued driving. "That's what this is about?"

To think of her any other way would be to remember...to remember my own part in this little drama. "I'm sorry. I can't—I can't—"

"You can't, what? Forgive her for maybe murdering her grandmother? Or forgive her for being engaged to Richard?"

Drew's words hung like a curtain between them. Bryan closed his eyes and cursed himself, again, for what he knew to be true.

Drew spoke slowly, as if trying to understand what he was saying. "You can't forgive her-"

"For sleeping with Richard Bennett, okay? I can't get past that she slept with him! I've gone over it and over it a hundred times in my head!" A familiar fury burned inside him. "It kills me, you have no idea."

246

"Aren't you making an assumption?"

"What, that maybe they didn't sleep together?" Bryan let out a mirthless laugh. "No, honestly, having met the man while he was actively screwing my wife, I have to say that the idea of him being engaged to someone, anyone, and denying himself that particular pleasure is not one I'll buy into."

"You met Richard when-" Drew broke off, for which Bryan was thankful. "Okay, I get it now." He whistled softly, tonelessly. "That explains why you hate him so much."

Don't go any further down this path, Drew.

"Bryan?" Drew's voice was still low, still even, but a note of dread now colored his words. He pulled the car to the side of the road. "Bryan, what happened when you got home...after Nate found that wallet?"

There it is. Bryan recognized Drew's businesslike tone, the tone he used when he was about to discipline a student. Opening one eye, he looked at Drew, who stared at him with an expression of concern and deep disappointment. *Tell him and end your life in Rock Harbor forever.* Bryan closed his eyes. *Just say it.* "I was the one who locked her in the barn. The back door is always locked unless the horses are out. I locked the front door. We argued and I locked her in the barn and left for Molly's."

"I thought Jenny-"

Bryan leaned forward and rested his head on the dashboard. "I'm surprised no one told you."

"Who would tell me that?"

"I don't know, one of the women. Molly's been with Shara every minute since the fire, she's bound to know everything. She tells Joanna everything and Jo tells you everything."

Drew stared at Bryan. "You should have told me everything."

Bryan turned his head just enough to look at Drew. "Oh, what, I'm just supposed to say, 'Drew, I locked Shara in the barn because I was crazy jealous, and it almost got her killed.' When, exactly, is the proper moment for an announcement like that?"

"Well that does explain why you've been trying so hard to convince yourself that she's guilty of murder."

Bryan stared at the floor. "At least, if she's guilty, it would give me some, I don't know, justification. The guilt of it is eating me up, but there's no way she'll ever forgive me, especially if she winds up being innocent."

"What did you argue about?"

"All this time, she lied to me, when I thought she was someone I could..." he paused and sat up in his seat. "She was in the barn, taking care of the horses. I threw the wallet at her and started yelling at her about how everything she ever said was a lie, it was all lies. She sat there and took it. I raved back and forth and she tried to defend herself. I wouldn't listen. She argued back, tried to explain, but I wasn't interested. All I could see was Jenny and Richard...it was like losing Jenny all over again to that bastard. I-I..." Bryan stopped, recalling the warmth of Shara's lips against his. "She must've known I wasn't really seeing her because she said, 'Bryan, look at me.' And I did, and Drew-I-I realized..." he stopped again and stared out the window.

Drew waited a beat. "Go on."

"I realized that everything I wanted in the whole world was standing right there in front of me, and I couldn't have her because she belonged to someone else. So I pushed her into a hay bale and locked the door."

Drew was silent for a moment, staring out the windshield, his hands on the steering wheel. "Then what?"

"I raved at Molly for a while, and she slapped me."

"You had it coming." A small degree of warmth crept into Drew's tone.

"And then Marva called and the barn was on fire and all I could think was 'Get her out, before it's too late.' But it's too late now."

"Well, you certainly haven't made it easy." Drew eased the car back onto the road. "As your friend, I'd suggest the two of you see a professional after this is over."

Like the two of us will be doing anything together again. "And as my principal?" *Because I'm fairly certain attempted murder is one those things that shatters that morals clause I signed when I started teaching here.*

248

Drew drove up Bryan's drive and put the car in park. "Did you know someone was going to set the barn on fire?"

"Of course not."

"Besides locking the door, what did you plan to do to Shara?"

Bryan looked at Drew, surprised. "I-I was going to call the police."

"You had no intention of hurting her?"

Did I want to hurt her? Bryan paused, shutting out the memory of the heat between them. "I wanted her to be miserable, like I was. I didn't want her injured."

"Once you realized the mistake you'd made, you went back to try and fix it?"

"Of course. Exhibit A." Bryan held up his hands. "Where is this going?"

"What do we teach the kids at school? We're human. We screw up. But there's hope, forgiveness. Take Richard out of the equation and think about your motivation. You had a suspected murderer in your barn. You had no way of knowing someone was going to set fire to the barn. Once you realized Shara was in danger, you went back to save her." Drew paused.

"So what, I'm forgiven, just like that?"

"Well, Jo and I do think of Shara as family," Drew frowned. "I do have an urge to punch you. But Jenny beat me to that. Besides, you can't fight back. It wouldn't be fair." He grew more solemn. "It's not my forgiveness you really need, you know that. Which is why I think you should go with me."

Bryan shook his head. "Even if I could get past the Richard thing, why would she want to have anything to do with me? I can't undo what I've said and done."

"There's always forgiveness. There's always a chance."

"Not this time." Bryan leaned against the window. "It's over." He opened the car door and stepped out into the rain. "There's no point to me going there today."

"You can't even harbor a bit of hope that she's not in love with Richard? Maybe, just maybe she's in love with you?"

Rain rolled down the back of Bryan's neck chilling him. "Maybe I don't have it in me to fight that battle again."

"Maybe you're an idiot." Drew shook his head. "I've got my cell. Call me if you…change your mind."

"Drew-" Bryan tried to stop his friend, but Drew barely waited for Bryan to close the car door before whipping backwards down the drive.

Bryan stood in the cold rain and watched him leave. He closed his eyes and leaned back, letting the chilling water wash over him. Finally, soaked and aching, he turned and went into the cabin.

The stench of burnt cloth and cigarettes hung heavy in the cabin. Bryan opened all the windows, gingerly, as his burn-stiffened fingers protested. He dragged the ruined coffee table onto the porch, next to the sodden pile of ruined quilt. The pain in his hands was a penance. Done clearing out the mess, he opened the hall closet to get the vacuum cleaner. There it was. *Bethany's coat.* The coat he'd given her on New Year's Eve.

He yanked it out of the closet, but his resolve melted as he held the soft denim to his face and inhaled a faint trace of her scent. His legs failed him and Bryan slid down the wall, holding the coat to his face and mourning the loss of its owner.

78: SHARA

There were few cars parked outside the school when Shara and Molly arrived. Shara, swathed in Molly's old wool jacket, shivered as a cold raindrop hit the back of her neck and rolled between her shoulder blades.

The meeting was in the teacher's lounge. Mr. James sat near the door, at the head of the big table. Molly ushered Shara to the seat closest to the door, next to Mr. James. She waited until Shara sat, then patted her on the shoulder. "We won't be far away."

Mr. James introduced her to the two detectives; a ruddy, barrel-chested man named Dinks and a quiet, colorless man named Chester. The only other person in the room was Kelly Fuller,

250

operating a video camera in the corner of the room. He gave Shara a thumbs-up sign, but his expression was grim.

She heard a commotion outside, and knew instantly the cause. Richard slid into the room and sat down next to her. "Sorry I kept you all waiting. I had business to attend to. How are you, Baby Doll?" He draped his arm around her shoulders, his hand dangling close to her breast.

Shara focused on his soft, manicured fingers. Her stomach convulsed at the heavy smell of his cologne. She shrugged out from under him. "Richard, my arm?"

"Oh. Oh sorry, Baby Doll."

Make it look like an accident.

The hair on the back of her neck prickled and Shara stiffened at this new flawed memory that wouldn't leave her alone. *Jennifer didn't say that. It was someone else.*

"I believe we're all here, if we can get started, please?" Chester's voice was soft, calm, in contrast to his partner, who paced back and forth behind the table. "Sheriff's Deputy Kelly Fuller is videotaping these proceedings. We are, today, questioning Shara Elisabeth Brandt, aka Shara Beth Brandt, aka Bethany Elias. Her lawyer is present-"

All those names make me sound like a criminal right off the bat.

"As is her fiancé, who should not be here," Dinks growled, pausing in his pacing to run his hands over his near-bald head.

"I think I have every right to be here. I am, as you said, her fiancé."

"Mr. Bennett, this is a police questioning. You can't be here. Get out."

"But Detective-" A very unattractive, whiny tone crept into Richard's voice.

Has Richard always been this annoying?

"Out." Dinks blustered, pointing a thick finger to the door.

Richard stood, and stroked Shara's hair a few times. "You be brave, baby, you hear? This will all be over soon, and then I'll take care of you. Like I always have." He kissed the top her head and left the teacher's lounge.

Shara stifled her gag reflex as the door closed behind him. *Did he always wear that much cologne? Have I never noticed just how girlie his hands look?* She shuddered away the last feel of his hand on her head, and recalled, fleetingly, the feel of Bryan's strong, calloused hands on her feet. *Bryan...*

Mr. James cleared his throat. "All right, gentleman, you may question my client."

"State your full name." Dinks glared at her, his hands on his hips.

Panic flooded her and the room swirled around Shara. She gripped the top of the table with her good hand to keep from slumping in her chair. Taking a deep breath to calm herself, she squared her shoulders and looked directly at the detective. "My name is Shara Elisabeth Brandt."

Speaking the words out loud drained her confidence, and the panic returned. Shara closed her eyes to fight off the white noise that threatened the edges of her consciousness.

Make it look like an accident.

79: MOLLY

"I cannot believe I have to wait in here with you people." Richard paced back and forth in Drew's office. Molly, Jo, and Drew were glued to the ancient intercom unit on Drew's desk. Drew switched it off the minute Richard spoke, so the occupants in the other room wouldn't realize the questioning was actually a broadcast. "I'm the one person who should be in there, taking care of her."

"Would you shut up?" Molly threw a cautionary glance over her shoulder at him. "It took Kelly the better part of last night to get this intercom working so we can hear what she's saying, but we can't have it on if you're yapping away."

"Oh, so the local law enforcement helped you listen in on what is supposed to be a serious interrogation? Nice. I love small towns. Everything's so by the book."

"You sound like you want her found guilty." Joanna's tone was icy.

"Guilty, not guilty, doesn't matter. It's not as if she's going to be able to answer any of those questions. Not without her medication." Richard leaned against the wall and crossed his arms.

Her medication. Molly turned her chair to look more closely at him. "Tell me, Richard, what kind of meds are we talking about? What was she medicated for?"

Richard clucked his tongue against his teeth. "Poor child, she's crazy. Clinically. Can't be trusted not to hurt anyone around her."

"Funny, she never had problems with the children." Joanna said in a low tone.

"Her grandmother told me, years ago, that insanity ran in the family…on her mother's side, of course…and that poor Shara, inherited the flaw. Lydia spent a considerable amount of time and money on doctors."

"For what?"

Richard gave a lazy shrug. "Bi-polar. Manic depression. Clinical depression. I didn't pay much attention. She's been taking lithium for about ten years."

"Lithium?"

"It's used to treat manic depressives." Richard spoke in a condescending tone.

"Don't lecture me on manic depression, you smarmy creep." Molly stood up and faced him, toe to toe. "I was a nurse more years than you've been an ass, and I know full well what lithium is for. What I want to know is why you think she needs it."

"I don't think she needs it. I know she does. Shara was…never easy when she wasn't medicated. She was temperamental, moody, when she was a child. Uncontrollable, Lydia called her."

"You're telling me that Lydia Brandt medicated her granddaughter because she sassed her?"

"I'm telling you that Shara Brandt has been under a doctor's care for a myriad of mental illnesses since she was thirteen."

Molly sat back down and stared at the intercom, picturing Shara as a small child. *Was there no end to the evil you had to endure?*

"Shut it all of you," Drew said. "I'm turning on the intercom."

"Tell us, Miss Brandt, what do you recall from the night in question?"

Everyone silenced to hear Shara's answers, but Molly, who already knew what she was going to say, watched Richard's face, instead. *He's going to give away something.*

"Did I miss anything?"

All eyes turned back to the door. There stood Bryan, holding the coat he'd given Shara for Christmas. Molly smiled. *It's about time.*

"How did you get here?" Joanna whispered, nodding to Bryan's hands.

"Marva dropped me off."

"You haven't missed anything." Drew snapped off the intercom. "Although we have learned from Richard all about Lithium and its uses."

"Got Kelly to fix the old system, huh?" Bryan stood behind Drew, and grinned at the intercom. "Lithium. Hmm. Well that is interesting." He cast a glance at Richard that Molly could not read. "Say, Drew, have you given that document any further thought since we read it?"

"I did." Drew tapped his fingers on his desk. "You?"

"That theory we were working on...I think I came across a new wrinkle."

"And that would be what?"

Bryan shot a pointed look at Richard, who, in Molly's estimation, cowered at the site of him. "I think if this Mr. James is good at his job, he already knows that I'm thinking. Has he mentioned the document?"

Drew leaned back in his chair. "I'm sure he will in time." He, too, glanced at Richard and this time, Molly thought, Richard blanched.

So Drew and Bryan read that will. What did they see in it?

Is it enough to clear Shara's name?

80: SHARA

"Miss Brandt, what do you remember from the night in question?"

Her throat burned as if filled with hot rocks. "I don't remember it completely. It comes in pieces. I was in Grandmother's office, reading magazines."

"Magazines?" Chester never stopped writing.

"Wedding magazines. I was to be married at Christmas."

"To Mr. Bennett."

"Yes."

"Mr. Bennett is much older than you are, correct?"

Shara frowned. *What does it matter how old he is?* "I'll be twenty-four in January, I believe he recently turned forty."

Dinks stopped his pacing again and inhaled and exhaled deeply. "Tell me, Miss Brandt, did you feel resentment, having your grandmother forcing you to marry a man much older than yourself?"

Shara blinked. "Detective, who told you I was being forced to marry Richard? I was marrying him of my own free will."

"Really?"

"Yes, of course." *Grandmother may have forced him into it, but not me.*

"Why?"

"What do you mean, why?"

"Why were you about to marry Mr. Bennett, as you say, of your own free will?"

Shara's eyes narrowed. "For all the reasons a woman marries a man, Detective. He was a loving man. He was kind to me. He was a good provider. He promised-"

Dinks suddenly looked eager, a cat ready to pounce. "He promised what?"

She shook her head. "He promised things that have no bearing on anything connected with my grandmother's murder."

"Why don't you let us decide that, Miss Brandt?"

Shara glanced at Mr. James, who nodded encouragement. "Fine. He promised that I could take whatever career path I wanted if I married him."

"You liked the idea."

"I did."

"You didn't want to take over your grandmother's business."

"I did not."

Dinks fired questions with the speed and tenor of a machine gun. "Not ever?"

"Not ever."

"Even though there's been a Brandt at the head of Brandt Motors for the last ninety years?"

"I could not have cared less about it."

"But you knew your grandmother wanted you to run the company one day?"

"Yes."

"How much did she want that?"

"Very much."

"Was Lydia aware that you did not want to work in the family business?"

"Yes. What does it matter?"

"Let me ask the questions right now, Miss Brandt. In spite of your personal desires, did she continue to try and groom you for the business?"

"Yes."

"Did you make your personal desires known?"

"Yes, of course."

"How did she react to that?"

"She was not happy."

"Were she alive now, would you be working in the business?"

Shara paused before answering and closed her eyes. Again the brown bottles with her name on them flashed before her eyes. *She tried to medicate me into submission, but I defeated that. She probably thought marrying Richard would do the trick, but he promised me otherwise. What else could she have done?* She looked again to Mr. James, who again said nothing but nodded encouragement. "Possibly."

"So she would be able to force you to take over the business?"

"Lydia generally got what she wanted."

"You're an intelligent, educated young woman. Your records from Marquette show that you graduated last year with a Bachelor's Degree in Business and a Bachelor's Degree in Elementary Education. You even took some pre-law courses, and it looks like you were accepted to law school."

"That's true."

"That's a lot of credits to cram in four years."

"Miss Shara is a supremely intelligent young woman." The pride in Mr. James' voice was unmistakable, and Shara smiled at him, grateful for the kind words. "Mrs. Brandt sensed that and...strongly encouraged Miss Shara to take as many college courses in high school as she could, which put her ahead of the game, so to speak, once she started college."

"Thank you for that unnecessary bit of information, Mr. James." Dinks glowered at the lawyer. "Two degrees from Marquette in four years...that's a lot of education."

"Yes, Detective, it is."

"Didn't leave much time for a social life, did it, Miss Brandt?"

Shara bit her lip, forming a careful answer before she spoke. "High school and college were not about being social, Detective. Grandmother was very interested in having me ready to take over quickly, she insisted I make the most of every minute."

"The Bachelor's in Education. You're a teacher?"

A faint smile crossed her face. "That was something I did on my own, Detective. I wanted to be a teacher, and Mr. James helped me enroll in night courses."

"So you snuck around behind her back in order to get what you wanted? You were that desperate to be out of the business?"

Shara shook her head. "I wouldn't call it desperate, Detective. I would call it following my own set of goals while fulfilling my obligations to my grandmother."

"So she couldn't stop you from doing exactly what you wanted to do, in the long run. So how is it you thought she could force you to take over the business?"

Again Shara looked to Mr. James, and cast a quick glance at the mirror. *They're all in there, waiting for my story.* "My childhood

257

was...not easy. Grandmother's rules were always law in the house, and if I disobeyed her, the punishment was severe." Here Shara inhaled, steeling herself for her next speech. "By the time I was a teenager, she was pretty much sick of my...strong willed ways. Grandmother convinced, or bribed, a doctor I was bipolar, or manic, something, and that I needed a number of different drugs, including lithium to control my mental illness. She found it much easier to keep me in line after that."

Mr. James' lips twitched as this information seemed to surprise the detectives, if only briefly. Chester stopped writing and glanced at her. Dinks, less phased, continued questioning. "So you've been on medication for some time?"

"I started with the medications when I was thirteen, yes."

"Taking lithium for about ten years? "

"I didn't say that."

Dinks leaned over the table and met her eye to eye. "Then how long have you been treated for a mental disorder?"

"I was thirteen the first time I went to see a psychiatrist, and I went to one twice a week until, until...that last night a year ago. I quit taking the drugs when I turned eighteen."

"Quit?" Dinks turned red.

"Quit." Shara smiled, recalling the pride she had the first day she felt no shakiness in her limbs. "It took me a while to realize what was happening to me, how I was losing myself a little bit more every day. I knew I couldn't quit on my own. Mr. James found a doctor who helped me. Grandmother never knew. No one did. The focus I gained back gave me the energy to go to night school."

"You see, gentlemen," Mr. James seemed unphased by the effect Shara's words on the detectives, "this brings into question whether my client is mentally diseased."

"Are you certain you want to tell us that, Counselor? Doesn't that take your insanity plea off the table?"

"I never intended to plead insanity." Mr. James pulled out the taped together document. "I always intended to plead not guilty, given what this document says. You gentlemen of course recognize this as Mrs. Lydia Brandt's last will."

Dinks and Chester both groaned quietly. "Look, Mr. James, we've been over that will. We've looked into all the allegations you've made. None of them panned out."

"None of them panned out quite so well as the theory that Miss Shara was repressed, rebellious, insane, and desperate." Mr. James held up the copy.

"Desperate enough to marry a much older man who promised her freedom. Desperate enough to sneak around to night school getting the degree she wants. I'd say that's desperate." Dinks kept his eyes away from the document. "Isn't that how it happened, Miss Brandt? The will has nothing to with why you shot your grandmother."

"Is that an official question?"

"Yes, Mr. James, it is."

"Then before I advise my client to answer, I'd like you to look at this document. Don't read it, just look at it." Mr. James waved the will in the air in front of Dinks.

"Who tore it up?" Chester paused in his note taking.

Shara blinked again, as if rousing herself from a dream. "Richard did. Yesterday, he tore it up and said I didn't need it, that he would take care of me like he always had."

"Why did he tear it up Miss Brandt?"

"I don't know, Detective Dinks. Mr. James is certain something here clears my name, but Richard seems to think that's not the case. Richard believes...he believes I did it, and he believes I'm quite ill." She bit her lip as a tear rolled down her cheek.

"He was the only eye witness. Other than you and your grandmother."

Shara nodded. "I know. I remember... very little from that night, but I do remember Richard...on the floor...bleeding..."

"You know he has stated that you were the one who pulled the trigger, both on him and on Mrs. Brandt."

"I have heard that." Her voice was little more than a raspy whisper.

"Is that why you ran away, Miss Brandt? Because you knew what Mr. Bennett would say about that night?"

"I didn't run away." Shara stared at the table. "I-I didn't run away, someone put me in the trunk of a car and drove me here."

The oxygen sucked itself out of the room. No one moved, no one spoke.

"I was sitting—on the floor— next to Richard. He was bleeding. And then, and then someone, a woman, grabbed me and put me in the trunk of a car."

Make it look like an accident.

"I'm sorry. Did you just whisper something?" Chester looked up.

Shara looked into the faces surrounding her. "Make it look like an accident. That's what-" She stopped, seeing her grandmother's office clearly for the first time. "Jennifer Tiel. She was in the office. Grandmother startled her. She fired twice. I knelt on the floor, next to Richard and he…"

The lounge door slammed open, the window glass shattering to the floor. Richard yanked Shara up out of her chair and gathered her into his arms. "That is enough! Can't you see she's out of her mind? I'm telling you, she's a frail woman, not one to stand up to all this stress." He pressed her tight against him. "There, there, Baby Doll. There, there. It's gonna be alright isn't it? I'll take care of you, just like I promised. We'll take you home and get you the help you need."

Looking over his shoulder, Shara caught a glimpse of the others standing in the doorway: Jo, Drew, and Molly…Bryan. Resolve washed through her, and she strained against Richard's arms. "Richard, you're hurting me-"

"Mr. Bennett, all of you, I don't know where you were listening to this conversation, but you need to leave. This is a formal police investigation and you are obstructing it!" Dinks slammed his hands on the table.

The crack of flesh against wood startled Richard just long enough for Shara to break away from him. "I remember everything now." She stepped away from Richard, closer to the door. She

260

nodded to Molly, who wore an expression of relief. *It's right there. All the pieces are suddenly right there, I see everything.* Ice gripped her soul as she turned her attention back to her fiancé "Why did you do it, Richard?"

"Why did I do what, Baby Doll?" A shadow of fear darkened his eyes.

Shara's eyes burned with the fury that churned inside her. "Why did you tell Jennifer Tiel to kill me and make it look like an accident?"

81: BRYAN

Standing in the shadowy hall, Bryan struggled to keep from laughing out loud at the expression Richard wore. *Something of a cross between fear and the flu.*

Richard, indeed was a deathly shade of pale, but managed a weak smile. "Shara, baby, you're mistaken. Jennifer Tiel? She's got nothing to do with this."

"Everyone get out right now!" Dinks shouted.

Mr. James spoke up. "No, Detective. Mr. Bennett should stay. I think Mr. Bennett needs to answer some questions."

"Shara, Baby, this is ridiculous. You're hallucinating. You don't even know what you're saying. You need to be in a hospital right now-"

Shara pushed him into a chair, a show of strength that amazed Bryan and made him proud. "Then humor the crazy woman, Richard. Answer the questions the detectives ask you. After-" she held up her hand to stop his protest, "Mr. James reads a bit of my grandmother's will that he might feel is pertinent. After all, sweetheart," her voice dripped with sickly sweet sarcasm, "you wouldn't want a single scrap of evidence that might clear me to be missed, would you...Baby?"

"No. No, of course not." Richard's smile was even weaker.

Now it makes sense. Bryan stood, unable to sit still any longer. He rocked back and forth on his heels, and looked to Drew, who looked as if he'd been struck by lightning. *Now it all makes sense.*

"Very well, Miss Shara. I believe there's just a single passage I need to read. Mr. Shepaski was good enough to high light it before he returned the damaged document to me." Mr. James adjusted his glasses and held up the paper. "According to this, Miss Brandt is the sole beneficiary of her grandmother's estate."

"We know all this Mr. James, really." Dinks paced back and forth, a caged animal ready to roar. "You're wasting our time. And you people should not be in here!"

No one budged as Mr. James hesitated.

"Go ahead, Mr. James, read who else benefits." Bryan couldn't stop himself from whispering. The lawyer, as if he heard Bryan, continued.

"However, should Miss Shara be deceased...or deemed mentally incompetent...then Mr. Richard Bennett inherits everything."

"Mr. James, we've been over this time and time again. While it might look as if Mr. Bennett had motive to murder Mrs. Brandt, it simply doesn't add up. We're supposed to believe that he shot the old woman and then turned the gun on himself, and then Miss Brandt just fled the scene for no reason?" Dinks' argument was smooth, rehearsed, as if he'd said it many times.

"I didn't flee the scene, Detective; Jennifer Tiel put me in the trunk of her car and drove me here." Shara closed her eyes. "Jennifer Tiel walked into the office that night. She started talking about how I would never have Richard, how I didn't deserve my family's money. Then Richard and Grandmother...they walked in and surprised her, I think. She just fired. Hit Richard first, because he was in front of Grandmother, and then hit Grandmother." Shara blinked. No one in either room breathed, waiting for her next words. "And then, Richard, you said... you said to her, 'Make it look like an accident.' Everything was dark then for a while." She turned cold eyes to her fiancé. "Why, Richard? Why?"

"Damage control." Bryan said under his breath.

Molly sidled back to him, a light of realization in her eyes. "He never intended to kill the old woman, did he?"

"He didn't plan to, I'm sure. But Jenny..." Bryan's head throbbed at the thought of his ex wife. "Jenny can be volatile."

"Gentlemen, I assure you, Miss Brandt is raving. Jennifer Tiel is a...business associate of mine. She's been quite helpful in the last few months, procuring business connections in parts of the state outside of Milwaukee." Richard wiped his forehead. "I assure you, she was no part of this, this scenario that Shara's poor mind has created."

"So you're denying any romantic involvement with Miss Tiel." Chester's pen flew across the page.

Deny it. Go ahead and deny it, and give me the supreme pleasure of kicking your dress shirted ass out of this building. Bryan grit his teeth at the very idea.

"Miss Tiel and I had a relationship some years ago, that's true. But we parted long before Miss Brandt and I were ever engaged."

"On good terms?"

"I-yes, yes of course."

"Really?" Shara got up out of her chair for the first time and took a step back from Richard. "You think you and Jennifer broke up on good terms?" She shook her head. "Richard, it wasn't even four years ago. I was young, not blind. Grandmother made you break up and you did it to protect your job."

All eyes turned to Richard, who held his hands out in a helpless gesture. "Do you now understand what I'm talking about? As if Lydia Brandt cared about anything her employees did outside of the office."

"Well, that's true, Richard, but she caught you and Jennifer inside the office...on your desk, I believe." The shadow of sad smile crossed her face.

"He does like to do things in unconventional places, doesn't he?" Bryan murmured through clenched teeth.

"Grandmother made you break up with Jennifer and fire her. Not three days later, Jennifer Tiel drove her car through the show room window."

"Well, Mr. Bennett, I wouldn't call that a break up on good terms." Dinks shook his head. "But that still doesn't prove anything, Mr. James. That doesn't prove Miss Tiel was there that night. There simply wasn't any evidence that anyone else was in the room, and only Miss Brandt's prints were on the gun." This time Dinks sounded almost sorry. "And there's still no motive for Mr. Bennett. If Miss Brandt's crazy, he inherits. If she's dead he inherits. Hell, if they're married, he gets it all. Why would he muddy the waters?"

"What I'm struggling with is the part about this Jennifer Tiel driving, Miss Brandt, some three hours away and letting you go."

"She didn't let me go. She got a flat or something and had to open the trunk. We struggled, and I got away."

"The sheriff's department never found an abandoned car on the highway. Miss Brandt didn't just fly here," Kelly added very helpfully. Bryan grinned, recalling how that small detail was so easily explained away the night before.

"There's one other bit in the will that I haven't read yet. And in light of Miss Shara's recollection, I believe this is pertinent, Detectives." Mr. James cleared his throat. "Mr. Bennett would inherit if Miss Shara were declared mentally incompetent, or were deceased, by natural causes." Here he lowered the will and gazed at Richard. "Should she be murdered, Mr. Bennett would not inherit." He cleared his throat again. "I cannot guess what was in her mind the day she drew up this will, Detectives, but as I've told you, Mrs. Brandt said to me, 'He swears to protect her, swears he's going to protect her from me. Well, my boy's going to protect her from everyone, including himself.'"

"Crap." Dinks bit his lip. "What was it Mr. Bennett allegedly said?"

Chester flipped through his notes. "'Make it look like an accident.'"

"That's what you said to Jennifer, Richard. And then she hit me over the head with something."

"And Mr. James' previous arguments about another person in there, with gloves or something, now that would hold up." Chester

264

looked up from his notes. "Things are a bit murky at any rate. I think we need to find this Jennifer Tiel."

"She's been seen around here the last couple of days."

That Kelly Fuller, a very helpful guy.

"I doubt you'll find her here, gentlemen. Miss Tiel used to live here and does not have…good memories of Rock Harbor." Richard turned smug eyes to the doorway. "She was in Green Bay on business earlier this week, but I haven't seen or heard from her in days. If Deputy Fuller says she's been in Rock Harbor, that's news to me."

He's still covering something up. Bryan ached to punch him again, but stayed as still as possible. *But why is Richard lying about Jennifer being here? He had to know she was up here.*

Unless he doesn't want anyone to know that he knew she was here.

82: SHARA

Everyone started talking at once, the din in the room growing to a roar. Shara's head swam with the sound. "I need to use the restroom." The conversations didn't quiet, so she cleared her throat and shouted. "Excuse me! I need to use the restroom!"

All mouths closed and all eyes focused again on her.

"Fine. Chester, take her." Dinks pointed a beefy finger at his partner.

"No, I'll go with her." Molly took a step towards Shara.

"No, I'm going to go all by myself."

"No, you're not, Miss Brandt. You're under arrest."

"Yes, I am Detective Dinks. The girls' restroom is two doors down from here. I'm going alone. You can continue deciding what, exactly, you're going to do with me, and I'll be right back before you are finished."

"How do we know you won't run away?"

Shara squared her shoulders. "Detective Dinks. Where, exactly, would I go, and how would I get there? In the last forty eight hours

I have been trapped in a burning building, nearly crushed by a horse, shuffled in and out of a hospital twice, been shot at, been arrested, and been questioned. Now I found out that my fiancé was part of a plot to have me murdered. I have a broken arm. I am tired beyond words. I have the most recognizable face in the state. All I want to do is go two doors down the hall, and use the restroom. Alone." She gave the collected audience in the room a look that dared anyone to speak. "No objections?" She glared at each face, daring them to question her. Seeing and hearing no objection, she turned and left the room.

The hallway was darker and quieter than the teachers' lounge. She pushed open the girls' restroom door with her shoulder and flipped on the light. The restroom was also the girls' locker room, and Shara stared at the far end of the room, through the shower room, through the lockers, where another heavy door lead to the gym. *If I had a prayer of running away, this would be my chance. But there's no point now, now that the truth is out.* She leaned against the sink and splashed some water on her face.

"Damn it, Richard." She spoke softly to her reflection in the mirror. "What could have been so hard about just loving me? We could have been happy."

"Doubtful."

Shara startled at the voice behind her. The face in the mirror, next to hers, was Jennifer Tiel's.

"Jennifer."

Jennifer smiled at her, moving slowly like a cat about to pounce, and positioned herself between Shara and the hallway door. "Yes."

Shara bit back the fear that bubbled up in her throat and tried to keep her calm. "What do you want from me?"

"I'm here to finish the job Richard gave me." Jennifer held up the handgun in a casual manner.

Shara touched her face as if she'd been slapped. "The job he gave you?"

"Of course. You know Richard. Every detail has to be checked and double checked." Jennifer looked at her reflection in the mirror and smoothed her hair.

Shara didn't miss the raw marks on Jennifer's wrists. "What happened to you?"

Jennifer blinked, as if trying to remember something. "Every detail has to be checked and double checked. Now I have to check you off the list." She made a check mark motion in the air with the handgun.

Shara kept her gaze locked on the gun. "You can't. Everyone's just down the hall, and if you make any noise, they'll come in here and catch you. Then you'll be the one with nothing."

Jennifer smiled again at her. "Poor, poor deluded Shara Brandt. I tried to explain this to you the last time. No one cares about you. Not your grandmother, not Richard. They see you as a means to an end. For your grandmother, it was all about keeping the family in the family business. For Richard, it was about the money, pure and simple."

"He would have gotten that if he'd married me." Shara kept her eyes glued on the gun. *It couldn't have been just about the money.* "I can't believe a word you say."

"I'm the only one who's being honest with you. Think about it, little girl. When he can have this," Jennifer swiveled her hips and tossed her hair, "why on earth should he look at you? It's the money. He didn't want to be saddled with you his whole life. He wanted me. No one's ever wanted you."

"That's not true." Shara stared at Jennifer, hypnotized by her purring voice and green eyes. *Bryan.*

As if reading her mind, Jennifer continued. "As for my ex husband, I saw that little moment you two had in the barn." Jennifer moved a step closer and lowered her voice even more. "You can't think for a moment that that had anything to do with him loving you, do you? That was all about me. He's never gotten over me." She laughed and tossed her hair again. "So you see, little girl, no one wants you. You may as well give up and put yourself out of everyone's misery." She leaned forward, her lips all but touching Shara's ear. "I'll make it painless for you, I promise."

"Shara, are you-"

Jennifer whirled around, slamming her weight against the door into Joanna. The spell broken, Shara leaped away and stumbled through the locker room. She shoved the heavy door open with her shoulder and ran into the darkened gym, Jennifer close behind.

83: BRYAN

Bored with the mini drama in the lounge, Bryan stepped in the less noisy hallway and watched as Joanna went to check on Shara. Joanna's startled cry of pain sparked Bryan to move before the others had time to react. "Jo, are you okay?"

"She, she slammed the door in my face..." Joanna, covered her face with her hands, but a trickle of blood seeped through from her nose.

Bryan helped her to her feet. "Shara slammed the door on you?"

"I don't think she's in there alone, Bryan. I thought I heard someone else talking." Fear clouded her eyes as she looked up at the crowd now assembled in the hall.

"Jenny." Bryan pushed open the locker room door. "We have to find them."

Mr. James helped Molly walk Joanna back to the teacher's lounge, while Kelly, Richard, Dinks, and Chester followed Bryan and Drew into the locker room. The sharp echo of single shot froze them in their tracks.

Bryan's stomach churned. *Jenny's here and she has a gun.* Fighting his gag reflex, Bryan kicked open the door and dove into the darkness of the gym.

84: SHARA

"Stand still so I can do this!" Jennifer's voice was raspy, a few feet behind Shara.

Crossing the gym, Shara made her way down the dark, windowless stairs to the school basement where she hoped she could escape through the kitchen.

Now in the stairwell behind her, Jennifer fired a second shot, this one hitting the stair wall inches above Shara's shoulder. *Jennifer can't see me, but she's getting closer.* Shara stayed quiet as possible, hoping she made herself difficult to track in the dark.

"No one wants you, just give up!"

The heavy gray light from the high, narrow windows in the kitchen was little better than the darkness of the stairs. Pain throbbed in Shara's arm as she groped the wall with her good hand to the windowless pantry. Breathless, she crouched in the dark near the shelves of canned goods and waited for Jennifer to run past her.

"I have to do this, Shara Brandt. With you still alive, I can never have Richard for myself. He'll stay true to your money; he'll stay true to you. But with you dead..." Jennifer tripped against a stainless steel table. "Dammit."

She's getting closer. Shara squinted in the darkness, but saw little. Bracing herself against the shelves, her hand brushed against a metal can. *Soup cans.* She armed herself with one and waited as Jennifer approached.

"It's over!" Jennifer fired blindly.

In the flash of the gun's muzzle Shara saw her enemy clearly. Summoning up a deep reserve of strength, Shara hurled the soup can in Jennifer's direction, making contact. Cursing loudly, Jennifer charged the pantry and crashed in to Shara, slamming her to the floor on her cast. Lightning bolts of pain shot through Shara's arm.

Cloaked in darkness, the two wrestled in the small space. Shara grasped another can and smashed it against Jennifer's head. Screeching with pain, Jennifer rolled away from her, just as the overhead light flared on. Momentarily blinded, Shara grasped one more can and chucked it hard. A male voice howled and somewhere, close to her, Bryan murmured, "Nice shot."

Shara blinked away the bright light and saw Detective Dinks, five feet away, rubbing his shoulder and glaring at her. She couldn't stifle a weak grin.

With a primal scream, Jennifer lunged at Shara, knocking her flat. Drew, Dinks, and Chester flew together as one, and pushed Jennifer back, pinning her against the far wall. Bryan knelt beside Shara, but she did not look at him. More than any pain in her body, she ached for the answers she knew Jennifer held. *This all ends now.*

"Wait a minute," Shara stood with Bryan's help and held a hand up to the men holding Jennifer. "Before you ...do whatever you're going to do...I have to ask Jennifer some questions."

"You got a minute." Dinks glared at her. "That's it."

"Jennifer." Shara's voice was low and calm as she stepped closer to the restrained woman. "Who came up with the idea to shoot me at the dealership?"

Jennifer's laugh was a sharp cackle. "That was all Richard. I was to sneak in, shoot you, tear up the place, leave before he and Lydia showed up." She stopped struggling and sagged against the wall. "He knew all about the will, about the murder part. He figured if you were murdered and he was actually with Lydia, she couldn't hold him responsible. Then he could have it all, and he wouldn't have to marry you." Jennifer's defiant tone faded to a low hiss as she glared from under the curtain of her red hair at Shara. "The problem was, you...you simply wouldn't die."

"I see." Shara blinked back angry tears. "Which means, Richard," she turned her gaze to Richard, who stood on the far side of the island counter. "You lied to me the entire time we were engaged, didn't you? It was all about the money."

"Shara..." Richard looked over his shoulder glancing at the accusing faces close to him. "Dinks, you cannot believe a word Jennifer Tiel says. She's insane."

"I gotta say there Mr. Bennett, either you're lying to us, which would be a huge mistake, or you have monumentally bad luck picking women, given that both the women you're involved with are mentally unstable, in your opinion." Dinks kept Jennifer still, but stared daggers at Richard. "I guess, Miss Brandt, since Mr. Bennett seems at a loss, maybe Miss Tiel can answer your question."

Shara shut all the faces around her and focused on Jennifer Tiel. "Jennifer, did Richard ever love me?"

Jennifer raised her head enough for Shara to see her vague smile. "He's incapable of love."

Shara swayed slightly, her legs threatening to give way. She sensed Bryan stepping closer behind her, but she ignored him. *I have to hear this. We all have to hear this.* "Prove it. Prove this was all his idea and not something you did out of jealousy and now you're lying to get out of trouble."

"Jealous? Of you? " Jennifer tossed her head back and laughed again. "Proving it is easy. Look at your ring."

"My ring?"

"Your engagement ring."

Molly, followed by Joanna, who held a wet bloody towel to her face, walked into the kitchen. "You weren't wearing a ring, when we found you, Shara. But you had been. When we found you, there was a ridge on your ring finger and some torn skin."

"The ring Richard gave me was a little too small. I was going to get it sized."

"You do have chubby fingers for someone so otherwise…unremarkable." Jennifer sneered, her lips curled back from her teeth. "You don't have it?"

"No. Do you?"

Jennifer nodded her head and cackled. "I took it. Richard packed you in the trunk, but I squeezed that ring off your fat little finger first."

"Jennifer, that's a lie!" Richard slammed his hands on the stainless steel table.

Jennifer blinked, a look of exaggerated innocence on her face. "No, I really did take the ring…oh, you mean packing her in the trunk. Well, I certainly didn't do it."

"You can't possibly believe a word she says! She shot me!"

"Wait a minute!" Dinks rubbed his face. "Miss Brandt said she knelt next to Bennett, that he was shot. But when we got there, he was sitting in the chair."

Richard made a strange choking sound. "What is that supposed to matter?"

"It matters because you told us Miss Brandt shot you and you fell into the chair." Dinks rubbed his face again. "Turns out, your memory might not be quite as …objective as we first thought."

Shara shot a glance to Richard, who looked like a rabid dog. "Why would you want it, Jennifer?"

"Oh, I'm a practical girl above everything else. I thought I might need it, someday." Jennifer looked at each face in the room, pausing as she stared at Richard. "Sort of my insurance policy. Shara, dear, why don't you describe the ring?" Jennifer didn't take her eyes off of Richard.

Neither did Shara, who watched Richard's composure crumble with every word. "It was silver. A square diamond and emeralds around it. It was a tall setting, too. I always snagged it on my sweaters." Behind her, Shara heard Bryan suck in his breath.

Jennifer let out an over dramatic sigh. "Platinum, little girl, not silver. But everything else you got right. And the inscription?"

"Inscription?" This question confused Shara. She looked from face to face for help, but everyone wore an expression of fascinated helplessness. Except for Bryan. Looking over her shoulder at him, Shara thought Bryan looked…angry.

Jennifer rolled her eyes at Shara. "Any words carved inside the band?"

"I-I never looked." Shara glanced again at Richard, who was leaning his full weight on the stainless steel table, his face ashen. *What could you have possibly had engraved in the ring that would be of use to Jennifer?*

Jennifer wore a triumphant smile. "Well, let's see if someone else in the room can't help you. Meddling Molly? Any guess? No? Mr. James? You know everything. Any thoughts? Detective Dinks, certainly you have an idea."

"Get on with it Jenny."

Shara turned around to look at Bryan. He was a pitiful figure, from the stitches in his scalp down to the tattered ribbons of gauze hanging from his hands. Yet there was a glimmer in his eyes, something fearsome and furious, that sparked a current deep inside her. Instinctively, she reached her hand out to him. *Your secret will be safe with me.*

He brushed her hand aside, but kept his eyes on her. "Guess it's my turn to answer a question, right?" He murmured just loudly enough for her to hear.

"Ah yes. My darling *ex* husband. Go ahead, Bryan. Maybe you can guess what's inscribed in the ring."

The fire left Bryan's eyes as he looked away from Shara and stood straighter. "'Two become one.' That's what it says."

"The hell it does! You're lying, Jacobs!" Richard shouted. "He's always hated me because his wife fell in love with me!" Richard's face contorted into something truly dark and ugly as he glowered at the gathered group. "Deputy," he turned wild eyes to Kelly, "you saw him punch me in the hospital yesterday! You know you can't believe anything Bryan Jacobs says about me!"

Kelly, still pinning Jennifer's left shoulder against the wall, glanced at Richard then shook his head. "I saw a brief scuffle between two men, Mr. Bennett. If you want my honest opinion, you started it." Kelly fired a grin to Shara so quickly, no one else saw it.

"I should've known, all you small town hicks are the same. Doesn't matter you're a cop, you're going to stand up for your buddy, aren't you?" Richard's face contorted into a sneer.

"Now, just a moment, Mr. Bennett." Chester loosed his grip on Jennifer's right shoulder. "Mr. Jacobs didn't say a word about you. He was talking about Miss Brandt's engagement ring. We could prove him wrong, if we had the ring."

Jennifer tossed her hair back and stood straighter, strangely calm. "Detective, if you'd like, the ring is in my left jacket pocket. There you go." She nodded to Chester, who retrieved a ring box from her, and opened it.

Squinting, Chester looked at the ring inside and out. "He's right. It's a little hard to see, but I think that's what it says."

"Damn it Jennifer! You stupid bitch!"

A creepy smile of triumph crossed her face as Jennifer ignored Richard's outburst. "Now, Bryan, dearest, how on earth would you know what's inscribed in the engagement ring Richard Bennett gave to Shara Brandt?"

"Because," Bryan swallowed hard, as if something bitter lingered in his mouth. "Because it's your ring, Jenny. It's the ring I gave you."

There was a general titter of disbelief, but it didn't register in Shara's consciousness. Switching her gaze from Bryan to Richard and back, she felt weak and dizzy. *Air. I need air. I need to get out of here.*

"So you see, Shara, dear, your precious Richard didn't love you enough to even bother buying you a ring. He borrowed mine and gave it to you, because he knew from the first that he wasn't going to marry you." Jennifer cackled. "Isn't that the bit of information you were really hoping I wouldn't tell, Richard, darling? Is that why you tied me to the bed last night?"

"We don't need to hear this!" Dinks moved to stand in front of her.

"Oh no, you have to hear it all, Detective, really. See, Richard was late getting to his hotel last night, wasn't he?"

"We didn't see him after he dropped us off."

"He stopped by my motel room last night. We had dinner...and dessert." Her green eyes flashed. "And then what did you do Richard? You tied me to the bed, but not for fun, right? You tied my hands to the bed legs and looped the rope around my throat, so that if I struggled, I'd choke myself to death. Look." She held her hand forward, revealing the raw, red marks on her wrists. "And look here." She tilted her head up to expose the red line across her throat. "Good thing the housekeeper's nosey, or people would think I killed myself." She relaxed, her hair falling over her face again. "Turns out, neither one of us is any good at killing people." Her voice was faint, weak.

274

"Richard." Shara took three steps toward him. He raised his eyes to her, and any doubt she had about the truth of Jennifer's words was washed away in the hateful light that glowed there. She took one more step toward him. "You lied to me. You plotted against me." *No more fear. No more.* "You shoved me in a trunk, and told your girlfriend to kill me." She cocked her head to the side, and studied his face, the fury that masked his underlying fear. "You can go to hell, you bastard." She swung at him, and her fist caught the corner of his perfect jaw. Pain and triumph shot up her arm.

Jennifer howled wildly with crazed mirth, swinging her body back and forth. Dinks and the others struggled to keep hold of her. With a last quick, hateful glance fired at Shara, Richard fled through the back door.

"Get him!" Dinks shouted at Chester and Kelly, who raced after Richard.

Bryan crumpled to the floor, bringing Jo and Molly to his side. The room erupted with noise and activity. Alone, Shara took stock of the chaos.

Air. I need air.

Without a word, she walked out the back door into the rain.

85: BRYAN

Sirens wailed in the distance. Bryan leaned against the sturdy leg of the stainless steel table and closed his eyes while Jo and Molly hovered over him. *It's over.* He closed his eyes, barely aware of the two women chirping comforting platitudes. He ached to do nothing more than sink into warm blackness. *Just float away and forget it all.*

"Where's Shara?"

"What do you mean?"

"She's not here in the kitchen, is she?"

Bryan ignored the commotion around him. *She's probably sitting in a corner and they can't see her.*

"She's not in here, Mol. She wouldn't have gone outside. It's pouring."

Bryan opened one eye and watched Joanna, the front of her shirt dappled with her own blood, stride across the length of the kitchen.

"She's got to be in here, Jo. Check the pantry. Shara? Shara?" Molly sat back on her haunches, looking around the kitchen.

"She's not in here, Mol. Where is she?"

Molly got up from the floor and joined the search. Closing his eyes again, Bryan listened to the women continue squawking back and forth, moving around the kitchen as if Shara would be hiding under some pot or pan. Elsewhere in the room, the detectives read Jennifer her rights and dragged her out the back door.

His eyes still closed, Bryan sensed someone squatting next to him. Wedging one eye open just a crack, he looked up at Drew. "What?"

"You okay?"

"I'll live."

"Good, because Shara is missing." Drew stood and walked to the stairwell.

Alone, Bryan sat on the floor of the school kitchen, listening to the jumble of sounds: sirens, male shouts, and the hiss of rain softening the harsh voices. Above it all, Bryan listened to Jennifer shrieking curses down on everyone. *Charming. How did I ever let her get away from me?*

Shara.

Bryan opened his eyes and looked around the kitchen. The rain beat hard against the windows. *It's a cold rain. She'll need a coat, wherever she goes.*

He pulled himself to a stand, wincing as his hands protested movement. The stairs, the gym, and hall to the teachers' lounge were empty. All activity was now in the school atrium, where voices, especially Jennifer's, were amplified by the height of the space. Somewhere, outside, someone shouted for Richard to stop running. *What does any of this matter? All that matters is that Shara is hiding again.*

Her coat lay where he'd left it, on the back of Drew's desk chair. Gingerly, he picked it up and tucked it over his arm. *Now, where is she?*

Where could she go in a short time, on foot?

Drew's house. Across the street to the church. These places, Bryan knew, Molly and Jo were scouring.

No, she won't be there. She'll be someplace outside, where no one is looking.

"Bryan," Drew trotted quickly up the dark hall, as if trying to outrun the symphony of voices in the atrium. "Where are you going?"

"The creek."

"Bryan, it's pouring."

"I'm aware of that." Bryan pulled away from his friend. Once outside, the rain slapped him like a cold hand. He crossed the parking lot, down the slope toward the creek. *This is where it all began. This is where she'll be.*

Bryan looked along the edge of the creek, and saw nothing. Glancing to his right, he saw her, draped on a swing like a wet blanket, rocking back and forth slowly. Stepping carefully over the rain-slick ground, Bryan walked up behind her. "Shara."

"That's my name."

His heart shattered. The anguish in her voice, so raw, sang to his bruised soul. He knelt beside her and put a hand on the swing chain. "Everyone's looking for you."

"Don't know why. It's not like I'd get far. Where, exactly, would I go?" She raised dead, tear stained eyes to him, her soft voice only an echo of those words she'd spoken to him a lifetime ago.

"Here," he covered her shoulders with the coat. "Thought you might want this."

"Thanks."

"You, uh, wanna come inside?"

"No."

"Okay, then." He knelt back down and waited.

"Why can't anyone love just me?"

The question caught him off guard and he wavered from his kneeling position as if pushed. "What-I mean...what?"

She shivered and hung her head lower. "No one's ever just loved me for me. It's all strings and conditions."

"Look, Shara," he moved around in front of her, and halted her back and forth motion. "Shara, there is nothing at all wrong with you." He closed his eyes, remembering his own contribution to her misery, "Real life just sort of beats the crap out of you." Bryan wiped raindrops out of his eyes and shook his head. "It's not you." He put his hands over her one good hand. "The rest of the world is messed up."

She peered at him from under her hair and her mouth trembled in a half smile. She looked back down and a teardrop fell to his hands in her lap. "Bryan-your hands!"

"Oh, yeah." He tried to pull them away, to hide them.

"What happened?" She kept a weak grip on them. Unable to struggle, he let his hands fall limp under her touch.

"I-uh-well, apparently, I'm not Superman and I am not impervious to fire."

She inhaled sharply, but did not look at him. "These are burns, from the fire?"

"Yes."

"How did you get burned?"

"No one told you?"

She shook her head. "No one told me much about you."

"They didn't want you to freak out, I'll bet." He forced a grin, hoping it looked more sincere to her than it felt to him. She didn't look up. "Anyway, I got burned lifting a beam from...from off of Rika."

"So it was you..."

"Yeah."

She was quiet for a moment, as if choosing her next words carefully. "You saved my life."

Bryan inhaled, trying to reign in the guilt that tightened his throat. *Just admit it all and be done.* "You wouldn't have needed saving if I hadn't locked you in the barn. Shara I'm..."

"This," she broke in, lifting a trembling fingers to his hairline. "This didn't come from the fire."

Her nearly imperceptible touch soothed the ache in Bryan's head a little. "That would be the work of the ex. She came to the cabin looking for you."

"I'm…sorry. I'm so sorry." The curtain fell between them again.

"No, no. There's nothing to be sorry about. You're not to blame for anything."

She raised tear-swollen eyes to him, the rain matting her hair to her scalp. "I am! If I'd told the truth from the first, no one would have been in danger; no one would have been hurt!" She gulped back a sob. "None of this would have happened."

"Listen to me!" He grasped her face in his hands, brushing wet hair from her eyes. "Listen to me, none of this is your fault! Do you hear me? What happened here," he held up a hand, " and here," he pointed to his head, " is because of what I did, because of my stupid, stupid jealousy, I couldn't bear the idea that you'd-that you'd been with *him*…" he stopped, unable to continue the thought. "I should have protected you, and instead I hurt you most of all." He took a deep breath. "As long as I live, I will never forgive myself for what's happened to you the last couple days." He sat silent, waiting for a response from her. There was none. *It's really over.* "Hey, look, it's getting really cold out here, how about if we go inside?" He stood and held out his hand.

Shara stood, but swayed unsteadily. Bryan reached out and caught her just as she was about to fall. "Easy there."

"S-sorry." Her voice quavered, her body shook from the cold rain.

"Let me carry you, okay?" Without response from her, Bryan scooped her up into his arms and held her close.

"B-but your hands…"

"Don't think about it." Her familiar scent of strawberries was diluted by the rain, and Bryan was reminded of that first day, so long ago. *This is where we started.* She rested her head in the hollow below his chin, and stayed still as he strode to the school.

The teachers' lounge was empty. He eased Shara onto the sofa. "I'm gonna go get some towels and blankets, okay? I'll be right back."

She shivered and nodded at him. He found towels in the cabinet in the first aid cabinet, next to a stack of quilts. *Good old Granny. Kept her mind active and kept RHCS stocked with hand-made quilts.* Loaded with towels and two quilts, he returned to the teachers' lounge.

Back at her side, Bryan tried to dry her off, but his hands were clumsy. "Screw it!" With his teeth he ripped off the remnants of wrappings from his right hand and then his left, and, ignoring the stinging protest of his raw, broken skin upon contact with the towel, he managed to help her dry off a bit and wrap her in a quilt. "Is that any better?"

Shara nodded and sunk into the battered sofa.

"You want something? Coffee, wait, I think we have some hot chocolate somewhere. Maybe some soup?" He hopped up to fetch things, anything. *Stay busy. Keep moving.*

"B-Bryan? I-I need-"

"Socks." He stared at her feet. "You need warm socks." He started out the door.

"Bryan, stop." This time her voice was stronger, almost commanding. "I need to say something."

He stopped, his back turned to her. "Okay." He tensed, waiting for her to say the words that would close the door between them forever. *And I deserve it.*

"I never slept with Richard." Her voice faded to a whisper. "I've never…slept with anyone."

A bolt of joy surged through him, instantly followed with an icy slap of comprehension. *That just makes me more of a bastard.* His shoulders sagged under the weight of his new guilt. Slowly, with heavy steps, he walked back to the sofa, ready for the condemnation he deserved. "Shara, I'll never be able to tell you how sorry I am for what happened in the barn. I wasn't thinking-we'd just found out, you know, about you. After Jenny, and it was Richard again and I-" he knelt at the side of the sofa, in a penitent position, his hands folded near her leg. He glanced at her and looked away quickly, ashamed to meet her gaze. "And you never- and I was so-I was such a monster." He paused, steeling himself for her response. "There's no forgiving what I've done."

"Yes, there is." Shara bowed forward and touched his shoulder. "You said it yourself. When two people love each other enough, they can forgive anything."

Her whispery caress broke him, and Bryan crumpled into her one-armed embrace.

"Do you believe that?" He kept his voice low, as if speaking out loud would wake her from whatever dream she was in and remind her of his part in her pain.

She moved her arm away and let him sit up on the edge of the sofa. "Yes."

"Shara." His voice husky, Bryan tucked a strand of wet hair behind her ear. Leaning forward, he cupped her face in his hands and touched his lips to hers.

In that still moment, all was forgiven. Bryan closed his eyes and let the warmth of her gentle touch wash over him. His last frozen edge of doubt thawed in one heartbeat that left him breathless.

He drew away from her, but still cradled her face. "That was how our first kiss was supposed to be."

Shara smiled at him. "Have you given any thought about our second kiss?"

Joy flooded him and he returned her smile. "As a matter of fact, yes."

She accepted his kiss again, this time responding with a passion of her own. Pain, sorrow, betrayal gave way to their mutual desire and the rest of the world melted away as they clung to each other.

86: MOLLY

"We've searched this place from top to bottom. You don't think they took off together, do you? Bryan can't drive, though. I mean, Drew said-"

"Jo, shhh," Molly waved her friend quiet as she stopped short in the doorway of the teachers' lounge. There, on the sofa, were Bryan and Shara, bonded in a kiss.

"Hey, did you two-"

"Drew-shhh!" Jo shushed her husband and pointed to the sofa.

As if suddenly aware they had an audience, Bryan and Shara separated, but smiled at each other, a smile of unbounded joy. Molly looked to the ceiling. *She's looking at him like I used to look at Robert.*

"If you guys are done getting your jollies watching us, come on in." Bryan never took his eyes from Shara as he spoke.

"About time you two figured it out," Jo gave Shara a quick shoulder hug.

"You realize, Bryan, there'll be no living with these two now," Drew grumbled, nodding at Molly and Jo. "I'll never stop hearing, 'I told you so,' for the rest of my life!"

"Bryan Jacobs, what on earth have you done to your bandages? And Shara, your cast!" Molly, unable to push aside her nursing instincts, knelt beside the two. "We have to get you guys back to the hospital."

"Okay, Mol." Shara didn't look at her.

"Right away." Bryan kept his gaze on Shara.

Joanna grinned at Molly. "Say, Molly, isn't that little brunette nurse still working a shift? I'll bet she'll just love to see Bryan for a third time, won't she? I mean, she can tell the town they're dating!"

Bryan laughed and made a face at Joanna. "She may want to." He returned his attention to Shara. "But this heart throb of Rock Harbor is officially off the market."

Molly watched Shara's face as it broke into a radiant smile. *We've done our job. Heaven help anyone who tries to break them up now.*

87: SHARA

A ring of pale skin on her left arm was the only souvenir Shara wore from the dramatic events two months earlier. As she walked down the aisle on Drew's arm, she looked out over the congregation, at all the faces of her family and friends. She found it impossible to remember being part of any community other than this.

Rock Harbor Community Church was a packed house. Emma led the procession to the altar where Nate, looking handsome and grown up in a suit, waited with Bryan. Everyone was there: Dave and all the Triple D girls; Bennie, the local newspaper editor, who had run a ten part series about her, a series that was picked up by every newspaper in the state, and two papers nationally; Molly, of course, waited with Joanna at the altar; Mr. James, who held Gracie and dabbed his eyes as she walked by in Joanna's smooth ivory satin wedding dress. And, in the far back corner, an older couple sat quietly. A tear welled in Shara's eye and she noticed the unmistakable resemblance the older man had to Bryan.

Bryan. Her heart sang at the very thought of him.

In two months she'd lived a lifetime in the friendly confines of the Shepaski home. She saw Bryan every day, but between her daily meetings with Mr. James about her grandmother's estate, the physical therapy both she and Bryan endured, and Bryan's school schedule, there was time for little more than a quick good night kiss on Drew's front stoop. A shiver ran up her spine as she recalled the barely contained desire that glowed between them, cooled only by the brisk fall air.

She'd been ready to give herself to Bryan, the moment they removed the bandages from his hands. But he staunchly refused and not, as she first thought, because of morals clause in his contract. It was more like he wanted to protect her virginity...from himself. *Like it's some precious gemstone or something.* She felt the color rise in her face as she thought about later...their first time together.

Looking over her shoulder at the assembled faithful, Shara knew the decision to live at the Shepaski house over those weeks was the

283

right one. Each smiling face glowed with support, love, and acceptance, devoid of any disapproval or condemnation. Even Mrs. King had given her a hearty hug just before the ceremony.

I might just be getting this whole church thing. Nothing in my past matters to them. All I had to do was live like an honorable person and they accept me. One small, insignificant string that binds them together. That binds me to them.

She recalled, again, the glimmer in Bryan's eyes. *But it hasn't been easy!*

Drew lifted the veil from her face, and gave her a quick kiss on the cheek. He paused, looking as if he wanted to say something. Drew's expression was so fatherly, Shara blinked back tears, and touched the locket resting lightly at the base of her throat. She doubted her own father could have been as loving as the man now stepping aside and taking his place as best man.

Taking Bryan's hand at the altar, Shara rubbed her thumb across the burn scar on his hand. While his skin would always be sensitive, Bryan had regained almost complete use of his hands. *And any other wounds we might have will heal in time.*

Shara closed her eyes as Pastor King read the words over them that had united couples for generations. She still startled at the sound of her full name spoken out loud. She'd wanted to change her name, legally, to Bethany Elias, but Bryan protested, pointing out that her parents gave her a name. To change it would cut her link to them.

Repeating after Pastor King, she and Bryan exchanged oaths and simple gold bands. No elaborate speeches, no intricate, sparkling gemstones needed or wanted to mark this union.

"You may now kiss the bride."

Bryan leaned forward and grinned at her. "Ready?"

She nodded, unsure of what he meant. He swooped her up in his arms, kissed her in a manner unsuitable for church, she was sure, and carried her out to thunderous applause. He deposited her in the passenger's seat of his Jeep, the grin firmly in place.

"Bryan Jacobs, you do have a flare for the dramatic, don't you?"

Bryan jumped into the drivers' seat and started up the Jeep. "I do, Shara Beth Jacobs." He kissed her quickly and laughed. "How dramatic would it be if we skipped the party and just went home?" He gave her another, more lingering kiss this time.

She kept her eyes closed, savoring his kiss. "Sounds very tempting. But no."

"No?" He gave her a disappointed look.

She batted his shoulder with her hand. "Are you kidding? This is going to be an awesome party, and I'm not missing it! Let's get going!"

Bryan threw the Jeep in gear and laughed, "My life as a married man begins!"

88: BRYAN

Dave's was filled to capacity and Teachers' Pets kept the party going. Proud as Bryan was of his new wife while she sang and entertained their guests, he was far more eager to get her home. Finally, at midnight, he nodded to Kelly Fuller to stop playing.

"Ladies and gentlemen, the bride and groom are going to leave now, but they wanted to thank everyone for coming tonight. They also ask that no one come out to the farm for the next couple days as they will be…busy."

Here a raucous cheer went up from the revelers. Kelly waved them to silence. "We, the guys in the band, have a gift for Shara and Bryan. Bryan, if you'd come up here and sit with Shara…"

Bryan eased through the crowd assembled around the stage and sat next to Shara. "Any idea what this is?"

Shara shook her head and looked back at Kelly.

"Most of you know that it was Shara here who pushed us to do original material. We owe a lot to her. I owe a lot to her." Kelly cleared his throat and blushed. "Bryan, you are the luckiest guy I know, getting Shara to marry you."

"Don't I know it," Bryan grinned at Kelly and put his arm around Shara.

"Anyway, we think you guys are great, really inspiring, and cool and…" Kelly stopped, turning a deeper shade of red as a titter of laughter spread through the crowd.

"Geez, already Kelly." Jake took the microphone from him. "What Kelly is trying to say is that Shara, if it hadn't been for you, we'd sound like every other cover band, but you convinced us to let Kelly play some of his stuff, and most of it doesn't suck. And, since you and Bryan had this completely out there kind of romance, we got inspired to write a killer song."

"So sing it already!" Someone shouted from the back of the room.

"Yeah, let's do that. Okay, Bryan and Shara, this song is for you."

The lights went down and Kelly's voice floated over the room, casting a mellow glow over everyone. Bryan ignored the band, and watched Shara as she lost herself in the song. Her eyes sparkled like stars in the dim light. Bryan couldn't take his eyes off of her. The expression she wore was something otherworldly, ethereal. *What will I ever do in my life to deserve her?*

As if reading his thoughts, she gave him a sidelong smile. He drew her into a lingering kiss as the song ended and the lights went up.

The crowd applauded and Kelly cleared his throat into the microphone. "I see the song had its desired effect!"

They broke apart and Bryan stood. "I think on that note, ladies and gents, Shara and I are going to head out. But you all," he waved a hand over the crowd who murmured dissent at his announcement, "stay here as long as you'd like, Dave will take care of you, right Dave?"

Dave waved a beefy hand at the stage. "Y'all just go and do what you gotta do Bryan. I'll take care of everyone!"

Taking Shara's hand, Bryan led her out of the room to cheers and well wishes. The air outside Dave's was chilly, and Shara shivered as she climbed into the Jeep. Bryan slipped off his suit coat and draped it over her shoulders. She smiled in thanks and sank into the jacket, reminding Bryan just how tiny she was.

As they drove through down the quiet roads, Bryan stole a glance here and there at his new bride, swallowing back words that threatened to spill out before they got home. Finally they pulled up into the drive and Bryan felt a peace, a completeness, settle over him. He turned off the engine and stared at the stars in the sky.

"It was a nice day." Shara snuggled into the crook of his shoulder, a perfect fit.

"It was. The first of many."

"Your parents were there."

The memory of seeing his parents for the first time in so many years, even for just a moment, brought a bittersweet smile to Bryan's face. "And someday you'll get to have a whole conversation with them."

"Your mom's sweet."

"And Dad?"

Shara snuggled deeper into his arm and sighed. "You Jacobs men have difficulty with first impressions."

Bryan hugged her closer to him and laughed into the frosty air. "Come on," he climbed out of the Jeep. "I have something to show you."

"Okay." She climbed out as well, wrapping his jacket closer to her. "It's colder out here than it was at Dave's."

"Well, this is outside. This isn't a packed dive with a grill in the back."

"Very funny. Where are we going?"

Bryan held her hand and led her up the path to the burned out farmhouse. "I want to show you something I've been working on."

"Can't this wait until morning? I mean, it's dark out here and the light from the..." Shara stopped in her tracks as motion sensitive lights flooded the area around the farmhouse. "Bryan-did you..." she stepped forward, away from him, staring at the building in front of her.

Bryan kept a step back and grinned with satisfaction. The burned out shell of a house was gone. He and the crew he hired had been able to keep the original foundation and some of the stone walls in the rebuilding project, a fact that made him proud. "I'm afraid I did. Well, I did have help."

Shara walked along the length of the house. "Why? Why did you do this? I mean, the cabin is perfect for us, you shouldn't put so much into this!"

He put up a hand to stop her. "First of all, stop. The cabin is perfect for us. It's not what you think. Look over here." He pointed to a sign on the door of the building.

"Orphans and Outcasts Studios." She turned a disbelieving face to him. "What is this?"

"This, my dear wife, is a state-of-the-art, spare no expense, recording studio for you and your band of brothers, as well as any other musical acts that catch your fancy. Mr. James helped me set it up. You are your own recording mogul."

Her face went slack in shock. "You-I-Thank you!" She leaped into his waiting arms and clasped her arms around his neck as he swung her in a circle.

"You are very welcome." He set her back down and grinned. "It's easy, being married to a millionaire and all."

"But Bryan, I told Mr. James…"

"Have a look around." Bryan opened the door to the studio and turned on the lights. "And yes, I know what you told Mr. James. And I understand better than anyone why you settled your grandmother's estate the way you did." He leaned against the wall and watched her study the soundboard like a small child looking at a wondrous toy. "Turning the dealerships over to Lydia's least favorite cousin, genius. Giving that big house in Shorewood to the state as a halfway house for people recovering from prescription drug addictions, inspired. Giving buckets of money to Drew, Molly, RHCS, Dave's, all awesome!"

She looked up at him. "You can't be mocking me for doing any of that. I mean, Molly always wanted to open a cat shelter, now she can. Drew and Jo get to be great parents and not worry about money. The school wants to do renovations, now they can. And Dave's needs new everything, you know he never wants to spend the money. I got to help with all that. I got to pay a little back for everything everyone gave me."

"You did, you did. But Shara," he put a hand on her shoulder, "you forgot about what you wanted."

"That's easy." She stood up and wrapped her arms around his waist. "I have what I want right here."

"Uh huh. Thank you. But seriously. Molly told me all you wanted was a chance to be your own person, free of any connection to your family or the family business. And, let's face it, Teacher's Pets is a good band, but you guys need to really let Kelly run loose with some songs. Mr. James and I got to talking and here ya go!" He kissed the top of her head. "I wanted to name it 'Insanely Jealous Husband who will Pound Anyone Looks at My Wife Records,' but Mr. James thought that was a bit wordy. You like it?"

Shara glanced around the room a little and looked back at him. "Bryan, I love it. I think this is the best thing anyone has ever done…ever!"

"That's what I was going for." Bryan brushed a strand of hair from her face and kissed her, gently at first, and then more possessively, allowing the desire he'd held at bay for so long to surface. He felt a slight quiver of hesitation run through her. *Be gentle with her.* Reigning in his natural instincts with some effort, Bryan pulled away from Shara and let her catch her breath. Her expression was cloudy and uncertain. *She's never been here before. Take it easy with her.*

"It's a little chilly in here," he rubbed her shoulders.

"Oh, is it?" Her voice was light and far away, like a summer breeze. "I guess I didn't notice."

"Yeah, well, it is. How about if we go to the house? I think Marva started a fire for us." Bryan felt the color rise in his face. *Jeez, could I be more lame?*

"Sure. Okay."

They walked back down the path to the cabin when Bryan stopped her at the porch. "We have to do this right, Mrs. Jacobs."

"What's that?"

"This!" He swooped her up in his arms again, his heart surging at the sound of her giggles. Reminded again of how he carried her that very first day, Bryan gazed at Shara's smiling, healthy face and marveled at the road that brought them together.

Still laughing, she shook her hair, and Bryan noticed that while she kept the wavy look, her hair was now almost to her shoulders, and the golden color he'd known as hers was fading to her natural lighter blonde. In the moonlight, her hair looked like spun silver, and her smooth face shone like porcelain. For heartbeat she was again the pale, sad girl with the enormous eyes. *And I was...hopeless.*

"Bryan? Hello?" She tapped his forehead with her finger. "Why so serious?"

"I was just thinking. Seems I'm always carrying you!" His laughter joined hers. Shaking his thoughts away, Bryan pushed the door open with his foot and carried her inside where, as he knew, Marva Blakely had started a fire in the fireplace for them not ten minutes earlier, after she finished bedding down the horses.

"Welcome home," he murmured as he set her down.

Shara seemed uncertain, as if seeing the room for the first time. He took her hand and led her closer to the sofa. Sitting, he patted the seat next to him, but she shook her head. "No, I...I need something to drink."

Let her go at her own speed. Bryan nodded over his shoulder to the fridge. "I stocked it just for you."

Her eyes flashed with gratefulness as she quickly crossed to the kitchen. "Bryan!" She cheered, opening the fridge.

He didn't need to see her face. Two cases of cola, one diet, one regular, side by side in the fridge, he knew, delighted her.

"Do you want any?"

"Sure." He took the can from her and quickly set it, unopened, on the end table closest to him. Extremes of cold and heat still bothered the tender skin on his hands. "How weird is it to not have a coffee table here?"

"Not all that weird. Makes this room larger, roomier, I think." She smiled at him as she tapped the top of her can, opened it with a hiss, took a sip, and set it on the opposite end table.

Then she stood before him, her face glowing in the moonlight that shone through the window, backlit with deep golden firelight. Without a word, she slid off his suit coat and draped it on the recliner. Standing there, in Joanna's simple, satin gown, she was ethereal, like a dream. Removing two sapphire clips from her hair, something Molly lent to her, Shara let her hair flow freely, completing the vision.

She took his breath away. Though he ached to touch her, to finally claim her for his own, Bryan feared any movement would startle this delicate spirit, and send her flying from him. As if reading his thoughts, she twirled around, the folds of her dress floating outward, glowing silver and gold in the double light.

I will never, ever be worthy of her.

She smiled at him, and reached a hand to him. He took her hand and strode to her, letting the joy that radiated from her wash over him.

But I will spend the rest of my life trying to be.

He cupped her face in his hands and kissed her slowly, gently. She stood on tiptoe to meet him, returning his kiss easily. He lifted her by the waist, up over his head and whirled her around, her laughter filling him with more joy that he'd ever thought possible. As he lowered her to her feet, she unbuttoned his shirt, which he slid off and let fall to the floor.

She stood on tiptoe again to kiss him, this time resting her hands on his shoulders. The feel of her touch on his skin roused Bryan, as from a trance. He reached around and unzipped her gown, sliding the straps off her shoulders. With a whisper, the whole thing slipped off of her body and to the floor, a shimmering cloud of white satin.

Now he kissed her, drawing her in to him. He kicked off his shoes and socks without releasing her from his kiss. Sensations long forgotten, or never known, flowed through him as he held her with one hand and removed his pants with the other.

He knelt before her, worshipful, and stripped away the last barriers to her beauty. Her skin glowed golden in the firelight, and her scent, sun warmed strawberries, washed over him. He drank fully the intoxicating scent and his head spun, dizzy with the thought of what was to come. He ached to claim her quickly, to release himself from the months of denial and desire. But, as Shara knelt and gazed at him in the flicker of the firelight, Bryan saw a shadow of hesitation on her face. *I will be patient with you. I will wait for you.* As if holding something delicate, he eased her down to the soft carpet, one arm protecting her, the other caressing her, waiting for her to open her one last secret to him.

She traced his shoulders and chest, and his body responded to her feather light touch. He kissed her, this time in askance, once, and again. Returning his kiss in answer, she trembled and pressed herself closer to him. The surging fever that heated his body radiated from her skin as well.

*Slowly, gently...*Bryan kissed her forehead, then each closed eyelid, then down to her lips, and to the sensitive spot at the base of her left ear. She whispered his name, her voice husky, heavy with desire. He hovered over her, keeping his full weight from her. She trembled as they slid together, and Bryan watched the glimmer of virginal hesitation flash from her eyes the moment they melted into each other.

She clung to him then, as if she would never free him. *As if I'd ever want to be free again. Not a chance.*

89: BRYAN: ONE YEAR LATER

Bryan Jacobs looked forward to evenings after school with the unbridled excitement of a schoolboy. The drive from RHCS home seemed longer, somehow, than it used to. The mere thought of what waited for him at home took his breath away and filled him with a grateful awe.

It was no surprise that there were several cars in the yard as he pulled into the drive. He parked the Jeep and climbed out, following the path to the studio where, he knew, Shara would be working. *I won't disturb her. I'll just peek in and make sure she's not working too hard.*

She sat at the soundboard, playing with the blinking buttons and knobs that befuddled him. In the studio, Jake and Kelly seemed to be in disagreement, as usual, about an arrangement. Bryan leaned against the doorframe and watched his wife.

Her hair was long now, a silvery blonde waterfall falling past her shoulders. She looked more like the girl he carried from the creek, than Drew and Jo's golden-haired nanny.

There were dark moments. As bright as life was now, Bryan could not completely exorcise the ghosts that haunted them both. There were nights he'd wake to her cries as she still battled the horrors of her newly remembered past. Love, Bryan realized, could ease, but not conquer, all. So, once a month, they traveled to Green Bay to visit a quiet woman who listened, who advised, but who prescribed nothing. Time, she told them, and security was all Shara needed to heal the wounds inflicted by her grandmother.

It was a prescription Bryan understood and respected completely.

He followed the legal events involving Richard and Jennifer. He testified in a pretrial hearing, an experience that left him bitter and weary. Shara flatly refused to testify in a courtroom in either case. After weeks of arguing and subpoenas, Mr. James convinced the judge in both cases to allow Shara to videotape her testimony in Rock Harbor. Once she testified, she closed the subject. Not even Benny, the local reporter and her biggest fan, could get her to comment on the trials as they unfolded with great drama in the Milwaukee media. News anchors referred to her as the "reclusive Shara Brandt." The term, Bryan knew, amused her. "I'm not a recluse," she'd tell him. "I simply don't want to say what they want to hear."

The project Shara undertook was to locate her parents' graves. Never allowed to attend a funeral or visit their gravesites, Shara had no idea where they might be. Even Mr. James, who knew every other secret Lydia Brandt had, did not know where Daniel and Lily Brandt were buried. After several months of searching, to no avail, Shara had two headstones set in the far corner of the Rock Harbor Community Church cemetery, near the creek. She put fresh flowers there each week.

Bryan watched her work, always amazed at her ability to pick up skills quickly. With Mr. James handling the legal end of things, Teacher's Pets was very close to releasing their first CD. It would be a regional release, but Bryan knew sales would soar. Shara's choice to use her real name was calculated to generate interest in the first CD. Shara Brandt was, after all, a woman with a great head for business.

His cell phone buzzed in his pocket. Not wanting to disturb Shara and the band, he stepped outside the door, still watching her as he spoke. "Hello?"

"Bryan? It's Archibald James."

"Hello Mr. James! I was just thinking about you."

"I wanted to let you know there is a verdict in Mr. Bennett's case."

That was faster than I thought. "Okay."

"Not guilty on all counts."

The phone fell from his hands as Bryan crumpled against a tree. *Not guilty?*

"Bryan? Bryan?"

Bryan picked up the phone and inhaled, trying to clear the furious white noise from his mind. "I'm here Mr. James. I'm...surprised."

"As we all are."

"How is it possible? Not guilty on all counts?"

"Well, the DA decided he couldn't make a case for the murder of Mrs. Brandt, so he focused on conspiracy, obstruction of justice, and the attempted murder of Miss Tiel. I was there for the whole trial, as you know. Mr. Bennett covered his tracks too well. I thought they might make obstruction stick, because of that body in Jefferson County."

"What about Shara's testimony...and Jennifer's?"

"A convicted murderer doesn't make a believable witness, and it doesn't help that her lawyer is appealing and still arguing diminished capacity. The jury tuned her out. The attempted murder at the motel in Rock Harbor boiled down to a he said/she said. Again, Mr. Bennett wins the point. As for Miss Shara's testimony, it was very compelling, but, even you have to admit, she doesn't have any hard facts. Everything he did, following Mrs. Brandt's murder, was done to make him look like the bereaved fiancé. He planned very carefully, and it paid off."

"But the ring, the will, what he said about it being an accident..." Bryan swallowed hard, fighting his gag reflex.

"All of it, put together, painted one picture for us, but in the hands of Mr. Bennett's attorney, painted quite another. Miss Shara's testimony was primarily ruled hearsay, since it was said to Miss Tiel, and since Miss Shara was, by her own admission, semiconscious at the time."

"So that's it, then?"

Mr. James did not answer right away. "We could file a civil suit against him for a number of things, but without a criminal conviction, it would be, at best, a long shot. It would be a very hard case to prove, given how clean Mr. Bennett kept his hands."

"No, I don't want to put Shara through anymore of that. Just keep the restraining order she has on him current. I guess that's the best we can do."

"I'll see to it, Bryan. I'm sorry we couldn't get more...justice."

In spite of the sick feeling in his stomach, Bryan smiled. "Mr. James, you are what we call up here, 'good people.' Don't worry anymore about Richard Bennett. I'm going to see to it that we don't."

"Very well. Now, on to happier things. How is Miss Shara feeling these days?"

Bryan watched Shara get out of her chair to hug Kelly and Jake as they prepared to leave the studio. Hugging was getting more and more difficult for her, given the size of her belly. Twins, the doctor said. A boy and a girl, Molly was certain. Joanna was delighted at the prospect of playmates for Gracie. All Bryan knew was there

295

was a beautiful glow around Shara all day long. "She is doing just fine. The babies are due in a couple of weeks, and she hasn't slowed down a bit. She did give up riding Spice, of course, but everything else is full steam ahead."

"Very unusual, they tell me, for a woman to experience no adverse effects of pregnancy. But Miss Shara is an unusual woman. Give her my best regards, will you?"

"I will do that, Mr. James. Thank you." Bryan closed his cell phone as Kelly and Jake left the studio.

"Geez, when is she going to have those kids already?"

"I don't know, Jake. Soon, I hope. It's hard to listen to her play piano, her fingers are so puffy, and she keeps hitting the wrong notes."

"Well, I just hope her weird sweating goes away. No way am I touring with a chick that sweats like a race horse. You'd think someone that sweat that much wouldn't be all swollen up. And how about having to play in that icebox? I swear, my fingers are frozen and she is still sweating!"

Kelly shook his head and grinned in Bryan's general direction. "Hi there, Mr. Jacobs."

"Hey Mr. Jacobs."

"Guys." Bryan knew that his former students would never address him as anything other than 'Mr. Jacobs.' Still, it made him feel old. "How are things?"

"Oh, good." Jake paused. "Those babies, they're coming soon, right?"

"And Shara will be back to...you know...her old self?" Kelly looked hopeful.

"Just before Thanksgiving." Bryan grinned, enjoying their discomfort, recalling his own feelings about Joanna's pregnancies. "And yes, she'll get back to normal."

"That's great. See ya Mr. Jacobs!"

Both younger men waved at him as they left the studio. Bryan waved back and walked down the hall to the sound room. Shara was arranging some papers at a desk. She turned and smiled. Her smile always took his breath away. *Those boys are clueless. Right there is the most beautiful woman in the world.* "Hey there Gorgeous."

"Ya know, Joanna told me you would be like this."

"Like what?"

She waddled to him and reached up to put her arms around his neck. "She told me that when she was pregnant, she was gross and sweaty and swollen and Drew wouldn't leave her alone. Said she was the most beautiful thing ever."

"And your point is?"

"Love is completely blind." She stood on tiptoe and kissed him. "Hungry?"

"Of course. What are we making tonight?" Bryan fully enjoyed Shara's cooking lessons…most of them ended in the bedroom.

"Well, the babies want wedding cake." Shara shot him a sidelong glance.

"I'm not sure I'm up to making butter cream frosting."

"Judy at the bakery gave me the extra layer from a wedding cake she made."

"Extra layer?"

"Yeah, apparently she does that when she knows there's a pregnant woman in town. White with a raspberry filling, and you know, it's exactly what the babies wanted?" Shara shrugged. "You'll have to scrounge for yourself tonight."

"Thanksgiving's just a few weeks away. Shouldn't I practice on turkey?"

"I don't know if you're ready for turkey." Shara gave him a mischievous grin. "Which reminds me: Your father called this morning."

"And?"

"They're coming for Thanksgiving. Said they couldn't wait to see us all. Also," she looked over her shoulder at the new barn, "they insist on staying in the loft. Apparently, your mom can't wait. She says it'll be like staying in a haunted hotel or something…with horses one floor below. I told her it was all rebuilt since the fire, but she said that did not matter."

"They're really coming?"

"Their flight number's on the fridge."

Joy surged through Bryan and he lifted Shara off her feet and swirled her in a circle. He set her down, gently, their laughter reaching the skies. Shara snuggled under the crook of his shoulder, a place she fit perfectly, and muffled her giggles into his rib cage. Waiting for her mirth to subside, Bryan gazed down the path toward the cabin. The oranges and reds of the sunset glowed over the cabin and in the brilliance of that light he saw it all: a new addition to the cabin; more horses in the pasture. A dark haired boy playing with a dump truck in the soft sand outside the front door, and a blonde girl, with eyes as dark as night, swinging on a tire swing in the side yard. And music, all kinds of music and wonderful cooking smells drifting all around, like a shield of love and peace.

"What are you thinking about?"

Bryan looked down into her dark eyes and smiled. "I'm thinking about how normal this all is." He kissed the top of her hair, inhaling her scent. "You, me, the babies coming, my parents coming for a visit. It's all normal, and peaceful, and..."

"And boring?" She gave him a mischievous grin.

"Not a chance." He pulled her closer to him. "No, more like an amazing gift that I didn't earn and don't deserve."

"You talked to Mr. James today, didn't you?" Concern clouded her dark eyes.

"Yes. Yes I did."

"And there was a verdict...in the second trial."

"Yes. Yes there was."

The dazzling colors of the sunset behind her paled in comparison to the smile on her face. "Bryan, it doesn't matter what happens...with them. That's over." She shrugged. "I know we still have to deal with...things. I'm aware of that. But...Richard and Jennifer..." she paused and took a breath, "they can't hurt us anymore, not ever."

And there, on the little hill behind the cabin, in the last shadows of the day, Bryan Jacobs realized she was absolutely right. He held her close to him, all of his concerns erased in the solid, secure feel of her next to him. "What would I ever do without you?"

She stood on tiptoe and kissed his cheek. "Well, I hope you can live with disappointment because we're not going to ever know the answer to that question."

Bryan looked down at Shara: his doubts and worries melting away into warm desire as he lost himself in her eyes. He kissed her, softly. She stood on tiptoe again and laced her fingers together behind his neck, pulling him closer to her. Dinner forgotten, they swayed together in the cooling shadows of evening. *This is our chance.* Bryan held Shara tighter breathing in her scent.

Acknowledgements
Sometimes it takes a village to write a book. Sometimes it takes a village and 30 years! I have to thank Linda Schmalz, my dear critique partner, who got me to the finish line and then pushed me farther. Thanks to friends and family who served as sounding boards for my ten million ideas for this book. Thank you also to my mother and editor who has the patience to fix my mistakes one word at a time!

"Lies in Chance" would never be in your hands right now if I hadn't been blessed to sit next to author J. A. Konrath at a book signing. He opened a whole new world of publishing possibilities for me, made me laugh, and shared his peanuts with me. I am a grateful fan!

Sarah J. Bradley
Sarah is a lifelong Upper Midwest girl who lives with her college sweetheart husband, her two children, and her five rescue cats in Waukesha, Wisconsin. When not writing or volunteering at her church, Sarah cheers for the Green Bay Packers, plays trivia games on the radio, and attends Rick Springfield concerts. Sarah's been writing since she was thirteen…when she started work on what is now "Lies in Chance."

Made in the USA
Monee, IL
19 September 2021

77583632R00167